Praise for Julianna Baggott:

'She has a flair for keeping the pages turning with a combination of short, sharp action beats and drip-fed revelations. Strong stuff, and gripping to boot' *SFX*

'Discomfiting and unforgettable' *New York Times*

'A great, gorgeous whirlwind of a novel, boundless in its imagination. You will be swept away' Justin Cronin, *New York Times* bestselling author of *The Passage*

'Baggott tells what might have been an overly grim tale with crystalline precision, offering a hint of hope in the novels to follow' *Guardian*

'If Katniss could jump out of her own book and pick a great friend, I think she'd find an excellent candidate in Pressia' Aimee Bender, *New York Times* bestselling author of *The Particular Sadness of Lemon Cake*

'Nearly impossible to stop reading . . . *Pure* packs one hell of an apocalypse' Daniel H. Wilson, *New York Times* bestselling author of *Robopocalypse*

The PURE Trilogy
by Julianna Baggott

PURE (2012)

FUSE (2013)

BURN (2014)

JULIANNA BAGGOTT

headline

First published in Great Britain in 2013
by HEADLINE PUBLISHING GROUP

First published in paperback in Great Britain in 2013
by HEADLINE PUBLISHING GROUP

3

Cataloguing in Publication Data is available from the British Library

ISBN 978 1 4722 0142 3

Typeset in Dante by Avon DataSet Ltd, Bidford-on-Avon, Warwickshire

Printed and bound in Great Britain by Clays Ltd, St Ives plc

Headline's policy is to use papers that are natural, renewable and
recyclable products and made from wood grown in sustainable
forests. The logging and manufacturing processes are expected
to conform to the environmental regulations of the country of origin.

HEADLINE PUBLISHING GROUP
An Hachette UK Company
338 Euston Road
London NW1 3BH

www.headline
www.hachette.co.uk

For my father, Bill Baggott.

Thank you for helping me build worlds, especially the original world of my childhood.

PROLOGUE

WILDA

*L*ying on a thin coat of snow, she sees gray earth meeting gray sky, and she knows she's back. The horizon looks clawed, but the claw marks are only three stunted trees. They stand in a row like they're stapling the ground to the sky.

She gasps, suddenly, a delayed reaction, as if someone is trying to steal her breath and she's pulling it back into her throat.

She sits up. She's still small, still just a nine-year-old girl. She feels like she's lost a lot of time, but she hasn't. Not really. Not years. Maybe only days, weeks.

She tugs her thick coat in tight around her ribs. The coat is proof. She touches its silver buttons. There's a scarf tucked down into the coat, wound twice around her neck. Who dressed her? Who wound the scarf twice? She looks at her boots — dark blue with thick laces, new — and her hands fitted into gloves, each finger encased in a taut cocoon.

A curl of her dark red hair sits on her jacket, her hair shining. The end of each strand is thick and perfect as if newly cut.

She pulls up the sleeve of the coat, exposing her arm. Just as it was *under the bright light, the bone is no longer warped. There are no thin plastic ridges bubbled along the skin. She isn't stippled with shards. Not even a mole or a freckle. Her skin is white – white, the way snow should be, maybe even whiter. She's never seen really white snow with her own eyes. The light veins ride blue beneath the white. She touches the soft inner skin of one wrist to her cheek, then her lips. Smooth skin on smooth skin.*

She looks around and knows they're close; she can feel the electricity of their bodies filling the air. She remembers what it was like when they first took her from the other strays; motherless, fatherless, they slept in a handmade lean-to near the markets. She isn't sure why she was chosen, lifted into the air, clutched. One cradled her in its arms and hurdled across the rubble while the others bounded around them. Its breath chugged, mechanically. Its legs pumped. Her eyes teared in the wind, so its angular face was blurry. She wasn't afraid, but now she is. They're here, their strong bodies buzzing like massive bees, but they're leaving her. She feels like a child in a fairy tale. In her mother's stories – she had a mother once – there was a woodsman who was supposed to take a girl's heart back to an evil queen, but he couldn't force himself to do it. Another sliced open a wolf to save the people it had eaten. The woodsmen were strong and good. But they left girls in the woods sometimes, girls who then had to fend for themselves.

Light snow falls. She stands slowly. The world lurches as if it's suddenly grown heavy. She falls to her knees and then hears voices in the woods; two are people walking toward her. Even from this distance, she can see the red scars on their faces. One wobbles from a limp. They're carrying sacks.

She tugs the scarf over her nose and mouth. She's supposed to be found. She's a foundling; she remembers this word was used in the room with the bright light. 'We want her to be a foundling.' It was a man's voice, quavering over a speaker. He was in charge, though she never saw him. Willux, Willux, *people whispered – people with smooth skin who weren't fused to anything. They moved easily around her bed, surrounded by metal posts where clear sacs of fluid were clamped and dripped into tubes, among little beeping machines and wires. It was like having mothers and fathers, too many to keep track.*

She remembers the wide light in the room, its brilliant bulb, so bright and close it kept her warm. She remembers how she first ran her hand over her skin, and when she touched her stomach, it too was smooth. Her navel – the thing her mother always called the button of her belly, and what the voices in that room called her umbilicus – was gone.

She reaches up under her coat and shirt and runs her hand over her stomach. Like before, there's only a stretch of skin and more skin.

'Healed,' the voices said behind white masks, but they were concerned. 'Still, a success,' they said. Some wanted to keep her for observation.

She starts to open her mouth to call to the distant figures carrying sacks, but her mouth doesn't open all the way. It's as if her lips are slightly stitched on either side – the edges sealed.

And what would she say? She can't think of any words. The words whirl in her mind. They're furred. She can't line them up or utter them. Finally she calls out, but the only words that form in her mouth are 'We want!' She doesn't know why. She tries again to call for help, but again she shouts, 'We want!'

They walk up, two young women. They're pickers; she can tell by the warts and scars on their fingers. They've touched a lot of poisonous bulbs, berries, morels. One of them has silver prongs, like those on an old fork, in place of two of her fingers. She's the one with the limp, and her face, though seared a deep red, is strangely pretty, mostly because of her eyes, which glow a golden orange like liquid metal – stained by the brightness of the bombs themselves. She's blind. She clutches the other picker's arm and says, 'Who's you?' It sounds like a birdcall. The girl heard birds in the bright room, recorded and piped in by the unseen speakers. Cooing, the girl thinks, and then she hears other birds in the woods. These birds have the kinds of calls she grew up with – not clear, sweet notes as in the bright room, but scratches and rattles.

The two young women are scared of her. Can they already tell she's different? She wants to tell them her name, but it's gone. The only words in her mind are Fire Flower. That's what her mother used to call her sometimes; born from fire and destruction, she took root and grew. She's never known her father, but she's pretty sure that he was lost in the fire and destruction.

And then her name appears: Wilda. She is Wilda.

She puts her hand on the cold ground. She wants to tell them that she's new. She wants to tell them that the world has changed forever. She says, 'We want our son.' The words startle her. Why did she say this?

The young women look at each other. The blind one says, 'What was that? Whose son?'

The other has a scar running down one cheek as if she had a braid fused to her face now covered in a layer of skin. She says, 'She's not right in the head.'

'Who's you?' the blind one says again.

The girl says, 'We want our son.' These are the only words that she can say.

The pickers look around suddenly, even the blind one. They hear the electrical synapses now, firing through the air. The creatures who took her are restless. 'There's many,' the one with the braided scar says, wide-eyed. 'They're protecting her. Can you feel 'em? They been sent by our Watchers to look over her.'

'Angels,' the blind one says. They start to back away.

But then Wilda pulls up her sleeve and exposes her arm – so white it seems to glow. 'We want,' she says again, slowly, 'our son returned.'

PART I

PART I

PRESSIA

MOTHS

THE LOBBY AT OSR HEADQUARTERS is dotted with a few glowing handmade oil lamps strung from the exposed beams of the high ceiling. The survivors are bedding down on blankets and mats, curled together to keep warm. Their bodies hold a collective humid heat despite the fact that the tall windows haven't been boarded. Their bare casements are fringed with the gauzy remains of curtains. Snow starts to flutter and gust, flutter and gust, in through the windows as if hundreds of moths have been lured in by the promise of lit bulbs to bash themselves against.

It's dark outside, but almost morning, and some of the early risers are waking. Pressia's stayed up all night again. Sometimes she gets so lost in her work that she loses track of time. She's holding a mechanical arm she's just made from scraps that El Capitan brings her – silver pincers, a ball-bearing elbow, old electrical cord to cinch it, and leather straps that have been measured to cuff the amputee's thin biceps. He's a nine-year-old with all five fingers fused together, almost webbed. She whispers the boy's name hoarsely. 'Perlo! Are you here?'

She makes her way through the survivors, who shift and mutter. She hears a sharp, mewling hiss. 'Hush it!' a woman says. Pressia sees something writhe beneath the woman's coat and then the silky black head of a cat appears at the side of her neck. A baby cries out. Someone curses. A song rises up from a man's throat, a lullaby . . . *The ghostly girls, the ghostly girls, the ghostly girls. Who can save them from this world? From this world? The river's wide, the current curls, the current calls, the current curls* . . . The baby goes quiet. Music still works, music calms people. *We're wretches but we're still capable of this – songs rising up inside us.* She'd like the people of the Dome to know this. *We're vicious, yes, but also capable of shocking tenderness, kindness, beauty. We're human, flawed, but still good, right?*

'Perlo?' she tries again, cradling the prosthetic arm to her chest. Sometimes in crowds like this she now looks for her father – even though she doesn't remember his face. Before Pressia's mother died, she showed Pressia the pulsing tattoos on her chest – one of which belonged to Pressia's father, proof that he's survived the Detonations. Of course, he isn't here. He probably isn't even on this continent – or what's left of it. But she can't help searching the faces of survivors for someone who looks a little like her – almond-shaped eyes, black shiny hair. She can't stop from searching, no matter how irrational it is to believe she might one day find him.

She's made it all the way across the lobby and comes to a wall plastered with posters. Instead of the black claw, which once struck fear in survivors, this is a poster of El Capitan's face – stern and tough-jawed. She looks down the row of posters, his eyes all lined up, his brother Helmud a small lump behind El Capitan's back. Above his head, it reads, ABLE AND STRONG? JOIN UP. SOLIDARITY WILL SAVE US. El Capitan made that up and he's proud of it. At the bottom, fine print promises an end to Death Sprees – the teams of OSR soldiers assigned to cull the weak, collect their dead in an enemy's field – and mandatory conscription at sixteen. For those who volunteer, El Capitan promises Food without Fear. Fear of what? OSR has a dark history. People were captured and hauled in, untaught how to read, used as live targets . . .

All of that is over. The posters have worked. There are more recruits now than ever. They wander up from the city, ragged and hungry, burned and fused. Sometimes, they come as families. He's told Pressia that he's got to start sending some back. 'This isn't a welfare state. I'm trying to build an army here.' But so far, she's always talked him into letting them stay.

'Perlo!' she whispers, walking along the wall, letting her hand slide over the rippled edges of the posters. Where is he? The curtains kick into the room. The snow is drawn in as if the large room were drawing in a deep breath.

One family has propped a blanket on a stick, creating a little tent to block the wind. She used to make little tents in the back of the burned-out barbershop when she was little, with a chair and her grandfather's cane to prop a sheet, playing house with her good friend, Fandra. Her grandfather called them *pup tents*, and she and Fandra would bark like puppies. He'd laugh so hard the fan in his throat would spin wildly. She feels a pang of loss – for her grandfather and Fandra, who are both dead, and her childhood, which is dead too.

Outside the windows, guards keep watch at fifty-foot intervals surrounding OSR's headquarters because Special Forces, released by the Dome, are multiplying. A few weeks ago, they were spotted bounding through the woods – their hulking figures bulked with animal muscle, their skin covered in something synthetic and camouflaged. They're agile, nearly silent, incredibly fast and strong, and well armed; their weapons are embedded in their bodies. They dart over the Rubble Fields, sprint among trees, race down alleys – quiet and stealthy, making routine sweeps of the city. They want Partridge – Pressia's half brother – most of all. Partridge is being protected by the mothers, along with Lyda – who is Pure, like Partridge, and was sent out of the Dome as a pawn – and Illia, who was married to the top leader of the OSR, her twisted husband, whom she killed. They get bits of information from sketchy reports sent in from OSR soldiers, who all deeply fear the mothers. One report noted that the mothers are teaching Lyda to fight. She's just a girl from the Dome with no preparation for the ashen wilds, much less life with the mothers, who can be loving and loyal but also barbaric. How is she doing? Another report mentioned that Illia wasn't holding up. She'd been protected in the farmhouse all these years, and now her lungs are struggling with the onslaught of swirling ash.

Everyone who was there at the end of Pressia's mother's life has to be careful. They're the ones who know the truth about Willux and the Dome, and perhaps they have something that Willux is still after – the vials. Bradwell and El Capitan stripped as much as they could from her mother's bunker after she was gone. Partridge has the vials now, and hopefully he's keeping them safe. They would mean a lot to Willux – with these vials and another ingredient and the formula of how to put them together, he could save his own life. Her mother's vials are potent, yes, but out here, they're too dangerous and unpredictable to be of use. They're souvenirs.

How long can the mothers keep Partridge hidden? Long enough for Partridge's father to die? This is the great hope – that Ellery Willux will die soon, and Partridge can take over from within the Dome itself. Sometimes Pressia feels like they're all held in a state of waiting, knowing that something is bound to give, and only then will the future take shape.

Freedle flutters in the pocket of her sweater. She slips her hand inside and runs a finger down the robotic cicada's back. 'Shhh,' she whispers. 'It's okay.' She didn't want to leave him in her small bedroom, alone. Or was it that she didn't want to be alone?

'Perlo!' she calls. 'Perlo!'

And, finally, she hears the boy. 'Here! I'm here!' He scuttles over to her, weaving around survivors. 'Did you finish it?'

Pressia kneels. 'Let's see if it fits.' She tucks the leather cuff around his upper arm, tightens it into place by the electrical-cord laces. His fused hand can make a tapping motion. She tells him to apply pressure to a small lever.

Perlo gives it a try. The pincer opens and then closes. 'It works.' He opens and closes the pincer quickly again and again.

'It's not perfect,' she says, 'but it'll help, I think.'

'Thank you!' He says it so loudly that he gets hushed by someone on the ground nearby. 'Maybe you can make something for yourself,' he whispers, looking at the doll head. 'I mean, maybe there's something . . .'

She tilts the doll so its eyes blink – one is slightly gummed with ash and so it clicks more slowly, out of sync with the other. 'I don't think there's anything that can be done for me,' she says. 'But I get by.'

The boy's mother whisper-calls for him. He whips around, raising the arm in the air triumphantly, and he darts off to show her.

And then there's a far-off gunshot, its rippling report. Pressia crouches instinctively and reaches into her pocket to protect Freedle. She lifts him and holds him to her chest. Perlo's mother pulls her son in close. Pressia knows it was probably an OSR soldier taking aim at shifting shadows. Errant gunshots aren't unusual. But that doesn't stop her chest from tightening around her heart. It's Perlo and his mother and a gunshot – the mix of it all – and she remembers the weight of the gun in her arms, lifting the gun, taking aim, firing. Even now her ears ring and she sees the bloody mist rising. It fills her vision. Red blooms before her eyes like the bursting flowers that shoot up in the Rubble Fields. She pulled the trigger, but now she can't remember if it was the right thing to do. She can't get it straight in her head. Her mother's dead. Dead.

She walks quickly, sticking to the edges of the lobby, the posters stretching on and on. She cups Freedle gently. When she comes to a window, she looks out, tentatively.

Wind. Snow. The clouds like clods of ash scuttling across the sky, she can see one bright star – a rarity – and below it, the edge of the woods, the brittle trees huddled and stooped. She can make out the soldiers' uniforms and the occasional glint of a gun, the thin veils of their breath rising in the cold on the sloping hill. She sees her mother's face lying on the forest floor and then it's obliterated. Gone.

Beyond the soldiers, her eyes stutter through the trees. Is something out there – something that wants in? She imagines Special Forces hunkered down in the snow. Do they even need sleep? Are they, in part, cold-blooded, their skins covered in thin scrims of ice? It's quiet, eerily so, but still there's a certain coiled energy. It snowed three days ago – a fine dusting at first, it turned heavy – and now the lawn is iced, dark and glassy, in three inches or more and snow is still flitting down.

She feels someone grab hold of her elbow. She turns. It's Bradwell, the double scars running up his cheek, his dark lashes, his full lips chapped by the cold. She looks at his hand, all ruddy and rough. His broad knuckles are scarred and beautiful. How can knuckles be beautiful? Pressia wonders. It's like Bradwell invented them.

But it's not like that between them anymore. 'Did you hear me calling you?' he says.

She feels like he's talking to her from underwater. Once, while the farmhouse burned, she had the courage to make him promise to find a home for them, but that was only because she didn't actually believe the moment would last. 'What is it?'

'Are you okay? You look dazed.'

'I just had to get an arm to a boy, and there was a gunshot. But it was nothing.' She wouldn't admit to seeing bright red bursting before her eyes any more than to her fear of falling in love with him. This is one thing Pressia knows is true: Everyone she's ever loved has died. In light of that fact, how could she ever love Bradwell? She looks at him now and the words drum in her head: *Don't love him. Don't love him.*

'Have you been up all night?' he asks.

'Yes.' She notices his hair is standing up messily on his head. They both have the ability to disappear for days. Bradwell gets devoured by his obsession with the six Black Boxes that tunneled up from the char and rubble of the farmhouse and holes up for days on end in the old morgue, where he now lives in the headquarters' basement. Pressia gets wrapped up in making the prosthetics. Bradwell is still bent on understanding the past, while she has devoted herself to helping people here and now. 'Have you been up all night too?'

'Um, yes. I guess so. It's morning?'

'Just about.'

'Yeah, then I was. I had a breakthrough with one of the Black Boxes. One of them bit me.'

'Bit you?' Freedle flits nervously in her hand.

He shows her a small puncture wound on his thumb. 'Not hard. Maybe just a warning. It likes me now, I think. It started following me around the morgue like a pet dog.' She starts walking down the hall, passing more of El Capitan's recruitment posters, and Bradwell follows. 'I've taken them all apart, put 'em back together. And they contain information about the past – as far as I can tell – but they aren't wired to transmit. They aren't spies for the Dome or anything like that, which I had to rule out. If they ever had those abilities, they've been lost.' Bradwell is on a tear, but Pressia isn't interested in the Black Boxes. She's tired of Bradwell's desire to prove his parents' Dome conspiracies right, his version of the truth, Shadow History, all of that. 'And this one, I can't explain it – this one is different. It's like it knows me.'

'What did you do to make it bite you?'

'I was talking.'

'About what?'

'I don't think you want to know.'

She stops and looks at him. He shoves his hands in his pockets. The birds in his back flutter their wings, agitated. 'Of course I want to know. It's how you unlocked the box, right? It's important.'

He takes a deep breath and holds it for a moment. He looks at the floor and shrugs. 'Okay, then,' he says, 'I was rambling about you.'

She and Bradwell have never talked about what happened at the farmhouse. She remembers the way he held her, the feel of his lips on hers. But this kind of love can't survive. Love's a luxury. He looks at her now, his head bowed, his eyes locked on hers. She feels heat drill through her body. *Don't love him.* She can't even look at him. 'Oh,' she says. 'I see.'

'Nope, you don't see. Not yet. Come with me.' He leads her down another hallway and then turns. And there, sitting by the door, waiting patiently, is a Black Box. It's about the size of a small dog, actually – the kind her grandfather used to call a terrier, the kind that likes to kill rats.

'I told him to stay and he stayed,' Bradwell says. 'This is Fignan.' Freedle noses up from her palm to see for himself. 'Does he know how to sit and shake hands?' Pressia asks.

'I think he knows a hell of a lot more than that.'

PARTRIDGE

BEETLE

THE ROOT CELLAR SMELLS LIKE pooled rain water and mildew. Bright red mold spores dot the walls and dirt floor. The walls are lined with the mothers' jars of strange vegetables pickling in vinegar. Mother Hestra, heavily armed, paces overhead. Each of her footsteps reminds him he's locked underground. Sometimes, he feels like her footsteps are heartbeats and he's trapped in the ribs of some enormous Beast.

He hasn't seen Lyda in six days. Time is hard to measure while he's alone and bent over the maps of the Dome he's been making, with only a crack in the cellar door to measure the light of day occasionally interrupted by the skimpy meals the mothers deliver – pale broths, clods of white roots, and occasionally a bite-size cube of meat.

He tells himself that aboveground is no better – the wasted detritus of suburbia. But, by God, he feels trapped, and worse than the feeling of being trapped is the boredom. The mothers gave him an old lamp so he has enough light to work by, and they've supplied large sheets of paper, pencils, and plywood that he's set on the floor and uses as a hard-top desk. He's making maps, trying to recall all the details of the blueprints that he memorized to get out of the Dome, trying to get everything down as quickly as possible. But hour after hour, minute after minute, footstep overhead after footstep . . . the boredom becomes blinding.

The truth is he's forced to rely on the mothers' protection at least until he decides on a plan. Part of him wants to wait until his father dies. His father is weakening. Decades of brain enhancements have caused a palsy and skin deterioration. Partridge's mother told him these were the signs of Rapid Cell Degeneration. Soon, his father's body will shut down, which might be the perfect time to return. The Dome would likely respect Partridge as his father's legacy. His father has ruled like a monarch, after all.

But the other part of him would like to take down his father while he's alive, defeat him for the right reasons. Don't the people of the Dome deserve to know the truth about what his father did? If he can get that truth to them and explain that there's another way to live – one in which they aren't just sheep following his father's orders, one in which they don't see the survivors as evil wretches who deserve their fate – they'd choose it over his father's reign. Partridge is sure of it.

He's got to find time with Lyda to make a plan. It feels inevitable that they'll go back, together.

Meanwhile, he focuses on finishing the maps, pushing through the solitary confinement, the blunt force of boredom, mold and spores, rationed food, and, stripped of all weapons, the awful feeling of needing the mothers, who treat him like a child and, at the same time, a dangerous criminal. They still consider him the enemy, especially because he comes from the Dome; he's a Death – a man, but, worse, a man from the Dome – and can't be trusted.

The mothers are interested in the maps, which is why they've given him supplies, but Partridge wants to get them to El Capitan. It's the one gift Partridge has to give. They may never be of use; what are the chances El Capitan will ever form a viable army capable of taking down the Dome? Still, it's something Partridge can contribute. As he works on the maps, he lets his mind drum over all the things his mother told him before she died. He's written down every word he could recall; all of it feels embedded with information, coded.

He puts down his pencil, opens and closes his fist. His hand's cramping, even his partially chopped-off pinky, which has healed to a shiny red nub. He rubs his fingers together, feeling the slickness of the waxy serum that the mothers recently had him bathe in, as preparation for an upcoming journey. The serum, extracted from a camphor tree and beeswax, is supposed to lock in his scent and mask it. His skin is stiff and shiny. There are reports that Special Forces have an excellent sense of smell, as do some of the other Beasts and Dusts. The mothers never let Partridge and Lyda stay in one place too long. They're protective, yes, but also Mother Hestra told Partridge that they can't risk Special Forces closing in on Partridge, putting them all in danger. Nomadic living is best.

He wonders if Lyda has been bathed in the serum too. He's always afraid that, one day, she won't come on the journey to the next place. So far she always has. He tries to imagine the feel of her skin encased in this waxiness.

Sitting on the dirt floor beside him is his mother's metal music box, first found in her drawer in the Personal Loss Archives;

Bradwell charred it in the butcher-shop basement. But he made sure that Partridge got it back. Bradwell's more sentimental than Partridge thought, and when it comes to things your parents have left behind, Bradwell has a soft spot. Partridge has rubbed the soot from the music box, but the gears are still blackened. Because all its parts are metal it still works, though it's off-key and a little muted now. It's the only thing the mothers let him keep – maybe because they're mothers themselves. He lifts the box, winds it, lets it play, the notes tinking in the close damp air. He misses his mother. He missed her for so much of his childhood, he's gotten good at missing her. Maybe it's why he's so good at missing Lyda. Years of practice.

When the notes die out, he looks at this most recent map, a cross section of the Dome's three upper tiers – Upper One, Upper Two, and Upper Three – and three subfloors called Sub One, Sub Two, and Sub Three, which include a section for the massive power generators. The ground floor is called Zero – home to the academy, where he spent most of his time.

He misses the academy with relentless longing. He shouldn't want to be back in his dorm room, hanging out with Hastings, begging Arvin Weed for his notes, hoping to avoid the herd – a group of boys who pretty much hate him – but he does. He even misses his classes. He thinks of Glassings, his history teacher, in that moment he pulled him aside in the hallway outside the dance. Partridge was just about to steal the knife, so, in retrospect, it was the moment when he could have turned back, continued on with his familiar life.

That's not how it went. Somehow he ended up here, powerless.

The irony is he has the vials, his mother's life's work – the vials are powerful. His father murdered for them – Pressia's adoptive grandfather, as well as his father's own oldest son and the woman his father supposedly loved, Partridge's mother.

The vials remind him of what his mother wanted him to become – a revolutionary, a leader.

Partridge walks to the mothers' pickled jars and picks one up, third from the corner. Under it there's a narrow, deep hole, and a few beetles skitter away. He fits his hands down in and lifts a tightly wrapped bundle, lightly caked in moist dirt. He carries the bundle to his cot and unwraps his mother's vials, four of them attached to syringes with hard plastic covers over the needles. After the farmhouse burned, Bradwell and El Capitan took them from his mother's bunker, along with anything else that might be of use – computers, radios, medicine, supplies, guns, ammunition. Afterward, it seemed smart to split the group in two – El Capitan, Helmud, Bradwell, and Pressia went to headquarters; Lyda, Partridge, and Illia went with the mothers because they have the greatest ability to keep Partridge hidden and heavily guarded. If one group was found by Special Forces, at least the others could carry on. Bradwell and El Capitan took the bulk of his mother's stuff, but Partridge hid the vials under his jacket.

He checks each vial. They're cool to the touch. Partridge's mother took Partridge to Japan as a baby at Partridge's father's urging, because the Japanese were ahead of everyone else in creating biomedical nanotechnology to repair trauma from detonations, in particular self-generating cells that would move into the body to repair it.

From a very young age, Partridge's father used brain enhancements – so much so that he lit up his brain with firing synapses – and now he has the telltale signs of Rapid Cell Degeneration: the palsy and skin deterioration, and eventual organ failure and death. It's not just him. Partridge remembers how, in the Dome, anyone who is sick, old, or weary is quickly whisked away to a cordoned-off wing of the medical center. In the last few weeks, he's realized one very dark truth: Rapid Cell Degeneration will also eventually affect Special Forces and all the academy boys who've been enhanced, including, one day, Partridge himself.

Before his mother died, she told him that if what's in these vials is paired with another substance as dictated by a formula – a formula that's gone missing – then this concoction could reverse Rapid Cell Degeneration. At the time, he'd been too overwhelmed with emotions – he hadn't seen his mother since he was a little boy – to fully grasp what she was telling him. But now, he wishes he'd been more clear-minded, more rational. He wishes he'd asked more questions.

His mother showed him a list of people within the Dome who were on her side, including Arvin Weed's parents, Algrin Firth's father, even Durand Glassings. They're part of a network within the Dome. When Lyda was sent out of the Dome as bait to lure Partridge, one of the people in the network whispered a message to her: *Tell the swan we're waiting.* When Partridge told his mother this, she whispered, 'The Cygnus,' which he still doesn't understand.

She told him that the liquid in these vials contains powerful cell-generating material. But also that the serum is unwieldy, imperfect, dangerous.

Holding up one of the vials to the dim light, he wants to know how, exactly, this liquid is unwieldy, imperfect, and dangerous. What would happen, for example, if it touched a living creature's skin? He wants to test it. Once the idea is there in his head, there's no talking himself out of it.

First, he needs something living to test the serum on.

A beetle.

He walks to the jars again and picks one up quickly. Again, a few beetles dash off, but he cups his hand over one of them. It has a glossy green back and a bright red head spiked with thornlike horns. Its legs fan out, knotted, bristled with spikes. He holds it in place until he feels the beetle tickling up his fingers.

'Sorry,' he whispers to the beetle. 'I really am.'

He carries it to the plywood, opens his mother's music box, gently nudges it into the box, and closes the lid. He hears the beetle scratching within it. He wishes Arvin Weed, the boy genius of the academy, were here. God, Partridge regrets not paying attention in labs.

He picks up one of the syringes, uncaps it, and fills it with fluid from one of the vials. The needle shines. He knows that this means he'll waste a drop. *Just one*, he tells himself. *Only that*.

He upends the music box. The beetle starts skittering across the plywood, but he pinches it and holds it delicately in place.

While its legs scurry, getting nowhere, a sharp tail curls up from under its wings, revealing a swaying stinger. Its small, rounded black eyes seem wet. Partridge looks at the needle, starts to depress the stopper when he feels the sting. His finger and thumb poised on either side of the beetle's shelled back are quickly covered with tiny prickles of searing heat. The burning moves up into his hand, and the shock of it causes him to shout, but he keeps his hold on the beetle.

As fast as he can, he moves the needle toward the beetle, but his hand feels so rigid with pain he has to let the beetle go. It clicks across the plywood, but not before a drop of liquid from the needle falls, landing – thick and wet – on one of its hind legs. The leg goes limp from the weighty trap of the liquid. The beetle drags itself forward.

The shout has alerted Mother Hestra. Her knuckles rap the cellar door. 'What was that noise?'

'Nothing!' Partridge wraps the syringes, his burning hand blotched now, and he crawls to the jar, lifts it, and slides the bundled syringes in the hole. The beetle pulls itself under the plywood to darkness.

The cellar door opens wide with a clang. Mother Hestra is backlit, dimly. 'What's the noise down here?' she asks.

'It's just a chant from the academy. It can get too quiet down here.' He rubs his burning hand but then stops. He doesn't want any more questions.

Mother Hestra has a thick body. Her son, Syden, a five-year-old, is permanently fused to her leg. She's wearing furs stitched together and fitted to the shape of her body with a hole for the boy's blotched head, just above her hip. Most of the mothers are Groupies, fused to children, and Partridge has never gotten used to it. During the Detonations, the mothers were holding their children or protecting them from the bright flashes, bent to them, tending to them. Partridge can't quite imagine being stunted in that form, never growing up, always locked into place within the confines of your mother's body. Syden's face has begun to age. Will he grow old like this?

Mother Hestra glares at Partridge. One of her cheeks is seared with words – a backward script burned into her skin during the Detonations – the impression of a blackened tattoo. Partridge doesn't let himself stare at it long enough to try to read it. He doesn't want to be rude. 'Well, stop with all that,' she says.

'I was just going to sleep anyway.'

'Good. We leave in the morning. I'll call on you early.'

'Lyda and Illia are coming too?' He'd rather not have Illia coming along. She's crazy. He can't fault her. She was locked away in the farmhouse, abused by her husband, forced to hide her scars beneath a stocking made to look like a second skin. Recently, she's reverted to wrapping herself in swathes of cloth – because she's ashamed of her skin? Or is it simply a habit? She murdered her husband – a scalpel to the back – and it messed her up good. Lyda is the only one he wants to see. Lyda.

'Lyda, yes. Illia? I don't know,' Mother Hestra says.

'Where are we going?' Partridge asks.

'Can't say.' And with that, she heaves herself out of view. The cellar door slams shut. For a second, Partridge is blinded by the news. No more confinement. He'll see Lyda tomorrow. Everything will be different soon; it's coming. He can feel it. God, he misses her.

That's when he hears the rasp, low and heavy. And then there's a noise like a shovel in dirt. But that's not it either – a thick scraping noise.

He feels like he's not alone.

His mother's music box lies in the dirt. He reaches for it and sees a long black talon on a thin spoke – the leg of an insect, a massive insect – sticking out from under the plywood. It's too big to be the beetle's leg. Still there's rasping.

He puts his hand on the plywood and begins to lift it. The leg crimps, disappears from view.

He takes a breath and yanks the plywood so hard it flips over; he forgets he's been coded with extra strength sometimes.

There's the beetle. Its tail clicking against its own shell, its wings convulsing wildly and uselessly, rasping as it struggles for breath.

It has one spiny, thick, massive leg.

The liquid in the vial worked. The cells of its leg weren't injured, and so, with incredible speed, the cells didn't repair trauma – they built on healthy tissue and bone; even the ornate spikes on this one hind leg have ordered themselves perfectly. And, for some reason, this seems familiar to him – the delicacy of rebuilding a small limb. Has he ever heard of something like it before?

Partridge doesn't want to touch it. His hand still tingles with heat. *Unwieldy, imperfect, dangerous.* That's what his mother called the serum. The beetle's leg jerks uncontrollably, gouging a claw mark in the dirt.

And Partridge feels a strange rush of power. He made this happen with one tiny drop of liquid. His head pounds and his ears ring, and he thinks of his father's power. What did the old man feel when the Detonations hit – blast after blast of bright blinding light pulsing around the earth?

My God, Partridge thinks. What if Partridge's father loved the power of it all? What if it made him feel like he was lit up? What if it felt like this infinitesimal moment expanded exponentially, infinitely, inside of him?

The beetle's wings fold in tightly to its body. The leg spasms a few more times, and then the beetle digs its powerful leg into the dirt like a knife and pushes itself up. Its small legs dart beneath it, and the massive leg contracts, then extends. The beetle springs into the air and flaps its wings. The leg is too heavy for the wings to support. It falls to the ground, but the massive leg is there to soften the landing. It contracts again, springs forward, flaps, lands, contracts, springs forward . . .

The beetle is no longer what it was moments ago.

It's a new species.

EL CAPITAN

NEW

IT'S BEEN SNOWING OFF AND ON, and now it's started up again. Snow shudders down from the sky, lightly drifting between the dark trees and scrub, settling on gnarled boughs. Many of the limbs have grown thick coats of fur this cold autumn. El Capitan runs his fingers up the spindly limb of a sapling, and there it is – not a fuzzy coating of something plantlike. No, this is the downy fur you'd find on the belly of a young cat. 'One day they'll grow legs and walk off,' he says to his brother, Helmud, the weight forever rooted to his back.

'Walk off,' Helmud whispers. He looks out over one of El Capitan's shoulders then bobs to the other. He seems anxious today.

'Stop shifting around,' El Capitan orders. 'Shifting around,' Helmud says.

El Capitan has given Helmud things to keep his hands busy. Helmud has always had nervous hands. Used to be that his brother was secretly fashioning a lariat to kill El Capitan, but then Helmud saved El Capitan's life. After that, El Capitan decided that he had to trust Helmud. He had no choice. To keep his hands busy, El Capitan gave Helmud a little penknife and things to whittle. 'You sure you want to do that?' Bradwell asked him once. El Capitan said, 'Of course I'm sure. He's my brother!' But the knife might just be a test, as if he's saying, *Go ahead. You want to kill me? You sure? I'll make it easy.* Sometimes when El Capitan leans forward, a small flurry of wood chips flutters to the ground. Helmud is whittling today, quite madly.

El Capitan sits down on the large root of a tree and sets his rifle at his boots. They left without breakfast and now he's hungry. From a sheet of waxed paper, he unwraps a sandwich made of bread heels. He prefers the heels – the extra toughness in his teeth. He says to Helmud, 'Time to eat, brother.'

El Capitan is used to Helmud's constant repetitions; usually they're just a dim-witted echo. Sometimes, though, the words mean something. And this time, Helmud repeats the phrase slightly differently. 'Time to eat brother,' he says, as if Helmud intends to devour El Capitan. It's a little joke, meant to keep El Capitan on his toes.

'Now, now,' El Capitan says, 'is that nice, Helmud? Is it?'

'Is it?' Helmud says.

'I shouldn't even share this sandwich with you. You know that?' Before they'd gotten involved with Pressia, El Capitan wouldn't have shared, but he's changed some. He feels it throughout his body, as if change happens cell by cell. He wonders if Helmud notices the change too, since they share so many cells. It's not that he's gotten sweet all of a sudden. No, El Capitan still feels a near-constant, fiery rage in his chest. But it's more about having a purpose, that there's something worth protecting. Is it Pressia herself?

Maybe it starts with her, but, no – it's larger than that.

El Capitan rips off a hunk of the bread and the small wedge of meat between the heels. He hands it to Helmud. He has to share with Helmud. Their hearts pump with shared blood, and if El Capitan is going to help bring down the Dome – and he'd like to live to see that day – he needs Helmud on his side and healthy. Being cruel to Helmud is the same as being cruel to himself. And maybe that's it. El Capitan hated himself plenty before he met Pressia, but that's eased up a little. He thought of himself as an abandoned kid. First abandoned by his father – some pilot kicked out of the air force for going mental. El Capitan tried to be like him – figuring out everything he could about flying jets – as if that could make him worthy of a father. Then his mother died. It seemed he wasn't worthy of having parents at all. He went a little mental himself, but he doesn't have to get stuck that way. Right? Pressia sees something worthwhile in him, and she could be right. 'See how nice I am?' he says to Helmud.

'Nice I am,' Helmud says.

El Capitan set out earlier this morning to follow the electrical pulses. He doesn't like the way they seem to be circling closer to headquarters. They've been eluding him. But now he's sure he senses something. Although he can't read the pulses, he can tell when they're moving at a higher rate, which means that one of them has sent out a call of some sort and the others are responding.

He folds a cloth over what's left of the sandwich, shoves it in his sack, and heads toward the pulses. He sees a set of tracks in the snow – each footprint crisscrossed with treading. A few figures darting up ahead. He follows at a respectful distance.

He comes to a clearing and stops. A few Special Forces cluster. They're beautiful and strong – almost majestic. Some are bulky, others sinewy. They seem unaffected by cold, as if their thin second skins are regulated to insulate them. They have a profound sense of smell. One lifts his head and tenses his nostrils, smelling El Capitan and Helmud, and then he locks eyes with El Capitan, who doesn't move but doesn't stiffen either. He doesn't want to seem fearful.

He's noticed over the last few weeks that this new group isn't as robust as the ones he and Helmud battled in the woods alongside Bradwell and Lyda. They seem not as fully formed, as if the changes to their bodies were rushed. They're not as agile. They sometimes lurch. They seem less comfortable with the weapons locked into their arms. When they cluster like this, it's like they need one another, a closeness – the way humans do.

The other three creatures also look at Helmud and El Capitan, alerted in some unseen way by the first. They never say a word to him, though he knows they can speak. It's as if they accept his presence as part of the environment, as they do the sharp *scree-scree* of an occasional wing-warped bird with a metal beak or the humanlike child-cry of an animal caught in one of El Capitan's traps. They aren't looking for him. That's not why they're here. They want Partridge, El Capitan is sure of it, and he's afraid they might be attuned to Pressia too – she shares a bloodline with her brother and she could be of use to the Dome, particularly to draw Partridge in.

El Capitan would like to talk to them. He knows their loyalty to the Dome is programmed, but there was one who went rogue when they fought near the bunker – Partridge's brother, Sedge. They're human, on the most buried level. He feels that one small connection would help. He's been waiting for the right moment.

He walks out from the trees and kneels down in the snow, the cold and wet seeping through his pants. He opens his arms, a gesture of supplication. He lowers his head, a bow of sorts.

He hears the scuttling of footsteps, the snapping of branches. He looks up and they're gone.

He sits back on his heels. 'Shit.'

'Shit,' Helmud says.

'Don't talk that way,' he says to his brother. 'It's a bad habit.'

He stands up, but then hears a sound behind him. He slowly pulls his rifle around to his chest. He turns.

A solitary Special Forces creature stands in the middle of the path not more than twenty feet away. El Capitan has never seen him before. He isn't sending out any low pulses, which reverberate off other Special Forces in the area. Interesting. Maybe he doesn't want anyone else to know where he is.

He's tall and the thinnest Special Forces soldier El Capitan has seen. In fact, his face still holds on to its humanness – and not just in the eyes, which always seem human in Special Forces, but also in the delicacy of his jaw and small nose and nostrils. His shoulders and thighs are strong but not hulking. He has two weapons embedded in his forearms, still shiny with polish – never used.

This one is very new.

He eyes El Capitan warily.

El Capitan raises his hands slowly. 'Listen, let's take this easy and calm.'

'Calm,' Helmud says, whittling nervously behind El Capitan's back.

'What do you want?' El Capitan says.

The creature cocks his head, sniffs the air.

'You want something to eat? If I'd known you were coming, I'd have packed more.'

The creature shakes his head. He leans down, clearing snow

from the path, exposing the bare, ashen dirt. He stands, then lifts his foot. One thick dagger pops from the boot's toe. El Capitan flinches, wondering if he's going to get gutted, but then the creature sticks the dagger into the dirt, raises his chin, looking out through the trees, and starts to claw out a word. El Capitan is fairly sure that the creature's eyes and ears are bugged – as Pressia's once were. He's played this game before. The creature wants to tell him something without recording it.

Beneath the word, the creature seems to draw some kind of symbol. It's all too far away to read. Plus, it's upside down.

The creature backs away, takes a few leaps into the woods, then jumps, gripping the girth of a tree – its top half gone and its pulp dug out by bugs.

El Capitan takes a tentative step forward. He looks at the creature, who is still staring off into the trees. El Capitan walks around the word and reads it to himself – HASTINGS. Is it a name? A place? He thinks of the word *battle*. Doesn't Hastings have to do with war somehow? El Capitan knows not to say the word aloud. He stares at the symbol. It's a cross, which is the way the Dome ended its Message – just after the Detonations – on small slips of paper that fell down from the sky. A cross with a circle around the center.

'I don't know what he wants from me,' El Capitan says to Helmud.

The soldier leaps from the tree and starts to run. But then he pauses.

'He wants us to follow,' El Capitan says.

'Follow,' Helmud says.

El Capitan nods and follows the soldier through the woods for almost a mile, keeping a brisk pace. Finally he comes to a clearing that overlooks the city, or what used to be the city. From this height, it's easy to see how it's been reduced to the Rubble Fields, black markets, hulls of old buildings, a grid of alleys, and nameless streets.

El Capitan looks around for the soldier. He's gone. El Capitan is breathless. Helmud's heart is beating fast too, but maybe only because El Capitan's heart has pumped the blood so hard. 'Damn it,' El Capitan mutters. 'Why'd he bring me here?'

'Bring me here,' Helmud says.

El Capitan can see the Dome too, the white curve of it on the distant hill, its cross glinting through the ashen sky. 'Did he think I didn't know where he came from?' He rubs his eyes with his knuckles.

'Where he came from,' Helmud says, and he points out across the barren, near-desert land that surrounds the Dome to a clump of people dragging timber and arranging it on the iced ground.

'Some crazies trying to build something out in front of the Dome?'

'In front of the Dome?' Helmud repeats.

Why in front of the Dome? Is this what the soldier wanted him to see? If so, why? El Capitan watches the way the people move. They're organized, shuttling things along like ants in ordered rows. 'I don't like it,' he says. 'Almost looks like they're going to try to build a fire.'

'Fire,' Helmud says.

El Capitan looks up at the Dome. 'Why the hell would they do that?'

PRESSIA

SEVEN

THE MORGUE IS COLD AND BARE with one long steel table. Since the last time she was here, a couple of weeks ago, Bradwell has spread out even more papers and books. Portions of his parents' unfinished manuscript are arranged in piles. On the wall, Bradwell has taped the Message, an original her grandfather kept for years. She gave it to Bradwell after he went back to the barbershop to pick up what was left. He's the archivist, after all.

We know you are here, our brothers and sisters.
We will, one day, emerge from the Dome
to join you in peace.
For now, we watch from afar, benevolently.

When the Message first fell from the hull of an airship to the ground in the days after the Detonations, it must have felt like a promise. Now it feels like a threat.

Bradwell slides a heavy bar across the door – a handmade lock bolted to the wall.

'Nice place you've got here,' she says.

He walks to his pallet and straightens the covers. 'No complaints.'

Pressia moves to the table where she sees the bell she gave him in the farmhouse. She found it in the burned-out barbershop just before she left home. It has no clapper. It sits on a news clipping that must have survived the Detonations, probably in Bradwell's parents' footlocker. It's not as ashen and charred as some of the other documents. He's taken good care of it. Bradwell has always taken care of the things from the past. After his parents were murdered before the Detonations – shot in their beds – Bradwell found their footlocker, which was sealed off in a hidden, reinforced room. It was filled with his parents' unfinished work, trying to take down Willux, as well as things Bradwell has preserved – old magazines, newspapers, packaging. The footlocker is shoved under a rusty stainless-steel sink. The bell hides part of the headline. The rest reads, DROWNING RULED ACCIDENT. There's a photograph of a young man in uniform, stone-faced, staring into the camera. Bradwell is using the bell as a paperweight. Is that all it means to him?

Pressia checks on Freedle. She opens her hand and sets him on the table. His eyes blink open and he looks around.

The Black Box motors past her feet. 'It *is* kind of like a pet dog,' Pressia says. 'You're right.'

'I had a dog once,' Bradwell says.

'You never told me that.'

'I told Partridge when we were looking for you out in the Meltlands. A friend of the family, Art Walrond, talked my parents into giving me a dog. He told them that an only child needs a dog. I named the dog Art Walrond.'

'Weird name for a dog.'

'I was a weird kid.'

'But when Art Walrond, friend of the family, and Art Walrond, family dog, were both in the room at the same time, and you said, "Sit down, Art Walrond," which one would sit?'

'Is that a philosophical question?'

'Maybe.' And it feels almost okay again between them. Maybe they can be friends, the kind who banter back and forth.

He reaches down and pats the Black Box like it's a dog. 'It's not quite the way I remember it.' She'd like to imagine him as a kid with a dog, weird and all. She'd like to know about herself as a child too. She spent most of her childhood trying to remember things that never happened, the life her grandfather invented for her. But he wasn't even her grandfather; he was a stranger who rescued her and made her his own. Was this lie hard for him? Maybe he'd had a wife and children who died and she was supposed to stand in for these losses. He's gone now, so she'll never know.

If the Detonations hadn't ever happened, she'd have liked to have met Bradwell – a reality in which there are no doll-head fists or scars or embedded birds, before all the losses. They might have had a first kiss under mistletoe – something her grandfather once told her about.

On the other side of the table, the room extends with three rows of what look like small square doors, three deep on one wall – nine total. She walks up to them, curiously. She touches one of the handles.

'That's where they kept the bodies,' Bradwell says. 'And the metal table was used for autopsies.'

The dead. Pressia imagines her mother's face – there and then gone. She draws her hand away from the drawers and looks at the far wall, its broken cinder block cracked through with dirt pushing in on the other side. 'It's a morgue. Of course they stored dead bodies here,' she says, more to herself than to him.

'And they still do every once in a while.'

She tries to lighten things. 'I guess that would be like having a roommate.'

'Kind of,' Bradwell says. 'I've had only one so far.'

'Who?'

'A kid who died out in the woods,' Bradwell says. 'Do you want to meet him?'

It's like an intruder has suddenly appeared. 'He's here now?'

'Soldiers on patrol found him. Cap brought the body here. He wants to know what killed the boy. And they're trying to find the family to come identify the body.'

'What if he doesn't have family?'

'I guess it'll be a fresh recruit's job to bury him.' He pulls one of the handles. She expects to see the boy's body. 'A morgue also happens to be the perfect place to lock up Black Boxes.' As the long slab slides out, she sees it's filled with the other five Black Boxes. They're still, their lights off. Each has a piece of paper covered with notes taped to the slab. Each note has a heading; he's named the boxes – Alfie, Barb, Champ, Dickens, Elderberry, alphabetical order. Fignan's on the floor, buzzing close to Bradwell's heels. Freedle flutters from the table and flaps around Fignan. A camera lens on a small arm extends from the top of the box and seems to take footage of Freedle in flight.

'Did you have to name them?'

'Easier to talk with them if they have names. I grew up alone. I can strike up a conversation with anything,' he says. With that, Pressia glimpses his childhood. At ten, he lived alone in the basement of a butcher shop and fended for himself. It was lonesome. How could it not have been? 'It doesn't really matter what I've named them, though. These five are all identical inside, designed to withstand extreme heat, pressure, radiation. They have this series of plugs.' He picks up one of the boxes and shows Pressia the small holes that the plugs revealed. 'I wedged the plugs off with the help of one of Cap's rigged-up blowtorches and then . . .' He picks up three pieces of wire and, simultaneously, fits them into the holes, a delicate operation. 'There you go.' The Black Box's lid is pulled back with a buzzing sound, and there inside is something red, oval, and made of heavy metal.

'What is it?'

'It's where all the information is stored. It's the brain. It responds to simple commands,' he says. 'Open egg.'

The red egg hums. Small sliding metal doors retract, revealing chips, wires, a vast network of synaptic-like connections.

'This is its brain. A thing of beauty.' He picks up the red egg, turns it in his hand. 'It holds an entire library of data.'

'Libraries,' Pressia says, awed. 'They were buildings that housed books, room after room of books, and they had people who tended to the books.'

'Librarians.'

'I've heard of them.' The concept is hard to fathom. 'And you could take the books home if you promised to bring them back.'

'Exactly,' Bradwell says. 'I had a library card as a kid. My name typed up next to my picture.' He looks wistful for a second. Pressia's jealous of the memory. She built a childhood from the things her grandfather told her, and now she has to dismantle that world, to unremember. She wishes she could recall something as simple as a library card with her name and picture. She thinks of her real name. *Emi* – two sounds that hum for that brief second on her lips. *Brigid* – like a bridge spanning a wide cold lake. *Imanaka* – the sound of sticks being struck together. Who was Emi Brigid Imanaka supposed to become?

Maybe that version of herself – Emi – could have fallen helplessly in love with Bradwell. She can't, not when it seems to guarantee losing him.

Bradwell turns his attention back to the boxes. 'I had to open the box to activate the egg, but now it can sit inside the Black Box and answer any question you can dream up.' He puts the egg back into the Black Box. 'Close.' The egg seals itself up and the box locks into place around it.

'What did you ask it?'

'First, I asked it what it was.'

'And?'

He leans over the box. 'What are you?'

A series of clicks rattle up from its center, and a mechanical, camera-like eyeball appears from its top. A beam of light shoots up above the eyeball, and an image of the egg itself appears and turns in the air. A young man's voice recites a brief history of recording devices, including Black Boxes, which were usually painted red or orange for easy recognition at a crash site. 'This box is part of a series of identical Black Boxes, a government-sanctioned and federally funded project to record cultural history and data in the case of a holocaust – nuclear or otherwise.' It gives the specific measurements of its aluminum housing, high-temperature insulation, stainless-steel shell, and radiation-resistant nanotechnology tubing.

'Wow,' Pressia says.

'They contain images of art and movies, science, history, pop culture,' Bradwell says. 'Everything.'

The idea of *everything* makes her feel almost light-headed. 'The Before,' Pressia says, awed.

'They contain a *version* of the Before. A digitized, cleaned-up version. Information isn't necessarily the truth.'

'My grandfather explained how the universe worked by rotating rocks in circles on the floor – the sun, planets, stars. He pretended to know things, because when he didn't, he could tell it made me nervous.'

'What is the universe?' Bradwell asks the Black Box.

Another widening beam of light shows planets and moons orbiting the sun, constellations dotting the air. Pressia reaches for a moon, expecting to nudge it, but her fingers glide through it. Freedle flutters up through the image too, then lands on his pronged feet and gazes at it, confused. 'This was what my grandfather was trying to explain. The universe.'

'Pretty hard to capture with rocks on the ground.'

Pressia feels lost. There's so much she doesn't know, can't even imagine. 'It's amazing! The amount of information we can have access to. It can really change people's lives. We'll have access to medical information, technology, science. We'll be able to make a real difference.'

'It's more than that, Pressia.'

'What do you mean? How can it be more than *everything*?'

'These boxes know only what they've been fed, and all of them were put on the same diet. Except Fignan. He's different.' Bradwell picks up the Black Box at his feet. 'Each of these boxes has a serial code on the bottom. But Fignan has only a copyright symbol.' He flips it over, showing her a circle around a crude three-line *C*.

Pressia runs her finger over it. 'What's a copyright?'

'It's a symbol to show ownership. It was widely used in the Before, but was usually followed by a year. This one isn't.'

Pressia gives the box a quarter turn. 'It could also be a *U* in a circle.' She turns it again, halfway this time. 'Or an unfinished square or a table.'

'Black Boxes aren't just boxes that happen to be black. They're the name of anything – a device or process – that's thought of in terms of input and output, when you can't see how it's being processed, what's going on inside. A white box or a glass box, those are things where you can put information in and you can see what happens to it.'

'The Dome is a Black Box,' Pressia says.

'From our perspective, it is,' Bradwell says. 'And so is the human brain.'

And so are you, she thinks. *And so am I.* She wonders if two human beings can ever be white boxes for each other.

He puts Fignan on the table. 'Fignan is an impostor. He's supposed to fit in, but he was made with a different audience in mind. But he won't just hand that information over to anybody. Some word made him light up and then he talked to me.' He puts his hands in his pockets and lowers his head. 'Should I recite what I was saying? About you? I mean, it's just us trying to figure this out. Nothing more than that, right?'

'Right.' She wants to stall. 'But first, it lit up and talked to you. What did it say?'

'It said *seven*.'

'The number seven?'

'It said *seven* over and over and then it stopped and beeped as if waiting for a response while seconds were ticking off a clock, and then it stopped. Time's up, like a game show.'

'A game show?' she asks. She knows that this is a reference to the Before, but she can't place it.

'You know, TV shows where people answered questions asked by a host who had a microphone and prizes like sets of luggage and Jet Skis, while the audience shouted things at them and clapped wildly. There was one where they gave electric shocks when the contestants answered wrong. People loved it.'

'Right, game shows,' she says, as if she remembers them. What's a Jet Ski? 'But why do we care if this one box opens up or not? We have everything we could possibly want from the other five!'

'Fignan holds secrets,' Bradwell says. 'He was programmed to guard them carefully.'

Pressia shakes her head. 'This is about uncovering the truth, the past, more lessons in Shadow History? Don't you know enough already?'

'Of course I don't know enough! How many times do I have to tell you that we have to fully understand the past or we're doomed to repeat it? And if we can understand Willux, the enemy, then—'

Pressia is furious. 'We can improve people's lives with what's in these boxes, but you have to go after the mystery, the holdout? Okay, fine. So do it again. Make him do the game-show thing again.'

Bradwell shakes his head and runs his hands through his hair. 'That's just it. I don't remember what I said exactly. Maybe I should retrace my verbal steps. You sure you're okay with that?'

'Of course.' Is he needling her?

'Well, I was . . . rambling . . . about you. It was the middle of the night, and I was, well, describing you . . . I was talking about what you looked like – your dark eyes, the shape of them, and how they look like liquid sometimes, and I was talking about the shine of your hair, and the burn around one of your eyes. I mentioned your hand, the lost one, but that it's not really gone, that it exists inside the doll, that the doll is as much a part of you as anything else.'

Pressia's cheeks flush. Why would he talk about her scars, her deformity? If he were in love, wouldn't his vision erase her flaws? Wouldn't he see only the best version of her? She turns away from him and looks at the rows of boxes. Their lights blink dimly, small twinkling repetitions.

He says, 'I might have mentioned your lips.'

The room is quiet now.

The flush in her cheeks spreads across her chest. She pinches the swan pendant and twists it nervously. 'Okay, so it said *seven*. Why do we care? Let's concentrate on the good boxes. Let it keep its secrets.'

Bradwell walks up to her and lightly cups her wrist. He stares at the necklace. His hand is rough but warm. 'Wait,' he says. 'I also mentioned the necklace, how the pendant sits right in the dip between your two collarbones. The swan pendant.'

The Black Box lights up. It beeps a short punctuated alarm and says, 'Seven, seven, seven, seven, seven, seven, seven.' They both stare at it, startled. The beeping continues as the clock ticks down, and then it goes silent.

'This has to do with my mother,' Pressia says. Her mother told her a lot of things that Pressia didn't understand. She spoke quickly, almost in a kind of shorthand. Pressia didn't ask her to clarify because she assumed there would be time later to hear everything she needed to know. But she does remember her mother talking about the importance of the swan as a symbol and the Seven. 'The Best and the Brightest,' Pressia says. 'It was a large, important program, recruiting the smartest kids they could find. And from that group, they made another, more elite group of twenty-two – and from that, Willux formed an inner seven. This was when they were our age. Early on.'

'The Seven,' he says.

'The swan was their symbol.' Fignan starts up again. 'Remember, I told you that they got tattoos, when they were all still together and young and idealistic, a row of six pulsing tattoos that ran over their own hearts, which was the seventh pulse.' Three of the pulsing heartbeats had stopped, but not her father's. Pressia knows she should be content that he survived. She shouldn't long to see him, but she can't stop herself from longing. Sometimes all she wants is to get out, to search for him. Even now, the thought of it makes her heart pound with extra beats, like the pulsing tattoos themselves.

Bradwell, El Capitan, and Partridge latched on to the idea of heartbeats still pulsing. It meant that other survivors, maybe other civilizations, exist beyond the Deadlands. But how far? For Pressia, it's personal.

She walks back to the box, leans down, and stares at it. 'Swan,' she says and it starts up again, repeating the word *seven*, seven times, then beeping. 'It's asking us for a password – or seven of them.'

'Do you know their names?' Bradwell asks.

She shakes her head. 'Not all of them.'

'Swan,' Bradwell says.

The Black Box says *seven* again and when it's done and the beeping starts, Bradwell says, 'Ellery Willux.' A green light blinks from a row of lights near the camera eye. 'Aribelle Cording.' Another green light sparks.

'Hideki Imanaka,' Pressia says, and it accepts this name too. She's said her father's name aloud so few times that this small green light feels like an affirmation. He truly exists. He is her father. She feels hopeful in a way she hasn't in a long time.

'And the others?' Bradwell asks.

She shakes her head. 'Caruso would have helped. He would have known.' Caruso lived in the bunker with her mother. When Bradwell and El Capitan went back to the bunker after the farmhouse burned, they thought they'd talk him into coming with them. But he'd killed himself. Bradwell never said how he did it, and Pressia didn't ask. 'I wish he'd known how much he could have helped us. If he'd known, maybe he wouldn't have . . .'

'Was Caruso one of them?' Bradwell asks.

'No.'

'Try to remember,' Bradwell says.

'I can't remember!' She squeezes her forehead. 'I don't even know that she said all the names.' Her mind is blank except for the image of her mother's death – her skull, the mist of blood.

'If we can get these passwords, who knows what we'll have access to.'

'No!' She's angry now. 'We have to focus on what we can do here, now, today, for these people. They're suffering. They need help. If we let ourselves get pulled into the past, we're turning our backs on the survivors.'

'The past?' Bradwell is furious. 'The past isn't just the past. It's the truth! The Dome has to be held accountable for what they did to the world. The truth has to be known.'

'Why? Why do we have to keep fighting the Dome?' Pressia has given up on the truth. 'What could the truth possibly matter when there's all this suffering and loss?'

'Pressia,' Bradwell says, his voice going soft, 'my parents died trying to get at the truth!'

'My mother's dead too. And I have to let her go.' She walks up to Bradwell. 'Let your parents go.'

He walks down the rows and stops in front of the drawer at the end. 'You should see the dead boy.'

'No, Bradwell . . .'

He grips a chest-high handle. 'I want you to see him.'

She takes a deep breath. He pulls the handle, and the slab slides out. She walks to his side.

The boy is about fifteen years old, bare chested, his lower half wrapped in a sheet. His skin has turned the color of a dark bruise, his lips purpled as if he'd eaten blackberries. His hands are curled up around his neck, twisted claws, and one foot pokes out of the bottom of the sheet. He has short, dark hair. What's most striking is that embedded in his bare chest is a silver bar that stretches from one side of his ribs to the other. He was a little kid when the Detonations hit, a kid on a tricycle. The handlebars are mottled with rust. They curve around him like an extra pair of ribs. His skin attached to the metal is thin, almost like webbing.

Pressia closes her eyes. She wraps her arms around her own ribs. 'What happened to him?'

'No one knows.' Bradwell pulls up the bottom of the sheet as Pressia opens her eyes. The boy has only one leg. The other is newly gone. The rupture is so jagged with exposed bone that Pressia gasps. 'The leg exploded,' Bradwell says, 'and he bled to death.' He walks to a counter near the sink, picks up a small cardboard box, and brings it to Pressia. The only thing she can imagine is a human heart, still beating.

He lifts the lid. The box is filled with scraps of metal and plastic. One piece has a metal joint connecting two smaller pieces of broken metal – each about an inch long. Bradwell says, 'This stuff was found near his body. Some shards were still embedded in what was left of the flesh on his leg.'

'What was it?'

'We don't know.' He closes the lid on the box and looks at the dead boy. 'The Dome did this. They aren't going away. Special Forces are only becoming more aggressive, hungrier. I'm not turning my back on *anybody*, Pressia. We have to find a way to push back.'

LYDA

METALTUBS

The ROOM IS AIRY WITH NOTHING in it but two large metal industrial-looking tubs and two chairs, lit by the dusky sunlight illuminating the battered windows. They've been bathing at night, but they were on lockdown during the last dark hours. Special Forces were buzzing nearby, so the baths were delayed.

Illia was let into the room first because she can't be naked in front of anyone. She doesn't even like to bare her face, which is now draped in gray cloth as she reclines in one of the tubs. As Lyda is led in, Illia says, 'You're here.'

'And so are you,' Lyda says, and she means not just here physically but emotionally too. The baths were first a recommendation for Illia. The ash of the Meltlands has collected in her lung pockets, the mothers fear, and bacteria has taken root. Illia needs rest and special care.

But then five nights ago, in these tubs, something miraculous happened. Illia, who'd been so vacant and silent, came to, like a fever broke. She started telling Lyda stories, odd, nameless, placeless stories about *the woman* and *the man*, myths or memories, perhaps from her own childhood.

Lyda told Mother Hestra about Illia's breakthrough, and Mother Hestra called it *a healing*. Lyda loves this. They never used the word *healing* in the rehabilitation center. Unlike her own mother, the mothers here are fierce but also fiercely loving. Ironically, for the first time in her life, she feels protected in a way that she never did within the protective bubble of the Dome.

Each day since the healing, they've bathed in the hope that it would continue. And it has. During the day, Illia is a dimmed light, coughing in a private room, but the bath changes her.

'Yours is not water tonight,' Illia says. Her voice is meek and soft, a little hoarse from disuse. 'It's something else.'

One of the mothers told Lyda that she needed to go all the way under. 'The serum must cover every inch of your skin, every hair on your head.' The air smells syrupy and medicinal. Lyda takes off her cape and hangs it on the back of a chair. She dips her fingers in the warm, cloudy bath. They turn slick and dry quickly, leaving a strange film.

'They say it'll mask the human scent,' Illia says. 'Safer for traveling tomorrow.'

'How does it feel?'

'Mine is water. I can't go and I don't want to.'

'Neither do I!' Lyda wants to see Partridge, desperately, but she likes it here. They've started her on combat training and hunting. Her muscles have grown strong. Her aim is good. She's learned to lie in wait silently. It's dangerous, but strangely peaceful. Even now, undressing, she isn't bashful like she was in the girls' academy locker room. She feels like she's in her skin, and that's good. She folds her clothes on the chair and climbs over the edge of the tub, lowering herself into the strange mixture.

'I'd prefer to die here,' Illia says.

'You're sick, not dying.' Lyda doesn't want to talk about death. In the Dome, it was rarely mentioned. The word itself wasn't appropriate. Lyda's father was escorted to the medical center, the quarantined wing, at the first sign of sickness, and she never saw him again. Disease and death are shameful, and she wonders now if her father, like Willux, had taken some enhancements that had started to wear him down. *Your father has passed on*, her mother told her. *Passed on*.

'Tell me a story! I look forward to them all day.' This is a half-truth. The stories also scare Lyda. There's something doomed about the telling – it's not a story that's going to end well.

'Not tonight.'

'You told me last time that the woman worked as the keeper of knowledge in the quiet place, and the man came to her and asked her to protect the seed of truth, a seed that would grow in the next world to come. What's next?'

'Did I tell you that the woman fell in love with the man?'

'Yes. You said it was like her heart was spinning.' Lyda understands. She feels this way when she thinks of Partridge, especially when she imagines him kissing her.

'Did I tell you that the man loved her?'

'Yes. That's where we left off. He wanted to marry her.'

She shakes her head. 'He can't marry her.'

'Why?'

'He's going to die.'

'Die?'

'And she can't die with him. She has to survive because she's the keeper of knowledge; she has the seed of truth. It holds secrets.'

'What kind of secrets?'

'Secrets that could save them all.'

Is the story true? Is it set during the Before? 'And how does he die?'

'He's dead. And she dies inside.'

'What happens to the seed of truth?' Lyda feels anxious. She tells herself that it's only a story, but she's not sure she believes that.

'She marries someone who is chosen to survive so the seed of truth can live. She marries a man who has connections. The End is coming.'

A chill runs through Lyda. Illia is talking about herself. The man who has connections must be, in fact, Ingership – Illia's husband, the one she killed. If Lyda brings up Ingership by name, she fears that Illia will retreat again. Isn't she telling the story this way because she can't face the truth of it, which is why it's healing? 'Tell me about the End,' Lyda whispers.

'An explosion of the sun. Everything became iridescent. Everything broke open as if objects and humans all contained light. It was the brightest entry into darkness.'

'And the keeper survived?'

Illia pulls down part of the gray cloth and looks at Lyda now with her hooded eyes. 'I'm here, aren't I? I'm here.'

Lyda nods. Of course. But if Illia knows that she's the keeper, why tell the story this way? 'Illia,' Lyda says, 'why not just say *I fell in love with a man*? Why not just tell me everything? Don't you trust me?'

'What if I'm not who you think I am? Some little housewife, all knit up in her stocking. Some little beaten housewife who never knew anything, who had no past, who'd never known love, who had no power.' She lifts her arms, shiny and wet, her hands clenched in fists. 'You don't know the difference between these scars and these? Do you? You don't know anything of scars.' Her arms are pocked and burned – a row of burns up one arm and a spray of shards in the other.

Lyda shakes her head. 'I don't.'

'I'm the keeper! So where's the seed? Huh? I ask you that. Where's the goddamn seed now?' Illia is furious. Her fists are shaking in the air. 'I don't know,' Lyda says. 'I'm sorry. I don't know what you're talking about. I don't know what you mean.' She grips the edge of the tub. 'Tell me. Tell me what you mean.'

'I couldn't deliver the truth to dead people. I had to keep it.' Her voice sounds distant and haunted.

'What dead people? Which ones?'

'There were so many . . .'

'Illia! I want you to tell me what this means. I want you to tell me the true story. Tell me. For your sake and mine. Get it out. Tell me everything.'

'And now I can't die until I have fulfilled my duty, until I have handed it over. I can't die until then, Lyda.' She looks at Lyda as if maybe she'd like to die. Lyda can't understand it. 'I can't die,' she says, as if confessing a deep sadness. 'Not yet.'

'You're not dying, Illia. Tell me what happened to you. Tell me, please. Don't talk about dying.'

'Don't talk about dying? You want me to talk about love. They're one and the same, child. One and the same.'

The room goes quiet. Lyda shrinks into the tub and closes her eyes and when she does, all she sees are Illia's wet arms – the spray of debris in one and the strange orderly row of risen welts on the other. It's the orderly scars that disturb her. The Detonations caused erratic fusings and scars, not tidy rows. She thinks of Ingership. She knows the difference between the two kinds of scars, after all. Some are from the Detonations. The others are from torture – nine years of torture.

She hears Illia draw in a sharp breath and then mutter to herself. At first Illia says, *I miss the truth. I miss art. I miss art. Life would be worth living if I had art.* Was she an artist? Lyda loves art. She once made a sculpture of a bird from wire. Illia then starts in about death. *I want to die! I want death. But the keeper can't die. The keeper can't die until she has fulfilled her role. The keeper must find the seed.* It's not a myth or even a story anymore; it's more like a mantra or a prayer.

But a dark prayer, a terrifying prayer. Lyda keeps her eyes closed – the serum must cover every inch of her body, every hair on her head, the mother explained. She slides down, her backbone bumping the metal. Submerged, everything is quiet. She feels like she's being held by the serum, the tub. Her held breath starts to burn her lungs. *Just another second of peace*, she thinks. *Just one more.*

PARTRIDGE

COLD

PARTRIDGE IS PACKED AND READY. The maps are rolled up in his backpack, the music box is in his coat pocket, and the vials are bound into place with a strip of cloth from his bedsheet, wrapped around his stomach. Still, when the cellar door slams open in the morning, he's shocked by the dusty light pouring in and the gust of cold air.

'It's time!' Mother Hestra shouts.

He barely slept. The beetle scrambled to the corner and shook spastically until finally it found a rat hole and disappeared. The image stuck in his head – the massive leg. But even without that pulsing behind his lids, he doesn't like sleeping because he dreams of finding his mother in the academy again and again; her bloody, amputated body under the bleachers by the playing fields, in the hushed library, and, worst of all, in the science lab – as if she's something his teacher expects him to dissect. He's sure she's dead, but then an eye will blink. Better not to sleep much.

He walks up the small set of wooden stairs. The wind gusts.

The sky is shot through with dark, billowing sashes. This was once a nice subdivision – rows of cream-colored houses that now look like bleached bones.

He sees Lyda standing by the corner of a fallen house. Her cape billowing around her hips, she holds a homemade spear – a sharp blade tethered to the tip of a broomstick. She looks at him at first like she's scared but then she breaks into a smile that lights her face. Her skin shines from the waxy serum too. Her blue eyes are tearing – because she's happy to see him, or is it the wind? Her hair is growing in, a soft fuzz on her head. With her hair short like this, he sees more of her beautiful face. He has the urge to run to her, lift her up, kiss her. But Mother Hestra would misinterpret it as aggression and might attack. Partridge and Lyda aren't allowed to be alone. This was another one of the conditions – total protection of the girl.

He smiles and winks. She winks back.

Lyda walks to Mother Hestra and ruffles Syden's hair.

Mother Hestra says, 'We'll travel in a line.'

'Illia isn't coming?' Partridge asks.

'The ash in her lungs has taken on disease. She'll stay here in the hope of recovery.'

'Has a doctor seen her?' Partridge asks.

'What doctor are they going to call?' Lyda says sharply.

'She is another victim of the Deaths,' Mother Hestra says coldly, eyeing Partridge. 'They created this ash, and her lungs are sickened by it. One day, she will likely die of it. Another murder.'

'I'm not a Death,' Partridge says defensively. 'I was a kid when the Detonations hit. You know that.'

'A Death is a Death,' Mother Hestra says. 'Get in line.'

Lyda is behind Mother Hestra and Partridge is at the end,

within three feet of Lyda. His stomach feels light. His heart pounds. 'Hi,' he whispers.

Lyda puts her hand behind the small of her back and waves.

'I missed you,' he whispers.

She glances over her shoulder and smiles.

'No talking!' Mother Hestra shouts. How did she hear him?

He wants to tell her about the vials, the beetle's leg, the strange feeling that it's familiar to him somehow. *We need a plan*, he wants to tell her. That's how they first got together, after all – his plan to steal the knife from the Domesticity Display, her keys to the knife case. He can't stay here, guarded by the mothers for the rest of his life. But there's no place for him and Lyda to run away to. They're stuck. Does she feel it too? She has to.

They're leaving the Meltlands, heading toward the Deadlands, which are barren, windy, and dangerous. He imagines what he and the other two look like – Mother Hestra dressed in furs limping with the weight of her son, Lyda with her billowing cape, and him glancing around nervously.

Weaponless, he's vulnerable and useless. Mother Hestra has a leather sack of lawn darts strapped to her back. He'd like to have something – *anything*, really. He'd gotten used to Bradwell's various butcher-shop knives and hooks. In fact, he feels weirdly relieved that, while still in the Dome, he got some special coding into his muscles – strength, speed, agility. The strange gratitude to his father for dosing him twists his stomach.

The Deadlands that lie before them were incinerated during the Detonations. They were stripped bare and still are – no trees, no new vegetation, only the remains of a crumbled highway, rust-rotted cars, melted rubber, toppled tollbooths.

Partridge slows and rubs his face, stiff with cold. He clenches his fists. The one stung by the beetle is still taut with pain. Cold radiates through his bones even down into the lost tip of his pinky, which seems impossible but he would swear to it.

They have to be careful now. Curved spines arch in the sand, which whips in spirals. Dusts are creatures that, during the Detonations, fused with the earth and rubble itself, and now they're trawling. Encrusted with dirt, stone, sand, they come in all sizes and shapes. They blink up from the ground, and can circle and attack. But Dusts know the mothers. They fear them.

Lyda has slowed, allowing space between her and Mother Hestra to grow so that she's closer to Partridge. On purpose? He picks up his step.

'Was it this bitter cold when we were little?' he asks.

'I had a blue parka and mittens that were connected by yarn and wound through the sleeves of my coat so I wouldn't lose them. We should be attached,' she says, 'so one of us doesn't get lost.' She stops. He keeps walking up to her. She glances at Mother Hestra and then she turns toward him. He kisses her. He can't help it. She quickly touches his cheek – their skins coated in that waxy ointment feel strange. 'Something happened,' she says, 'with Illia.'

'What is it?' Partridge says.

'She knows things. She says she can't die until she plays her role. She kept talking about the seed of truth.'

'Is she hallucinating or something? What does that mean?'

'I don't know,' Lyda says. Before Mother Hestra has a chance to yell at them, Lyda turns and strides quickly to reclaim her place in line.

Mother Hestra stops at the edge of a rise. Below is a splintered gas station and billboard half devoured in sand. 'Stay here. I'll call you when it's safe to follow.'

Partridge looks at Mother Hestra's son's head bobbing beside

her as she heads down an incline toward the beaten highway.
'I'm still not used to it.'

'Used to what?'

'Children fused to the mothers' bodies. It's, I don't know,
disturbing.'

'I think it's nice to see kids for a change,' Lyda says. Because of
limited resources in the Dome, only certain couples are granted
procreation rights. But still this exchange feels like a rift between
Lyda and him. 'There were so many children during the Before,'
she adds. 'Gone.' *The Before* – that's a phrase that the wretches
use. She's already picking up the mothers' habits and language?
The change makes him feel uneasy. She's the only one who
really understands him here. What if she becomes one of them?
He hates himself for even thinking this way – *us, them* – but it's
ingrained.

'Are you happy here?' he asks.

She glances back at him again. 'Maybe.'

'It might not be that you're happy *here*. But just happy in
general. You know, one of those people who starts whistling the
moment they wake up.' She can't really be happy *because* she's
here, can she?

'I don't know how to whistle.'

'Lyda,' he says, his voice so forceful it surprises him, 'I don't
want to go back. But it's inevitable. Home is no longer a place.'
Partridge hears his father's voice in his head saying, *Partridge, it's
over. You're one of us. Come home.* There is no home.

'If home isn't a place, what is it?'

He tries to imagine what this place was like before it was
wrecked and the drifts of sand blew in. 'A feeling,' Partridge says.

'Of what?'

'Like something perfect just out of reach. It was stolen. Home used to be simple.' He can see Mother Hestra and Syden making their way to the next rise. She might wave to them to follow at any second. He says to Lyda, 'I know what's in the vials. I experimented a little.'

'Experimented?'

'I saw the stuff grow cells, build them up. I doused a beetle's leg and it grew and grew. My father wants what's in those vials, and now I know how potent it is.'

'Like that kid who won first prize in the science fair last year.'

'What? Who?'

'I don't know his name. He was the kid who always won, every year.'

'Arvin Weed?'

'Yes! That's his name.'

'What the hell did Weed win for?'

'Did you go?'

'Yeah, I think so. I vaguely remember walking around the booths with Hastings.'

'I was on a team that made a new kind of sensitive-skin detergent.'

'Nice!'

'Don't patronize me.'

'Sorry. I didn't mean to. I didn't make anything for it, not even a volcano with baking soda.'

'Well, Arvin Weed was documenting how he'd regrown the leg of a mouse that had lost a limb in a trap.'

'Are you kidding me?' But then he remembers it, how Hastings said something sarcastic like 'Excellent work, Weed. You've discovered the three-and-a-half-legged mouse. An incredible species.' Weed had glared at him, and as Hastings had loped off, Weed grabbed Partridge's arm and told him that he should care about his experiment, that it could save people. 'Save people from three-and-a-half-legged mice?' Partridge had said.

The memory jolts Partridge. 'Jesus,' he whispers. 'He's already figured it out! So the Dome already has access to what's in these vials. When my father had me followed to my mother's bunker, he was after the other two things – the missing ingredient and the formula. He was already a step ahead. He has one of the three things he needs to reverse his Rapid Cell Degeneration and save his own life.' It's a race suddenly, and his father's winning. Partridge's mother told him that his father knew the brain enhancements would catch up to him, but he thought he could find a solution, and once he had it, he could live forever. 'What if my father never dies?'

'All fathers die.'

Partridge thinks of the thick black muscular leg of the beetle. 'My father's not like other fathers.' He reaches out and grabs Lyda's hand. She seems surprised by the suddenness. He says, 'We need a plan on how we're going to get back into the Dome, how we're going to get the truth out once we're there.'

She stares at him, her eyes watery with fear.

'It's okay,' he says. 'We'll figure it out.'

'It wasn't okay for Sedge,' she says.

For years, Partridge's father let him believe that his older brother, Sedge, had killed himself. But the truth was that Partridge's father killed Sedge, his oldest son. How many times had Partridge imagined Sedge fitting the muzzle of a gun into his mouth? It was a lie. But now his brother is truly dead. *Partridge, it's over. You're one of us. Come home.* Partridge despises, most of all, the way his father said it – his voice going soft as if he loved Partridge, as if his father could ever understand something like that. It'll never be over. He isn't one of them. There is no home.

'He could kill you,' Lyda says. 'You know that.'

Partridge nods. 'I know.'

One of the Dusts suddenly rears from the ground so close to Lyda's foot that the earth crumbles and she loses her footing.

Partridge's enhanced vision crystallizes. As the Dust's jaws widen, he jumps and, midair, kicks the Dust in its rocky head. The Dust's head cracking against his boot feels good.

Lyda is on her feet, spear in hand.

The Dust now has its eyes locked on Partridge. 'Come on,' Partridge urges. 'Come on!' His body burns to be put to fighting use. His heart pounds in his chest; his muscles feel coiled, ready to spring loose.

But Mother Hestra shouts from the ridge on the other side of the highway, drawing the Dust's attention. As it turns, she whips out a lawn dart, launches it expertly from a great distance, hitting the Dust's forehead, dead-on. The Dust sags.

Partridge shouts, 'Why'd you do that? I had it!'

Lyda walks to the Dust, the living element of its body sifting into the dirt, and pulls out the dart, wipes the dark blood on her skirt. 'Did you really have it?'

'Of course I did.'

She shakes her head, as if scolding him. 'I would have taken care of it myself.'

Partridge lets out a deep breath. 'Are you okay?'

'Fine.' She dusts off her cape. There's some look in her eye that he doesn't recognize.

Mother Hestra waves them on, and when they're close enough, Lyda shouts, 'How much farther?'

'A couple of miles. Keep the line straight. No talking.'

They walk in silence for what seems like hours until finally they come to a row of fallen prisons – two of them are still standing.

Their steel structures and parts of the foundation are still there, but the rest is crumbled. Across from the prisons lie the remains of a factory of some sort. One smokestack still stands, but the other two are felled like trees, smashed on impact.

Mother Hestra stops at a long, jagged scar in the earth and a sheet of metal staked to the ground on two homemade hinges. She searches the distant skeletons of the steel. A mother must be up there, somewhere, as a lookout, because Mother Hestra raises her arm and seemingly waits for a sign. Partridge scans the structure but doesn't see a soul.

Eventually, Mother Hestra must be satisfied by a kind of all clear. She lowers her hand and says, 'We're here.' She pulls the metal sheet up from the ground against the tide of the wind.

The opening leads to a dark tunnel. 'What's down there?' Lyda asks.

'Subway train,' Mother Hestra says. 'We knew it was out here by tracing the route of the subway line that ran in and out of the suburbs. During the Detonations, the train tunnels jacked underground.' Partridge imagines the cars shouldering up hunks of earth, creating this buckle. 'We knew what the long tear in the ground was when we saw it and then dug down to it.'

'Weren't people trapped in there?' Lyda asks, peering into the slanted hole.

'Long dead by the time we found them. We gave them proper burials. Our Good Mother wanted to honor them as they gave us something we needed. There's bounty out in the Deadlands. Often you have to dig for it.'

Lyda crawls in on her hands and knees. Partridge isn't as eager. If people didn't die on impact, they were buried alive. He glances at Mother Hestra. 'Ladies first?'

She shakes her head. 'You go.'

Partridge gets down on his hands and knees too, the ground cold and hard. Mother Hestra, now inside the tunnel behind him, slams the door. The tunnel goes dark.

Then, suddenly, a bright glow illuminates the end of the tunnel. Lyda's face appears, bathed in golden light. 'It's perfect,' she says, and, for a moment, Partridge imagines that his entire childhood is waiting for him at the end of the tunnel – dyed Easter eggs, baby teeth, his father just a hardworking architect, a middle-aged bureaucrat, his mother feeding damp clothes into the open mouth of the dryer. A home, the thing that was stolen. Perfect, as if perfect *ever* existed.

EL CAPITAN

PYRE

EL CAPITAN TRUDGES DOWNHILL. Brambles like small claws nick his pants, but he keeps his pace. The wind cuts in, but he feels charged. *Hastings*. Maybe it's not a battle or a greeting, but something as simple as the soldier's name. It didn't come to him at first, because El Capitan doesn't think of Special Forces as being human enough to have names, but of course they were once just normal kids – actually, better than normal. They turned out to be the most privileged kids in the world.

Or was El Capitan supposed to recognize some meaning? *Haste* – he knows the meaning: to go quickly. Tidings are greetings. They're always *glad* tidings, never *hostile* tidings, which would be more appropriate here. *Haste* and *tidings* equals *Hastings*, right? El Capitan wasn't ever good with words. He likes guns, engines, and electricity.

'Hastings,' he says aloud. Helmud doesn't repeat it; El Capitan had figured he was asleep, but in the cold, Helmud tucks his chin behind El Capitan's shoulders and pulls his long skinny arms in tight and dozes. At a distance, El Capitan might even look like a man, all alone. He imagines Pressia seeing him this way. She looks at Helmud sometimes when they're talking, but not like everyone else does – glancing at some deformity. She looks at him more like he's part of the conversation. Still, El Capitan would like Pressia to see just him for once. Just him alone.

He wonders if the soldier will show up again, if he'll offer real information. *Damn*, El Capitan thinks, *what if I've got an informant? Someone on the inside?* He thinks of telling Bradwell and Pressia, but he likes the idea of knowing something they don't – the little rush of power.

He's closing in on the survivors building the pyre and can see that they've collected sticks, dragged in split logs, arranged narrow saplings in such a way that they could get a big fire going, though the wood looks green and damp. There are a few men with handcarts. They glance at him out of the corners of their eyes but keep moving.

Three girls are sitting on the ground, making up a song together. The girls are all Posts – born during the After – and just like all Posts, they're still deformed. The Detonations impacted cells down to the spirals of DNA. No one was spared – not even this generation. One of the girls has a closely shorn head as if she'd been recently deloused, which lays bare her skull's knotted bones, bowed on one side as if there's more than just a brain lodged within it. Another girl's shoulder juts forward under her coat. All three have mottled skin and pinched eyes.

When the girls see him, they stand and bow their heads. The OSR uniform has been associated with fear for a long time, and there isn't much he can do about it, so he uses the fear. Fear can be an asset.

'At ease,' he says. The girl with the jutted shoulder looks up and shudders, frightened by Helmud, who must have just lifted his head. 'Just my brother is all.'

One of the men walks up. He has a bloated belly, maybe a growth that's widened his ribs. 'We don't mean any harm. We're for the greater good.'

'Just curious what might be going on here,' El Capitan says, swinging the rifle around in front of him.

'We got word,' the man says.

A tall, older girl with a raised braid of skin on the side of her face says, 'She's real! They can save us. She's the living proof. I was one that found her. That's what. Not far from here.'

'Hold on,' El Capitan says. 'It seems like you want to build a fire.'

'Fire,' Helmud says, and everyone gawks at him.

'We want them to see that we found her and we got these three to offer,' the young woman with the braided face says. 'We'll line 'em up and wait.'

'That one in the middle's mine,' the wide-ribbed man says, pointing to the girl with the shorn head.

'Who'd you find out here?' El Capitan says. 'What girl?'

'What girl?' Helmud says.

'The Girl with the New Message,' the young woman says. 'Proof they can save us all!'

'When did you find this girl?'

'This is the third holy day,' the young woman says.

'And who can save us, exactly?' El Capitan asks, but he knows the answer. The Dome has sent a message through a child. Is this why the soldier led him here?

The young woman smiles, the braid on her cheek bunching up. She lifts her hands to the Dome. 'The Benevolent,' she says. 'Our Watchers.' El Capitan has heard this kind of talk before

– the Dome followers, the ones who've confused Willux and his people with gods and the Dome with heaven.

He rubs the muzzle of the rifle, just to remind them that there are more powers than the Dome to contend with. 'I don't think this is a good idea,' he says calmly. 'I'm going to have to ask you to disperse.'

'But we're preparing the Girl with the New Message for the pyre,' the young woman says. Her face is lit up like she's been stricken by something. Her eyes have lost focus.

'Are you going to burn her?'

'Burn her?' Helmud whispers. El Capitan hears Helmud's penknife click open.

'We're going to worship and adore her. And hope they take the others.' She sways as she speaks and her skirt brushes her shins, which are pale and ashen.

El Capitan looks over at the three girls again. They squint and tilt their heads. They don't even seem scared, which makes El Capitan nervous.

'The angels,' the wide-ribbed man says, 'are never far off.'

The young woman says, 'Can't you hear the buzz of their holy spirits?'

'Special Forces? That's no holy buzzing, I can guarantee that.'

'Guarantee,' Helmud says.

'You don't believe,' the young woman says. 'But you will.'

He points the gun at the man with the wheelbarrow. 'How about somebody brings me the girl, now!'

'Now,' Helmud whispers.

The young woman looks at the man with the wheelbarrow. He nods.

'She's in the city, being kept,' the young woman says. 'I can show you.' She starts to walk toward the other edge of the woods. El Capitan follows her. She looks over her shoulder, showing the bulbous, braided cheek, and says, 'She's real, I tell you. She's proof. She'll tell you herself.'

But as soon as the young woman with the braided face finishes her sentence, her eyes dart behind El Capitan and then widen. Her voice awed, she whispers, 'Look!'

El Capitan doesn't want to look. This can't be good. Helmud arches on his back, pivoting to see what's behind them. El Capitan takes a deep breath and turns.

Beyond the pyre, the massive Dome stands on a hill, its bulk lording over them, the cross piercing coal-dark clouds. At first he doesn't see anything unusual, except for a few small black dots. Then he sees that the dots are moving. They have legs. They're not dots but small, black, spiderlike creatures, crawling out of a small opening at the base of the Dome. Shiny and robotic, they skitter over and around one another.

'They're sending gifts!' the young woman says.

'I don't think so. No, not gifts,' El Capitan says.

Helmud says, 'Not gifts.'

Even from this far off, El Capitan swears he can hear the clicking of their metallic bodies, the rustling of sand under their pronged feet. Wicked creatures, Dome creations. He'll need to get word to Bradwell and Pressia. 'We don't have much time,' he says to the young woman. 'Let's move.'

On the walk into the city, El Capitan learns that the young woman with the braided face is named Margit. She talks the entire time – about picking morels and finding the girl with her blind friend – but El Capitan barely listens. If she slows down, he nudges her in the back with his gun. How long before the robotic spiders make it to the city? Their legs were small but swift.

El Capitan and Margit walk quickly down alleys of darkened shanties built from piled rocks, plywood, tarps. The city is always rotting – the sharp stench of death, the sick-sweet ripening of bodies, meat churning on spits.

Skirting the Rubble Fields, El Capitan counts the trails of smoke, a habit. Each trail piping up from the rocks represents a cavity filled with Dusts or Beasts that feed on survivors they drag down. El Capitan has lost a lot of soldiers in the Rubble Fields.

He keeps an eye out for the Special Forces who sweep the city. There are none, which makes him uneasy. Have they evacuated because they know the spiders are coming?

Margit leads him to a culvert guarded by a Groupie – two men with conjoined torsos and a woman, half of her body melded into one of the men's backs. They could have been strangers, knocked together by the Detonations while at a bus stop or in a bank line. At least El Capitan is fused to someone he knows. Family.

One of the Groupies has a chain, the other a rock, and the woman behind them glares from beneath a dark hood. They see the gun, the uniform, and back off a little.

Margit says, 'He wants to see her with his very own eyes.'

They nod and step aside.

The culvert is caved in on one side but seems solid. El Capitan and Margit are both too tall to stand upright, and so they bow to enter and walk hunched. Helmud's back rubs the top of the culvert. He whimpers.

'Stop complaining,' El Capitan says.

'Complaining,' Helmud says back.

El Capitan sees a homemade oil lamp and a few people

huddled around it. He stops and tells Margit, 'I want to see her alone. No one else around.'

'She's too precious,' she says.

'Too bad.'

'Can two of us stay with you? The ones who found her? We'll keep quiet.'

El Capitan looks at the faces, pitted with shadows. 'Fine, but get all these others out.'

'Others,' Helmud says, as if he's better than they are because he gets to stay. Where would he go anyway?

Margit walks over. They argue, briefly, and then disperse, scooting past El Capitan as they scuttle down the culvert.

In addition to Margit, only two figures remain, sitting on the ground – one bigger than the other, a blind picker and the girl.

As El Capitan approaches, Margit says, 'This man wants to talk to you. He wants to know the truth.'

El Capitan swings the rifle around Helmud's back and kneels. Closer to the light, he can see the blind picker's eyes – burned out from the Detonations. There are plenty of blind people like her. The cataracts aren't milky like El Capitan's grandmother's were in the Before. No, these eyes seem to glow, more cat than human.

'This girl is holy,' the blind woman says. 'Angels guarded her until we arrived, and then they left her to us for keeping.' She reaches up and touches the girl's pale face.

There's a hitch in the girl's breath, and then she starts to cry.

'Her voice . . .' the blind picker says. 'It isn't the same as ours. Been made Pure. No roughness to it. It's like bells!'

'It's 'cause she's been made new!' Margit says. 'She's the Girl with the New Message, who will save us all!'

'I might be able to help,' El Capitan says to the girl. 'I hope I can.'

The girl looks up at him, pulls her hair back from her face, which is pale and creamy like milk.

'You say she's been made Pure?' El Capitan says.

'Pure?' Helmud says, leaning forward for a closer look.

'Pull up them sleeves,' Margit says. 'See with your eyes, if that's what you need to believe.'

'I don't need it,' the blind picker says proudly.

El Capitan looks at the girl first, and then cups her wrist. She doesn't seem afraid. In fact, she seems to be pleading. He tugs one sleeve, revealing pristine flesh. Disbelieving, he pulls up the other sleeve. This arm is equally flawless. 'She wasn't born in the Dome? She's not a Pure?'

'She was mangled and living with strays. Some of those orphans identified her,' Margit says.

'What's your name?' El Capitan asks the girl.

She doesn't move, doesn't say a word.

'Her name is Wilda,' Margit says. 'The orphans said it, and she nods to it.'

'Tell him the New Message,' the blind picker says, reaching out and touching the girl's shiny hair. 'Tell him.'

The girl knits her fingers together, pulls them to her chin, and retreats into herself.

El Capitan says, 'Something you want to tell me?'

Helmud's hand appears over El Capitan's shoulder. He's holding a small boat, whittled from wood. *Damn*, El Capitan thinks, *Helmud made that?* It's so delicate and beautiful that El Capitan feels a little choked up. His eyes flood and he presses them shut.

The boat is a gift. El Capitan opens his eyes and watches as the girl accepts it, cups it in her hands. 'Tell me,' Helmud says to her. 'Tell me.'

PRESSIA

CADET

'HAVE YOU ASKED THE BOXES personal questions?' Pressia says to Bradwell. 'You know, about your parents?' They're eating waxy meat from tins at the cleared end of the metal table.

He nods. 'Yeah, I have.'

Fignan sits on the floor, next to a radiator that occasionally gives a weak blast of steamy heat, his arms and legs retracted into his body. His lights are dim. She walks over and kneels next to him. 'He likes to keep warm?'

'I think he's leaching energy, actually. He seems drawn to the sockets, the lamp I use for reading, and the radiator when it starts to buzz. I don't know how he gets energy from them, but it explains how he survives.'

'And the others?'

'Whenever I let them out of the drawer, they do the same thing.'

As soon as he mentions the drawer, Pressia thinks of the bruised dead boy with the handlebar in his ribs. She can't shake the sight of his body stretched out on the slab. Her mind quickly races through the deaths she's seen in the past few months. She shudders. 'So you think about your parents still?'

'Now more than ever.'

'Why?'

'I'm getting closer to them, not farther away. Ingership said that Willux knew my parents. They're still connected to this world – by their work to try to stop Willux and by me. Like with your mother, right? She's still here. The swan, the Seven. It's all jumbled, but it means something.'

'I guess so.'

'I'm not like El Capitan. He wants to bring the Dome down. And Partridge, he wants to get back at his father. I just want everyone to know the truth.'

'I'm sorry about what I said earlier. I know that your parents risked everything for the truth. I want to know the difference between what's real and what was made up and handed to you as the truth.' But she doesn't mean it the same way Bradwell does. He wants to know the truth about the world. She wants to know only the truth about herself in that world. It seems like such a selfish desire – small and petty. *Emi Brigid Imanaka*. They're just three words. And *Pressia Belze* is an invention.

He says, 'Good,' but when she glances at him, he's looking at her in such a way that she's pretty sure he doesn't quite believe her. Maybe he knows what she wants. 'Go ahead. Ask Fignan about your mother and father.'

She rests her hand lightly on the top of the box. 'Should I?'

'Only if you want to.'

'I feel like it might be cheating.' She pulls her hand away. 'I want to remember them on my own, but I don't think I can. Why don't I remember the Detonations? Or, really, anything much from the Before?'

'Have you ever wanted to?'

'I need to,' she says. 'I mean, I have to tunnel back through that part if I want to get to the Before. I feel like it's a locked door to an attic. If I open it, I'll find the things my mind has blanked out from the Detonations, and, deeper in the attic, maybe memories of my mother and father.'

'You know, I thought of this the other day; you used to be fluent in Japanese,' Bradwell says. 'You lived there, raised by your father and aunt. The language is inside of you, down deep.'

'I guess so, locked away like everything else.'

'Maybe that was part of it – a lack of language for what was going on. You couldn't process all of it.'

'I knew the words to the song about the girl with the swaying dress on the porch that my mother sang to me.'

'That's a safe memory,' Bradwell says.

'Are you saying I don't have the guts to remember the hard stuff?'

'I just meant that—' Someone pounds on the door. Fignan lights up, his engine growling to life.

'Bradwell!' a man shouts.

Bradwell walks to the door. 'Who is it?'

'We got news from El Capitan. It's important.'

Bradwell lifts the bar and steps into the hall.

Pressia can tell by the tenor of the voices that the message is urgent. Something has gone wrong. Her stomach turns. She looks at the row of lights, lined up like a series of eyes on Fignan's back. *Seven swans a-swimming,* Pressia thinks, but she has no idea where the words come from. Fignan stares at her, like a dog that knows only one trick.

She kneels down, leans in close, and whispers, 'Would you tell me about my parents, if I asked?' As she says it, she wonders if she's afraid to know about her parents. Will it only make her miss them more? Will there be information that she doesn't want to know? She's a bastard, after all, a secret.

Fignan rises up. One of his arms darts out, grabs a few wisps of her hair, and pulls, yanking them from her head.

'Ouch!' she says, standing up, rubbing the spot. 'What the hell was that for?' The hair disappears like thread being quickly wound by a motor within the box. Startled, she backs away from Fignan, bumping into the metal table, jostling the bell that gets kicked to its side. It rolls off the table and clangs against the floor.

She picks it up and starts to put it back, but first, she looks down at the newspaper clipping. The entire headline is readable now: INTERNATIONAL CADET'S DROWNING RULED ACCIDENT. The boy's name appears under his photograph – CADET IVAN NOVIKOV. Pressia picks up the clipping, which explains that the training operation was an international effort. The Best and Brightest from a number of countries were brought together in a diplomatic effort in an open exchange of cultures. From what Pressia can tell, it was a branch of the Best and the Brightest, bringing in the most elite kids from around the globe, which explains how her Japanese father was invited. Ivan Novikov hailed from Ukraine. The boy's face looks haunted, but maybe that's only because she knows he's long dead. He's handsome and serious. Under this clipping, there's another. The headline reads, CADET AWARDED SILVER STAR FOR HEROISM. Again, there's a picture of a cadet, but this face she recognizes – though he's younger and his eyes look darker and more alive. CADET ELLERY WILLUX. She skims the article. *Willux, aged 19, tried to save Cadet Novikov in a training accident. 'It's a shame because the boy [Novikov] had been feeling sick for quite some time,' Officer Decker said. 'He was just now on the mend. It was his first swim of the season.'* There was a funeral and, later the same day, a ceremony to award the medal. She skims the article, her eyes locking on one specific quote. *'It's a sad day, but heroism is being rewarded,' said Cadet Walrond.*

Walrond, as in *Arthur Walrond*, the friend of the family who talked Bradwell's parents into getting him a dog – a dog named Art Walrond? Was he one of the Best and the Brightest? Was this training facility the place where Willux and her mother and her father first met? Was this before or after they became the Seven? Why hasn't Bradwell mentioned any of this to her?

She puts the two articles down just as she found them, the bell on top. Fignan buzzes toward her. She backs away. He stops and his lights blink playfully. He whines then. It's almost plaintive. Is he apologizing?

She tilts her head, lifts her eyes. 'What do you want from us?' she asks.

The Black Box doesn't say a word. Maybe he's not programmed to want. She wonders if he understands desire and fear.

Bradwell walks back into the room and says, 'Talking to a box? Not bad company, are they?'

She's embarrassed. 'What's El Capitan's message?'

'I'm meeting him near the Rubble Fields. There's this girl. A strange case. And spiders. Something about spiders.'

'He doesn't want me to come too?'

'It's too dangerous out there.'

'I'm coming with you. I want to help.'

'Cap would kill me if I let you come.'

'Am I being guarded for my own sake or am I a prisoner here?'

'You know the answer to that. Cap just wants—'

'If I feel like a prisoner, I am one.'

Bradwell shoves his hands in his pockets and sighs.

'I'm not fragile.' But she isn't sure if it's the truth. Is there now a fissure inside of her – she pulled the trigger; her mother is dead – and is it a fissure that will never really heal?

He lifts his eyes, looks at her. 'It's too soon.'

'You forgot something.' She recognizes this voice – quiet but sure.

'What?'

'I make my own decisions, and this isn't up to you.'

LYDA

SUBWAY CAR

As A CHILD, LYDA NEVER RODE the subway. The wrong element rode underground – revolutionaries, the viral, and the poor, whom God didn't love enough to bless with riches. Righteous Red Wave films showed scenes of ferreting out the wrong element on subways. Her father was fond of these films and the video games that came with them.

But she never expected that a subway car would look like this. The floor is tilted and littered with glass shards and debris. The windows are shattered in spiderweb patterns. The rest of the car is intact – the orange plastic seats, the silver poles, the subway maps and advertisements under splintered Plexiglas. The lantern casts everything in shifting shadows as if there were ghosts darting behind the seats.

'So this will be home for a while,' Lyda says. 'How long?'

Mother Hestra is trying to fix the Christmas lights the mothers had strung up and connected to a small battery. The lights flicker. 'Can't say. Days or weeks. Until it's no longer safe.'

Partridge and Lyda pass close enough that their elbows brush. Lyda checks if Mother Hestra saw them. She didn't.

'What will we eat?' Lyda asks.

'I've carried provisions for a few days. After that, someone will come with more.'

Lyda is afraid to talk to Partridge. He wants them to return to the Dome together, to make a plan? He's drawn backward – that's the way she thinks of the Dome, as something she left behind, the past, another world. How could she go back? But she's drawn to him. She moves close to him, lifting the lantern to an advertisement for a line of sunny cleaning products – SPRUCE UP YOUR HOME THE RIGHT WAY – and a lemony sparkling soda with smiling bubbles. The one beside it simply shows a young woman staring out a window. NEED HELP? It gives a phone number. 'Do you think she's depressed? Suicidal?'

'Or pregnant and unmarried?' Partridge whispers. This makes Lyda blush. It's not possible to be pregnant and unmarried. Is it? 'Maybe the operators standing by didn't care. They had one answer for everything.'

'Asylums,' Lyda whispers. 'What do you think about Illia? She told me this story about a man and a woman and a seed of truth. It sounds like make-believe, but it isn't. I'm sure . . .' She stops mid-sentence. Partridge's eyes are roaming her face. 'What?' she whispers.

'God. How long are we going to be trapped here?' Partridge whispers. 'I won't be able to take it – not with you here.'

The comment stings. 'What do you mean?'

'This close,' he says, 'and not allowed to kiss you?'

Her stomach flips. She covers her face with her hands, and then whispers, 'I feel the same way.' They've been monitored all their lives, counted like sheep, put in rows, taught to read in groups, turning the pages in unison – during the Before and in the Dome. So it seems cruel that they find themselves here, where everything is wild and uncharted, and instead of being wild themselves, they're monitored, once again.

She places her hand on the Plexiglas and he does too. Her pinky touches his wounded one – proof of the mothers' wildness. Although she's sorry that his pinky is gone, she loves the barbarism of the mothers. She loves the weight of the spear in her grip, throwing it with all her might, the thick sound it makes when it strikes the target. After her childhood of battened-down emotions, the constant tamping of anger, the denial of fear, the embarrassment of love, barbarism seems honest.

Mother Hestra says, 'Three feet between you two, please. Three feet!' Partridge lifts his hands, as if to say, *No contact. Promise!* Lyda and Partridge step away from each other.

Mother Hestra has told her that if Lyda and Partridge were left alone, he'd 'make unwanted advances,' and he might even 'do her harm.' But Lyda would love to tell Mother Hestra that she's got it wrong. Lyda's always liked Partridge more than he liked her. She'd love to be alone with him, to kiss his lips, to run her hands over his skin, and have him run his hands on her. She knows what married couples do when they're alone – or she's heard rumors, at least. They keep most of that away from the girls in school. *A happy heart is a healthy heart* – that's what passes for health education; that covers the issues of the body.

'Let's work on the maps,' Partridge says. 'We have to get them done before . . .'

Before what?

'Mother Hestra,' Partridge calls, 'can Lyda help me with the maps?'

Mother Hestra has a small morsel of food that she pops into Syden's open mouth. She mulls it over and finally nods.

He pulls the maps from his backpack and spreads them on a section of the floor that's been swept clean of debris. 'Maybe you should start your own map.' He walks to the advertisement about sprucing up your home. He picks at some shards of Plexiglas until he can get an edge of the poster and pulls it free. He hands it to her. The back of it is bare.

She looks at Partridge. *We need a plan on how we're going to get back into the Dome.*

That's what he said. *We.* The two of them *together.* It's what she's been waiting to hear, in some way, isn't it? She was raised to become a wife, a *we*, and who better to be with than Partridge? But now she looks at him, and she thinks there is no such thing as *we*. Each of us is an individual. Odd that she'd realize that here, among the mothers, among those fused together. But there it is: Everyone is alone, for life, and maybe that's not a bad thing.

She feels numb, suddenly, as if cold has burrowed into her ribs. She grips the poster and looks around the subway car, and it's as if the train car is a rib cage too and each of them is a chamber of the pounding heart. She feels like she could die here. Trapped and pounding. That's why some of the windows have the spiderweb shatters – people banged their fists on them in the hope of getting out.

There was no way out.

PRESSIA

SNOWMAN

Bᴙᴀᴅᴡᴇʟʟ DRIVES, HUNCHED forward so as not to apply pressure to the birds rustling beneath his shirt. Pressia likes to look at his hands on the wheel, red and nicked up. He fiddles with the knobs that turn on the heat, but no heat comes. He hits the button for the windshield wipers to brush away the ash and light snow. Only one of them works. It wags across the windshield like a broken tail. Fignan, who sits on the seat between them, lifts one of his spindly arms, moving it in unison with the wiper, as if the wiper is waving and the Black Box is waving back. She checks on Freedle, snug in her pocket.

She rubs her hand over her doll-head fist then looks at Bradwell, the jagged twin scars running up his cheek. 'How did you get those scars?'

He reaches up and touches them. 'Groupies,' he says. 'They caught me off guard, almost killed me. But your grandfather did a good job, didn't he?'

'I always wished he could fix me,' she says.

'Fix you?' Bradwell says, then glances at the doll head. 'Oh.'

'What about the birds?' she asks. 'Didn't you ever want someone to come in and be able to remove them, magically?'

'No.'

'Never? Not once? You've never wanted them out? Just to be free of them?'

He shakes his head. 'The people who died instantly all over this earth and the ones who died slowly of burns and disease and poisoning, they're free of everything, right? The birds meant that I survived. Fine with me.'

'I don't believe you.'

'You don't have to.'

'Maybe it's different for you because you can't see them.' She thinks about this for a moment. 'Have you ever seen the birds?'

'I don't get undressed in front of a lot of full-length mirrors.'

'Do you even know what kinds of birds they are?'

He shakes his head. 'Waterbirds,' he says. 'Terns, I think. I'm not sure.'

For some reason this makes her feel better, consoled. Bradwell doesn't know the most basic things about himself either. They're strangers to each other, but to themselves too. 'I like that,' she says.

'You like what?'

'That you don't know something. You should try it more often.'

'Are you calling me a know-it-all?'

'As a know-it-all, you should know you're a know-it-all.'

'Which is proof that I'm not.'

He turns down an alley not far from her old home. Pressia used to like scavenging for parts, bartering in the markets – anything to get out of the back room of the barbershop where she lived with her grandfather – but she doesn't like open spaces anymore. They make her feel exposed. Everything feels tinged with falsehood. When she walked these streets, she was someone else.

They turn out of an alley onto a street. The barbershop is up ahead. It's her first time back since her mother's death. What's startling is how little things have changed when, for Pressia, everything has changed. This simple thought disturbs her: Her grandfather is gone, and she's still here. She feels guilty for being alive.

They pass the exploded hull of the barbershop. Out front, someone's built a snowman – blackened, sooty. Each of its three sections is flecked with detritus – small barbs of metal, bits of glass, rocks – from being rolled on the street. Its form is slightly melted. Weary, it tilts to one side.

'Stop,' she says. 'Just for a second.'

'What is it?' He stops the car and puts it in park.

She cups her hand to the car window and peers into the barbershop's blasted front – the old striped pole, melted and warped, and the row of shattered mirrors and demolished chairs, except for the last chair, which is still intact.

She remembers a fevered dream from her childhood, counting telephone poles – in the dream, this was her job. But instead of *one, two, three*, she whispered, *Itchy knee. Sun, she go*. But why did her knee itch? Why did she talk about the sun going? Was she dreaming of the sun blotted by ash after the Detonations? Was that where the sun went? Some of the telephone poles were on fire; some were already blackened and toppled, the electrical wires snapped loose, but she knew not to touch them. Someone else did, and the body rattled to the ground then went limp. In her dream, there was also a body without a head. There was a dog without feet. There was a sheep – pale and hairless, scalded a deep scarlet. It didn't look like a sheep anymore.

'The last time I was here, I picked up that bell, the one I gave to you,' she says. 'Why are you using it as a paperweight?'

'It holds down things that are important to me. You want it to be of use, don't you?'

She fiddles with the knobs on the dead radio. 'Things that are so important you haven't told me about them?' she says.

'What are you talking about?'

'Arthur Walrond, Willux, the dead cadet?' She looks at him squarely.

'Just something I found, but I don't know what it all means. Not yet.' He sighs. 'Can we go now? El Capitan's waiting.'

She looks back at the snowman – its bulbous body of ice, metal, glass, rocks. One of the snowman's eyes is melting down its face.

'It's one of us,' Bradwell says.

She can see beauty in the smallest details in this dark world, but this? 'It hits a little too close to home,' Pressia says.

'I don't know much about art,' Bradwell says, 'but I think that's what it's supposed to do sometimes.'

And then Pressia sees something skitter up the snowman's shoulder. 'What was that?'

'Spider?' Bradwell says.

Another spider – thick and metallic – darts in front of the car. 'Another one,' she says.

'And more,' Bradwell says, pointing at two of them climbing over the broken, snow-covered pavement, crab-like, and another on an exposed drainage pipe.

He jerks the car into gear and guns it. 'Is that what El Capitan meant? *Robotic* spiders?'

More are crawling along the window ledge of a splintered storefront.

'They're all the same,' Pressia says. 'Newly constructed. They have to be from the Dome. There's no other explanation.' She grips the seat as the car bangs over potholes.

'You know what they do, don't you?' Bradwell says grimly.

Pressia feels sick. She recognizes the black metal, the ball-bearing joints in the spiders' legs. 'The dead boy in the morgue.'

'One of these things blew off his leg.'

'El Capitan could have given a little more info on the spiders,' Pressia says.

'Maybe he doesn't know what they're capable of. Yet.' He glances at her. 'Glad you came?'

She'd rather be here than at headquarters. She needs to be out in the world again. She has to prove she's not fragile – maybe to herself most of all.

Bradwell pulls the car over a rut and parks. El Capitan stands next to a crumbled brick wall, Helmud's thin arms gripping his shoulders.

Pressia and Bradwell climb out of the car. Both eye the ground for spiders.

The street is empty except for a Groupie – two large men and, slightly behind them, a woman – standing at El Capitan's side. The air is deeply familiar here – the densely packed housing of lean-tos and tarp-covered huts, the smoky atmosphere, the falling ash a near-constant dusting. It smells like home, something sharp and sulfuric in the back of Pressia's throat. It smells like childhood, and she's allowed to be nostalgic for it; even a poisoned, desolate childhood can be missed.

'What the hell is Pressia doing here?' El Capitan says.

'Pressia,' Helmud says with a smile.

'Hi, Helmud,' Pressia says, then she says to El Capitan, 'Thanks for the tip on the spiders. A little more description next time?'

'What? You were expecting some daddy longlegs?' El Capitan says, and then he knows it was mean. Pressia knows he struggles to be a better person now, but it's not easy. 'Sorry,' he mutters.

'Longlegs,' Helmud says.

'They're deadly, Cap,' Bradwell says. 'You know that.'

'Deadly?'

'The boy found in the woods,' Bradwell says. 'Remember how his leg looked? The hooks in the flesh? He may have been killed by a prototype – you know, a little trial kit.'

Helmud leans forward, glancing at his brother's expression, maybe trying to gauge his fear.

'Well, we've got other issues here.' El Capitan strikes a match and tosses it into a metal pail of bundled clothes. 'Make sure these burn to ash,' he says to the Groupie. He strides toward the opening of a nearby culvert. 'No sudden moves. Eyes out for spiders. Most haven't made it this far, but they're coming.'

Inside the irrigation pipe, Pressia remembers this place. Her grandfather brought her one rainy night, telling her that she was to hide here once she escaped through the back panel in the cabinets. She was supposed to come here the night she headed to Bradwell's, when she met Partridge – or was led to him. If she had hidden in this pipe, would she still be that other girl who went scavenging through the city? Would her grandfather still be her grandfather? Would he still be alive?

'You okay?' Bradwell whispers. She must look dazed.

'Fine,' she says, shaking off the chill.

'The girl's a survivor, a Post,' El Capitan continues. 'The Dome took her, made her Pure, brought her back. She's got a message.'

'Made her Pure?' Pressia whispers. 'That's not possible.'

'Now it is,' El Capitan says.

'It is!' Helmud says, eyes glinting.

Heat prickles across Pressia's back. *It's possible to make someone Pure?*

They walk up to two young women Pressia's age and a younger girl, hunched against the wall. El Capitan introduces the one with a twisted lump of skin on one side of her face as Margit. The other is a friend of Margit's who's blind. El Capitan doesn't give her name. 'Dome worshippers,' he says with disgust.

The blind one says defensively, 'What would you have us worship instead?'

Bradwell hates Dome worshippers. He shoots back, 'The Dome's your enemy, not your god.'

Margit says, 'When you hear the New Message, you'll turn your tongue.'

Bradwell opens his mouth, but Pressia grabs his arm. 'Let it go.' She walks toward the young girl they've been talking about – pale and clear-eyed with dark red hair.

'Name is Wilda,' El Capitan says. 'Burned the clothes in case of any kind of surveillance.'

Wilda is wearing an old, ill-fitting dress that gapes at her neck, the sleeves rolled up past her elbows. Pressia hasn't seen a Pure other than Partridge and Lyda. Because this girl is so young, she seems doubly Pure and vulnerable. Pressia wants to protect the girl, maybe because of the way the girl looks at her, so desperate and lonesome.

'A girl who's a Pure but not a Pure?' Pressia says.

'Whatever she is she's got a New Message from the Dome,' El Capitan says.

'The truth!' Margit says.

Wilda has a small wooden boat in her hands. 'What's that?' Pressia asks.

Helmud shouts, 'The truth!'

'It's a boat. Helmud whittled it from wood. Gave it to the girl.'

Pressia looks at the little boat. 'I like your boat,' she says to the girl. 'Nice work, Helmud. I didn't know you whittled.' He lowers his head, suddenly shy.

El Capitan squats down, imbalanced by the weight of Helmud on his back. 'Say it for them. Tell 'em.'

Helmud shakes his head. He doesn't want to hear it.

The girl tucks the boat in her pocket and looks at all of them. 'We want our son returned,' she says, her lips pursed as if her mouth doesn't open all the way.

Pressia nods, encouraging Wilda to continue.

'This girl is proof that we can save you all,' she says and then pulls her lips into a thin tight line, her chin to her chest. Pressia is alarmed by how a face that's so perfect can look so anguished. Wilda's cheeks flush and stiffen. Her lips look as hard as knuckles. Still, more words come. 'If you ignore our plea, we will kill our hostages . . .' She squeezes her eyes shut, shakes her head wildly back and forth. She doesn't want to say another word, but they're in her throat, working her lips. 'One at a time.' She starts to lift her right hand, but she grips her own wrist, stopping herself, and starts to sob.

'It's okay,' Pressia says. She looks at El Capitan and Margit. 'Tell her she can stop.'

'Stop!' Helmud says, rubbing his ears.

'But she can't,' El Capitan says. 'She's not programmed to stop.'

Even though Wilda looks at Pressia wide-eyed, pleadingly, the girl still wrestles her arm from her own grip and makes a small cross on the center of her chest then marks it with a circle.

'The New Message,' El Capitan says wearily.

'What does it mean, *They can save us all?*' Pressia never got to be a girl like this – without scars and marks and fusings. This was denied her. They made this girl Pure. Could Pressia have her Purity back? Could she one day see her hand – her real bare hand – again? Could the crescent-shaped burn on her face be erased? What about Bradwell's birds? What if El Capitan and Helmud could be their own people?

'Hostages, Pressia!' Bradwell says. 'They're going to kill people.' Pressia's embarrassed that her first thought was of being made Pure again, but doesn't like Bradwell correcting her either. He puts his hand on the curved wall of the culvert and shakes his head.

Margit says, 'They're going to save us. The hostages will be made new!'

'New,' Helmud whispers to Pressia. 'New!'

'The Dome isn't going to abduct people to make them shiny and new!' Bradwell says.

'The spiders,' Pressia says. 'That's how people will be held hostage and killed. That's why they're here.'

'If we give them their son, they can make us all Pure!' the blind woman says.

'Partridge,' El Capitan says, under his breath.

The girl stands up, totters a moment, and then starts to walk toward the entrance.

'Wilda!' Pressia calls.

Margit runs to Wilda and twists her elbow. 'You can't go nowhere,' she says. 'You got to tell them to save us!'

Pressia shouts at Margit, 'Let go of her! You're scaring her!'

Margit releases Wilda's arm. Wilda pulls her arm quickly to her chest, rubbing it, and shouts, 'We want our son returned!' But it's more of a rebuke than a message.

The blind woman staggers to her feet and sways as if drunk. 'We can be made Pure! It's the way of the First Bible. God gave us his only son. We must return him!'

'Stop worshipping your oppressors!' Bradwell says. 'You know why you're blind? They did that to you. They did all of this!'

The blind woman hisses, 'What proof have you got? I've got the Dome itself ! I've got this girl! This Pure girl!'

'This Pure girl,' Helmud says, his voice full of hope. Does Helmud think that the Dome can save him? Separate him from his brother and make him Pure? Pressia would love to believe she could be made Pure, shiny, and new, as Bradwell put it. 'This Pure girl!'

'Shut up, Helmud!' El Capitan shouts, and then all the voices rise up so loud that they bounce around the culvert walls – even Helmud yells back at his brother, 'Shut up! Shut up! Shut up!'

Wilda squeezes her eyes shut and screams, 'This girl is proof that we can save you all! We can save you all! If you ignore our plea, ignore our plea! We will kill our hostages, one at a time.' She then scrapes a cross on her chest and makes a circle around it so roughly that it must hurt.

The air goes quiet.

Wilda opens her eyes. Pressia goes to her and kneels. The girl looks at the doll head, touches it gently. Pressia offers it to the girl, and she cradles it and Pressia's arm, rocking back and forth, soothing herself. 'We want our son returned. This girl is proof.' She climbs onto Pressia's lap.

Pressia rocks her as she rocks the doll head. 'Hush. It's okay.' Pressia has memorized the first Message, the one written on small slips of paper that flurried down from some kind of airship. She recites it: 'We know you are here, our brothers and sisters. We will, one day, emerge from the Dome to join you in peace. For now, we watch from afar, benevolently.'

The girl nods. They're speaking the same language.

The blind woman says, 'What's happening?'

'Hush,' Margit says. 'Just hush.'

'The cross,' Pressia says softly to the others. 'The kind with the wreath around the center point. It's the same one printed at the end of the first Message.' She looks at Bradwell. 'The two Messages are almost identical in some way, right?'

'In what way?' Bradwell says.

'I don't know. They just feel like they're the same length, the same form. You know?'

El Capitan says, 'Twenty-nine.'

'Twenty-nine?' Bradwell asks.

'Words. Each Message has exactly twenty-nine words,' El Capitan says.

'It's going to be okay,' Pressia whispers to Wilda and rubs her narrow back.

'Okay, okay,' Helmud coos.

Holding the doll head tightly, the girl whispers, 'We want our son returned.'

'I know,' Pressia says. 'We're going to take care of you.'

EL CAPITAN

SPIDERS

BRADWELL LIFTS THE GIRL, who's still gripping Pressia's doll-head fist, while the blind woman curses and claws at Bradwell. 'She's ours! Let her go!'

'Back off!' Pressia shouts, and she shoves the woman. She and Bradwell carry the girl off quickly.

Margit yells at El Capitan, 'Let us all be Pure! You know their son! I know you do! Hand him over! If you don't hand him over, we will hunt him down ourselves!'

'Don't threaten me!' El Capitan says.

'It's not a threat!'

The blind woman says, 'Didn't the Message open your heart?'

'Shut up about my heart!' El Capitan says.

'My heart!' Helmud says.

'Hand over their son!' Margit shouts.

The blind woman screams, 'Pure! We can be Pure!'

'Pure! Pure!' Helmud calls back, like it's some kind of birdcall.

Margit grabs Helmud's shirt and yanks as hard as she can. El Capitan swings the rifle around and aims it at her. 'Don't give me a reason. I'm trigger-happy. Call off your friend too.'

'We're willing to die for the New Message!'

'Kill us!' the blind woman shouts.

'Really?' El Capitan says. He cocks the rifle. They're both quiet. The blind woman knows the sounds of a gun. Helmud shrinks on El Capitan's back, laying one cheek flat against his neck.

Margit takes her friend's hand. 'Jazellia, the angels will watch over her every step! Have faith!'

Up ahead, Bradwell's voice rings out. 'Spiders! They made it!'

El Capitan and the two women run out of the culvert. Spiders are everywhere. The Groupie is gone. The pale, burned clothes smolder. Bradwell, gripping Wilda to his chest, and Pressia run to the car. Helmud's whittled boat pops out of the girl's pocket and falls in the snow. No going back for it. They slam the doors as spiders click over the hood.

One of the spiders gets too close to El Capitan. He fires at it, misses.

The blind woman screams. Margit says, 'The Dome sent these creatures. The Dome is good!' Her eyes snap to one spider, skittering over a rock, and she watches its small, swift movements. She reaches for it.

'Don't!' El Capitan calls out.

But it's too late. The spider crouches and springs at her. It hooks its pronged feet through her sleeve and into the meat of her upper arm. Her eyes go wide as a red bead of light flashes on its bulbous body. Blood seeps from her skin into her sleeve. Her face goes pale. She raises her hands in the air. 'It chose me!' Her voice is a mix of joy and pain.

Another spider is circling close to the blind woman's leg. El Capitan shoots at it, misses. 'Run!' he shouts. 'Or I'll kill you! Go, go, go!'

'Go,' Helmud says.

The blind woman pulls on Margit's arms. They turn and run. El Capitan sprints to the car. In the backseat, Pressia holds the girl, who keeps her eyes on the doll's eyes; maybe she's in shock.

'Get in!' Bradwell shouts from the driver's seat. He revs the engine.

El Capitan sees the boat in the snow. He could make it, he's pretty sure. 'I should get your goddamn boat, Helmud. You made that beautiful goddamn boat!'

'Get in!' Helmud says, throwing his weight toward the door.

A spider runs over the toe of El Capitan's boot. He jumps. Fires. A plume of snow and dirt rises from the bullet hole. He grips the handle of the passenger door just as a young man runs toward him screaming. A metallic spider is embedded in his thigh; his pant leg runs dark with blood. *Too late for you*, El Capitan thinks. Maybe it's too late for all of them. His army isn't ready. It probably never will be. The Dome has sent little spiders to kill them.

El Capitan's going to leave the guy there. What can he do? But Pressia jumps out of the car and runs to the man.

'Leave him,' El Capitan urges her. 'Spiders are everywhere!' He tells Bradwell to stay with the girl. He runs to Pressia.

'We can't help,' El Capitan tells her. 'We have to go.'

'We *can* help!' Her fingers run lightly over the spider's back, which glows with a red digital clock: *00:00:06 . . . 00:00:05*. 'It's counting down!'

'Down!' Helmud cries out like a command. 'Down, down!'

El Capitan grabs Pressia by the ribs and lifts her and runs.

Helmud grips his neck. The spider emits a long, slow beep. El Capitan dives.

The spider, locked onto the man's leg, explodes.

His ears are ringing. His vision is black. His shoulder feels like it's plowed into a wall. His breath is caught in his throat. Helmud moans.

Pressia puts her hands on his chest. 'El Capitan? Can you hear me?' Her voice is tinny and distant.

'Yeah,' El Capitan says gruffly, as her face – her perfect face – comes into view. She's reaching over his shoulder and tending to Helmud.

She tries to pull them up. El Capitan stands so fast his vision fades again for a second. Pressia steadies him, but he pushes her away. 'I'm fine.' She runs to the car, looking back to make sure he's following. He is, though his steps are leaden.

'Don't look!' he hears Bradwell shout, maybe to the little girl. 'Don't look!'

Helmud repeats it, burying his face behind El Capitan's back. 'Don't look. Don't.' But El Capitan does look back at the exploded man – his body already charred, his clothes on fire, smoke trailing in the air.

El Capitan reaches the car and puts his hands on the hood to keep his balance. He presses his forehead to the window for a second. Cool glass.

'Hurry up, Cap!' Bradwell shouts.

'Hurry,' Helmud says.

Something darts up the heel of El Capitan's boot. He sees a small bulky movement under his pant leg – a spider's on him. He whips off his rifle and rams his calf with its butt, but the spider's legs pierce his skin and drive into his muscle. He feels sick, but he straightens up, blood trickling down into his boot. *Don't look,* he tells himself. *Don't look*. The others are in the car, calling his name. They can't see the lower half of his body, so he tugs up his pant leg, and there, above the cuff of his boot, in the densest part of his calf muscle, is a robotic spider. Its black humped back shows a timer, counting down. *07:13:49 . . . 07:13:48 . . . 07:13:47.* The rest of his life and Helmud's too, meted out in hours, minutes, seconds.

'Goddamn,' El Capitan says.

'God,' Helmud says, pleadingly. 'God, God, God!'

PRESSIA

GAZEBO

It's like the city has grown a layer of movable skin, a clicking black scrim that's covering everything in sight – the hunched buildings, the broken walls, the plywood roofs on handmade lean-tos. Pressia closes her eyes, but the clicking sounds like the eyes of a thousand dolls.

Bradwell jerks the gears, tugs the wheel as spiders pop and crunch under the tires. Luckily, this doesn't cause them to detonate; they're probably programmed to explode only when attached to flesh, which they've done expertly. Survivors stagger and call out to one another. Some run and climb. Others smash spiders with bricks. But some just give in and have half a dozen or more spiders locked onto their bodies like thick black ticks.

Wilda is between Pressia and El Capitan and Helmud in the backseat. Fignan seems to be putting on a light show for the girl, as if to distract her from the window. Pressia warns her that sometimes Fignan bites and pulls hair. And, sure enough, moments later, she sees Fignan scratch the girl's arm, but it's not too rough and barely leaves a mark. The girl doesn't seem to mind. She goes back to the light show.

'The Dome wants Partridge back. *Our son returned* . . . What the hell are we going to do?' El Capitan says.

'Partridge can't hand himself over,' Pressia says. 'It would be a death sentence.'

'He's Willux's son,' Bradwell says. 'That has its privileges.'

'What's the alternative?' El Capitan says. 'Is he going to let everyone die, one by one?'

'We need to get to him,' Pressia says.

'Before the Dome worshippers get their hands on him,' El Capitan says. 'They say they want to hand him over, but they're insane. They might hand him over by burning him up and sending his ashes off in the first stiff wind!'

'The mothers hear everything. They're the eyes and ears,' Bradwell says, hitting a straightaway. The spiders under the wheels sound like crushed bones. 'They'll know we're headed there before we even show up.'

'Okay then,' El Capitan says. He still looks pale from the blast.

'Thanks for grabbing me back there,' Pressia says.

'It was nothing. Don't even think about it.'

'Think about it,' Helmud whispers.

Wilda stares up at Pressia. 'We want our son,' she says. Pressia guesses that she's tired.

Pressia pats her shoulder. 'Rest your head.'

The girl leans on Pressia, lifts her arms. Pressia lets her hold the doll head to her chest, and then Wilda closes her eyes. Pressia thinks about the lullaby her mother used to sing to her, and her mother's face appears in her mind. The bloody mist. She thinks of El Capitan saving her from the explosion. Couldn't she have done that for her mother? There must have been something she could have done. Pressia leans close to Wilda's ear and sings the song that pops to mind, the one sung by the man in the crowded, snowy lobby of OSR headquarters.

> The ghostly girls, the ghostly girls, the ghostly girls.
> Who can save them from this world? From this world?
> The river's wide, the current curls, the current calls, the current curls.
> They wade in water to be healed, their wounds to be sealed, to be healed. Death by drowning, their skin all peeled, their skin all pearled, their skin all peeled.

Her grandfather told her that she went to an all-girls school for kindergarten in a plaid pleated skirt and a white blouse with a Peter Pan collar. She knows who Peter Pan was – a boy who stayed young forever. Was this *her* childhood? Had her grandfather stolen this childhood from someone else? This song is about boarding-school girls who survived the blasts and walked to the river singing their school anthem. Some of the girls were blind because they'd been lying in the grass, staring up at the sky when the Detonations lit it up – at least that's the way people tell it. They huddled by the river. Some waded in. Water was good because it soothed the burns, even though the water was warmed by the Detonations. Their skins turned papery, peeling away from their arms, curling like lace collars at their necks. In the end, people knew them by their uniforms – what was left of them.

> Marching blind their voices singing, voices keening, voices singing.
> We hear them 'til our ears are ringing, ears are screaming, ears are ringing.

The way the story goes, people wanted to save them but the girls didn't want to be saved. They wanted to die together and they did, singing.

> They need a saint and savior, saint and sailor, saint and savior.
> They'll haunt and roam this shore forever, haunt and roam this
>   shore forever.

In some versions, they fused with trees that still stand by the riverside. In others, they became Dusts and rove the banks, and if you come close, they'll devour you. In some versions, they fused with animals and became foxes or waterbirds. But in every version, no one can ever get them back.

> The ghostly girls, the ghastly girls, the ghostly girls.
> Who can save them from this world? From this world?
> The river's wide, the current curls, the current calls, the current
>   curls.

Pressia thought of the ghostly girls often when she was Wilda's age, haunting the shore in tattered uniforms and lace collars of peeled skin, a detail so grotesquely specific she was sure it had to be true. She tries to think of a happier story to tell Wilda, but the girl's breath has gone deep. Her eyelids flutter with dreams. Pressia wonders what her dreams might look like. Hasn't she been to the Dome and back? What did she see there? A fleeting smile plays across her lips; then it's gone. Wilda's grip on the doll head has loosened. Pressia puts her hand on the girl's hand and feels a faint vibration. It's not just the car rattling on the road, but trembling – from within Wilda herself.

And Pressia thinks of Willux, his tremor, the result of years of brain enhancements, ones that will hopefully result in his death sometime soon. But she remembers, in a sickening flash, asking her mother in the bunker why she didn't dose Pressia with some resistance to enhancements, why they didn't leach the meds she'd developed into the drinking water. Her mother said the doses that would work for an adult could kill a child. She could give Partridge resistance to only one form of enhancements, and she chose behavioral coding. She wanted him to have his own will. And why didn't she give any to Pressia? Well, she was just that much younger. It was too dangerous.

What have they done to Wilda to make her Pure? Is the cure a new disease, just like Willux's Rapid Cell Degeneration? Is it crashing her system? Is this trembling the very first sign?

An hour later, Bradwell parks on a hill between two fallen houses on the edge of the Meltlands. They have a view of the footprints of slab foundations, cracked cement holes that were once swimming pools – circular, oval, kidney-shaped – burned metal skulls of cars, and indistinct blobs of melted playground equipment. The semicircular streets fan into the dust bowl of the Deadlands.

Bradwell gets out and paces in front of the car. El Capitan and Helmud get out too and sit on the hood. Pressia stays with Wilda, who's sleeping, her hands curled near her chest, shivering, ever so slightly. But then she stirs, sits bolt upright, and says, 'Proof that we can save you all?' She looks out the window.

'We're waiting for help,' Pressia tells her. The girl grabs the door handle and jiggles it. 'Do you want to see where we are?'

She nods.

Pressia unlocks the door and opens it. They step out and look at the Meltlands below, soot and snow dragged across them in dark billowing sheets. 'Any sign of the mothers?' Pressia asks.

'Not yet,' Bradwell says.

'Can't be sure if they'll show up as caretakers or warriors,' El Capitan says. 'Unpredictable lot.'

Wilda starts to walk toward one of the toppled homes.

'Call to us if you see them,' Pressia says, following the girl.

They both nod, Helmud too, staring out across the landscape.

Pressia stays close to Wilda, following her to the back of a house where there's the impression of a cement pool. The deep end is cluttered with patio furniture and what might have once been a gazebo – crooked, splintered, and covered in ash and snow. It leans to one side like an off-kilter hoop skirt. Wilda sits on the edge of the shallow end, pushes herself off, and lands. 'Wait,' Pressia says. She climbs in after her. Wilda walks over to the gazebo and sits down inside, cross-legged, on its floor. Pressia joins her. 'It's like playing house,' Pressia says. 'Do you like to do that?'

The girl nods.

'I wonder,' Pressia says, taking Freedle from her pocket and letting him flit around, 'if kids play house in the Dome.' If you weren't always searching for a real home, if you lived in a safe and happy place, would you still need to play house? For a fleeting second, she imagines cooking in a cheery kitchen, and there's Bradwell working with her. She has her doll head fused to her fist. His birds are still there nestled in his back. No. It can't work. In fact, the idea of the two of them in a cheery kitchen scares her. It seems to invite only doom and loss.

Wilda looks at Pressia, startled. 'If you ignore our plea, we will kill our hostages.'

'So you're saying they were bad? It was scary in there?'

She looks across the pool and slowly shakes her head.

'Was it nice?'

Wilda shakes her head again.

'It wasn't scary and it wasn't nice. What was it?'

Wilda lies down, closes her eyes, and then opens them, blinking like there's a bright light shining down on her. She presses fingers to thumb, opens and closes them – gesturing someone talking over her head. She does it with the other hand. Another person talking. The hands look down at her then to each other. More talking.

'You weren't a hostage as much as you were a specimen? Something to be experimented on?'

Wilda nods. She sits up, pulls her legs to her chest, and rests her chin on her knees.

'You didn't see how they lived or what was in their homes or anything much at all?'

Wilda shakes her head. No. She looks like she's going to cry, so Pressia changes the subject. 'Do you know how to swim?'

The girl stares at her.

Pressia lies down and pretends to swim on her back. 'I don't know if I ever really learned how to swim,' she says. 'Funny. It's something you think I should know about myself, right?'

Wilda lies down and pretends to swim too.

Then they hear a thud – Bradwell's boots landing in the shallow end. He walks over. 'They've been sighted. Not far off. What are you two doing?'

'Swimming. What else? We're in a pool,' Pressia says.

He ducks into the gazebo. 'Of course,' he says with a smile.

'Do you know how to swim?' she asks him.

He nods.

She sits up. 'Too bad the cadet didn't know how to swim.'

He looks at her.

'I read the clippings in the morgue.'

'Were you snooping?'

'Were you hiding them?'

'No.'

'Then I wasn't snooping,' she says. 'Why do you have them out?'

Wilda gets up and starts chasing after Freedle, who dances around her head.

'After my parents' funeral, I found them in a small plastic ziplock bag in their footlocker. My parents were building a case to bring Willux down. They thought they might have a lead.'

'But Willux was awarded the Silver Star for trying to save the cadet. What kind of dirt were they looking for?'

'I'll never really know.'

'In the clipping, Walrond called Willux's attempt to save the cadet *heroism*. Maybe Walrond and Novikov were members of the Seven. My mother said that one of the Seven died young, just after the tattoos were put in.'

'I don't know about Novikov, but Walrond wasn't.'

'How can you be so sure?'

'I just am.'

'Are you saying you're going with your instincts here, ignoring reason and fact?'

He shakes his head. 'I've done research. After my parents were murdered, I followed every lead. The day of the Detonations, my aunt told me to stay close to the house. My uncle was working on the car. They were on the inside, awaiting word. But I didn't know what was at stake for them that day. I told them I wouldn't go far, but I rode my bike to the old training grounds. That's where I was when the Detonations hit. Why do you think I've got *water*birds in my back? I was running from the bounce of light on the river. My bike fused to the tree I'd leaned it against. It took me hours to get back to my aunt and uncle's, where I found them wrecked and dying. It went on for days. You know all that. I was in bad shape, and there was the dead cat in the box, the engine, the way he begged her to turn the key.'

'Yes.' Pressia imagines Bradwell alone by a river, dazed by the bright white light, the searing pain of the burns and the feel of daggers in his back. 'I'm sorry.'

'About what? I don't want your pity any more than you want mine.'

'Okay then,' Pressia says. 'Tell me one good reason Walrond can't be one of the Seven. Just one.'

'Because if he was one of the Seven, it means he became friends with my parents only to pump them for info. It means he was a double agent, and he might have been playing both sides against each other, which could have gotten my parents killed. And even in that stupid little newspaper clipping, did he mean what he said to the reporter, or was he already playing everyone? Was it heroism, or did he know the truth about the cadet?'

Pressia looks at Bradwell. He's staring out through the gazebo's tilted frame. His eyes look red, his cheeks flushed and streaked with ash. 'What's the truth?'

'It was murder.'

'What kind of murder?'

'Willux's first.'

Pressia remembers the grainy newspaper photograph of Ivan Novikov – his seriousness, the haunted expression. She sighs. 'Novikov and Walrond were connected to Willux at the time when the Seven was first started – tightly connected. They're two important names. There's no way around it.'

'He was good to me,' Bradwell says, and he looks at Pressia. 'You know what I mean?'

She nods. 'But it doesn't mean he was all good, all the time, to everyone.'

'We should go. The mothers should be here.'

Wilda is holding Freedle in her cupped hands. She gives the cicada to Pressia, who tucks him back in her pocket and gets up. They walk back to the shallow end and hoist themselves out of the pool. Pressia glances back and tries to imagine what it was like before the Detonations – the blue water, the gazebo, tall and white with gauzy curtains. Who lived this life?

'They're here,' Bradwell says.

'One at a time,' Wilda says, and she makes the sign of the cross and its circle on her chest.

El Capitan has laid down his gun. He's kneeling on the ground, bowed at her feet. Helmud has tightened to a fearful knot on his back. And Pressia has the answer to her question. One of the mothers stands before them – scarred, burned, one child fused to her shoulders, legs wrapped and lost around her waist. She's weary, tough, and lean. The mothers once lived these lives. They once had houses with pools and gazebos. This is the earth they've inherited.

Wilda wraps her hand around Pressia's doll-head fist and whispers, 'We want our son returned? This girl?' Pressia is sure she means, *Who's this and what's going to happen to us now?*

EL CAPITAN

BASEMENT BOYS

THEY'RE IN A NICER PART of the Meltlands. The houses' footprints are larger and more have swimming pools, now just pits of crumbling cement. The mothers agreed to take them to Partridge, but Bradwell and El Capitan had to leave all their weapons. El Capitan locked the car with his rifle inside. The mothers only let Bradwell strap Fignan to his back because Pressia convinced them that he wasn't a bomb, only a kind of library.

El Capitan's calf muscle burns deep into the core. The robotic spider's legs are locked in almost as deep as the bone. Every time he flexes his foot, the pain spikes, shooting up his leg. It reminds him of the scorched ache after the Detonations, when Helmud was fused to him. The pain whispers, 'Remember me? Remember that suffering? Feel it still?'

He remembers the morning of the Detonations. His brother was a chatty kid, smart and funny – smarter than El Capitan, that was for sure. The last thing El Capitan said to his brother? 'Don't be a moron, Helmud. Don't be such a friggin' moron.' Helmud was on the back of the motorbike with El Capitan driving. They were going Dumpster diving at a minimart. Helmud said he'd distract people by singing. Thing was, Helmud had a beautiful voice. Their mother said God was in it. Their mom was gone by this point, and they both missed her.

And now? Helmud is a friggin' moron, and all these years of keeping them both alive are about done. They're going to die in five hours and twenty-three minutes and fifteen seconds – last he checked. Strange to know the exact second you're going to die. A little mystery snipped out of your life.

At some point he and Helmud will peel off, the way dogs sometimes run away to die.

The mother stops and waves them in close. 'The air's uneasy.'

Then a hand-whittled arrow sinks into the ground near their feet. Another skips off a concrete pad. 'Basement Boys!' she shouts. 'Run for it!'

Basement Boys? What the hell is a Basement Boy? And please, El Capitan thinks, *anything but run for it*. His leg's on fire. Jesus. He might not make it. Pressia whips the girl into her arms and takes off. Bradwell's beside her. El Capitan tries to keep up, but he's hobbled by pain. He can feel the remains of Helmud's thighs; the muscles flex as if El Capitan's a horse that Helmud wants to get going faster. 'Ease up, Helmud! Jesus!'

'Jesus!' Helmud says.

Up ahead, the mother has dived behind a corroded water tank lying on its side next to a low wall. A few more arrows whine through the air. She pulls out a section of metal pipe and a case of thin darts, probably poisoned. She takes aim at a raised lid by the flattened remains of a house across the street.

El Capitan runs to her spot and curls against the water tank.

'What the hell's a Basement Boy?' He grabs his thigh, wincing.

'Teenagers when the Detonations hit,' the mother explains. 'They were home from school, their parents worked, and they survived cocooned in basements, playing video games. We've tried to tend to them, but they want their independence. Some of their hands are seared to plastic controllers. They hacked them down but the remains are there in their palms. They've got homemade weapons.'

'Ah.'

'Pale snipers, they burrow into an area underground. Rumor has it there's one rogue band of them that killed a few of those Death Dealers, stripped them of weapons, and are now heavily armed.'

'Death Dealers? You mean Special Forces. Smart.' He looks at her sweetly and says, 'Too bad we had to leave our weapons.'

The mother eyes him suspiciously.

'What can I say? I'd like to help,' El Capitan says with a smile.

She digs through her heavy skirts into unseen holsters. 'You know how to use blow darts?'

'It's an art.' He'd dabbled in it during one hunting phase early on. 'I'm probably rusty.'

She pulls out a second pipe and a set of darts. 'Careful,' she says. 'Poison-tipped.' Her blue-eyed kid looks at him.

'I'll be careful!'

'Careful!' Helmud says.

He looks around the edge of the tank and sees a shadowy flicker near the concrete pad across the street. He raises the pipe to his lips and blows just as a pale head appears. The dart rips the Basement Boy's ear. He cups the ear with his hand as blood pours down his neck. He disappears.

'Nice,' the mother says.

'Nice,' Helmud says back to her, almost as a greeting.

They push on from an old Jacuzzi to a wall someone made from pavers and flagstone to a beat-up, stripped-down minivan. They pick off Basement Boys one by one until they make it out of their territory. El Capitan's leg feels shot through with fire.

Bradwell, Pressia, and the girl are hiding behind a collapsed two-car garage.

'We're clear,' the mother says.

Pressia says to El Capitan, 'You were limping all the way.' She was watching him?

'Muscle cramp,' he says. 'I'm fine.'

'I'm fine,' Helmud says, as if she'd asked.

'Stay straight on this path. Due west,' the mother says.

'You're not coming with us?' El Capitan says. 'I thought we made a good team.'

She pulls off her jacket. Her shoulder's been grazed. 'Not the only ones who know how to poison. Leave us. We'll never make it.'

'We'll go for help!' Pressia says.

El Capitan knows that he can't volunteer to run for help. He might blow up in the process. No time.

'No,' she says. 'We'll be found. Mothers will come for us.'

'Freedle,' Bradwell says. 'He can get a bird's-eye view and find other mothers. Draw them here.'

Pressia pulls Freedle from her pocket. 'Should we add a note?'

'Just let him go,' the mother says, sitting down and cupping her child's head. 'They will know.'

Pressia cups Freedle. 'Get help. Find mothers, lead them here,' she says. She lifts her hands and Freedle takes off, batting his wings, flitting off into the ashen air.

'Go now. You'll be fine,' the mother says.

'You sure about that?' El Capitan says.

She squints up at him. 'No. I'm not sure of anything.'

PARTRIDGE

TWO BY TWO

FOR THE LAST FEW HOURS, Partridge and Lyda have worked steadily on the maps. Lyda's been adding details of the girls' academy, the rehabilitation center, the street where she once lived, its parks and shops.

Partridge feels like a kid again, an art project sprawled on the floor, lying on his stomach across from Lyda. He wants to hold on to this moment – the Christmas lights blinking overhead, Mother Hestra telling Syden a story about a fox, and Lyda bent over her work. Mother Hestra is letting them whisper.

'I just realized,' Lyda says, 'that Christmas is coming.'

In the Dome, they exchange simple gifts – no need to create a lot of products with limited resources to fill up a limited space. The women are encouraged to make aprons and pot holders (even though no one cooks much anymore), scarves (even though the Dome is temperature-controlled), and beaded jewelry that the men buy from one woman to give to another – identical bead necklaces trading hands.

'I'm glad we'll miss it,' Partridge says. 'Last Christmas, my father gave me file folders – assorted colors.'

'I'll miss the way the little kids make paper snowflakes and stick them to windows.'

'I stayed with my science teacher, Mr Hollenback, and his family. We went to the zoo.'

'You didn't go home?'

'My father's always in the middle of something. And with Sedge gone, what was the point?'

She looks down at her map. Does she feel sorry for him? He wasn't trying to elicit sympathy. 'What's the zoo like at Christmas?' she asks.

The academy boys were dragged there on so many field trips that Partridge grew to despise it. Even Hollenback's two kids seemed to hate it. Julby complained about her saggy balloon, and Mrs Hollenback kept trying to get Jarv, the two-year-old, to repeat animal noises. 'The lion says "roar!"' But Jarv refused – either stubborn or not ready. Partridge hated the bleached-out smell of cleansers, the animals' dimmed expressions, and the guards with their tranquilizer guns. 'It was worse at Christmas – as if the animals should have been merry. But they're never merry, and what do they know about Christmas?' Lyda nods. 'You know how most people call it the Two-by-Two?' It was a Noah's ark reference that stuck. 'My friends call it the Cage's Cage because that's what it feels like – one set of caged animals looking at another set of caged animals.'

'One Christmas,' Lyda says, 'before my father left, he gave me a snow globe of children sledding. He told me to shake it. So, I did. And the snow swirled up.' She stops speaking.

'What?'

'I just knew in that moment that I was a girl in a dome shaking a dome with a girl in it.'

'That's the way I always felt at the zoo. A boy in a cage staring at animals in cages.'

She tilts her head and smiles sadly. 'We'll miss the winter formal.'

He remembers dancing with her under the streamers and fake stars. 'I'd like to feed you some of those cupcakes,' he whispers.

'I'm going to make you a present,' she says.

'What kind of present?'

'I'll think of something.'

There's a knock at the end of the tunnel leading to the subway car, and he knows this moment is over. It's that kind of knock – sharp, urgent, bad news. 'Don't move,' Mother Hestra says then limps to the tunnel, Syden bobbing along with her, and crawls up.

Partridge pulls himself forward on his elbows like a soldier until his face and Lyda's are just an inch apart. He tilts his head toward hers and kisses her. Her lips are sweet and soft. 'Paper snowflakes,' he whispers. 'Is that all it would take to make you happy?' They kiss again.

'Yes,' she whispers. 'And you.' She kisses him. 'This.'

The hatch is opened; light spills down. There's rustling. Lyda jerks away and leans into her map, smiling.

Mother Hestra reappears. 'They intercepted a message,' she says, brushing dirt from her clothes. 'Your people are here.'

'Our people?' Partridge says.

'Something's wrong in the city. Trouble from the Dome. I'm going to leave you; I've got to go for reinforcements.'

'Leave us?' Lyda asks.

'Who's here?' Partridge says.

After Mother Hestra departs, there's more noise in the tunnel. A voice says, 'Where the hell does this take us?'

And then the dim echo: 'Take us.'

El Capitan arrives, boots first. 'We made it,' he says, dirt-streaked and ashen. He reaches for the back of one of the subway seats and eases himself into it with a grunt.

'Who's *we*?' Partridge says. Hard to say if he means just Helmud and him or someone else.

Bradwell emerges from the tunnel next, then Pressia.

Partridge's sister. His *sister*!

They're dirty, sooty, breathless.

Pressia turns to help someone. And there's a little girl. She's pale and wide-eyed with shiny red hair – a child from the Dome? A Pure? For a second, he thinks of Christmas again – the academy girls, flanked by chaperones, caroling down the halls of the boys' dormitory. But they aren't here to sing. Partridge feels a buzz of excitement in his limbs. He didn't know that some part of himself was waiting for them to arrive – to free Lyda and him from the mothers? He wants out.

But then too there's a sick churn in his gut. Something's wrong. 'This isn't good, is it?' he says.

'Nope,' Bradwell says, shaking his head. 'And nice to see you again too.'

─

Within a few minutes, the subway car is abuzz. Lyda is getting food and water for everyone, using their provisions, but it's necessary. The group is haggard. Partridge can't look away from Pressia. He sees his mother in her freckles, the way she dips her head when she smiles, and the gentle way she leads this little girl to a seat, whispering something that makes the girl smile, even though she looks scared. Who is this girl with no marks or fusings?

Lyda whispers to Partridge, 'Is she a Pure?'

He shrugs.

Partridge walks up to Pressia. Should he hug her? She doesn't seem the type. She holds the girl's hand. 'How are you doing?' he asks quietly. He wonders if she dreams about their mom the way he does, doomed to find her dead body everywhere he goes. Would Pressia ever confess to dreams like his? He doubts it. She holds things in. Still, she knows what it's like to have found your mother after years of thinking she was dead, only to have her taken again. If they never talk about it, it's still something they share.

'I've been okay.' She clearly doesn't want to get into it.

'I try not to think about it too much.' It's cowardly to refer to Sedge and his mother's murders as *it*. 'Sorry,' he says, not exactly sure what he's apologizing for – maybe the past itself. 'I didn't mean to—'

'It's okay.' She says it sincerely – a forgiveness.

'Cap, look at these.' Bradwell points at the maps on the floor.

El Capitan takes a look – Helmud too, leaning over his shoulder. 'You do these?' El Capitan asks Partridge.

'Lyda's helped,' he says. 'They're not perfect at all, but I thought they might help one day if . . .'

'Is that what it's like inside?' El Capitan kneels down, wincing. What did they battle to get here?

'We're not done with them yet,' Partridge explains.

'Why are you here?' Lyda asks.

'Everything's turned,' Pressia says.

'Turned?' Partridge says.

Bradwell unstraps one of the Black Boxes from his back and places it near the power source that works the Christmas lights, which immediately dim. 'We've got things to tell you and questions to ask.'

'And' – Pressia glances around, unsure how to start – 'this is Wilda.' The girl looks up. She isn't a Pure. There's something off about her that he can't pinpoint.

Bradwell sits down, rubs his hands together. 'Dome worshippers found her near the woods. They say Special Forces dropped her there.'

El Capitan picks at dried blood on his pant leg.

'What the hell's going on? Special Forces?' Partridge asks.

'I was led to the girl by a Special Forces soldier.' El Capitan looks pale. 'He wrote a kind of message. Just one word: *Hastings*.'

'Hastings?' Partridge says.

'As in Silas Hastings?' Lyda asks Partridge.

'You know him?' El Capitan says.

'He was my roommate,' Partridge says. 'Jesus, they got to Hastings! How bad off was he?'

El Capitan rubs one of his knees as if it's aching him. 'Still very human. I could still see the real person in his eyes.' And then he asks, 'Is Hastings trustworthy?'

'He wasn't the toughest or the most reliable, but he's loyal.' He imagines Hastings at the dance, tall and awkward, chatting up some girl. 'The enhancements change people, but if he can, he'll help.'

'We'll need all the help we can get,' El Capitan says.

'What's wrong?' Partridge asks. 'Help with what?'

Pressia says, 'Wilda has a New Message from the Dome – from your father.'

'My father? How do you know that?' He knows he sounds a little defensive.

'It has the same structure as the first Message,' El Capitan says. 'Twenty-nine words and the cross with the circle.'

'The Celtic cross,' Lyda says. 'It's Irish.'

'Special Forces took her into the Dome,' El Capitan says. 'Wiped her clean.'

Partridge grabs a pole overhead and sits down. 'Wiped her clean?'

'She was a wretch,' Pressia says.

'Jesus,' Partridge says, 'they have what they need, don't they? If my father can reverse the effects of fusings, he can rebuild himself. He's probably already regenerated his own cells. I did this experiment with the vials.' He untucks his shirt and shows them the vials strapped around him. 'They're dangerous, like my mother said, but if my father can . . .' He leans forward, looking at the girl's perfect skin. 'If he can do this, he can fix himself, right?' He looks at all of them. 'He can live forever!'

'No,' Pressia says. She holds out her hand and lays the girl's hand on hers, flat. It shakes. The girl already has a palsy, like his father's. 'She's young. Remember why our mother could protect only one strand of your coding? And why she couldn't dose me at all? I was just a year and a half younger.'

Partridge nods. It was too dangerous but he doesn't want to say this in front of the girl. She looks scared enough as it is.

'Enhancements in the Dome don't start on boys until they're seventeen,' Lyda says. 'For girls, it can be even later.'

'Rapid Cell Degeneration,' Partridge says. The younger you are when you get enhanced, the worse the effects. His father started young – in his teens – and has kept up heavy brain enhancements for decades. The girl is only, what? Nine years old? She's already shaking. How long will she last? Months, weeks, days? 'How could he do this?' Partridge's chest goes hot with fury.

'He doesn't know how to reverse the side effects,' El Capitan says.

'If he ever figures that out,' Pressia says, 'he could save his own life, and . . .' She glances at Bradwell. She doesn't have to finish. Partridge gets it. He could undo all their fusings, make them all Pures, with no downsides.

'All I know is she's a messenger,' Bradwell says. 'One who your father knew would get our attention.'

'What's the Message?' Lyda asks.

The girl buries her head in Pressia's arm. 'It's okay. You don't have to do it.'

El Capitan says, 'We want our son returned. This girl is proof that we can save you all. If you ignore our plea, we will kill our hostages, one at a time.' He then draws a Celtic cross on his chest with his finger.

'Where are they getting hostages?' Lyda asks.

Bradwell sighs and says, 'They've sent robotic spiders into the city that have lodged in people's bodies – they're hostages. If we don't hand Partridge over, they'll keep detonating the spiders, killing people.'

'They've already started?' Partridge asks Pressia.

She nods.

So this is what no one wanted to tell him. He feels a little lightheaded. Lyda makes a small sound. Has she started to cry? He refuses to look at her. If it weren't for him, she'd be living a quiet life in the Dome, making Christmas pot holders.

'They're crawling all over the city. We saw one detonate. The person exploded. Gone – just gone!' El Capitan winces as if the memory pains him. 'And another one was found dead in the woods.'

'Gone!' Helmud says.

'The Dome followers have gone nuts over the girl. They think she's holy,' Bradwell says.

'She *looks* Pure,' Lyda says, gazing at Wilda.

'Why do we have to keep using that word?' Bradwell mutters under his breath.

Pressia shoots him a look.

'They're offering salvation and damnation in one fell swoop.' El Capitan leans over with his elbows on his knees. He and Helmud both look pale with a glaze of sweat and caked ash.

Partridge bends down in front of the girl. 'Did they put you in a kind of body cast? Did they put medicine in your body through tubes?'

The girl nods and makes the sign of the cross and its circle on her chest.

'Did it go exactly the way they wanted it to?'

She shakes her head.

'What went wrong?' Partridge asks.

Wilda looks at Pressia. She takes her hand and presses it to her stomach, then glides it back and forth. Pressia touches the girl's stomach then pulls her hand back instinctively. 'They healed too much of her.' She looks up at Partridge. 'She has no navel.'

A shiver shoots down Partridge's spine. The subway car is silent for a moment. Wilda hugs Pressia, who holds her close.

Finally, Bradwell turns to Partridge and says, 'Are you going to give yourself up?'

Partridge remembers the feeling he had when his mother told him that there was a secret group of people in the Dome awaiting word from the swan to revolt, to put Partridge in a position of power. He was the one supposed to lead from within. Would going back into the Dome be an admission of defeat? Or would it be his chance to lead – like his mother thought he could? He wants to take down his father, yes, and at least give people a chance to choose a better life. But does he have it in him to lead? Where would he even begin?

Lyda starts to cry. 'He can't turn himself in. There has to be a way around it. Maybe someone can talk to his father.'

'Right, talk to his father. Because he's such a reasonable man,' Bradwell says sarcastically.

'She doesn't want to send Partridge on a suicide mission,' Pressia says. 'Fair enough.'

Bradwell runs his hand through his hair, frustrated. 'If anyone can think of an alternative, I'm all ears. But it better be quick.'

No one says a word.

'It's not a suicide mission. Willux won't kill him,' El Capitan says. 'If he wanted him dead, he'd have blown us all up by now. One thing Willux knows is destruction.'

Partridge looks at Lyda, who reaches out and squeezes Partridge's hand so tightly that their palms become hot. With her by his side, he could do it, couldn't he? This feels like fate. No way around it. 'I wish I'd finished the maps,' Partridge says. 'There are some more details, crucial ones. You'll need the points of entrance through the air-filtration system. More on how Lyda got out, that loading dock she saw. The way in. If I had more time, I could get them down.'

'More time . . . ,' El Capitan says, his voice trailing off.

'Time,' Helmud says.

'And we need you to look at the box,' Bradwell says. 'Do you remember the names of the Seven?'

'Do we have time for this?' Pressia says. 'We have to get him aboveground and to Special Forces as fast as possible.'

'If we ever bring down the Dome, it will *save* lives,' Bradwell says. 'Don't you get it?'

El Capitan looks awful – gaunt and pained. He furrows his brow and lets out a slow, jagged breath. 'Sometimes people are willing to sacrifice their lives for the greater good,' he says. 'We can't ask them to, but the truth is, some of them will say, *Let's at least have a fighting chance.* Mark down the points of interest, and take a look at the box. It all matters.'

LYDA

SNOW GLOVE

LYDA PASSES THE BLACK BOX to Partridge, gently, like a
baby – or maybe more like a bomb. Bradwell's explaining how
the other five Black Boxes are identical encyclopedias, really –
massive libraries of information. But this one's different. 'Flip it,'
he says.

Partridge turns it over, and Lyda runs a finger over a small
symbol.

'The others have serial numbers, but this one has a copyright,'
Bradwell says, 'without a date.'

'It could be a lot of things,' Pressia says. 'Let them come at it
with open minds.'

'Or the symbol for pi,' Partridge says. 'Three point one four.
In a circle.'

Lyda wonders what this means. *Pie? In a circle?* It's likely one of
the many things the academy teaches boys but not girls.

'Whatever it is, the box is linked to your mother,' Bradwell
tells Partridge. 'It means something.'

Partridge looks at Pressia. 'Our mother? How? And who is Fignan?'

'The box is Fignan, and when someone says *swan*,' Pressia begins, but she's cut off by the box, which lights up and performs the ritual. 'Seven, seven, seven . . .' Partridge is so surprised he bobbles the Black Box.

When it's over, beeping and all, Pressia says, 'He wants the names of the Seven. Do you remember them?'

'She didn't tell us all of them,' Partridge says.

Lyda sees a thin metal arm unfold from the box's body. It has a shiny, sharp tip on the end of it. 'What's that?'

The tip rears and quickly pierces the skin on Partridge's wrist. A small dot of blood beads up. Partridge snatches Fignan's arm and holds up the box like a rat by the tail. 'What the hell was that?'

'It's just his way of getting to know you,' Bradwell says.

'Like I needed that! Here.' Partridge hands him back to Bradwell and dabs the blood with his sleeve.

Lyda says, 'What names do you have?' She leans in close, but not too close. She doesn't want to get nipped.

'We've got Aribelle Cording, Willux, Hideki Imanaka,' Pressia says. 'And there was the one who died young. We think his name might have been Novikov.'

'And Kelly,' Partridge says. 'Bartrand Kelly and Avna Ghosh. I wrote everything down that I could remember my mother saying.'

'Kelly and Ghosh,' Pressia says.

'So that's six. Who's the seventh?' El Capitan asks. He looks shaken, ghostly pale. Is he sick? Fevered?

Pressia looks at Bradwell expectantly, her eyebrows raised. It's as if she's waiting for him to say a name – challenging him in some way. Lyda wonders what's passed between them.

Bradwell looks down at his hands.

Pressia says, 'It's probably Art Walrond.'

'God, I hope it's not Walrond. If he was in that deep with your father from the beginning,' Bradwell says to Partridge accusatorially, 'it'll kill me. Not Art. Not him.'

'Art,' Lyda says, thinking of the strange things Illia was saying about missing art. Lyda wonders if she misunderstood her. 'I miss art or I miss Art?'

'What are you talking about?' Bradwell says.

'Illia. She said she'd like to die, but she hasn't fulfilled her role.' Lyda stares at the box in Bradwell's arms. 'She told me a story about a man and a woman in love. He gave her the seed of truth to protect. After he died, she became the keeper of the truth. She had to marry someone who would survive the Detonations so that the seed could survive, and she can't die until she gets it to the right person. She told me, *I miss art.* I thought she meant "art" as in the beauty of things made. But what if she meant *Art* Walrond? She was the woman in the story. What if Art was the man? And Ingership was the man she married just to survive. What if the truth is in that Black Box?'

'Maybe she worked for the government-funded program, uploading the boxes with information. Maybe Art found her there . . . ,' Pressia says.

'And used her,' Bradwell says. 'He was a womanizer.'

'No,' Lyda says, 'they loved each other.'

'Does it matter?' Partridge says.

'It does to me. Remember in the farmhouse, Illia said that I reminded her of a boy she once knew?' Bradwell says.

'Maybe it wasn't a boy *like* you,' Pressia says.

'Maybe it *was* me.' Bradwell sits down heavily. Lyda doesn't know much about Bradwell, but she can imagine what it would be like if there was no one left in the world who knew him before the Detonations – no one at all. It's a kind of lonesomeness that you'd want to end. The birds on his back go still. 'What truth?' he says. 'What goddamn truth was she keeping for Art Walrond, huh?'

Pressia turns to Fignan. 'Swan!'

Fignan lights up and says *seven*, seven times, and as he begins to beep, they all feed him names – Ellery Willux, Aribelle Cording, Ivan Novikov, Hideki Imanaka, Bartrand Kelly, Avna Ghosh. Fignan accepts each name with a green light.

'Arthur Walrond,' Bradwell says, finally.

And there's the final green light. Wilda reaches out and holds Pressia's hand.

They wait – for what? Lyda isn't sure, but nothing happens. Fignan's lights dull.

'That's it?' Pressia says.

'What?' El Capitan says.

Helmud echoes him sadly.

'No!' Bradwell says, shocked. 'It's not possible.'

'I guess it's just a box,' Partridge says. 'Maybe some of the past should just stay in the past.'

'I guess that makes sense coming from someone who survived in a nice little tidy bubble world,' Bradwell says, 'all spruced up with a brand-new paint job and a sweet little school and your school pals and your doting girlfriend.'

'Shut up,' Partridge says. 'I don't need a lecture.'

'And I'm not a doting girlfriend,' Lyda says, clenching her jaw. Partridge looks at her. Has she surprised him? Part of her hopes she has.

'We don't have time to fight,' El Capitan says.

'No,' Bradwell says, standing up and looming over Partridge.

'It's him! Fignan wouldn't tell secrets in front of Willux's son – not if someone on the inside programmed the box.'

'Maybe you're giving Fignan a little too much credit,' Pressia says. 'You think he knows who we are and who our parents are? That's crazy.'

'No, it's not,' Partridge says, looking at his wrist. 'Fignan took a sample of my blood.'

'And he got a sample from me too,' Bradwell says. 'My thumb.'

'He pulled my hair,' Pressia says, touching a few wispy strands.

Just then there are footsteps overhead.

'We might be getting very low on time,' El Capitan says.

Someone throws open the door to the tunnel and climbs down. It's Mother Hestra. 'They're moving in.'

'Who?' El Capitan says. 'Special Forces?'

She and Syden both nod. 'Coming in fast too,' she says.

Partridge grabs the map. He pulls out one of his pencils. 'Here,' he says, making an X on the map and drawing a line that leads deep into the medical center. He scrawls the number of fans in the system, the number of fan blades, the filter barriers, the intervals of time when they shut down – three minutes and forty-two seconds. 'Lyda, tell 'em where you think the loading dock is.'

She's not sure. 'Here, I think. There was a hill, and I could see distant woods. So, wait – maybe here?'

'It's okay,' Pressia says.

Bradwell gathers the maps. Footsteps pound overhead. Everyone looks up, as if they can see through the subway's ceiling, the layers of dirt.

Lyda has to tell Partridge the truth: She can't go back. She'd rather live out here in the wilds for the rest of her life and suffer than go back.

Partridge lifts his shirt. 'These vials can't come with me,' he says. He slowly and carefully unwraps them from his stomach. 'They contain an ingredient I think my father already has, but still – I don't want him to know we have it. Maybe it'll help you. But be careful. The contents of these vials are a kind of cure. They can do miraculous things – rebuilding cells and all that. But they're out of control.' He keeps them individually swaddled and hands them to Pressia. 'She'd want you to have them.'

Pressia cradles them gently. 'If things go badly, and you don't come back out,' Pressia says to Partridge, 'we'll go in after you.'

'Thanks,' Partridge says.

'We'll stay down here with the girl until it's all clear,' Bradwell says.

'Be careful up there,' El Capitan says.

'Careful,' Helmud says.

Partridge turns and looks at Lyda. He fits his hand around hers and squeezes it. 'Lyda and I will stick together.' And in that moment, that small collection of words, Lyda feels like her fate is sealed. Could she tell him, right here, in front of everyone, that she's not coming with him? He's sacrificing everything. Shouldn't she sacrifice too? She can imagine the mothers, urging her to stay, but she also knows her role – the one that's been drilled into her head her entire life. She should be a helpmate. She should follow.

'We'll be fine,' Lyda says, letting go of his hand and putting on her cape. She steps into the tunnel after Partridge, and as he begins to open the flat metal door, there is at first just a quick flutter of light, and she remembers her cell in the rehabilitation center, the fake panel of sunlight on the wall as if it were streaming in through a window and how sometimes it would flicker like a bird had fluttered by, casting a quick shadow and then it was gone. A fake bird, a mere projection, flitting in fake sun on the other side of a nonexistent window – inside a prison.

The Dome is a cage, a snow globe. She's going back in.

PARTRIDGE

SPEAR

PARTRIDGE GRABS THE HANDLE and pushes it outward. The brightness dazes him, and when he pulls himself out of the tunnel, he hears the clicks of guns. As his eyes adjust to the light, he sees they're all trained on him. He lifts his hands in the air. 'Easy now,' he says. 'We're coming peacefully.'

The wind picks up snow and swirls it around him. Partridge scans the crowd for Silas Hastings and the other academy boys from his year – the herd, as he used to call them: Vic Wellingsly, Algrin Firth, the Elmsford twins. They'll be hard to recognize – pumped with enhancements, made into mechanical creatures. There are remnants of their former selves locked inside them somewhere – former selves who hated Partridge. The last time he was with them, Vic offered to beat his ass, and Partridge talked him down with one word. 'Really?' But everyone knew what Partridge meant: It probably wouldn't be too smart to beat up Willux's son. Partridge was disgusted with himself for saying it, but Wellingsly backed down, though he was probably seething – and now he may be heavily armed.

Lyda appears beside him, knitting her hands on her head. The guns shift. Red target lights dot her chest and head. It makes him sick. He remembers the beams trained on them in the woods where his mother and brother were murdered. That old rage rumbles back. 'Can you all back off?' Partridge shouts. 'We're handing ourselves over! What more do you want?'

'We want the others,' one of the officers says. He steps forward, close enough that his gun muzzle presses into Partridge's ribs.

'What others? It's just us.' Where's Hastings? Partridge keeps scanning the thick jaws and massive craniums and knotted temples. Nothing.

'Take the girl!' the officer shouts, and two other soldiers grab her arms, pulling her about thirty feet away.

'She's coming in with me! It's a condition of my surrender!'

'You don't set the conditions,' the officer says. 'We do.' He bends over the hatch and shouts, 'Everyone out!'

He should have known Special Forces wouldn't be content with just him. 'What are your orders?' Partridge says. 'What are you going to do with them?' Partridge doesn't like the way one of the soldiers grips Lyda's waist.

The officer doesn't answer. One of the soldiers takes a small step forward from the line, tilting his head at Partridge. He's tall and thin, insect-like almost. Silas Hastings? Could it be him?

Partridge jerks his head the way Hastings used to, flipping the hair out of his eyes. The soldier repeats the action even though his head is shaved. Hastings. Clearly. Is he offering to help?

As the others climb out of the tunnel, each is shoved along by a soldier and lined up. They put their hands in the air –

El Capitan and Helmud, Pressia's doll-head fist. Bradwell has left Fignan and the maps behind.

Partridge quickly takes in the landscape – do the others have any shot of escape? Out past the fallen smokestacks there's a wispy spiral – a Dust? A spiny back crests and falls like a wave of dirt. Where are the reinforcements the mothers had promised? Have the Dusts had enough time to learn to fear Special Forces the way they do the mothers? He doesn't want to get shot, but he doesn't want to get eaten by Dusts either. 'I have a right to know what your orders are,' Partridge says.

The officer walks up. Despite massive thighs and broad shoulders, he's strangely light on his feet. He says to Partridge, 'Do you have any rights?'

Partridge glares into his beady eyes. 'I know he wants me brought in alive. I'm no use to my father dead.'

With the sharp knob of his elbow, the officer strikes a blow to Partridge's ribs, knocking the air out of him. Partridge folds, almost falls to one knee, but refuses. He wrenches his body upright. He sucks air, chokes it down into his lungs.

'Execute them,' the officer says. 'Return this prisoner to the Dome.'

'What? No!' Partridge lunges at the officer. 'I'm Willux's goddamn son! I outrank you!'

The officer punches him with a gun riding into the muscle and bone of his hand and arm. Partridge hears his jaw pop and tastes blood. He spins and falls.

He hears Pressia's voice. 'This girl is Pure. You sent her here. You can't kill her.'

Partridge wipes blood from his mouth and sees Pressia pushing Wilda out of the line toward the soldiers. Bradwell and El Capitan wear steely expressions, unreadable. It's as if this is how they always thought they'd die. Helmud's already closed his eyes, bracing for death.

'She's done her duty,' the officer yells. 'Step back in the line!'

Wilda takes a step back toward Pressia.

'I've got an army now,' El Capitan says. 'They *will* avenge our deaths.'

'Listen to him!' Partridge shouts. 'Please stop! Let's talk this out!' And then he locks eyes with Lyda. She's lowered her arms and is gripping her ribs. He expects terror but he sees something else – clenched jaw, stiffened arms. She isn't scared. She's angry.

The officer looks at Partridge coolly. 'On three,' he shouts to the soldiers.

Lyda calls, 'Mother Hestra!'

Bradwell tries to stall. 'Listen, we're of use to you. We've got some information—'

The officer ignores all the noise. 'One!'

'Jesus!' Partridge shouts and he charges one of the soldiers, tackling him. The soldier quickly flips Partridge and pins him, slamming his head into the ground. With sharp gunmetal pressed down on his windpipe, Partridge bucks and twists, trying to get up.

'Two!'

'Not the girl!' Pressia shouts. 'Just not her!'

And then there's a shot. One of the trigger-happy soldiers firing before the officer even gets to three? Who was hit? The soldier holding Partridge down slumps on top of him, bullet to the temple, deadweight. Partridge starts to push the dead soldier off, but there's crossfire. Everyone scatters. Bradwell, Pressia, and Wilda run for cover on the other side of the earth buckled from the subway. El Capitan? Lyda? He can't see them. The bullets are zinging the air. Partridge huddles under the dead soldier, hoping he absorbs bullets. Two more soldiers are hit and fall to the ground.

The soldiers drop to their bellies and fire back in the direction of the smokestacks. At first Partridge thought it was the mothers, the reinforcements arriving with their knives, lawn darts, and spears, but instead, the soldiers are being taken out with real guns – automatics.

Partridge sees Lyda. She's loose and on the run. One of the soldiers spots her, sprints after her, and grabs her cape, which rips and tears loose from her neck, revealing the homemade spear. She must have gone back for it when he was already crawling out of the tunnel. She pulls it out, chokes up on the handle, and pierces the soldier in the throat. The gun in one of his arms lets out a stutter of bullets, spraying across the snow.

Partridge is stunned. Lyda looks around – raw and wind-whipped – then turns and keeps running toward the fallen prisons. Why? He's not sure, but he's not going to let her be out there alone. It's too dangerous.

He looks over his shoulder, ready to make a run for it. Faint silhouettes of small, pale bodies dart between the rubble of the smokestacks, firing with sniper-like precision. The horizon is spinning with Dusts now, rising up from the earth. Death is coming and they want to feed.

Bradwell jumps over the buckle in the earth, yanks open the hatch to the tunnel, and dives down, probably going back for Fignan and the maps.

Partridge gets out from under the dead soldier and starts running. His boots pound across the hard, snow-covered earth. It feels so good to surge with this much speed.

But then he takes a blow to the back of his head. He falls forward, skinning his palms. Looming over him is one lone soldier. With his thickened cranium and hard-jutted jaw, he leans down into Partridge's face and hisses, 'I'd be happy to beat your ass now, Partridge. How about it?'

Vic Wellingsly. Partridge looks him in the eye and says, 'I didn't know the Dome's little sock puppets had such good memories.'

Wellingsly kicks Partridge in the stomach, knocking the wind from him. This won't be a fair fight. Wellingsly is incredibly enhanced and was a strapping kid to begin with. He punches the ground near Partridge's face. 'How'd you get out?'

'What?' Partridge mutters.

'I wanted out. We all wanted out. And now this is what I am.'

'I didn't do this to you. I never wanted—'

But Wellingsly isn't listening. He's cocked his fist again. Partridge rolls left. Then Wellingsly gets struck from behind, crashing to the ground. It's Hastings. He looks at Partridge but doesn't say a word.

Partridge says, 'Thanks.'

Hastings nods. He means, *Go. Run.*

As Partridge gets up and starts running as fast as he can, he looks back and sees Wellingsly scramble to his knees and tackle Hastings, wrestling him to the ground. They're brawling – a flurry of fists and rising dust and snow – quick and vicious.

Partridge keeps running. The Dusts are moving closer to the fighting – the draw of blood. Partridge sees the two fallen prisons ahead and a shape moving quickly over rubble – Lyda.

He glances back one more time; the Dusts have risen up thick and monstrous, cluttering the air with snow, sand, dirt, teeth, claws.

He can't look. He calls for Lyda. She doesn't turn back.

Between the two fallen prison buildings, cocooned from the Detonations, are the skeletal remains of a house.

A lonesome, tilting, roofless house.

Lyda steps into its dark, gaping doorway.

PRESSIA

SMOKESTACK

Basement boys. too many to count. And they're armed with real guns. They aren't here on a rescue mission. They're tracking big game – Special Forces. Pressia watches them take out soldiers, one by one, while the Dusts circle and claw. She and Wilda have their backs pressed to the middle fallen smokestack, its top axed off and shattered like a glass bulb.

El Capitan shouts her name.

'Here! We're here!' Pressia calls to him.

He and Helmud appear at the end of the smokestack. He limps and drops to a knee. 'Where's Bradwell?'

'He went back to get Fignan and the maps. We're waiting for him.'

'We should get out while we can. I'll carry Wilda. He knows where we're headed. He'll follow.'

'We can't leave him,' she says, looking out across the dusty, loud, snow-covered battlefield. 'What's wrong with your leg anyway?'

'It's just an old injury coming back to haunt.'

'I thought you said it was a muscle cramp.'

'That was the injury,' he says. He coughs into the bend of his arm. 'The air here – if a Dust doesn't choke you, it will.'

He's hiding something. She looks at Helmud, who stares at her, wide-eyed with fear. 'Choke,' he says. 'Choke.'

Pressia looks down at El Capitan's leg. 'There's blood on your pant leg. Muscle cramps don't gush blood.' She reaches for his leg, and he staggers back.

'Don't. It's nothing.'

'Nothing?' Helmud says.

'You have to show me,' she says.

El Capitan shakes his head and stares up at the sky, letting out a deep breath.

And then Pressia knows what it is. One of the spiders. She whispers, 'No.'

He nods.

'You've had it on you since the city?'

'Yes. It got me just outside the car.'

'It got me,' Helmud says. If his brother explodes, he does too.

Pressia's throat cinches. 'When you were saving me?'

He looks away, and she knows that's when it happened. She feels ripped through with guilt. She reaches out and touches El Capitan's chest, just above his heart. 'How long do you have left?'

'About two hours. Long enough to get us to the medical outpost.' Her surge of guilt is quickly overrun by anger. 'We could have taken this time to get you to a doctor back at headquarters! We could have left the city immediately and—'

'No,' he says. 'It would have distracted everyone, wasted time—'

'But' – she's rethinking all the decisions made in the subway car – 'you were the one who convinced me to let Partridge and

Bradwell have more time together to figure out the box, to finish the maps . . .'

'I said that sometimes people are willing to sacrifice their lives for the greater good. That's the truth.'

She's furious with him. 'There's still time, isn't there? We have to get you—' There's a massive explosion. The bottom hunk of the smokestack explodes into dust and shards. She's blown onto her back, slammed by a dozen fist-size chunks of cement and mortar, her breath shoved from her lungs. All sound is muffled. Special Forces are pulling out the heavy artillery. She runs her fingers over the vials nervously. They're all intact. She rolls to her stomach and looks around. Smoke and dust fill the air. 'Wilda!'

'Here!' El Capitan is holding her in his arms, protecting her with his body.

Another blast hits the ground between them.

'Run!' Pressia shouts. 'Take her and run!'

El Capitan gets on his feet.

'We'll see each other again!' she shouts. 'This isn't the end!' It can't be.

He smiles at her sadly, then turns and runs, hobbled by his bad leg. As they head off through the smoke, Helmud raises his spindly arm in the air. A wave goodbye.

Her chest feels like it could tear open at any moment. The spider locked on El Capitan while he was saving her, and now how much time does he have left? Only two hours? She has to focus. She blinks tears from her eyes and looks onto the battle scene.

Bradwell. She has to find Bradwell.

And where are Partridge and Lyda? Are they already being led to the Dome?

She runs down the ruins of the shattered smokestack, her legs heavy. A small cluster huddles about two hundred feet away, their motions frantic. She thinks at first that it's a Groupie but then realizes it's a pack of Basement Boys who've dragged a compact and broadly muscular Special Forces soldier, now dead, away from the battle. They're gutting the body for weapons and parts. She feels sick. She hates this world.

Bradwell. Where the hell is he? Is he ever coming back? What if he's dead already? Gone?

Off in the distance, the Basement Boys start to fight over what's left of the dismantled soldier. At the center of it, something small and sharp spins through the air and then thuds into the ground.

A lawn dart.

And then another.

The mothers are here, rooted on the far side of the buckle. They kick up a wild spray of lawn darts, spears, arrows. Why the sudden upsurge? But then she figures it out. The mothers are laying down cover for Bradwell, who's now running toward her through the dust and snow, Fignan under one arm and the rolled maps under the other. Alive. Her chest feels swollen suddenly, tight with . . . relief ? Joy?

'Bradwell! Here!' she screams.

Bullets whine and crack, hitting the fallen smokestack. His eyebrows are covered in dust, his face streaked with dirt. She's filled with relief. And then he's down. Taken by a bullet? He's still got hold of Fignan and the maps, but a Dust has him by the leg, a claw clutching an ankle. Pressia runs to him as fast as she can. Bradwell kicks the Dust with his free boot as viciously as he can, digging in with his elbows to hold his ground.

Pressia pulls a stray lawn dart out of the ground and plunges it deep into the ripple of rising and falling ribs – into the heart of the Dust. She hears a guttural cry and hiss as she then rips it from its body.

She helps Bradwell stagger to his feet. The remaining hunk of the fallen tower bursts open and rains down. The artillery is deafening.

They run in the direction of distant trees, the woods that lead to the river, and make it to an old outbuilding with a cinder-block foundation. They stop to catch their breath.

'El Capitan and Helmud,' she says. 'A spider. Lodged in his calf. He's got only a couple of hours left.'

'Why didn't he—'

'He didn't want to distract us.'

'Where is he? Where's Wilda?'

'He's taking her to the medical outpost, past the river.' The river. Pressia's never been out that far. 'He said you know the way.'

'I do,' Bradwell says. 'More or less.'

'Do you think they'll make it?' She was lying when she said to El Capitan, *We'll see each other again. This isn't the end.* She was lying to him and to herself. And he knew it. She remembers his look of sad resignation. Shouldering his brother all these years, he's always accepted the truth of his life – now his death. 'He's gone,' she says, and it feels like a part of her is gone. She had no idea how empty and vulnerable and disoriented she would feel at the *idea* of losing him. She raises her hand to her throat and looks out across the dusty terrain. Smoke has clouded everything.

'El Capitan?' Bradwell says. 'Never count him out.'

LYDA

BRASS

THE HOUSE IS PROPPED ON one side by a chimney and on the other by a staircase. The outer walls are gone for the most part, making the house feel exposed. A piano stripped of keys and strings and pedals sits on its side, a slain carcass. She hears someone behind her, turns. It's Partridge. Just him. They're alone.

'Did they follow us?' she asks. Her heart beats quickly in her chest, but, for some reason, she feels calm.

'I don't think so.' He touches a cracked windowsill. 'This may be the warden's house. Some of them lived near the prisons in big, beautiful houses.'

She tries to imagine this house as beautiful. It's now ravaged.

They take the stairs, which have survived a fire. Whorls of black soot stain the walls. The handrail has detached and lies on the stairs, useless. Silky ash makes the stairs slippery.

'Where are we going?' Partridge asks. 'Up.'

On the third floor, there's only air overhead. *A roof of sky*, she thinks. She'll miss the sky – dusky as it is. She'll miss wind, air, and cold. The walls have nearly crumbled away, and the room is bare except for a tall four-poster brass bed frame. It's a miracle – this bed frame. The mattress, sheets, blanket, dust ruffle are long gone, swept up with the roof or looted. But this brass frame, covered in soot, remains.

Lyda wipes the brass ball on one of the posts. She sees her own reflection, and behind her Partridge, warped and rounded. 'It feels like a gift,' she says.

'Maybe it's our Christmas gift,' he says.

She steps over the rails into the middle, where the mattress once was, and says, 'Maybe so.' She sits down and, in slow motion, pretends to throw herself back onto the soft blankets.

'How will we get back into the Dome now?' Partridge says.

Lyda doesn't want to talk about it. 'We have to wait out the battle. We can't do anything until the soldiers and Dusts are gone at least.' She smiles. 'We need to plump the pillows.'

Partridge steps over the rails, picks up a pretend pillow, gives it a few punches, and hands it to her.

'Share it with me,' she says, pretending to put it down on the bed. He lies down next to her. Side by side, they stare up at the clouds. Partridge rolls toward her. 'Lyda,' he says.

She kisses him. She doesn't want to hear anything he has to say. They're in this windy world in a house without a roof in a bed that's no longer a bed. They're free of the Dome's chaperones and the mothers. They're alone. No one knows where they are. No one at all. They don't even have to exist. What they're doing is make-believe.

Partridge's mouth is on hers and then on her neck. His hot breath sends shivers across her skin.

She pulls off his coat. There are the small, delicate buttons of their shirts, and then the shirts are gone. His skin touches hers – so hot it surprises her. With wind this cold, how could such warmth exist?

They cocoon themselves in his coat. Her body rubs against his. She's surprised by how good it all feels – his lips on her ear, her neck, and her shoulders. She feels flushed, but not just her cheeks – her whole body. In fact, his body and hers – what's the difference? There's this abundance of skin, all of it tingling as if it's just come alive for the first time.

The waxy sheen from the baths turns slick. Is this how it should be between a husband and wife? She thinks back to her health lessons in the girls' academy – *a happy heart is a healthy heart*. They said nothing of love and sex, though she knows bits of these, the small amounts of science that the girls are allowed to know, what some mothers will whisper to daughters and girls will whisper among themselves, which gets spread so thin who knows what's true and what's a lie?

He takes off the rest of his clothes, and she undresses too. All of it gone. Is this even happening? They're completely alone, unseen, unwatched, and she feels something like hunger, but it's not hunger exactly. She loves his lips on hers. She runs her hands through his hair. She wraps herself around him, arms and legs.

Partridge pulls back. He looks surprised, scared even. He says, 'Are you sure?'

She doesn't know what he's talking about. Is she sure she's coming with him into the Dome? She didn't know she had a choice. But of course she has a choice. This isn't the girls' academy. This is the real earth and sky, and she's alive in it. Maybe she can stay here. She doesn't want to ruin this moment by telling him the truth – if she doesn't have to go back into the Dome, she won't. She says, 'I'm sure.' She'll explain it to him later. Why waste this precious time?

And then he's inside of her. She feels a sharp, brief pain, then pressure. An expansion of herself. She lets out a gasp.

'Should I stop?' he asks.

Is this what he meant? Was she sure that they should do *this*, something she's only heard rumors about – stories of grunting animals and husbands and blood and babies?

She should tell him to stop, but she doesn't want him to. His skin and his lips and their bodies – where does his body end and where does hers begin? They're fused – this is what comes to her now. The two of them are Pures, but fused. She loves him in this moment. Everything feels so warm and wet and fascinating and new that she doesn't want it to end. 'Don't stop,' she whispers.

What if this is the last time they see each other before they're separated forever? Now that she knows she's not going with him, she's desperately sad as well as freed. She wants to be his wife – if in no other moment than this one, all they might ever have.

He says, 'I love you. I'll always love you.'

And she says, 'I love you too.' She loves the way it sounds.

She's sure there's blood. She's sure that this is wrong, but at the same time, she doesn't want to do anything differently. He shivers and lets out a soft sound. He holds her then, close.

She looks up at the sky over Partridge's shoulder – the scudding clouds, the windswept ash – and she imagines she's above them, atop a roofless house, two bodies locked together in the center of an empty four-poster bed.

She misses him already. She can already feel herself longing for him. He's going to go. She's going to stay. What will happen to the two of them without each other?

'Goodbye.' She whispers it so softly that she isn't sure whether he's heard it or not.

EL CAPITAN

SING, SING, SING

THEY'RE WINDING THROUGH TREES, heading uphill. El
Capitan can hear the river, can almost smell it. He walks behind
Wilda, keeps his eyes moving, but they blur with sweat. The pain
keeps trying to draw on his old pain, but he tells it to shut up.
Some were vaporized so fast that their bodies left only a shadowy
stain behind. Some turned to char. After the Detonations, he
found a woman in her yard, bent over her melted rabbit cages
– a thick coal statue. He reached out and touched her shoulder,
hoping she'd turn; instead, a chunk of her shoulder fell to the
ground in a puff of ash. His fingers were stained gray. He was
lucky he wasn't char. He was lucky he didn't drink the black rain
even though he was dying of thirst. He found an old water tank,
and he and Helmud drank from it instead. So he didn't die, days
later, from the inside out. He and Helmud were both sick and
weak, but they ate canned tangerines – something his mother
used to put in a dessert with apples and coconut flakes.

The pain winds its way up through his body. Now his chest

hurts. His heart pounds. He steadies himself by putting his hand on the rough bark of a sapling. The pain reminds him of the other kinds of suffering – loss. His mother. The plastic bag of coconut flakes – gritty in your teeth and sweet on your tongue.

He grunts.

Helmud grunts.

El Capitan touches the girl's shoulder. 'This way.' They push past saplings. The river opens up. It's deep here, but up a little farther it's shallow enough to pass. They follow the bank, then El Capitan stops. 'I'll have to carry you,' he tells Wilda.

She looks up at him and raises her arms.

He lifts her and the pain is brutal. Oddly, though, with her gripping his chest and Helmud on his back, he finds a new equilibrium. The water is frigid. It seeps quickly into his boots and up his pants. As soon as the iciness hits the wounds from the robotic spider, he wonders if the water will fry the little thing. Maybe it's that simple.

The thought spurs him quickly to the other side of the river. He puts Wilda down and looks at his calf. While the girl is distracted, he inches up the wet pant leg, dark with blood. His eyes sting so much he has to blink and squint. It's not fried. The timer reads, *1:12:04 . . . 1:12:03 . . . 1:12:02.*

It's close to dusk. The sunlight is low in the trees.

'Helmud,' he says, 'I'm going to try to make it, but if I don't, we have to get the girl—'

'Don't,' Helmud says, and it's one of those moments when Helmud doesn't feel like an echo. He seems to know that El Capitan is about to go soft, and he wants him to stop. These moments are rare but, God, El Capitan lives for them. It's like having his real brother back again – that kid who buried guns with him, the smart one who sang.

'Okay,' El Capitan says. The fact is, if El Capitan dies, Helmud will too. He wants to tell Helmud what's going on, just to say it aloud, just to have someone help shoulder the emotional weight of it. But Helmud understands what's at stake.

The truth is that if it weren't for Helmud, El Capitan probably wouldn't have made it. He'd have already given up without someone to protect, even in his own twisted, love-hate way.

He continues walking. He's got to at least try to deliver the girl to the outpost safely before the spider explodes. He wishes he could get there in time to try to dismantle it, but chances are they'd only set it off and die in the effort.

Wilda looks at him.

'It's just a little farther. We'll follow the edge of the woods around the meadow to the right. After that, we'll see the roof of the outpost.'

Wilda is ahead of him on the narrow path. He keeps trudging forward, each step more excruciating than the one before it. He's slowing down. Maybe he should just tell her to keep going. Maybe this is as far as he'll get.

His knee buckles. He staggers, reaches out, and grabs a tree. He drops and lands with his bad leg kicked out to one side. Helmud hugs his neck.

Wilda rushes back to him.

'You're going to have to make a run for it yourself,' El Capitan says. 'Don't come back.' He worries about OSR soldiers guarding the outpost. If they hear her running, they'll open fire. 'Can you sing?'

She shrugs.

'Sing the message as you run. Sing all the way. Sing!'

She turns and starts running through the woods, jumping over brush. Her dress flashes through the trees, then disappears.

She's not singing. 'Sing!' El Capitan shouts, using all his breath. 'Sing or they'll shoot you!'

'Shoot you!' Helmud says. They might shoot her anyway.

By God, she's still not singing. *Sing, sing, sing!* he begs her in his mind.

And just when he figures that maybe she really can't, a voice rises up, clear, sweet, melodic. 'We want our son returned!' Wilda sings, and it reminds him of Helmud's voice when he was a kid, during the Before. Angelic. It made their mother cry sometimes. 'This girl is proof that we can save you all!' Wilda holds the last note and it rings through the trees.

El Capitan closes his eyes, lets the song swell in his head. *We want our son returned* . . . And El Capitan wants to be returned. Coconut and tangerines. His mother mixing them in a bowl. Return, return. He feels a tug on his pant leg. *I'm hurt,* he would tell his mother if she were here. *I'm hurt.*

His eyes flit open. Helmud's face bobs into focus for a moment, then is gone. He feels his brother rummaging behind El Capitan's back, then he hears the click of Helmud's penknife. He shows El Capitan the shiny blade.

'No, Helmud. Jesus. No,' El Capitan says through grunts of pain. 'You think you're going to dig the spider's legs out of me? Like whittling a piece of wood?'

'Like whittling a piece of wood,' Helmud says calmly.

'It's too dangerous. What if you trip the explosive? What if . . .'

'What if ?' Helmud says.

He's right. They've got nothing to lose. 'Oh, God. Helmud.'

'God Helmud!'

For once, their lives are in Helmud's hands. There is no other alternative.

'The girl isn't around, right? I don't want her to be anywhere near us.'

'The girl isn't around.'

El Capitan bows his head. 'Okay.'

Helmud twists around. His arms are long enough to apply pressure to El Capitan's ankle, a firm hold. There's a breeze and then a pain so sharp he punches the dirt. 'Shit!' El Capitan screams.

Helmud takes just a bit of the word this time – 'Shhh. Shhh. Shhh' – and keeps digging.

PRESSIA

RIVER

ONCE THEY'RE DEEP ENOUGH into the woods and stop to catch their breath, Bradwell says, 'Let's try it again.'

'Try what?'

'Fignan.' The Black Box has been keeping pace, using a mix of wheels and long arms to get him over uneven ground. 'I haven't stopped thinking about it. I want to try it again with all seven names and Partridge not here. Just us.'

'Okay,' Pressia says, 'but this time don't—'

'Don't what?' She was going to tell him not to pin his hopes on Fignan, but she can't. His voice is so passionate, his gaze so forceful, how could she tell him not to have hope? How could she tell anyone out here in these wrecked wilds not to have hope?

'Nothing,' she says. 'Let's try it.'

They both kneel down on either side of Fignan. 'Swan,' Bradwell says.

After Fignan finishes his litany of *sevens*, Bradwell quickly rattles off the names. 'Aribelle Cording, Ellery Willux, Hideki

Imanaka, Ivan Novikov, Bartrand Kelly, Avna Ghosh, and Arthur Walrond.' A green light flashes after each one. The eye of a camera appears on the top of the box. It gazes at Bradwell and then Pressia. 'He knows us,' Bradwell says. 'He must be matching our faces with the DNA samples he took.'

Fignan's inner motor churns, as if he's having trouble computing. Finally he says, 'Matching Otten Bradwell and Silva Bernt. Male. Matching Aribelle Cording and Hideki Imanaka. Female.'

'That's us,' Bradwell says. 'See?'

Pressia is stunned.

'Clearance,' Fignan says. 'Playing message for Otten Bradwell and Silva Bernt.'

And then a flickering bright ribbon of light spirals up from Fignan into a cone and there, hovering, is lit air – motes of ash riding on the wind.

'It worked!' Pressia says, amazed.

'I told you it would,' Bradwell says.

A face appears through static, one that Pressia doesn't recognize – a man in his thirties with messy blond hair and a blond mustache. He blinks erratically as if he's been too wired to sleep and has been awake for days on end. He says, 'If you're seeing this, it means you're someone I trust. You're one of the Seven who I still have faith in, or you're Silva and Otten, who I trust with my life.' He stops, presses his hand flat to his chest. His eyes tear up. 'And you're alive.'

Bradwell leans close to the man's face. He's stunned, like seeing a ghost.

Pressia reaches up and touches Bradwell's sleeve. 'It's Walrond?'

He doesn't look away from the man, only nods and mutters, 'It's him.'

'By the time you're watching this, I'm probably dead. Maybe the whole world is dead. Maybe nothing we're trying to do right now will work. But I had to try. And the box knows,' Walrond says. 'Sorry about the DNA sampling. It was an extra layer of security. I had to do it.' He looks around, bleary-eyed. He steps out of frame for a moment, maybe looking for something or someone, being watchful, but then he's back. 'This box contains all the notes, from the very beginning, since the inception of the Seven – all of Ellery's ideas that went into it. All of his madness.'

He crosses his arms on his chest. 'People don't just decide young to be mass murderers. A person has to work up to an act of annihilation, and Ellery has. He still is. But he started small. I was there early on. I should have done something then. I see that now, looking back. The thing is, he killed the one person who could have saved him. That's the irony.'

Bradwell's eyes are filled with tears, but he's not crying. He loved Walrond. The pain is etched in his face.

'It's all here for you and it'll lead you to the formula,' Walrond says.

The formula. Walrond had it and can lead them to it – still? After all this time?

'It's not all laid out pretty. I couldn't risk something that simple. And listen, if you get to a point in your search and you can't go any further, remember that I knew Willux's mind as well as anyone. I pored over these notes and I had to look into the future. This box wasn't safe enough for me. I couldn't simply store everything here. If you know Willux's mind – and you all do – it became our life's work, didn't it? Trying to figure out his next move and all that. Well, if you just think about his mind, his logic, you'll be able to understand the decisions I've made.

And when you get to the end, the box isn't a box at all. It's a key. Remember that. The box is a key and time is of the essence.'

He leaves the camera's field of vision again. Is there a window nearby? Is he checking for people following him? When he returns, he says, 'I can feel them closing in on me. We're running out of time. If you're hearing this, it means all our attempts here have failed.' He almost laughs – or is it a sob? Pressia can't tell. The man's chest heaves for a second and then he says, 'Willux – he's a romantic when all's said and done, right? He wants his glorious story to live on. I hope one of you hears this, and I hope you give his story *an ending*. Promise me that.' He stares up at the ceiling. The image sputters for a moment and then returns. 'Not that I deserve your word, especially not Silva and Otten. Your word is too good for me. I've broken so many promises. You two are better than me,' Walrond says. 'You always have been. And Bradwell's the best of both of you put together.' He looks directly at the camera then, directly at Bradwell. 'In fact,' Walrond says, 'what if he's the one to survive out of all of us? Maybe I'll add one more feature, just in case. All your kids,' he whispers. 'God, I hope they outlive us all. I hope they survive what's coming. I hope they have a world left to survive in.'

The light fades. The small camera that projected the hologram clicks down into the Black Box.

It's quiet.

'Are you okay?' Pressia says. She can't imagine the shock of seeing Walrond again.

'Fine. Just fine,' he says, staring at Fignan. 'It's the formula after all that. He's got it in there somehow. The formula. So, there you go.' He takes a deep breath. 'Let's go.' While Fignan's inner motor keeps churning, he starts walking so fast that Pressia has to run to catch up.

'Wait,' she says. 'What did you want from Walrond? Isn't the formula good news? If we can get it, we need only one more ingredient and then we can save Wilda and—'

'It is good news for you, I suppose.'

'What's that mean?'

'The Dome can Purify people. They've figured it out, but it causes Rapid Cell Degeneration,' Bradwell says. 'And then there's this hope, this little chance that if you could get your mother's vials and one other ingredient plus the formula on how they would work together, the Dome could Purify people, and then have some meds to offset the side effects. Life would be perfect, right?'

'When Willux and the people of the Dome decide the earth is clean enough again for them to return, Willux has it worked so there will be two obvious classes – the Pures and the wretches who'll serve them,' Pressia says. 'This could erase his plan.'

'Or they could come out here and face us. Face what they did to us, and accept us for who we are.'

'You can't ignore the fact that a cure is an interesting possibility.'

'You mean a *tantalizing* possibility.'

'Don't tell me what I mean!'

'I know what you're hoping for, Pressia. You want your hand back. You want to erase your burns. You want to be like them.'

'Is there something so wrong with that? Really? Is wanting not to be disfigured and burned such a crime?'

'And if you got what you wanted, Pressia, what would that really change?'

She isn't sure, but it feels like she'd get some part of *herself* back. She says, 'I still have this memory of who I was. I want that person to exist. I want to be wholly me.'

'You *are* whole,' Bradwell says. 'This is who I am – scars, birds in my back. I'm whole now. I accept that. You go around seeing beauty in all this wreckage, but when will you see it in yourself?' He reaches up and runs his finger along the curve of the crescent scar around her eye. 'This self.'

Pressia wants to jerk her head away, but she doesn't. It's the way he looks at her – so intensely. 'At least the formula is real. You just wanted to dig around in the past. You just wanted old truths, didn't you?'

'There is one truth,' he says. 'We have to find it and keep it.'

'I don't know,' Pressia says. 'Sometimes I think you believe everyone else's truth is malleable, changeable, untrustworthy – but not yours.'

Finally she turns her head and looks across the river. A light fog drifts across the surface. Something rustles in the underbrush not far away. They both peer through the leaves.

'It'll be dark soon,' Pressia says.

Bradwell looks up at the sky broken by limbs. 'Why would time be of the essence?' he says. 'It's like Walrond forgot that we'd be listening to that message after the Detonations. Time was only of the essence during the Before, when they could still hope to stop Willux. It doesn't make sense.'

'How could he have really fully imagined all this? Back then, time had to have meant something different,' Pressia says. 'We have to keep moving.' Time, right now, makes her think of El Capitan. Has enough time passed that the spider embedded in his leg has exploded? She has no watch. What if he and Helmud are dead now? It's something they don't talk about. Can't.

PARTRIDGE

DOWN

STILL LYING ON HIS BACK, Partridge opens his eyes to the ashen bowl of the dark night sky, so much of it, stretching on like a cloudy ocean. The moon offers some frail light. When Lyda whispered goodbye, he was thinking the same thing – goodbye to this world, its ash, sky, wind. The world outside the Dome has a wild heartbeat all its own, a vicious, pumping heart that makes everything – even the air – feel violently alive. He doesn't want to go back to the Dome's stale, trapped air, its punctuality, scoured cleanliness, all of that well-mannered hypocrisy. And yet he would love to be warm, in a real bed – with Lyda.

She's already dressed and standing at the edge of the exposed wall, which comes to her hips. It's like she's looking off the prow of a tall ship.

He sits up and gets dressed. He says her name. She doesn't turn around.

Partridge grabs his coat and walks over to her. He slides his hands around her waist from behind and kisses her cheek. 'Do you want my coat?'

'I'm fine.'

'You should take it.' He wraps it around her shoulders.

'It's a matter of time,' she says. 'I've seen Hastings out there.'

'Where?'

'He was walking the rubble of the prisons, alone. He must have split from the others. He's probably looking for you.'

'Maybe he'll be the one to take us in. Better him than Wellingsly. It'd help his reputation to be the one who hands me over.'

'He won't be the one to bring us in,' Lyda says.

'What do you mean?'

'Not us.' She pulls away from him.

'I don't understand.'

She whispers, 'I'm not going with you.'

'But we're going back in together.'

'I can't go back.'

'You'll be with me. I can make sure you're protected.'

'That's just it,' she says, her eyes tearing, her voice suddenly desperate. 'I don't want to be protected anymore.'

Partridge doesn't believe her. It makes no sense. He looks out at the decimated landscape. 'It's barbaric out here. I can make sure—' He's about to tell her that he can make sure she's taken care of, but he knows that's not what she wants to hear either.

'It's barbaric in there too. The only difference is that in the Dome they lie about it.'

She's right, of course. He watches the Dusts rise and then disappear, roving just beneath the surface of dirt and snow. *Trawling* – that's the word that comes to mind. 'You might not need me, but what if I need you?'

'I can't.' Her voice is firm, unwavering. It surprises him.

'But you were going to come with me. You said goodbye to all this. I heard you say it.'

She shakes her head. 'I wasn't saying goodbye to all this,' she says. 'I was saying goodbye to you.'

Partridge feels choked, like he's been punched in the chest. He looks at the fallen prison. A thin beam of light floats over the fallen girders. It's Hastings picking his way along the rubble. He stops, as if sensing someone watching him. He turns and looks at Partridge, lighting Partridge's face and chest. Hastings is outfitted with excellent vision. He would be able to see Partridge in great detail. Hastings gives Partridge a nod, then doubles back over the wreckage, starting to make his way to the house.

'Hastings is coming,' Partridge says. He turns and looks at Lyda, her cheeks pink from the wind, which makes her blue eyes even bluer. 'What can I say to make you come? Tell me. I'll promise you anything.' He's afraid he might cry.

'You'll need this.' She holds the coat to his chest. For a moment, he refuses to take it from her, as if this will keep her with him – a coat she can't return. Then he takes it and looks away. She kisses his cheek.

'You shouldn't be alone out here,' he says.

'The mothers will come for me.'

He can hear his own heart and then Hastings' boots downstairs. He reaches into the coat pocket and pulls out the music box. 'Here.' At first she won't even lift her hands, but then she looks him in the eye. 'Please,' he says.

She takes it.

He calls to Hastings, 'I'm coming!'

'Be careful,' she says. 'I'm afraid of what your father might do to you.'

'I know better than anyone he can't be trusted,' he says defensively.

'I know,' Lyda says. 'But you still want him to love you.'

It's true. He can't even fight her on it. It's what makes Partridge so vulnerable. 'You said goodbye, but I'm not,' Partridge says, 'because we'll find each other again. I'm sure of it.' And then because he can't bear the thought of her leaving him, he shouts to Hastings again and runs down the stairs.

PRESSIA

GHOSTLY GIRLS

THEY'VE BEEN FOLLOWING THE RIVER along the bank where the reeds are high. Occasionally, a Beast growls from the reeds. Once, she saw a dark muzzle and then the quick shine of bared teeth. Bradwell is supposed to know where it's low enough to cross, but he hasn't found it yet. The river is deep and dark. Rivers. Has she seen one before? Is there a memory here that's her own? She can almost feel it, but she fears it too. If there's a memory, she's not sure it's one she wants to surface.

The air is windy and cold. The reeds, covered in thin layers of ice, click together. Near the bank where the mud isn't as stiff with cold, it suctions Pressia's boots, as if there's something alive in it, something with tentacles. Bradwell has Fignan under an arm and the two maps – now dirty and crushed – tucked into his belt.

The current is quick. Pressia thinks of the ghostly girls. She sings the song softly: *'The river's wide, the current curls, the current calls, the current curls.'*

'The outpost we're headed to was the school the girls in that song went to, supposedly,' Bradwell says.

'Really?'

'I've heard it was bad here. Well, you know how it was anywhere there was water. Swimming pools, duck ponds on golf courses, rivers like this one.' The reeds rattle. A small, furred body slips through the underbrush.

Pressia knows what he'd heard. Everyone moved toward water – a procession of death – because there were fiery tornadoes, and the world was, for a while, a tinderbox. Everything went up in flames. People found water – like the ghostly girls – and the rivers became glutted with bodies. There, burned and bleeding, the people died. But she has no memory of this. None at all. She looks out across the river. 'You know what I'd like to know? If I can swim. It feels like something you should know about yourself, doesn't it?'

'Yeah, it does.'

More dark forms rummage nearby. There's scattered growling now.

He turns around and looks at Pressia. 'So how would you like to test it?'

'Swimming? Are you crazy? The water's freezing. Where's the place to cross?'

'Yeah, about that,' he says. 'I'm not sure if it's a mile ahead of us or a mile behind. And these Beasts are giving us an ultimatum.'

'I'm not getting into that freezing water. Whether I can swim or not is beside the point. We'll die of the cold in there!'

Upstream, reeds are clicking. A small, lean animal darts through them. The growls are growing louder.

Bradwell starts untying his boots. 'More likely we'll get eaten by whatever's growling.'

'What are they?' Pressia whispers.

'I don't know, but their hackles are up. See the tin roof over there?' Bradwell asks.

Pressia squints across the river. She can barely make out the distant tip of a roof through the trees. 'Is that the outpost?'

'Yep.'

'Hasn't someone built a bridge or something?'

'Like beavers?'

'Like whoever.'

'Do you see one?'

'Maybe if we shout, someone at the outpost will hear us.'

'Over the sounds of the river? And what would they do if they did hear us? Join hands and make a bridge for us to walk across?'

A bridge of bodies. A river. There is a memory here. She feels sick, the saliva in her mouth hot. She leans over and spits.

'What's wrong?'

'Nothing. I'm fine.'

'You don't look fine.'

'I am.' *They wade in water to be healed, their wounds to be sealed, to be healed. Death by drowning, their skin all peeled, their skin all pearled, their skin all peeled.* She can see the ghostly girls in her mind's eye, leading one another, blindly, singing their school song. Bodies of water. Bodies. Bradwell said, *Well, you know how it was anywhere there was water. Swimming pools, duck ponds on golf courses, rivers like this one.* Does she know?

'Look.' Bradwell takes off his jacket. 'If you can just float, I'll swim you across.'

Marching blind their voices singing, voices keening, voices singing. We hear them 'til our ears are ringing, ears are screaming, ears are ringing. She looks around. All the bushes take on the hunched look of animals. She doesn't want to think of floating in a river. Isn't that how the girls' bodies bobbed to the surface once dead? 'The maps will get wet.'

'They will. But they're written in pencil, not pen. That helps.' He pulls his shirt off over his head – maybe so that he can move through the water more easily. His chest is broader and stronger than she remembers it. The wounds on each of his muscular shoulders have healed, leaving pinkish red scars. He's beautiful and tough – and more beautiful because he looks so tough. She can hear the birds' wings but can't see them. Is he keeping his back to the woods because he doesn't want her to see them? He'd never admit it, but it's probably true.

'You should take off some of your heavy stuff,' he says. 'You don't want to be weighed down.' He unhooks his belt then stops. He rubs his arms briskly.

Fignan motors to the edge of the water. He draws in his arms and wheels. Thin, webbed spokes appear at his sides. They look delicate but strong. 'You think he'll be okay?' Pressia asks.

'He was built with the apocalypse in mind. We're the delicate ones.' *The delicate ones.* She thinks of the ghostly girls again – so delicate. 'Are we doing this?'

Pressia looks across the water. She sees a swirl that quickly disappears. She thinks of the fevered dream she had as a kid, the horror all around her and how she counted the telephone poles. And when there were no telephone poles, her grandfather told her to close her eyes and imagine telephone poles to count. *Itchy knee. Sun, she go.* 'All I have to do is float?'

The low vibrato of growls reverberates through the reeds. Pressia sees dozens of shining eyes, muzzles, and teeth.

'Yes,' Bradwell says, glancing at the animals. 'Just keep calm, relax, and float. I'll do the rest.'

She shrugs off her coat and quickly unlaces her boots, ripping them off by their cold, mud-packed heels.

Bradwell takes off his pants. He's wearing loose shorts underneath. He pulls the belt from its loops, picks up the maps, tightens the belt against his stomach – the maps pressed to his skin.

'You're really serious about not being weighed down,' she says. 'Yep.' He wades out into the water, winces with the pain of the cold.

She sees his birds now, shining feathers, their bright orange feet. Waterbirds.

'The vials,' she says, making sure they're still safely intact.

'Come on!' One of the Beasts has edged out. She sees a flash of shiny hair – almost mane-like. The growling is low and gruff. The Beast's silky mane parts like a curtain; a dark, muddy arm emerges, a thin, human arm – a ghostly girl? No, they're just a myth. A myth. She edges backward into the freezing water. It swirls around her legs. It's so cold it burns. The iciness scares her. She raises her arms over her head as the water reaches her hips. Bradwell grabs her hand, strong and firm. She bounces on her toes, feeling the buoyancy now.

'Let the water hold you up. I'm beside you.' He hooks his wet, bare arm around her waist. He pulls her forward on her stomach. She reaches one arm lightly around Bradwell's neck and lifts her legs. Her skin starts to numb.

Pressia looks back and sees Fignan motor into the water, starting to thrum his webbed spokes, then disappears into the deep.

She holds her breath, keeps her chin high. Bradwell pushes off the riverbed and starts kicking. 'You can kick too,' he says, 'if inspired.'

She kicks but feels light-headed. She lets out her breath, draws it in again quickly. She wishes she had taken off more of her clothes. They're weighty.

'You're doing great,' Bradwell tells her, huffing.

Then Pressia feels something glide around her legs. She pulls them to her chest and tightens her hold around Bradwell's neck. 'Something's down there!'

'Probably a fish. That's all.' She can tell by the way he eyes the water that he's scared too.

The water is too dark and clouded to see into. 'No,' she says. 'It wasn't anything like that.' The ghostly girls. What if they're here, all around them, in the woods, now beastly, growling in the reeds, underwater?

'Kick!' Bradwell says.

'I can't.'

'Let go of my neck!' he shouts, but she feels the swishing around her legs again. This time, it feels like a hand fitted around her ankle, then gone.

She screams and clutches Bradwell so hard his head goes underwater. She pushes off him to stay up, climbing up his body, forcing him down. It's an instinct. Is she drowning him? She feels panic clawing through her. Thrashing, she screams his name across the river. She dips under now too – suddenly feeling deaf and blind and airless.

She flails her arms, breaks the surface, gasps, chopping the water, pounding it with the doll-head fist, but she goes under again. Her eyes are wide, but still she sees only wide-eyed darkness. Quiet rushing fills her ears. She tries to force her way to the surface, but the more she moves her arms and legs, the deeper she sinks in the icy water. Air locked in her lungs, her chest feels like a cavity, freezing from the outside in.

Can her heart freeze before she even has time to drown? Her skin will turn to ice. Her hair will become stiff. Her clothes hard. Her body – dead and blue – will be dragged out to sea. *Itchy knee* – the words from her dream appear in her mind again – *sun, she go.*

Her lungs feel like they could burst, and Pressia sees a body of water after the Detonations; the image flashes in her mind. A bridge spanning halfway into the air, and below was a bridge of bodies. Her grandfather told her that they couldn't swim across. She remembers it all now. They had to crawl across the bodies, and for this, there was no counting. For this, there was no reciting of itchy knees and suns and going. And there was no closing her eyes. She had to make it across, on her hands and knees, over bodies. She remembers the give of the bodies as layers of them took on her small weight. It fits with her dream of counting toppled telephone poles on fire, the electrical wires snapped loose, a body without a head, a dog without feet, the scalded sheep. These weren't in a dream. The bodies in the water weren't a dream. This is a memory. Her own. Panic rises inside of her. She will be swallowed by this river. It won't ever let her go. Her lungs ache and burn. She could open her mouth, let the water fill her, and drown.

She could let it happen now.

She closes her eyes to the darkness and there's only more darkness. Where is Bradwell? Is he already dead? Will their bodies be dragged out to the same glassy ocean?

And then, from below, she feels pressure – as if there are two hands on her back. Another hand grips her doll-head fist and pulls. Pressia tries to yank the doll head back, but then she realizes that maybe she's being saved. Maybe these hands will deliver her to air. The ghostly girls – she imagines their hair fanning around their faces, their uniform shirts slowly rippling in the water.

Finally, she breaks the surface. She pulls air into her lungs, which sting and spasm. Her foot strikes the river's floor. She stands, heavily, the water still rushing around her. She gasps and coughs.

She hears her name being called. It's Bradwell's voice. She then hears him splashing toward her, saying her name over and over. He lifts her off her feet and hauls her toward the shore.

He falls onto the bank, still wet, the soaking maps on the ground. The feathers of the birds' wings on his back bead with droplets. His chest and arms glisten.

Pressia coughs. Her body holds on to the deepest chill and she feels limp, heavy, exhausted. Her soaked shirt and pants are pressed to her skin, freezing cold. She blinks, looking up at the faded moon, and then Bradwell's face is beside the moon, his beautiful face. He brushes her wet hair from her cheek. 'Breathe,' he says. 'Just keep breathing.'

She reaches up, placing her hand on his cold, wet, scarred cheek. 'I didn't kill you,' she says.

'No, I thought I'd lost you.'

'I thought we were both dead.'

'It was my fault.' His lashes are wet and dark. Water drips from his chin onto her neck.

'They saved me,' Pressia says. 'Who saved you?'

'The ghostly girls.' She knows it sounds crazy, but everything has become a blur. It could be true.

Fignan buzzes up on the bank. His lights flit across their faces as if he's happy to see them.

'She's okay, Fignan,' Bradwell says. 'She's alive.' He rubs her arms. 'You were right. It was too cold.'

She's shaking. Her breaths are light and quick. 'I'm okay,' she says, but the words feel slow and stiff in her mouth and she can't feel him rubbing her arms. It's as if her skin has grown rubbery like her doll head, her nerve endings almost deadened.

'We have to get you out of the wind.' He takes her arm, wraps it around his shoulder, and pulls her to her feet. She can't stiffen her knees to hold her own weight. He bends and lifts her, cradling her to his chest.

'I'm sorry,' she says – for being a burden, but she can't get the rest out. Her jaw is rattling. Her teeth chatter. She's shaking so hard that it's actually making it hard for him to carry her. Could she have been saved by the ghostly girls only to die of the cold? She knows that her body temperature has dropped. She was in the cold water for too long. The wind is too strong. Her clothes weighed her down and now they're like cold compresses. When she was crossing that river of dead bodies as a little girl, all anyone wanted was a cold compress to the skin, and now this is how she will die.

They're moving through the trees. Fignan lights the narrow path. Bradwell follows. He's shaking too. She can feel the trembling in his arms, in the herky-jerky way he's walking.

'I'm sorry,' she says again.

'Don't say you're sorry.' He staggers then pitches forward. They land hard. He gets on his knees, lifts her again, rising unsteadily to his feet. He trudges on, his bare skin bright red. He says, 'Pressia.' She looks at him – his firm jaw, his wet head, his dark eyes. 'Think of something warm,' he whispers. 'Think of heat. Think of something good.' Pressia can tell that he's afraid. His breathing is ragged.

She thinks of the moment he gave her the mechanical butterfly, the one he'd saved from her home, how he said that it seemed like a miracle – that something that beautiful could survive. He has a way of making her flush. It's a memory of warmth, heat, goodness. She'd tell him if she thought she could form the words.

Bradwell falls again. This time he curses under his breath. He tries to lift her again, but he can't. The ground is hard and cold. 'Fignan,' he says. 'Keep going. Follow this path to the outpost. Can you do that? Are you listening? Find someone. Get help.'

Pressia hears Fignan's motor. It keeps buzzing along. But she doubts he'll be able to find anyone, much less bring them back here to save them.

Bradwell moves to a stand of trees surrounded by a thicket of underbrush and dense leaves. He digs in the leaves, lays her down. 'You can't stay in wet clothes. You've got to stay alive. Do you hear me? I can't make it any farther.'

She nods. She sees his face in pieces – an eyebrow then his lips then his hands. She has to stay alive.

He unbuttons her pants, his fingers shaking badly, and tugs them off her. He pulls her shirt over her head. Her arms feel brittle. He lies on his side – to avoid smothering the birds – absorbing the cold earth for her. He pulls the leaves in close around them and wraps his arms around her. The birds barely flinch, barely move.

Her ribs facing his, she imagines them locked together, ribs hooked to ribs. They breathe their quick breaths, white clouds rising from their red lips. Her cheek on his chest, he holds her, rubbing her back, her arms, but his movements are jerky and slow now. He pulls her cold, wet hair away from her skin. He says, 'Stay alive. Say something. Talk.'

She wants to tell him that she'd rather die here than without him in the cold river. She wants to tell him that if they die now, they might be locked together forever – ribs within ribs, frozen.

And then there'd come the thaw – grass and weeds, the forest's mossy floor covering them.

'Pressia? Speak to me. Can you talk?'

Can she talk? She thinks back to being a little girl crossing the river full of dead bodies. Could she talk then? She said words that no one understood. And, eventually, there were no words for the things she was seeing and feeling – the give of a body that bobs when you put your weight on it, bumping a body that exists beneath it. 'Itchy knee,' she whispers now through chattering teeth.

'Itchy knee?' Bradwell repeats, and then as if he has unlocked the mysterious part of her mind, as if he knows her thoughts, he says, 'Itchy knee. Sun, she go?'

She doesn't know what it means or how he could possibly have known the words. She nods, but it's more of a jerk of her head. 'Itchy knee. Sun, she go.'

They say it together. 'Itchy knee. Sun, she go.'

EL CAPITAN

BOAR

EL CAPITAN HEARS FOOTSTEPS tramping toward them through the woods, and he's relieved. The deactivated spider lies in pieces on the cold ground. Helmud wrapped the wounds tightly with a piece of cloth ripped from his own shirt. While El Capitan lies there on his side, the agony in his leg subsiding a little, Helmud is holding his hand and petting it like a kitten. El Capitan lets him because he's indebted. And, too, each time he tries to wrench his hand free, Helmud whimpers. The noise could attract Beasts. Vicious ones roam at night – ones that have mutated and interbred so much, it's hard to tell if you're staring down a wild boar or a wolf with gnarled tusks or something part collie. It's worse when there's something human about them – some slip of skin, knuckles, that fleeting glimpse of humanity in their eyes. Some say survivalists out here were eaten by trees but are still alive, trapped within. He thinks of Old Man Zander, who taught him how to bury the guns before the Detonations. He owes the man his life. Was he eaten by trees? Is it a myth?

Now there's help on the way. 'I hear them coming,' he says. 'Can I have my hand back?'

'My hand back?' Helmud says, as if El Capitan's hand belongs to Helmud too.

'Helmud!' El Capitan scolds him, and Helmud unlocks his hold. 'Thanks,' El Capitan says, flexing the hand.

He sees Wilda first. She's holding a flashlight, which bobbles wildly as she runs. Two soldiers follow – one male and one female, wearing coats with hoods pulled tight, and El Capitan can't make out their marks and fusings in the dark. The boy has an uneven gait. The girl has a humped back. Both look too young to be soldiers. El Capitan thought of himself as a warrior at their age, though. In fact, he was fending for himself and Helmud by the time he was Wilda's age. This strikes him as a little tragic now.

Wilda jogs to him and abruptly stops, pointing the beam of light at his chest as if to say, *There, see? This is what I was trying to tell you.*

'El Capitan?' the girl soldier says, startled. 'Yeah, it's me.'

The two straighten up – the girl still stooped by her hump – and salute.

Wilda kneels down next to El Capitan, hugging his arm. It makes him uneasy. He doesn't want her to start relying on him – like he needs another mouth to feed. He ignores her and addresses the soldiers. 'Who are you?'

'Riggs,' the boy says.

'Darce,' the girl says.

'At ease,' El Capitan tells them. It's possible that they've never been in El Capitan's presence. They seem nervous. They've likely heard only rumors – is he the old El Capitan out in the woods hunting down fresh recruits as live targets? Or the new El

Capitan, who's promised them fresh water, food, arms? Or is he some strange mixture of both versions?

Wings buffet overhead. They all look up. A bleached owl perches on a nearby tree limb, which bobs with the bird's weight. 'They're like vultures now – those pale owls,' El Capitan says. 'I've seen them attack a soldier that was only half dead.'

'Half dead?' Riggs ask. 'Half dead how?'

'What do you mean, "half dead how"? Not fully dead. That's how.'

'That's how,' Helmud says.

'It smells blood. Others will gather soon,' El Capitan says. 'They're like sharks and there's blood in the water.'

'I don't know anything about sharks,' Riggs says.

'Did I ask you?'

Riggs shakes his head, his chin dented with worry.

'I'll need a hand getting to the outpost. Has anyone else shown up at the outpost tonight? Anyone at all?'

'Anyone at all?' Helmud asks.

'No, sir. I don't think so,' Riggs says. 'Should we be expecting someone?'

'I was hoping that Pressia Belze and Bradwell would show. Radio back and ask.'

The soldiers exchange a look.

'You don't have walkie-talkies?' He left his own in the car – the mother's orders.

'No, sir. We haven't earned 'em yet,' Riggs says. 'Only on week two.'

'Great,' El Capitan says.

Another bleached owl alights on a nearby branch. El Capitan doesn't like that this one has a bloody beak. It's been feasting on something already tonight. He hopes it's not anyone he knows.

'At least you're armed,' El Capitan says. He's had enough puncture wounds today. 'One of you should run back to the outpost – whichever one is the fastest with the clearest set of lungs. Ask for Pressia and Bradwell. If no one's reported them, send soldiers out into the woods on recon. Do you understand?'

'I'm faster,' Darce says.

'Really? Under that hump?' El Capitan says.

The girl opens her mouth to say something, then shuts it fast. Was she going to make a crack about what El Capitan has on his own back? Is this what's going to happen to him now that they think he's gone soft? 'What? Say it.'

'Riggs' legs don't work as well.'

'Fine,' El Capitan says. 'What the hell are you waiting for, then? Go!'

'Go!' Helmud says.

Darce salutes again and takes off running. A few more bleached owls flutter through the trees.

'And you, Riggs, are going to prop me up and get me to the outpost. Okay? You'll be my crutch.'

'Yes, sir,' Riggs says.

El Capitan hefts his and Helmud's combined weight forward. Riggs squats down. El Capitan wraps his arm around Riggs' shoulder. 'On three,' El Capitan says. 'One, two, three.' Riggs hefts El Capitan and Helmud up until El Capitan is balancing on one leg. El Capitan tries to put a little weight on the bad leg. Searing pain rips up his calf. The puncture wounds are deep, and Helmud wrapped them so tightly that his leg throbs. 'Okay. Let's move.'

'Move,' Helmud says.

Wilda quickly picks up the parts of the robotic spider. El Capitan almost yells at her to leave them, but what do they matter now, dead as they are? The girl lost her boat, so go ahead – take the spider parts.

Riggs is a runt. He's some help but not much. The ground is rocky. Wilda leads the way again, holding the flashlight. El Capitan's calf feels fiery, as if already infected – and maybe it is. Maybe that's the scent the bleached owls have followed. There are more of them – a flock – beating their wings overhead.

El Capitan hears snorting in the underbrush. He says to Riggs, 'Let's pick up the pace.'

He wonders if Darce has found Pressia and Bradwell at the outpost; maybe they're sitting by the fireplace in the headmaster's old house. Maybe they'll see a search party heading out into the woods any moment now. They'll find Bradwell and Pressia – hopefully alive – if, that is, they made it out of the Deadlands at all.

One of the bleached owls gets bold. It dips down low enough to El Capitan's head that when he takes a swing, he almost makes contact. His fist brushes the outer wings.

'Give me your rifle,' El Capitan says. 'Two weeks in? I think I'm a better shot, even a little off balance and with a moving target.'

Riggs stops and pulls the rifle off his back and helps El Capitan secure the strap. It feels good to hold a rifle again. Guns – they always make him feel better. He hears the snorting again and sees a yellowed, twisted tusk poke through some brush, but just as quickly it's gone.

Wilda sings nervously, her voice trembling, like her hands. 'If you ignore our plea, we will kill our hostages.'

El Capitan can see the clearing just beyond the trees. He knows the rest by heart – the broken road leading to what was once a brick archway now toppled and blackened. The road winds between rows of stooped trees and leads to the spokes of a shattered greenhouse, twisted goalposts, hedges that have grown wild, nearly woolly stalks that offer tainted berries in the springtime, and brittle ivy that's climbed over the stones, blooming yellow flowers with ragged-sharp petals in summer, multiple crusty seed heads that remind El Capitan of three-headed babies. The place feels haunted.

But then Wilda stops and points the flashlight at one spot in the underbrush.

El Capitan tells Riggs to stop. They're at the edge of the woods. 'What is it?'

'I don't know,' Riggs says. 'She's spooked.'

'Wilda,' El Capitan says. 'What is it?'

The girl bows down, shifting her head so that she can get a better look through the brambles.

'Step away very slowly, Wilda,' El Capitan says softly.

She doesn't listen. She lifts her hand to touch something.

El Capitan shouts, 'No!'

The wild boar snarls and pounces.

The flashlight thuds to the ground. Wilda snatches her hand to her chest and falls backward. The wild boar – furred like a coyote – lunges onto her narrow chest.

El Capitan shoves Riggs out of the way and swings the gun to his chest, but then a bleached owl swoops down, batting him with wings, and without the soldier's support, El Capitan tilts forward, catching himself on his bad leg, which gives. His shot goes off, but it burrows into the dirt.

Wilda screams – like a shrill whistle – which momentarily stuns the furred boar. It looks up sharply, sniffs the air with its rubbery snout. It opens its jaws wide to show sharp fangs and lets out an ungodly squeal.

El Capitan tries to get in position to get off another shot, but as he balances against a tree he knows he's probably too late, the boar is going to kill Wilda. They go for the jugulars. And she's going to die here in the woods, under his watch. He told Pressia he was going to get her to the outpost. He's going to fail.

But then the boar pitches backward and cries – an injured, whimpering cry. There's a wash of blood from a tiny bullet wound in the meat of its upper thigh. In seconds, the boar goes limp. Could it be dead? The wound wasn't enough to kill it.

Wilda is paralyzed with fear. Her eyes glaze over as if she's still staring at the Beast, as if it's still bearing down on her. El Capitan goes to her, cups her chin. 'It's okay now. It's gone.'

The bleached owls circle and dip. Riggs swings at them, takes one out with a strong blow.

El Capitan scrambles for the flashlight, batting the bleached owls away from Wilda. He grabs her and holds her to his chest. He shines the flashlight on the boar, whose back haunch is marbled with blood, but its ribs rise and fall. Whatever hit it was loaded with a sedative of some sort.

One of the bleached owls strikes Helmud. El Capitan can't take it anymore. He lets go of Wilda, drops the flashlight, lies back, letting Helmud take his weight, and shoots at the birds. Some fall to the ground, a bloody spray of feathers. Others dart off into the trees.

Soon, they are surrounded by the dead owls. The flashlight's beam stares out across the hard ground.

'What the hell hit that boar?' El Capitan says breathlessly.

'What the hell?' Helmud says.

And then the Black Box buzzes up to the lit ground, as if moving into a spotlight.

'You did that?' El Capitan says.

Fignan's lights bob. Yes.

If the box made it this far, it's a good sign. El Capitan takes a deep breath – almost too filled with hope to ask. 'Are Pressia and Bradwell alive?'

Fignan doesn't move. He doesn't know.

LYDA

WIRE CAGE

LYDA CLIMBS BACK INTO the confines of the four-poster brass bed frame and curls up as tightly as she can against the cold. The mothers might come for her or they might not. Either way, she's alone now. When has she really ever been alone in her entire life? Truly alone? Free?

She isn't like the bird she once made of wire, locked in a wire cage. Her bones are not that frail and malleable. She's a hardened knot all her own. She's the way she first started out, a bundle of cells, organized to make her – not just anyone. *Her*. And she's stunned to find herself here alone – this is what those cells have become. This person who isn't a girl anymore. This person who isn't going to follow Partridge back to an old life. She isn't walking across the Deadlands, trailing behind him. And as good as this feels – an incredible freedom, like nothing she's ever felt in her life – it's met by the sharp ache of Partridge's absence. And, for a second, she also misses the person she was before she told Partridge that she couldn't go with him. That person is absent too. She's someone else, someone she only barely recognizes. She's new. She turns her face to the sky because she can, because it's there. It's snowing again. A snow so light that it swirls up as much as it's lighting down.

Snow.

PARTRIDGE

TRAITOR

PARTRIDGE AND HASTINGS have been walking in silence for hours. Hastings has probably been programmed to be practical with his speech, to use it wisely, cautiously, clearly. But what's Partridge's excuse? He hasn't felt like talking. He keeps seeing Lyda's face, her expression when she'd just kissed his cheek. Already gone. Already shut off from him. She'd said her goodbye.

Partridge can see the white Dome cresting in the north, caught in the blur of gray snowflakes. He's more alone than ever; a spike of fear shoots through him. 'So, Hastings,' Partridge says, looking for distraction, 'how are your parents?' He assumes Hastings won't answer.

But Hastings stares at him sharply – as if he's just remembered that he has parents – and then his eyes scan the horizon calmly, as if the question had never been asked.

'Your mom always sent cupcakes in those circular tins, remember? And your father always told jokes when she wasn't around.' They were an angular couple, tall and thin like their son. His father's jokes were bawdy, like he wanted to be one of the guys – the way Hastings did. Hastings wanted to fit in. Now he does, in a way. Does that make him happy? Are Special Forces capable of feeling emotions like joy? Do his parents know they've lost their son even though he's still alive?

Partridge wants to jog Hastings' memory and maybe some old, dormant emotions. What part of his friend is still there and what part of him is gone? 'Did Weed ever get the girl he was trying to talk to? You know, using that laser pen on the lawn of the commons? Remember how you called him a dork, trying to communicate with some dork girl?'

'Arvin Weed is valuable.'

This seems like a start. 'Valuable?'

Hastings nods.

'Did you ever get with the girl from the dance? Remember that one you were talking to?'

Hastings stops walking. He fiddles with the mechanisms of his weaponry, as if checking the action.

'So Lyda's staying behind. I guess you realize that much. But it's not over between us.'

Hastings pauses and glances at Partridge, an expression that borders on sympathy. Is sympathy the emotion to aim for?

'And my father – what do you think he's going to do with me in the Dome, Hastings? Any ideas? Any thoughts on that?'

Hastings doesn't respond.

Partridge punches Hastings in the arm – a little harder than he meant to. 'Damn it, Hastings. Talk to me. What the hell am I in for?'

Hastings looks up at the Dome. His eyes are watery. He shakes his head.

'It's bad in there? Worse now?'

He says, 'Flynn, Aria. Age: seventeen. Approximate height: five foot three inches. Approximate weight: one hundred and fourteen pounds. Eye color: hazel. Medical record: clear.'

'Aria Flynn. That's the name of the girl at the dance! The Flynn girls – she has a sister too. Suzette.'

Hastings walks on, quickly now.

Partridge runs to catch up. 'If you remember Aria Flynn, you remember what it was like before I left. Right?'

'That was a very small world,' Hastings says. 'There's more to this world.'

'Yeah, but isn't it just more of the same – the world all scorched?'

Hastings doesn't respond.

'They've got you bugged, right? Eyes, ears, a ticker in your head?'

Hastings keeps walking.

Partridge grabs him by the arm – the meat of his biceps, a spot where there are no weapons, just flesh, nerve endings, a real person. Hastings turns and looks at him. 'Why did you come for me?' Partridge asks, knowing that Hastings can't answer him, that every word might be recorded, but he can't stop himself from pressing. 'Are you on my side? Can I trust you?'

Hastings doesn't answer. The dirty snow flutters around his head – like Lyda's memory of the snow globe, shaking it and feeling trapped inside of it at the same time.

'None of this went the way I expected. Everything fell apart out here, Hastings. My father killed my brother and my mother. Sedge was Special Forces like you and he had a ticker in his head. Remember when we talked about tickers the night of the dance? And I said they weren't real and you thought they were? You were right. And now they're gone – Sedge and my mother. Dead. He could kill both of us too.'

'My orders are to return you to the Dome.' And then he stiffens and turns, his nostrils sensing something in the air. 'They're coming.'

'Who?'

'They will take you the rest of the way. Not me. They're coming from the Dome.'

Partridge looks toward the Dome now, and he sees shapes emerging from a small door. 'There was a door? All along? It was as simple as a door?'

'They will bind your hands like a prisoner.'

'Is that what I am?'

'We're all prisoners now,' Hastings says, stoic.

'Listen, you need to get back to El Capitan. Find him.'

'I'm a soldier. I'm loyal. You're the traitor.' He stands tall and points his gun at Partridge. It's clear now that Hastings has captured him – for real or for show? Partridge can't tell.

The other soldiers are coming at Hastings and Partridge with great speed.

'What should I do?'

'Raise your hands. Be very still.'

The soldiers are grotesque, deformed by overgrown muscles, misshapen bones, and protruding skulls. Their weapons are burrowed so deeply into their bodies that they might be fused to bone. One soldier quickly swipes Partridge's feet out from under him. He lands hard. 'I know you're still you, Hastings. I know it. Find El Capitan. Promise me that!'

Hastings doesn't respond.

A soldier yanks Partridge's arms behind his back, ties his wrists with plastic cuffs. 'Are you still in there, Hastings?' Partridge shouts from the ground, dirt and snow in his mouth. 'The real thing? You? Are you going to stand up for what you believe in?'

Hastings reaches down and pulls Partridge to his feet, roughly. Hastings is much taller than Partridge, so when Hastings leans in, he bows his head until his face is close to Partridge's, and in a low, angry voice that seems almost steely, as if his voice box relies, in part, on electrical wiring, he says, 'I could ask the same of you.'

EL CAPITAN

SWALLOWS

El CAPITAN SITS IN AN old folding chair, reinforced with ropes to keep it held together. His bum leg is straight in front of him, the foot splayed. He's waiting for someone to douse it with antiseptic and rewrap it. Meanwhile, he refuses to look at the wounds. Bent-beaked swallows coo in the eaves. Helmud coos back at them. Riggs has stoked the fire and gone off for supplies. The chimney is supposed to reach all three floors of the house, but the top two floors are gone. The first floor is capped by a new roof, a mess of a thing – warped and buckling, completely gone in one corner. El Capitan can see the smoke rising up the half-gone chimney before it drifts off – the ash mixing with the wafting snow.

Wilda is asleep on a pallet in a corner where the roof is good. It's quiet. Even the people out in the tents are hushed. He won't be able to sleep without news about Pressia and Bradwell. Darce sent a search party out to find them, but as soon as they arrived here, El Capitan sent out another party, with Fignan as their guide. He's so restless with nerves, he wishes he could pace to get the anxiety out of his body.

Riggs walks back into the room with a jug of alcohol and fresh bandages.

'Can't I get someone with a medical background?' El Capitan says.

'They sent me.'

El Capitan sighs. Helmud does too. Riggs kneels down and unwraps the bloody strips of Helmud's shirt.

'How bad is it? Festering?' El Capitan asks.

'Dark red, swollen, some pus.' He opens the jug. 'This is going to hurt.'

'I've been through worse.'

'Worse,' Helmud says.

'Do it fast.'

The rubbing alcohol sets each puncture blazing. El Capitan draws in a sharp, quick breath. Helmud does too – out of sympathy?

Riggs wraps the wound again quickly.

El Capitan sits back, letting Helmud prop his back. He says, 'Riggs?'

'Yes, sir?'

'What have you heard about me? What am I to you?'

'I don't know, sir.'

'Yes, you do. What do people say?'

'They say all kinds of things. You're a leader, though, so I don't think any of it matters.'

He thinks of Pressia, waiting by the smokestack for Bradwell. Would she have waited for El Capitan? Would he and Helmud have been worth it? 'I think it might matter what people think of me,' El Capitan says. 'It might.'

He stares out the hole in the roof. What's snow and what's ash? Both are gray and light and whirling. He can't tell the difference from here.

PRESSIA

ICE

PRESSIA'S EAR IS PRESSED to Bradwell's chest, her head weighty, and she hears his faint heartbeat, like a slow watch wrapped in cotton. His breaths have gone soft. His arm has lost its hold on her and now lies on the ground, limp. She pulls it in close to their bodies, sees the imbricate skin of ice that's formed over it. Her own arm is glittering with snow, a thin new skin of shining gray crystals. She has no voice. Her lashes are dusted with snowflakes, heavy. She wants to close her eyes. She wants the snow to cover the two of them in a gray blanket. She wants to be buried in this lace.

Her own breaths are shallow. She's tired. It's night. She whispers, 'Good night,' knowing it might be the last words she ever says.

Her eyes are heavy – too heavy to keep open. And as she closes them, she knows she isn't falling asleep. She's dying because she sees spokes of light blinking through the trees. The ghostly girls now angels . . . She hears their voices drifting toward her as if carried by the snow.

PART II

PART II

PARTRIDGE

CLEAN

He'll never be pure again. It's not possible, but this is how they will make him clean.

Transfusions of new blood, new marrow, a rush of new cells. His mummy mold still exists – lightweight, durable. It fits more snugly than before because he's gotten stronger. His body disappears into it for hours. There's still nothing to be done about his behavioral coding. But they try different angles, applying new advances. Nothing works. There has been a cold sheet pack, his body iced and restrained. 'Lumbar puncture,' someone says once, and a needle is injected into his spinal column.

He's drugged to sleep and to stay awake and to talk – a white-tiled room with a recording device on a table. The words rattle up from his mind, his chest. As soon as they whirl in his mind, they're on his tongue.

Sometimes, he hears his father's voice over an intercom. He hasn't seen the man even though he's asked again and again.

Where's my father? When will I see my father? Tell my father I want to see him.

He thinks of Lyda. Sometimes he calls out for her, her name ringing in the room before he realizes that he's the one calling. Once he reached for a white coat. He grabbed a fistful and said, 'Lyda! Where is she?' The tech pulled away, and Partridge's hand hit a tray of sharp, steely instruments, which clattered. 'Goddamn it!' someone shouted. 'Sterilize those!'

A woman in a lab coat will sometimes tell him what day it is, not based on the calendar but on his arrival here.

You're on day twelve. You're on day fifteen. You're on day seventeen. When will this end? She won't say.

His pinky is another way to mark time. Lyda was right. Arvin Weed figured it out with his three-and-a-half-legged mouse. My God. And if he's gotten this down, is he closing in on a cure for his father? The fine collaboration of Partridge's bones, tissue, muscle, ligaments, and skin cells is being re-created through repeated injections. The stump is capped by a fiberglass cast that his finger will grow to fit. The laboratory technicians, surgeons, and nurses look at the pinky through scopes. Sometimes they apply needlelike points of heat, as if soldering.

It's regenerating nicely. We're pleased. The coloration of the skin is nearly flawless.

Starfish can do this. Do starfish still exist somewhere?

The thing is, he doesn't want the finger back. He sacrificed, and now that sacrifice is being erased. The past, the world out there, what happened to him and the others, the death of his mother and his brother – it seems to exist less, to fade, with the infinitesimal growth of cells.

Twice, Arvin Weed appears. His eyes hover over Partridge's head – the rest of his face hidden by a mask. Partridge would talk but there's a tube in his throat. He's strapped to an examination table.

Arvin doesn't address him, but, once, Arvin winked at him. The wink was so quick it almost looked like a twitch. But Partridge believes it was more than that. Arvin is here; he's going to make sure Partridge is taken care of, right? Partridge wants to tell Weed about Hastings and what's happened on the outside. He wants to say the name *Lyda*.

He wakes up without a memory of falling asleep. His head is heavy, eyes swollen, the tube gone. He's being rolled along on a gurney, its wheels clicking over the tiles. He passes a bank of windows. Behind them, there are rows of babies in incubators. Tiny babies – almost the size of puppies, but human nonetheless. They fit in the palm of a nurse's hand. Could there be this many premature babies being born at the same time in the Dome? But the babies aren't perfect, aren't Pure. They have scars and burns and are flecked with debris. Is he dreaming of wretch babies? What's real? The incubators stretch on and on.

There's another room. His father's voice rings over an intercom. 'He's a child. There must be punishment. The punishment will Purify him. The Purification will be by water. A baptism.'

The woman tells him that this is day twenty-one.

His head is securely strapped to a heavy white board, tilted so his head is low. His shoulders are pinned. He can't move. They've made such progress with the pinky – which has grown incrementally and is tingling with nerves – that they must be careful. It can't get wet.

The white board is motorized to lower him into the water slowly. The technicians stand by, following orders with timers and small handheld devices. Partridge's head feels the water first, cool but not cold, soaking his hair, filling his ears, creeping up the sides of his face. He pushes out his breath and quickly pulls one in. He holds his breath, tries to jerk himself loose. His eyes are wide. The water is clear and bright. The room is lit by fluorescent bulbs. He can see the warped faces of the technicians.

He lets some air escape from his nose. Just a bit. How long will he be held here? His father doesn't want him to die but maybe to get to know death. He lets out more air. His lungs feel pinched.

Just when he can't take anymore he feels the small tug of the white board. His chin emerges, his mouth. He drags air back into his lungs. Is the baptism over? Has he been saved? He feels the motor again, reversing him back into the water. He pleads with the technicians, 'No, no, no!' It's possible that their ears are sealed in some way to protect them from his begging.

He can't shake his head, can't arch his back for air.

He's submerged again and again – a baptism that just won't take? He stops pleading. He works to time his breaths. He tries to develop a method. His mind loses track of time. He's only trying to meet the surface, to be in the air.

He tries to hold on to the image of Lyda's face, the exact color of her eyes. He comes up for air and his larynx spasms, closes shut. This time, there is no air. No sound. No breath. He tries to signal his panic to the technicians with his eyes.

They make notes.

The motor hums again. He's going back under without having taken a breath.

One of the technicians seems to understand that something's gone wrong. He reaches for an intercom.

But Partridge is now submerged. He can't hear what's being

said. He can't breathe even if he wanted to draw water into his lungs. That's when the bright glossy light of the room fades to a smear of darkness – ash. He thinks of ash and snow and Lyda – her face coming apart piece by piece and floating up into the sky.

PRESSIA

MOSS

PRESSIA AND BRADWELL are living in a small cottage, where the search party brought them the night they almost died. Small, with stone walls covered in moss both inside and out, it was chosen because it was easy to heat with its potbelly stove. Pressia rebounded quickly from hypothermia, but Bradwell's lungs have taken on water. One thing survivors know well is labored breathing, coughs, how to determine which are serious. Pneumonia causes short grunts at the end of each exhale.

For three weeks now, Pressia has dedicated herself to two things – poring over Fignan and all the notes that Walrond left behind, and tending to Bradwell, who mostly sleeps.

She started writing on paper, which is precious, but soon ran out and began writing on the surface of a narrow table. When she ran out of room there, she started writing on a small chopping block, and then on stones she's brought in from the orchard. She keeps her print tiny. In cones of light flickering in the air above him, Fignan projects video clips, images of scanned documents

– birth certificates, marriage licenses, death notices, diplomas, transcripts – and Willux's handwritten notes about books he's reading, giving page numbers without titles or authors, and convoluted screeds. Pressia jots it all down.

Meanwhile Bradwell rouses just enough to take a sip of water or pork broth. El Capitan has arranged for soldiers to bring food, and nurses visit. Fignan offers medical information and data about pneumonia, various risks and treatments and medicines that they don't have access to. She can't fault him. He's trying to be helpful.

El Capitan begged Pressia not to stay with Bradwell, whose sickness could be contagious. She told him she couldn't leave him. 'I'm a loyal friend.'

Friend – is that still what they are? Pressia remembers his body, stripped of clothes, wet. Sometimes, she thinks of him seeing her undressed, almost completely naked. She knows it's silly to be embarrassed. They were dying. So what if he saw her undressed? He saved her life. But now, just thinking about it, she feels suddenly shy – flushed, nervous – as if it's happening at that very moment. Her mind wanders to the feeling of his skin against hers, trembling because of the cold, and she feels like she's falling again, headlong, down into some unknowable darkness, a terrifying rush. Falling, falling, falling – in love?

Right now, it's selfish and stupid to even think about things like that. She sits on the edge of his cot, waiting for that moment when Bradwell comes to, blinking into the light, knowing who she is. The alternative is that he doesn't get better, that his lungs fill with too much fluid and he drowns from within. She can't let herself think of it. She has to work. She has to have something to show him when he emerges. She emerged once from drowning. He will too.

She stands and leans against one of the lichen-covered walls. From all the video clips that Fignan has stored within him, there's one she keeps coming back to – the one of her parents when they were both young. Pressia's taken detailed notes about it. It feels like an indulgence each time she asks him to play it, but now as a reward for slogging through Willux's notes, she says, 'Show me again, Fignan, that footage of my parents.'

Fignan turns on, creating a flickering cone of light. There's Pressia's mother, laughing in the sun and brushing her curly hair from her eyes, then a young man who must be Pressia's father. He has dark, almond-shaped eyes, like hers, and a quick, unpredictable smile. They're in a field, wearing their cadet uniforms, open-collared, untucked. They wave to the camera.

Pressia wants to walk into that sunlight, to grab the hands of her mother and father, to tell them, *It's me. I'm your daughter. I'm here. Right here.* The image of her parents – so beautiful, so real – is punishing and wonderful. It allows her to miss them specifically, in incredible detail.

In the background, she sees Willux – she'd recognize him anywhere – with his notebook. He's talking to the guy whose face Pressia remembers from the clipping, tucked under the bell back at the morgue – the cadet whose death was ruled an accident. Ivan Novikov. Their heads are bent in quick conversation. Her mother walks up to them, showing them that the camera is on. She's telling them to wave. She reaches for a hand, and she takes the dead cadet's hand – Ivan Novikov's, not Willux's, not Pressia's father's. Ivan pulls her close and kisses her. Willux tucks the notebook under his arm. He waves then puts his hand in his pocket and walks away.

Pressia turns from the flickering light, which makes the moss-covered walls shimmer. Does that kiss mean her mother was dating Ivan? Did *everyone* love her mother? Who was Aribelle Cording anyway? Pressia can't imagine how someone could give and take love so easily. Did her mother have a weak constitution? She followed her heart, not her head. Pressia should be thankful for it; it's the reason she was born. But still, she wishes her mother had been . . . what? Stronger? Less susceptible to love? Love is a luxury. It's something that people are allowed to indulge in when they're not simply trying to survive and keep other people alive. Pressia can't help but think of her mother as love-rich, love-spoiled, and what good did it do her?

Bradwell moans. One of his feet kicks the covers. She says his name, hoping this is the moment he'll come to, but then his body is still again. If he did open his eyes just now and recognize her, what would she say to him?

Pressia knows that it's fear that keeps her love in check. But what if falling in love is a sign not of weakness but of courage? What if it isn't falling or crashing but taking a leap?

The footage stutters to its end. The room dims. She runs her hands over all of the stones, covered in her hand-scrawled notes. The nurse has told her to talk to Bradwell. 'It's good for him. He really might be able to hear you, even in his dreams.'

And Pressia has kept him updated. She's told him that even though they don't know for certain that Partridge is back in the Dome, they suppose he is because the robotic spiders have been deactivated. The day after they made it to the outpost, word came from the city that the robotic spiders all crackled with life for a moment, their legs seized, and then their screens went blank. She's told Bradwell that El Capitan is in a medic station set up in the city, where he's been removing the robotic spiders, which are all still lodged in people's bodies.

She hasn't told him the bad news – more children have

disappeared. Some have been returned. A few days ago, one was found asleep in the woods. Two more were wandering the market. Another was in his bed as if he'd never been gone except, like Wilda and the others, his body was perfected. These children have had every scar or burn healed, all amputations regrown, and their umbilical wounds covered in new skin. El Capitan has them all brought here and guarded in the dormitory so they don't fall into the hands of the growing cult of Dome worshippers. Wilda lives here too. Pressia misses her, but she can't visit; Bradwell might be contagious, and Wilda's immune system might be slipping as her cells degenerate.

Like Wilda, each of the children is programmed to say very little. 'Propaganda,' El Capitan calls it. 'Little spokesmodels for the Dome.' And their messages end, as Wilda's does, with the gestured sign of the Celtic cross.

They call them Purified, as they aren't really Pure, but remade. And all of them have developed tremors in their hands and heads.

Pressia hopes that they will be able to find the formula in combination with her mother's vials and the third mysterious ingredient. Maybe they can save the children before they're too far gone. She would never confess to Bradwell that she stares at her doll-head fist sometimes, squints until her eyes blur with tears, and tries to imagine the hand beneath it. The doll head gone? Maybe it's another reason why she works so hard.

And now she says, 'Willux is a stranger to me, Bradwell.' How do you organize the ravings of a crazy person? How is she to find some pattern that would make sense to one of the Seven or Bradwell's parents? Walrond left clues for them after all. Bradwell knows Willux better than she does. 'I need you,' she says. 'Wake up and help me.' But she's not sure if he would help even if he were awake. He desperately wants the truth, but not the formula.

From a restless sleep, he coughs. His cheeks turn a deep ruddy color. The birds on his back contract, as if their air is dependent on his breaths.

'Easy now,' she says. 'It's okay.' Fignan buzzes to his bedside. His coughing subsides.

The fire is fading a little. She puts on her new boots and coat – OSR-issued, gifts from El Capitan. She slides the iron bolt that El Capitan installed, and opens the door. A cottage is tucked deep in an orchard. The trees' black branches bow so low that the limbs have started to root back into the ground. The air is cuttingly cold. She supposes Partridge is sleeping in some completely static temperature – and what would that be? Seventy-two degrees or seventy-three? She wonders if he ever thinks of her out here. There's a chance they'll never see each other again, and, for a moment, it's as if it's all over. Nothing will change. This will be her life. Here forever. And that will be his.

And if Bradwell dies, Pressia will live out her days here in this orchard cottage surrounded by trees that seem wired to the earth, alone.

Because the moon is full – though, as always, partially lost in a skein of ash – she can see the low, crumbling cement wall in the distance and, beyond that, to one side, the glowing fires of the tent dwellers and, to the other, an old dormitory, half of which is collapsed. That's where Wilda stays.

There's a light on in the dormitory and Pressia wonders if it's Wilda's light. What if nothing comes of Walrond's Black Box? The girl will die.

She picks up an armful of wood from the neatly stacked pile and imagines what this place was like during the Before. When the ghostly girls were alive and well, did they pull fruit from the trees? She squints through the orchard – these stalks of wilting bouquets, rows and rows of blackened tethered limbs – and she sees movement. A shape darts so quickly that the fog swirls. Then nothing.

She looks at the small cottage. She hears Bradwell coughing again and then his voice – rough and raw. 'Pressia!'

She drops the firewood, runs to the cottage, and finds him thrashing. She kneels next to the bed. His eyes are open but he's still lost. 'I'm here,' she says. 'I'm still here.'

He coughs raggedly. She gets a cup of water. She lifts his head and puts the cup to his lips. 'Take a sip,' she says. 'You need to drink something.'

His eyes close, and he drinks a little then pulls away. She eases him onto his side.

She stands and paces. Finally, she rests her forehead against the stone wall, flattens her hand to the moss, and rubs it away. 'Bradwell,' she says, 'why don't you come back? This can't be the end.' She waits for Bradwell to respond even though she knows he won't.

Pressia lifts her hand from the wall and sees colors – a bit of blue, a smear of red. She looks closely at the lichen. Are these reds and blues just another kind of mold?

She reaches up and rubs off more lichen, and beneath it, she sees more color – paint. She rubs and rubs, until she sees the side of a face – an eye, a cheek, an ear.

Who lived here after the Detonations? An artist? Did the artist keep painting in this little cottage and after running out of canvases, take to painting the walls?

Pressia grabs a washcloth and lightly dabs the moss away, careful not to damage the colors underneath. Faces emerge – one girl after the other – as if they were locked away. Ghostly girls. *Who can save them from this world? The river's wide, the current curls, the current calls, the current curls.*

Was the artist trying to hold on to all those who were lost? Pressia remembers the feeling of being pushed up to the surface – those small hands at her back. True or not, she felt it. *They wade in water to be healed, their wounds to be sealed, to be healed. Death by drowning, their skin all peeled, their skin all pearled, their skin all peeled.*

Pressia knows what it's like to be trapped underwater, and now it feels like she's bringing each of them to the surface, one by one. There's another mouth, open, as if holding the note of a song. *Marching blind their voices singing, voices keening, voices singing. We hear them 'til our ears are ringing, ears are screaming, ears are ringing.* A blue eye, half closed, pained. There is a cheek, rounded and full. *They need a saint and savior, saint and sailor, saint and savior. They'll haunt and roam this shore forever, haunt and roam this shore forever.* Another eye, lifted sadly by a worried brow. Lips, this time pursed as if about to say a word.

Bradwell breathes jaggedly, but it's as if the girls are breathing. They breathe in, *Will*; they exhale, *ux*. He is their murderer. He killed them. The walls are filled with their faces. The room is filled with their breathing.

Will.

Ux.

Will.

Ux.

Pressia turns and finds Fignan at her feet. Walrond said to remember that he knew Willux's mind. To know the secret, she has to know the man. To know the man, the mass murderer – the killer of these girls as well as most of the world – she has to enter his mind.

Will.

Ux.

She has to think his thoughts, walk his steps, breathe his breaths.

Will, the girls whisper in unison, *ux.*

LYDA

NINE

Her cot is number nine on the right. This is a new place, a new room – temporary, as the mothers tend to be nomadic. But her number isn't temporary. The next place the mothers move, she will still be number nine, even if it's a row of pallets on the floor, even if it's a row of bodies in a dirt dwelling. Maybe even if it's a row of graves.

Why number nine? After the mothers found her, they gave her this cot, which belonged to one of the mothers who died in the recent battle. It seems cruel for Lyda to take her place. It's hard to lie here, heart pounding into the bedsprings, knowing it should be someone else's heart. But there's no way around it. The mothers believe in order.

It's night. The room is dark. Some of the children are still restlessly fighting sleep. She hears them asking for water, the mothers humming, the whispers of nightly prayers. It's an incantation that helps her sleep.

But tonight she's not sleeping. She's been told that she's finally allowed to see Illia. She's wanted to see her every day since she returned, but she was told that Illia had gotten worse and was under quarantine.

Lyda's requests have finally been granted, though, because Illia's body is barely holding on. 'The soul case is wearing thin,' Mother Hestra told Lyda. 'Her time is coming.'

Lyda rests her head on her pillow, shared with Freedle. He was given to her when she arrived. She's to keep him safe for Pressia. His wings creak when he flutters them, but he's still swift. She strokes his head.

When she was little, she had a stuffed ladybug that she shared her pillow with. Lyda was in charge of putting herself to bed. Her mother followed the method that told parents not to come when their kids called out at night. And now she is surrounded by an abundance of mothers. It feels good, safe. She's earned a place here through hard work. Her muscles burn with fatigue. She's learning to aim darts – the important action of the wrist. She's practiced gutting Dusts and Beasts and hauled dirt from a new burrow being excavated. She's dug up roots and, hunched over a bucket, skinned them for meals.

All the while she tries not to think of Partridge. The mothers have taught her that men are a weakness. They will only betray your love. Of course, Partridge isn't a Death. He's not one of those men the mothers hate with such conviction. But she's still afraid that the more she misses him – his face, his skin, the way he looked at her – and the more hope she has that she'll see him again, the more she has to lose.

The door opens; light sweeps into the room. Mother Hestra whispers her name.

Lyda pats Freedle quickly and runs to the door.

Mother Hestra says, 'It's time,' and leads her down the hall into a small room. Lyda needs to tell Illia about the Black Box, the seed of truth.

Illia is gaunt and pale. Her face is bare, covered with burns and scars from the Detonations and from Ingership's abuse. Maybe she's come to peace with it or is too tired to hide it. Lyda sits in the chair beside her bed. Illia stares at the ceiling. Lyda takes her hand and whispers her name. Illia doesn't respond.

'The seed of truth,' Lyda says, 'is in good hands. It's with the people who will know what to do. Good people.'

Illia doesn't move. Can she hear Lyda?

'Illia,' she whispers. 'The truth is in good hands. You fulfilled your role.' Is she giving Illia permission to die? It's been ingrained in Lyda to fight sickness and death, to fear them above all else. One day her father was sick; the next day he was gone – shuttled away to a distant ward. She never got a chance to say goodbye. They got a notice saying he was dead. But the mothers have taught her death is part of life.

Lyda looks at Mother Hestra. 'Has she been gone like this for a long time?'

'She's half here and half in the beyond. Between life and death.'

'Illia,' Lyda says. 'I know what you meant when you said "I miss Art." I know you meant Art Walrond.'

Her eyes flutter. She turns her head and stares at Lyda.

'The seed of truth – it's alive. It exists. You did what he needed you to do.'

'Art,' she whispers. 'I've seen him. He's there; he's waiting.'

Lyda's eyes fill with tears. 'You can go to him,' she whispers. 'It's okay now.'

Illia raises her hand and touches Lyda's cheek. 'If I'd had a daughter . . .' And then she lays her hand on her heart and closes her eyes.

'Illia,' Lyda whispers. 'Illia, are you still with us?' She turns to Mother Hestra. 'Do something! I think she's—'

'She is going,' Mother Hestra says calmly. 'You knew that. She is going, and it's okay.'

Lyda stares at Illia's ribs, looking for breath. They're still. 'She's gone.'

'She is. Yes.'

Mother Hestra hooks her arm around Lyda's and says, 'Let's go back now. We will take care of her body.'

'Let me sit with her a minute.'

'Yes,' Mother Hestra says.

Lyda closes her eyes and says a bedtime prayer, one she used to whisper to her stuffed ladybug toy about the joy of morning light.

After a while, Lyda walks, nearly blind, back through the hall to cot number nine. She wants to tell them, *Someone's died. Someone just left us.* But there's no need to wake them. It was natural. Death is part of life.

She lies down and tries to sleep, but she doesn't have the ability to rein in her thoughts. She imagines Illia and Art Walrond reunited in a place like heaven. Is it possible? Her mind darts to Partridge. Where is he now? Is he safe? Is he thinking of her?

She remembers the last thing he said to her. *You said goodbye, but I'm not. Because we'll find each other again. I'm sure of it.*

Now he's returned to some version of the life they once lived. It has rules, social order, and rigor. It has bath towels, starched shirts, and fresh paint. People expect things from him. The Dome has a way of changing you – beyond enhancements and drugs – just by the stifled air you breathe. In the Dome, she accepted what she was told. Her greatest fear was disappointing those around her. And yet the truth was there if she'd looked for it. She accepted – so easily, so readily, so *happily* – that those on the outside were less than human. She doesn't despise her old self as much as she fears her. Her trapped life was so comfortable that she'd still be in it if she'd been allowed a choice. If her old self had been told that she would one day find herself out here, living among the wretches, she would have pitied her new self. But she's lucky she got out.

When she's sure everyone's asleep, even Freedle, she pulls out the music box Partridge gave her – the one that belonged to his mother. She winds it and lifts the lid but lets only a few stray notes float on the air. Illia and Art – can they hear this tune? Where does the soul go after death?

She slips the music box back under her pillow.

How can Partridge remember the world outside – hold on to the strange idea of it – once inside the Dome?

She'll be erased. She knows it. The Dome won't allow her to exist. She let him go once. Every day demands that she release him over and over again.

She clenches her fists and thinks, *Will he find me again?*

And she tells herself, *No. Don't want this. Let him go.*

She opens her hands, spreads her fingers wide.

PRESSIA

STONES

PRESSIA IS BENT TO HER NOTES written on wood and stones. The problem is clear. Willux was crazy. He was crazy when he detonated the planet and he was a crazy young man. On one page, he scrawled *Good Ole Buck* in one corner, *Collins* in another – buddies of his? – and the rest of the page is filled with entwined snakes. One page is just the numbers 20.62, 42.03, NQ4, and the words *I was forged by fire. Made new by flames.* What does it mean? He seemed fond of poetry and appeared to be working on one that shows up a few times with various alterations.

> *She rises every day to the top of the sky,*
> *Brushing over the holy mound with the tip of a wing.*
> *I'd tell you this but my voice is shy*
> *Because your beauty is, too, a sacred thing.*

He drew an arrow from *I'd tell you this but my voice is shy* to an alternative line, *The truth is written up there on high,* and then a list of words to rhyme with *wing – sing, swing, bring, adjourning –* and then *sky – sigh, lie, pry, fly. A romantic –* that's what Walrond called him. Were these poems written to Pressia's mother? The thought sickens her.

She'd really like to stumble upon formulas, discussions of cells, degeneration, renewal, nanobiology . . . Instead, she's just found pages of what look to be constellations and birds and curlicues, ever-tightening spirals – pages of them.

She stares up at the lit motes swirling in the image of a page projecting up from Fignan. She feels so alone. She looks at Bradwell's shoulder, rising and falling with each breath, his jaw, his cheek. Since he called her name, he sits up to eat and can walk a little, one hand on the wall – touching the ghostly girls' faces, which he doesn't seem to notice. He looks at Pressia as if he's trying to see her across a canyon. Sometimes he whispers her name or says, 'Thank you.' And Pressia feels like the ground is shifting under her feet. Falling, falling – that's what it's like when her name is on his lips. Still he sleeps most of the time, and then she returns to one question: How did Walrond get inside Willux's mind? The room seems to spin with the faces of all the ghostly girls looking on, urgent and goading. What if nothing ever makes sense?

She knows the answer. The ghostly girls will hound her. They won't ever let her walk away. *They'll haunt and roam this shore forever, haunt and roam this shore forever.*

She says to Fignan, 'Turn the page,' and a new page from Willux's notebooks appears. Again, birds.

But this time, in the margin, there's a word: *Brigid.* Her middle name. Emi Brigid Imanaka. Willux didn't name her. He didn't even know she existed until years after her birth, so why does he have a note with her middle name in it – over a decade before she was even born? She feels a flush fueled by anger.

It feels personal, as if he's goading her. What does he want from her? She stands up and says to Bradwell, who's still sleeping soundly, 'Okay, let's go over this again.' She points to the upper-right corner of the table. 'All this refers to the Seven – how it started, what it meant to Willux. Each of the members of the Seven has their own area.' After Willux, notes on her father and mother are the fullest. Maybe she should be ashamed of spending so much time with them. She couldn't help it. She loves the way her father smiles. She sees her face in his – a bit here and there. She's amazed by him. Even the simplest gesture – picking up something someone dropped and handing it to them. She had to start somewhere – why not her father, the lost part of herself?

'This large stone is where I write all references to *swan*; this portion of the chopping block is devoted to numbers – Willux had certain numbers that he loved. This stone is where I jot references to domes of any sort.' Young Ellery Willux was obsessed with domes.

She moves back to the table, leans down on it, one palm flat and the doll-head fist pressed into the box reserved for Ivan Novikov. She might not be able to get into the head of Ellery Willux, but what about Ivan Novikov, Willux's first victim? She remembers the video of him holding her mother's hand.

She walks the edges of the room, looking into the eyes of all the ghostly girls. There's one who always makes her pause – there's something about this girl's face, a flash of light in her eyes, that reminds Pressia of her friend Fandra, her good friend from childhood. Fandra and her brother Gorse ran away before they could get taken by OSR. Fandra had golden hair that brushed her shoulders, blue eyes, and a shriveled left arm. She snorted sometimes when she laughed, which made Pressia laugh. Pressia ran into Gorse not long ago – at one of Bradwell's old underground meetings on Shadow History that she'd gone to – and was stunned to find him alive. She started to ask about Fandra, and he said, 'No.' Fandra was gone.

And even though this girl doesn't have golden hair, Pressia feels like Fandra exists in the image somewhere. 'Fandra,' she whispers now. 'What am I doing?'

She knows what Fandra would do. She'd keep going.

Pressia needs a new stone, one reserved for the word *Brigid*. She says to Bradwell, 'I'll be right back.' She shuts the door tightly behind her as she leaves.

She can't shake Willux's words – *I was forged by fire. Made new by flames* – and the image of the entwined snakes, always two wrapped around each other, loosely spiraling up. 'Ivan Novikov,' she says to herself, dipping under the branches. What did the clipping say about his death? Willux tried to save him during training. Young Cadet Walrond said that it was a sad day. An officer said that it was Ivan's first swim of the season, that he'd been sick but had just gotten well.

Pressia bends down and finds a large oval stone. She cradles it to her chest. She remembers Willux's expression when her mother held Ivan's hand. Did Willux have a crush on her? Was he jealous?

She remembers nearly drowning in the cold, dark river, the hands – she was so sure they were hands – pushing her up, and she imagines Ivan Novikov, but Willux's hands are pushing him down. Looking down from above, who can tell whether the struggle is to save someone or drown them? And if Walrond thought the world of Willux, he'd assume the best. Ivan was sickly, so that might have made it easier to believe he was drowning, to believe the rescue was doomed. Willux had no visible motive. Ivan was his friend.

She walks quickly back to the cottage, closing the door behind herself once inside. Bradwell is restless. The birds flutter on his back. She sets the stone on the table.

'Fignan, show me Walrond's message, the one meant for the Seven.'

Fignan powers on, and there is Art Walrond again, broad and blond. 'Fast-forward,' Pressia says. The image speeds up. 'Stop.'

Art crosses his arms and says, 'People don't just decide young to be mass murderers. A person has to work up to an act of annihilation, and Ellery has. He still is. But he started small. I was there early on. I should have done something then. I see that now, looking back. The thing is, he killed the one person who could have saved him. That's the irony.'

He killed the one person who could have saved him. Ivan Novikov. Was he the one who had the formula?

'I want to see the medical records again,' she says to Fignan. 'Ivan Novikov.' Fignan lights up Ivan's folder. She reads the doctor's handwritten scrawl.

. . . *Tremors of the extremities. Slight palsy of the head. Hearing diminished. Eyesight decreased from 20/20 to 20/100* . . .

Pressia recognizes the symptoms. Rapid Cell Degeneration. Willux started brain enhancements young, a little at a time, her mother had said. Maybe that was one of the points of the international branch of the Best and Brightest – a global effort to ensure that the best minds were even better. If Novikov and Willux had both started up brain enhancements, neither of them would have had adverse effects for a long time. Wilda shakes because her body was too young to accept the intense doses all at once. Willux shakes now because of the accumulation of enhancements over decades. Maybe Novikov had some underlying medical condition causing the enhancements to hit him harder, or maybe he did more than Willux, more than anyone else . . .

Willux killed the one person who could save him.

She starts over. Novikov had Rapid Cell Degeneration, from what the medical reports indicate, and then he didn't. He was better. Maybe Novikov knew that the enhancements would have a downside. Maybe he induced the Rapid Cell Degeneration himself because he had a way to reverse it and he wanted to test it.

'Novikov's notes,' she says to Fignan. 'I want anything that Walrond collected from him that's personal, written in his own handwriting.'

The cone of light above Fignan yields one result – a file: *Novikov Notations*. She says, 'Open file.'

The file is empty.

Why would Walrond make a file of Novikov's notes if he didn't have any?

Unless Walrond was sending a message that he had notes, but now they're gone.

'Walrond's message again,' Pressia says to Fignan.

The Black Box shows Walrond's face. He gives his introduction, and as the message plays on, his eyes go teary. 'It's all here for you and it'll lead you to the formula,' Walrond says. 'It's not all laid out pretty. I couldn't risk something that simple. And listen, if you get to a point in your search and you can't go any further, remember that I knew Willux's mind as well as anyone. I pored over these notes and I had to look into the future.'

She whispers, '*I had to look into the future.* Why?' She looks at the stacks all around her.

'This box wasn't safe enough for me,' Walrond's image says. 'I couldn't simply store everything here. If you know Willux's mind – and you all do – it became our life's work, didn't it? Trying to figure out his next move and all that. Well, if you just think about his mind, his logic, you'll be able to understand the decisions I've made. And when you get to the end, the box isn't a box at all. It's a key. Remember that. The box is a key and time is of the essence.'

'Stop,' Pressia says.

Fignan holds the image frozen in midair. She remembers Bradwell questioning Walrond. Time was of the essence back when they hoped to stop Willux. Not now. It makes no sense. And Walrond couldn't trust the box to hold the formula. The file was a placeholder. It tells Pressia that the formula exists, but that maybe Walrond hid it. 'Where?' She sits down on the edge of Bradwell's bed. She's suddenly angry at Bradwell, even though that's not fair or logical. She needs his help. She takes a deep breath. 'Continue,' she says to Fignan.

Walrond disappears off screen but then returns and says, 'I can feel them closing in on me. We're running out of time. If you're hearing this, it means all our attempts here have failed.' He laughs and cries at the same time for a second and then he says, 'Willux – he's a romantic when all's said and done, right? He wants his glorious story to live on. I hope one of you hears this, and I hope you give his story *an ending*. Promise me that.'

'Stop,' Pressia says. The image stops. The small cottage goes quiet. The wind is sharp outside. A small sprig of ivy taps the window. She should tell Fignan to power down, but she likes the extra light. It's getting dark outside. Her mind is whirring.

Bradwell's birds rustle under his shirt. She lifts his shirt to see if they're okay, revealing Bradwell's broad, muscular back. His skin holds on to a deep flush. The birds seem better. Their eyes glint. She strokes their feathers. They're beautiful – regal almost.

She wonders, *What is it like to be joined to something alive, to have those three small beating hearts with you, always?*

Pressia lowers the shirt, hoping they'll sleep. She's tired too.

Bradwell turns. She wants to be close to him and warm. She's been sleeping on a pallet on the floor, but it's cold. Ice is crystallizing on the windowpanes. She doesn't want to sleep on the cold floor alone. Pressia wants to feel safe. She doesn't want to think of what might be lurking in the orchard or of Willux drowning Ivan Novikov. She doesn't want to wonder why her middle name is in the margins of Willux's notebook.

She lies down next to Bradwell, slips under the blanket, lifts his heavy arm, and lays it over her shoulder.

She feels his warm breath on her ear.

Loyal friends. That's what they are – friends – and that's why this is okay. If it were more, she would stop herself. She likes the feeling of his warm breath on her neck.

And then she hears his voice. 'Are you taking advantage of me?'

She sits up and scrambles out of the bed. 'Bradwell.'

His eyes are clear. 'I'm in a weakened condition, you know.' He smiles. 'You shouldn't take advantage of someone at a time like that.'

'I was cold!' Pressia says, wrapping herself in her arms. 'That's all.'

'Is that right?' His eyes are shining.

'You're awake. You're really awake,' she says.

He nods. 'More or less.'

'I'm glad you're back.' And she is. She feels giddy with happiness. 'You're really back!'

'I never left.'

'You saved me out there,' she says.

'And you saved me in here.'

PARTRIDGE

WARM

Partridge WAKES UP warm and dry. He opens his eyes and sees a billowing white canopy. There's a breeze. Sunlight thrown from a window falls on the blanket. He lifts his hand – which feels impossibly heavy and bruised to the bone – and rests it on the sunny square.

It's warm. Is that possible? Where is he?

He smells food being cooked – something fatty and fried. Maybe bacon. He hasn't smelled frying bacon since he was a child, but some things stick with you forever, he thinks, and bacon is one of them.

The canopy is attached to a large oak bed and he's in the middle of it. He lifts his head, which starts pounding, and struggles to his elbows, as if his body is waterlogged. A door across the room leads to a pale blue tiled bathroom.

There's a plumped pillow beside him. He punches it softly, his fist sinking into feathers. A feather pillow? It's too real to be a dream.

He wonders if this is some version of heaven. If so, will Lyda meet him here? This could be their bedroom, with a tall wardrobe, a bedside table, a lamp, and a *real* bed. Attached to the ceiling is a slow fan with wide blades made of wicker, churning air.

He looks out the window – it's open and screenless, but windows in the Dome are only for show. They never open; it's the same temperature outside as it is inside – except during the winter when they reduce the outside temperature by ten degrees to give the impression of a season change.

Outside the window, there's a crystal-blue ocean. Small waves are rolling up on golden sand. It's empty except for an old man with a metal detector. He remembers old men with metal detectors on the beach from his childhood. They wore black socks and thick rubber shoes, just like this one. This beach is like an advertisement for a Caribbean vacation.

But there's his fiberglass cast on his pinky. He wedges it off, revealing a stub – three-quarters of the way formed, sealed with his own skin.

He's in the Dome.

Something chafes the soft skin under his chin. He touches a strange collar, locked around his throat. It's made of thin metal, slightly malleable. A box of about two square inches is attached to it, vibrating with electricity. He feels a grooved pattern on the box – a keyhole?

He's a prisoner here.

There's a knock at the door, and for a second, he wonders if it's Lyda. Anything could happen.

'Come in,' he says.

The door opens. Like the bed, it's ornately designed. A woman in a pink skirt and white blouse appears. She's wearing a beaded necklace. Partridge remembers the mother with a beaded necklace grown over with skin so it looked like a fleshy tumor.

She walks over to him and sets a tray of food on the bedside table. Bacon, eggs, a stout glass of orange juice clouded with pulp. A piece of toast is glazed with what seems to be butter and honey. He's hungry yet his stomach feels weak.

She leans over him with familiarity and puts a cool hand on his forehead. 'Partridge,' she says, 'you seem to be feeling better!' She smiles as if she's been missing him and he's finally arrived.

There's something vaguely familiar about her face. Has he seen her at functions he was dragged to as a kid back when his father gave more public addresses?

'Yeah.' He swallows and his throat aches. 'How do we know each other again?'

'I knew you'd know me. He said no and I said, "Wait and see!"' She tilts her head. 'We go way back, Partridge. But we've never met – not formally. I'm Mimi,' she says. 'I've been taking care of you here.' She sits on the edge of the bed. 'My daughter has helped too. She's downstairs, practicing the piano.'

Partridge has no idea what Mimi is talking about. She's said a lot of words, but somehow he understands less than before. 'Where am I?'

She smiles. 'Where do you want to be?'

He rubs his eyes. He's tired. 'I want to know where I am.'

Mimi gets up and takes little steps to the door – her hands dance around her head, her skirt swishes around her calves. 'Listen,' she says. 'A Beethoven sonata. Hear it?' Partridge hears a classical tune. 'She's taken lessons for years. She doesn't have the most natural ear for it, but she's a perfectionist. That makes up for just about everything, doesn't it?'

He's not sure if that's true or not, so he doesn't answer. 'Where's my father?'

'He's at work. He works so hard. Hours and hours.'

'How do you know him?'

'I've known him for years, Partridge. By gosh, I've watched you grow up – from afar, of course. My daughter and I have been on the outskirts of your life, so to speak; you know how it is.'

He has no idea how it is. He needs to focus. He needs to find Arvin Weed and Glassings – people who were on his mother's list as those he can trust.

'Haven't you felt it?' she says. 'A set of maternal eyes, keeping watch? I've begged him to let you in. Begged and begged. But he said that it would be too disruptive. But here you are!' Mimi takes her mincing steps to the edge of his bed and kneels. She grips the bedspread and looks like she might cry.

With great exertion, he sits up, his back to the headboard. At first, her face doubles. But he squints, concentrates, and her face is pretty, in an angular way, and strangely ageless. She looks to be ten years younger than his parents, but at the same time she seems older. Is it her gestures? Her speech? She has no wrinkles, even now that she's smiling at him expectantly. Her face is taut.

Now it hits him that Mimi might assume some intimacy with him because she has established intimacy with his father. She and her daughter have had to live on the outskirts. She's been an extra set of maternal eyes on him – for *years*? He says, 'Are you . . .' He doesn't know how to put it. 'Are you my father's . . .' *Mistress*? Is that the word he's looking for?

'I'm his *wife*,' Mimi says, beaming.

'What?'

'We're newlyweds, technically, but we've been together all these years. He loves me, and I love him. I hope you can accept that.'

Partridge feels sick. 'He killed my mother and then he turned around and married you?' He kicks off the blanket and sheets, his leg muscles burning. He pushes himself to the other side of the bed, swinging his legs to the floor. 'Was that an added bonus to exploding her head? That he'd be a free man?'

'He's not a murderer,' Mimi says softly. 'You're confusing the facts.'

'He had me tortured! Do you know that? I'm lucky to be alive.' He still feels close to death, as if it has burrowed deep into his body.

'You could have a father who doesn't care about you at all. You could have a father who abandoned you – like my daughter. Your father took me in when no one else would have. He saved our lives.' Mimi is still smiling at him – the smile is nearly exhausted but expresses grave patience.

'I have a father who's a mass murderer.' He pulls on the collar around his neck.

She shakes her head and clucks her tongue. Is she scolding him? Does she really think that she's his *mother*? He wants to slap her. 'You've been out there too long,' she says. 'We were hoping you'd have seen the light.' She gets up and brushes her skirt. 'I won't tell your father that you've said these things. It would only upset him and get you into more trouble.' She walks to the window and looks out. He despises her, but he knows that whatever is broken and twisted in Mimi is likely his father's fault.

Patridge looks out past her. The old man is on the beach again, walking in the same direction he was before, waving the metal detector back and forth. 'Watch this,' Mimi says, and she leans out the window and calls, 'Hello! How are you doing this morning?'

The old man stops, takes off his small cap, and gives a big wave.

Mimi says, 'He used to just ignore me. But I told your father how much this upset me and Iralene, my daughter, and your father fixed it. One little mention and in a few days, that stupid old man was waving. I hate him, actually. But now he stops and waves. It's better this way, isn't it?' Mimi is terrifying. She seethes with love, hurt, fury – flipping between emotions in a matter of seconds. She turns and looks at Partridge. 'You know, I made this trip in person. I didn't have to, but I asked permission and your father allowed it because meeting you was very important to me. I hope it wasn't a waste of time. I hate to waste real time.'

He can't help but be smart-mouthed. 'How do you feel about wasting fake time?'

'You mean *suspended* time?'

He shrugs and says, 'Yeah, *suspended* time.'

'I have all the suspended time I want. There's no such thing as wasting it, is there? I mean, this might sound too philosophical for you to really comprehend—'

'Try me.'

'Suspended time is, by definition, time not spent. It exists alongside time as we know it. So it can't be wasted, can it?'

'I guess not.'

She smiles at Partridge and walks to the door.

Partridge remembers Pressia's story of being poisoned in the farmhouse. He says, 'This food isn't going to make me sick, is it?'

'Are you crazy?'

'I don't know. Are you?'

'Don't be rude.'

'You know what's rude? Putting an electrical collar on someone you're supposedly feeling all maternal about. How far can I go without being zapped?'

'I wouldn't wander far. It's for your own protection.'

'Well, in that case, thank you. Thank you so very, *very* much.'

'I hope you enjoy your breakfast, Partridge. If I were you,

I'd be thankful for everything. Every little handmade detail.'
It sounds like a warning. She winks, nods, and walks out the
door, leaving it open enough for Partridge to hear her daughter,
Iralene, playing the sonata.

Partridge falls back into the bed, his arms and legs leaden. He
closes his eyes; the music picks into his brain, but he can't tell if
the music is being played or if it's recorded. Does Iralene exist? Is
there even a piano at all?

EL CAPITAN

STITCHES

M OST OF THE OPERATIONS are much more complex than Helmud digging spider legs out with a penknife. El Capitan is lucky that his robotic spider was lodged in the meatier part of his calf, not actually digging into and splintering bone. Most of all, he's lucky that he had only one spider lodged in him – the record now stands at thirteen in one body alone. Just shy of a month, and there are still hundreds of people to tend to.

Between studying and copying Fignan's sedative bullets and the information that El Capitan has gathered over the years about different plants he's found in the woods – ones he tested on fresh recruits – they've created ways to put people under for surgery, more or less.

Helmud shoots serum into patients' bloodstreams and assists. El Capitan asks for alcohol, swabs, tweezers, scalpels, needles, and thin, clean spools of wire used to noose the gaping holes. Helmud delivers. For the first time in their lives, they work like one man with four arms. Another soldier swabs the instruments with alcohol and stands by in case a patient comes to in the middle, in which case the soldier and El Capitan hold the patient down until another shot is injected.

Helmud is fascinated by the surgeries. He leans so far over El Capitan's shoulder that El Capitan sometimes has to tell him to back off.

'Stop breathing on me,' El Capitan says now during a surgery.

'Stop breathing,' Helmud says.

The rusty smell of blood hits El Capitan so hard he feels sick. He finishes up with this patient quickly. 'I've got to see if any more children have gone missing,' he tells the soldier. Twelve kids have disappeared and been returned since Wilda, with rumors of a new one found in the early-morning hours in an abandoned lean-to at the edge of the Rubble Fields.

As they step out of the tent, Helmud shivers in the brisk air. El Capitan swings his rifle around to his chest and walks to the market. There's the normal bustle, some shoving, hawkers shouting about their wares, their meat, their strange vegetation – edible? Maybe, maybe not. He walks past a number of lit oil drums, people huddled around them, warming their hands. Everyone eyes him as he passes. Some bow their heads.

Special Forces haven't returned to the city. Now that Partridge is back in the Dome, perhaps they see no need. El Capitan has seen a few in the woods, though, and he always hopes to come across Hastings again. Partridge said he was trustworthy. El Capitan has even thought of trying to set a trap for him. But how on earth would you trap a Special Forces soldier? Not even a bear trap would hold one.

El Capitan comes across a little boy handing out sheets of paper. *Is your soul worthy of Purification? Prepare!* 'What's this about?' El Capitan asks.

A metal splint holds up one side of the boy's face. He says, 'The Dome is all-good and all-knowing.'

'No. The Dome's been exploding people. Did you miss that part?'

The boy shrugs and hands out more of the papers to people walking by.

'What do you want? A chance to be mute except for the words that get programmed into your skull? A chance to get pumped with their Purification only to get eaten alive by it?'

'Purity comes with a price! They're martyrs in the eyes of our Watchers!'

'They got you pretty thoroughly brainwashed, don't they?'

The boy looks at him, his face bright with hope. 'It's more than just kids, now. Even you have a chance!'

'What do you mean, more than just kids?'

'Mother and daughter. Father and son. Always from the same family. Three pairs so far. All taken in the broad sunshine.'

'In daylight?'

'We light the pyres and hope and pray to be chosen.'

'Are you kidding me? You line up and let Special Forces take you? Just like that?' He growls, 'What the hell?'

'Hell!' Helmud says.

El Capitan snatches the papers from the boy's hands. 'Where did you get these?'

'The Dome had a son,' the boy says. 'He made it to earth. He was our redeemer. The Dome wanted him back. We were held hostage, and when he was returned to the Dome – where he sits with his righteous father – we were shown mercy, set free.'

'I get it. I get it. Very old-world.' El Capitan knows enough about biblical stuff to catch the references. 'Children weren't enough? Now they want families? Have any of them been sent back yet?'

'Only one pairing,' the boy says. 'The others are staying in paradise!' His eyes gleam.

'And the one pairing? How are they? Are they programmed only to spout Dome propaganda?'

'They're dead. They were unworthy. We're writing a new gospel. We're adding on to the Word. We'll have all-new prophets.'

'That's lovely,' El Capitan says. 'Where are the bodies?'

'The pyre,' the boy says. 'We sacrificed them, and they made their way on the ash winds.'

'How were they killed?'

'Found by the pyre one morning. They were perfect, like God intended, but for a ring of scars around their heads – like a crown of thorns.'

'Scars? What kinds of scars?'

'Tidy,' he says. 'Stitched up good. You know God made clothes for Adam and Eve in the garden? God's seamstress.'

'God's seamstress lives in the Dome? Yeah, that makes *perfect* sense!'

'Perfect sense!' Helmud says.

'Where's Margit and her blind friend? They still alive?'

The boy nods.

'Does Margit still have a spider in her arm?'

'Yes, a gift from God.'

'Tell her it's a gift from God that's going to get infected.'

El Capitan walks off, pushing his way through the crowd, and the boy yells, 'When they come for me, I will be ready. Pure within. Will you? That's the question. Will *you*?'

El Capitan makes it back to the tent quickly. He pulls open

a fluttering flap, yanks it closed behind him. 'Enough for today. Send the rest home.'

The soldier is cleaning up.

El Capitan picks up the bag of sedative vials. 'Let's pack.' He notices the pile of dead robotic spiders – some whole, most in parts. El Capitan picks one. It feels heavy and dense in his hand, like a grenade. He says to the soldier, 'Collect all these parts. Bag 'em.'

'Why's that, sir?'

'Metal and explosives,' he says. 'They might make a nice gift.'

PARTRIDGE

SOUL

PARTRIDGE STARTLES AWAKE. He's still in the large oak bed, somewhere in the Dome. There's moonlight coming in the window. He's not alone.

He turns his head, the collar cutting into his skin. A thin figure is standing beside the bed. He sees the outline of a skirt, two pale legs, and high heels. 'Mimi?' he whispers. 'What the hell are you doing here?' Has she been watching him sleep?

'It's not Mimi.' The voice is soft, almost childlike. The figure takes a step into the moonlight. It's a girl about Partridge's age, maybe a little younger. A few inches shorter than Partridge, she holds a piece of fruit, red like an apple but the size of a melon. She's pretty and looks a little like Mimi, except her face is softer, her lips fuller. Her skin seems thin, so frail that Partridge can see a pale blue vein etched across her temple. She's nervous, maybe even scared. 'I'm Iralene.'

Mimi's daughter, the pianist. 'Is that for me?' He points at the fruit.

'Kind of.'

'It is the middle of the night, right? Or is that fake too?'

'I think it's night.'

'Why are you here?'

She straightens up and says, in a rehearsed way, 'I've heard you aren't completely happy here. I can help remedy that. You can be anywhere you want while you recuperate, Partridge. Anywhere in the world.'

'Well, that's great, Iralene. Thank you so much,' he says sarcastically.

'Maybe you don't understand,' Iralene says. '*Anywhere* in the *world*!'

'I've got it. I've seen the old man on the beach wave at your mother. I'm impressed, okay? You can tell my father that this is a really fantastic magic trick. Good stuff.'

Iralene looks a little panic-stricken. 'I can't tell your father that.'

'When I was little, we got new industrial-strength carpet padding, and the advertising said you could bounce an egg on it. My dad did and the egg bounced. So just tell him that this is even better. Okay? Even better than bouncing an egg.'

'I don't know anything about bouncing eggs,' Iralene says, looking teary.

'How is my old man these days?'

Her eyes dart around nervously, as if she's expecting him to appear. 'He's not well. He had bouts of illnesses. I'm sure he'll get better!' She pauses as if trying to decide whether to say more. Partridge lets the silence hang awkwardly, hoping she'll want to fill it, and she does. 'His skin is dry. His voice is . . .' She stops herself as if the memory of his voice is chilling. 'One hand has started to curl inward.' She lightly twists her hand until it looks misshapen, pulling it toward her collarbones. 'Some of the fingertips are turning bluish.'

'Bluish?'

'He has wonderful doctors! And the research is top-notch. I'm sure they'll fix all his little medical problems soon.'

'What does he want from me, huh?'

She lifts the fruit and holds it out for Partridge to see. It's not an apple or a melon. It's a highly polished computer of some sort, red and made of a waxy-looking, hardened plastic. 'You can be anywhere in the world while you recuperate!' she repeats. 'I can reprogram the room. We can go there together.' Iralene's voice is filled with forced wonder.

'Is this a game?'

'Do you want to play a game?'

'Stop it.'

'Stop what?'

He turns on a lamp on the bedside table.

Iralene smoothes her hair, nervously, and Partridge can tell that she's terrified.

'What's wrong?' he says. 'Why are you so scared?'

'I'm not scared,' she says and then she pouts her lips and looks at him flirtatiously. 'Are you scared, Partridge?'

'Did my father send you because he wanted me to fall for you?'

'Fall for me? I'm real,' she says. 'I know that for a fact.'

'It's a little upsetting that you're stating that you're real,' Partridge says. 'Do you know that?'

'I don't want to upset you. I want you to really like me. Don't you like me? Aren't I pleasing?'

'You're my stepsister. Has my father explained that to you? Your mother and my father are married.'

'But it's not a *blood* relation, so it doesn't count against us!'

'There is no *us*,' Partridge says gently. 'There isn't ever going to be an *us*.'

'Don't say that! I've been held for you. Stopped and held. Suspended. I've been waiting for a long time.'

'Suspended? What does that mean exactly?'

'You know what it means. My mother told me everything that you talked about.' She holds up the small red computer and says again, more insistently this time, 'You can be anywhere you want while you recuperate, Partridge! Anywhere in the *world*!'

'Okay,' Partridge says. He needs to know how this place works so that he can escape. Maybe he can win Iralene's trust, maybe weasel some info out of her – more about his father, more about this lovely prison. 'You pick.'

'Yes!' She's very excited. 'London!' She presses a screen that's wedged into the side of the computer, inserting information. She looks at Partridge and smiles, making sure that he's enjoying this. He's not, but he raises his eyebrows to appease her. Iralene is fragile. If he's not excited enough, who knows what could happen? She might crumble.

She puts the orb on the floor, and the room changes all around them. It's spectral. A tea tray appears with dainty cups and saucers. Portraits of kings and queens appear on the walls. The window is draped in brocade curtains that are pulled back to reveal a view of a giant Ferris wheel, a bridge, and a cathedral. She walks to the window. 'The London Eye,' she says, 'and Westminster Bridge. And Westminster Abbey's close too. I like London.'

The blanket has changed to a yellow brocade to match the stitching in the curtains. Partridge touches it, but the change in stitching is a projection. The blanket feels the same as the one before. 'You could take me for a walk on a leash like a British bulldog.'

'What?'

'It's a joke about my collar.'

'Oh. It's funny. Very funny!' She doesn't laugh.

'How far can I go with this on?'

'Anywhere in the apartment. It has two floors and goes on and on. I think, though, they'd like to keep you safely locked in for your own—'

'Protection. Yeah, I get it.' He runs a finger under the collar just to get it away from his skin. 'Is there a key to it?'

'How would I know anything about that?'

'Just asking.'

'Let's talk about something else.'

'Okay. Here's a question.' Partridge needs to find Glassings. He was on the list his mother showed him in the bunker, the list of people waiting for the swan to return. *Cygnus* – that's the word she whispered when she talked about it. 'Do a lot of people know that I'm here?'

'I know that you're here.'

'I know you know, and the techs who almost killed me know, and your mother and my father. But the general public? Anyone out there?'

'Did they even know you were gone?'

This hadn't ever dawned on him. His father has sent robotic spiders – thousands of them – to hold survivors hostage until Partridge turned himself in. But inside the Dome he might have wanted to keep the news of Partridge's escape a secret. It might have been a great embarrassment. 'Some people had to notice.'

'There are always rumors, and there are always secrets. And secrets within secrets. They protect us. The truth can be manipulated. But we live within a secret within a secret within a secret. That's why we can make anything happen, Partridge. Anything at all.'

'Do you like living within a secret within a secret within a secret?'

'It can get lonesome. That's why I'm glad you're here.' She glances at him, smiling, and for the first time, he feels like she's spoken the truth. She turns away and taps on the window. 'It's going to start raining,' she says. 'The raindrops will bead up on the glass.'

He swings his feet to the floor. Iralene walks to the bedside and cups his elbow. 'I can do it,' he says. He gets up and walks to a painting, his head heavy and dizzy. He touches it, but instead of the hardened strokes of oil, there's only the smooth wall.

'It's not as perfected as the Caribbean. My mother loves that one,' Iralene says. 'But it's not bad, is it?'

'Not bad at all.'

'Do you know how few people in the Dome even know that this kind of a room exists? Do you know how many people have seen a bead of rain on glass like this since . . .' She doesn't mention the Detonations.

'How many?'

It's apparent that she wasn't expecting him to ask the question. 'Not many. Not many at all. Maybe only a handful. And you're part of that handful now, Partridge. You and I both are.'

'Yeah, but what's London look like now?'

'Who would want to see that?'

'I would.'

'No, you wouldn't.' She laughs.

'Yes, I would. In fact, if you can project anywhere in the world onto these walls, I want the outside world just beyond the Dome. Not the past. Now. Dusts and Beasts and wretches. Let's see that.' He thinks of Lyda, out there somewhere.

'We don't have it.' She picks up the orb and turns off London. The room reverts to the beach. The breeze is back. The ceiling fan churns slowly overhead.

'You said anywhere in the world.'

'But I meant the preserved version of it.' She puts the orb on the bedside table.

'I want *now*. Anywhere in the world. But from *now*.'

'Stop saying that.' She grips the flesh of her upper arms.

'Tell my father that's what I want.'

'I can't.'

'Yes, you can.'

'No. I'll have failed. I can't tell him that I've failed.'

'Tell him that his son would like to join him in the real now.'

'You hate me. Why do you hate me?'

'I don't hate you.'

'Yes, you do. And now I'm worthless. I've waited all this time. Just for you to hate me.'

Partridge walks up to her. 'Iralene,' he whispers. Her grip on her arms is so tight that the pinched flesh has blotched red. He touches her wrist. 'Stop. You're hurting yourself.'

'I'm too old, Partridge. I'm too old to find a mate.'

'Too old? You're only what – sixteen?'

She smiles as if he's said the sweetest thing. 'That's right. Sixteen.'

'I can help you and you can help me, Iralene.'

'Do you need me?'

'I do.'

'How?'

'I need to get out of here.'

'But here *is* out of here. You can stay here and live anywhere in the world! There's nothing better than here. My mother and I . . .'

He brushes her hair back over her shoulder and whispers in her ear, 'Iralene, listen to me. I need to get to Durand Glassings. I need to get out of here – not to something better, only to somewhere real. Can you help me?'

They stand very close together. She looks around the room.

'Don't tell anyone I asked this of you, Iralene,' he whispers. 'Okay? This is our secret.'

She puts her lips to his ear. 'I won't tell a soul. Not a soul. Not anyone. I won't breathe a word, Partridge. Not a word, not a breath, not a soul. And will you help me?'

'Anything, Iralene. Tell me what you need.'

She looks at him, stunned, as if she's never considered what she needed. She opens her mouth, but then, as if she has nothing to say, she closes it.

'Iralene,' he says.

'I don't play the piano, Partridge,' she says, her cheeks burning.

'That's okay.'

'But you should follow the music,' she whispers. This is a gift. She's given him something essential. 'Now you owe me.'

He feels uneasy. What will this gift cost him? 'We'll both help each other.'

'This is our secret,' she whispers. 'It's *ours*.'

EL CAPITAN

FREE

As THE TRUCK LABORS UPHILL, El Capitan downshifts. Helmud is whistling behind El Capitan's back.

The soldier who assisted him in the surgeries is in the back of the truck. They're on their way to the outpost. It's dusk. El Capitan is looking for boars and those damn bleached owls. He doesn't regret taking out as many of those birds as he could – only that they weren't edible. The boar was, though. It had beautiful, marbled meat, and it's been prepared and eaten.

Out the passenger's window, he sees a flicker close to the ground. It disappears. He doesn't know whether to speed up or slow down. Could be a boar with twisted horns. He'd love to have more of that meat. Helmud jerks on his back.

'You see something?' El Capitan asks.

'See something!' Helmud says.

El Capitan stops the truck. 'What is it?' He hunches to get a good view out the passenger's window. But Helmud turns the other way, then cries out.

El Capitan's head snaps to the other window, and there is the elongated face and muscular upper body of a Special Forces soldier. El Capitan draws in a quick breath. Hastings! Hastings steps away from the truck, his weapons so sleek they look wet. 'It's okay, Helmud. It's okay,' El Capitan says. He turns to the soldier in the back of the truck. 'Don't get out, okay? Don't move. I'll be back.'

El Capitan grips the handle, hopes Hastings hasn't been reprogrammed to kill him, then gets out of the truck, raising his hands in the air. Just in case Hastings is outfitted with a ticker that can explode his head, El Capitan keeps his distance. 'What can I do for you?' he says.

Hastings' chest rises and falls, heavy and quick. He paces back and forth in front of El Capitan. Helmud has curled down as low as he can, hiding behind El Capitan's shoulders.

'What do you want?' El Capitan asks again.

Hastings walks up close. He towers over El Capitan and stares at him. El Capitan hears a click and looks down. The knife in Hastings' boot – a claw of a knife – has popped out.

'Easy now,' El Capitan says as he looks back up at him.

'Easy now,' Helmud whispers.

Hastings steps back and claws at the dirt, writing.

Set me free.

El Capitan doesn't say anything for a moment. He's trying to process this. Hastings is asking for what, exactly? How could he be set free? He belongs to the Dome. He's their creation.

Hastings walks over to a rock.

'Wait,' El Capitan says. Could he actually set Hastings free? He and Helmud have been surgeons these past weeks. If they could sedate him and debug him, he'd be free and extremely valuable. Hastings stares at him pleadingly. He knows the look – *put me out of my misery*. The last time he saw it he was with Pressia in the woods. He shot a boy caught in a trap. He's not asking to be killed, though, is he?

Hastings pushes the heavy rock toward El Capitan and turns his back, kneeling down. He bows his head and opens his arms wide.

El Capitan opens the back of the truck. 'Hand me that bag.' The soldier gives him the sedatives. He walks back to Hastings, who's still on his knees.

He touches Hastings' massive shoulder then squeezes it tight. Hastings stiffens – expecting a blow to the head? El Capitan sees Hastings' pulsing jugular, slips the needle under the skin, releases the sedative into his bloodstream, then pulls the needle out. He watches as Hastings slouches forward, catching himself with one locked arm. He twists and looks up at El Capitan, his eyes floating with tears. He's confused at first then strangely relieved. He smiles, ever so slightly. As his elbow buckles, he falls hard to the ground.

'Looks like we've got another patient, Helmud – a big one.'

PRESSIA

CYGNUS

PRESSIA HAS EXPLAINED to Bradwell everything she's learned, including her theory about the death of Ivan Novikov, plus the strange images and phrases that repeat – entwined snakes and talk of being forged by fire, made new by flames, strange sets of numbers, the poetry, and the appearance of her middle name, Brigid. They've split up the work. She's devoted the day to Willux's number obsessions, and Bradwell has concentrated on words and patterns. They've taken turns using Fignan – who buzzes happily when being put to good use – and have agreed not to interrupt each other unless absolutely necessary.

Still, she's aware of Bradwell's every move. Sometimes he breathes in like he's about to say something. She stops and turns. 'What is it?' He looks up and stares at her for a moment. Their eyes catch. She wonders if he's lost his train of thought. He looks down at his papers again and says, 'Nothing. Just trying to put things together.'

Now it's dusk, and Bradwell starts to cough like he has

croup – harsh, seal-like barks that make him wheeze. He sits on the edge of the bed, hunched over, each cough racking his lungs.

Pressia says, 'Let's get some air.'

Fignan beeps.

'You can come,' she says.

They put on their coats quickly, the birds on his back shifting their wings. On their way out, Pressia points out one of the faces painted on the wall – the one that reminds her of Fandra. 'I had a friend who looked like this girl. Fandra.'

Bradwell leans in close. 'Gorse's sister? She was one of the last' – he starts coughing again, but then draws some slow, deep breaths – 'one of the last to use the underground before we shut it down.'

'We were like sisters, and then one day she was gone.'

They step into the open air. Fignan sticks close to their boots. As Pressia bolts the door, she asks where the underground led.

'We hoped to get people out, but the territories surrounding this place are deadly. We wanted to think there was a place on the other side where people were surviving – maybe peacefully, maybe living pretty well. Her brother Gorse came back alone after they tried to make it out and said he'd lost Fandra.'

'Why did you shut the underground down?' They head into the orchard, dipping under the limbs rooted into the ground, stepping over the bulbous roots.

'We sent people out and few came back. They told brutal stories. A lot were simply missing and others died. We lost hope. Or nerve, or both.' Bradwell pauses, maybe to catch his breath. He leans against a tree. 'I still hold out hope that some survived, but what if they all died out there? It's a thought that I can't shake.'

'If they didn't try to make it out, they were probably going to get picked up by OSR and, back then, that meant they'd have to start killing people in Death Sprees or, worse, get used as live targets. What choices did they have? You were doing your best.'

'I'm sorry,' Bradwell says, 'about Fandra.'

She shakes her head. 'I hold out hope too. I can't help it. I do.'

They continue on, passing a set of fallen stables, a shattered greenhouse. Fignan buzzes along and then uses his arms to walk over roots, stones, and shards of glass. Bradwell takes deep breaths, pulling the cold into his lungs.

Pressia sees the dormitory where Wilda is probably getting ready for bed. She stares at one of the lights in the windows. Wilda. She wants to tell her that they're trying to figure it out.

Bradwell stops in front of a spot where the cement wall was buffered by a demolished school building and survived intact. When Pressia stops, too, and studies the wall for a moment, she sees what he's looking at: the shadow-stain of a person left on the wall, someone who was reaching down to pick something up when they were vaporized on the spot.

'There used to be so many of these throughout the city,' Bradwell says. 'Some were made into small shrines.'

'My grandfather pointed them out. They used to scare me when I was little, like they were dark ghosts.'

'But they're beautiful,' Bradwell says.

'You're right.' Pressia remembers what he said to her about finding beauty everywhere but never in herself. She looks at her doll-head fist, ugly, beaten, ashen. He's right, she thinks.

The wind whips up then dies. Fignan situates himself between Bradwell's boots.

'I think Partridge was right about something,' Pressia says.

Bradwell doesn't like it when Partridge is proven right. 'About what?' he says a little sullenly.

'The mark on Fignan, what you thought was a copyright, is pi.'

Fignan lights up at the sound of his name. 'Walrond was giving us a clue. There were twenty-two of the Best and the Brightest who were selected for an End-of-World scenario, and from that Willux chose seven. I looked up pi, and Fignan says that people usually expressed pi as three point one four but also as twenty-two divided by seven. Remember when El Capitan counted the number of words in the two messages from the Dome?'

'Twenty-two plus seven is twenty-nine,' he says. 'But that could be just a coincidence.'

'Every coincidence is worth looking at closely. Willux's mind is still thinking in obsessive ways. Pi is a number that goes on forever. And, most important, it's necessary for circles. *Domes* are circles. He was obsessed with domes.'

'Huh,' Bradwell says, and it sounds like a small concession. 'Domes. Let's say that Walrond created an empty file for the formula, as a clue, and hid the formula somewhere. He says on the video that he had to look into the future.'

'I've thought about that too,' Pressia says. 'He would have had to look into the future to find a place to hide the formula that might survive the Detonations. What if Willux wanted to spare certain places – ones he found holy? He was in charge of the Detonations – the strategic annihilation – so he could have left some places untouched.'

'Walrond did call him a romantic, right?' Bradwell says. 'Maybe domes were a soft spot.'

'Exactly,' Pressia says.

'But domes existed everywhere, in every culture. Which dome was the most holy?'

'I guess that's where things fall apart.' She reaches out and touches the shadow-stain.

'Willux has this string of numbers, mixed with a few letters.

I keep trying to fit them into Fignan, but no matches come up.'

'What are they?' Pressia asks.

'Twenty point sixty-two, forty-two point oh three, NQ-four.'

'They sound like coordinates.'

'I can't find a place anywhere on this entire planet that they'd work for.'

Bradwell tilts his head and looks up at the sky. His neck is strong, his collar loose enough that she can see his collarbones. He's gotten thinner since he got sick, leaner, his cheekbones more cut.

'Maybe they're not for this planet,' Pressia says. 'If the formula is hidden somewhere out there in the universe, we're screwed.'

'There *are* coordinates for stars.' Bradwell looks down at Fignan. 'Run the series of numbers I just mentioned and see if they match anything beyond us – out there, in the universe: constellations, stars, planets.'

Fignan buzzes quietly, the inner red egg whirring. Pressia doesn't know much about the night sky. The stars have been dimmed by ash for so long that it's rare to see them. Her grandfather drew them for her – Orion, the Big Dipper, the Milky Way. He told her that there were myths about stars but that was about it. Fignan finally lights up and shows a slowly rotating model of the night sky. The words *right ascension: 20.62 h; declination: +42.03°; quadrant: NQ4; area: 804 sq. deg.* are written next to a constellation that reads, *The Northern Cross (Cygnus).*

'Cygnus?' Bradwell shakes his head, mystified. 'All roads lead back to that word.'

'What do you mean?'

'I spent some time on your middle name today,' Bradwell says. '*Brigid* means "fiery arrow." And Brigid was a saint and before that a pagan goddess. She's associated with fire and was known for poetry, healing, and blacksmithing. She invented the whistle, of all things. She was the first to keen – a way of mourning by crying out. Her son died. Half of her face was beautiful, half of it was ugly.'

Pressia looks at the ground. She can feel the burn marks around her eye, a flush as if the burn is fresh and spreading a searing heat across her face. Doesn't that describe Pressia – half herself, half destroyed?

'But most of all, Pressia, her symbol was the swan.'

The wind stings Pressia's eyes. She reaches up and touches the swan pendant that sits in the dip of her collarbones. Pressia's *mother* was the swan, not Pressia. She looks at the sky, which is windy and dark, gauzy with ash. She feels a great pang of loss, an unexpected welling of sorrow mixed with confusion.

'Your mom must have wanted to pass that down to you for some reason,' Bradwell says quietly. 'It's a good legacy. To have that part of her.'

'I don't want it. What good did it do my mother to be the swan wife? To be caught between two powerful men? To have to hide me away like a shameful secret? I'm not the swan. I don't want anything to do with her legacy.'

'Sorry,' Bradwell says. 'I thought it might make you happy.'

She points to the light – the one she imagines belongs to Wilda's room. 'If we're going to save Wilda, the only thing that's important to ask is why Willux was so obsessed with the swan. What did it mean to *him*? That's what we have to focus on now. We have to be simple and practical.' She puts her hand on the shadow-stain. 'You said fire, right? Brigid is associated with fire, a fiery arrow. Willux said that he was forged by fire. What does that mean?'

'I don't know.'

'At some point, I think we're going to have to accept that there are mysteries we can't solve.' She thinks of Willux's stupid love poems and those damn entwined snakes that he drew again and again. Maybe that's just the weird kind of thing a disturbed young man would doodle, madly, for no real reason.

'Maybe we can get enough answers. Just enough. That's what Walrond said – the box will unlock the next move. That's all we need.'

'So we're not asking the right questions,' Pressia says.

'What do you have in mind?'

'I don't know. I mean, okay, my middle name means something, so what about Partridge's and Sedge's names?'

'Do you know their full names?'

She shakes her head. 'Ingership called Partridge by his full name once. I know his first name is really Ripkard but I don't remember the whole thing.'

'And Sedge?'

She shrugs.

Bradwell asks Fignan to pull up the full bio on Ellery Willux.

A cone of light brightens above their heads; it shows a document. 'Two sons,' she says. 'Ripkard Crick Willux and Sedge Watson Willux.'

'Watson and Crick,' Bradwell says excitedly.

'What about them?'

'They discovered the structure of DNA.'

'But how does that fit with anything?' Pressia sighs.

'The snakes,' Bradwell says.

'What about them?'

'You said there were always two snakes entwined, right?'

She nods.

'DNA – the double helix. That's how DNA is structured.'

For some reason this only makes her angry. 'That's fantastic,' she says sarcastically. 'It doesn't help, though. I swear, this feels personal. Willux is messing with us. Isn't it enough that he killed my mother?' It's the first time she's ever said it out loud. She feels the sting of tears, pressure building in her chest. She presses her hand against the wall, covers her eyes, and tries not to cry.

'Pressia,' Bradwell says, 'it's okay to be angry and miss her.'

'I don't want to talk about it.'

'I think you *should* talk about it.'

'No.' She uncovers her eyes and looks at the shadow-stain again. A ghostly girl, most likely. Here, then gone.

'Pressia,' Bradwell says, 'I'm serious about this. It'll eat you up. Trust me. I know.'

'You don't talk about them.'

'My parents?'

She nods.

'I was so angry for so long, and I still can get angry. But it's different now. I've had time.'

She removes her hand from the wall and bends to match the shadow-stain's shape. 'What do you think she was reaching for?'

'Maybe something she'd lost and then found again.'

She tries to imagine the girl who was vaporized on this spot so quickly her shadow was all that was left of her.

She looks up at the dormitories again. 'I want to see Wilda.'

'What about the possible contagion?'

'I know I can't be near her. But I just want to see that she's okay. You should go back with Fignan and get more information about swans and Cygnus and Brigid. Everything we can get.'

'You sure you want to be alone?' he says.

'Yes.'

'Okay.'

She gets up and starts to walk off toward the dormitory but then stops. There's something she can't let go of. 'When we were . . .' How would she put it? *When we were lying on the cold ground, practically naked, dying in each other's arms?*

She doesn't have to say it. Bradwell knows what she's talking about. 'Yeah, in the woods.'

In the woods. It's a relief that they now have a phrase for it. *In the woods.* Not naked, not dying, not lying with each other, skin touching skin. 'Right,' she says, 'in the woods. I said *Itchy knee*, and you said *Sun, she go.* You knew what I was saying. How did you know that? Where does it come from?'

'Japan was my father's area of interest. It's how he stumbled on the stories of the fusings from the bombs on Hiroshima and Nagasaki in the first place. I know some Japanese, and you do too, or you did as a child. I told you that it was still inside of you.'

'I was speaking in Japanese? I wasn't talking about an itchy knee and the sun going away?'

She remembers being a little girl right after the Detonations – all these new memories that have risen up: the singed sheep, the body snapping with electricity, the dead bobbing in the water. She had her old language. She was holding on to what she knew.

'You were counting,' Bradwell says. 'You were saying one, two, three, four, five. I counted with you.'

PARTRIDGE

PIANO

AFTER IRALENE LEAVES, he can't sleep. His mind wanders to Lyda. Just the idea that his father seems to want him to be pleased by Iralene feels like betrayal. He wonders where Lyda is now. Is she safe? Are the mothers taking care of her? He hears piano music – the sonata again. Iralene told him to follow the music. That was her way of helping him. He feels a surge of hope. Maybe Iralene will prove useful, but he feels the gnawing of dread too. He doesn't want to be indebted to her now.

Moonlight shines through the window. He gets out of bed, hobbles to the door – his joints aching – and jiggles the knob. It's locked.

Did she realize that he was locked in? He searches the bedside table drawers, the bathroom, even the window hinges for anything that would help him jimmy the lock. He flips up the bed skirt. On the edge of the mattress, there's a rounded plastic corner that has a few inches on either side that run long and flat. He kneels down and pries it loose.

He walks to the door, wedges the plastic into the lock. He twists the knob. The door swings open. No alarm. He wonders if he's supposed to leave the room, if this is part of someone's plan.

Afraid of a shock, he edges toward the threshold slowly, waiting for a tingling sensation. He doesn't feel anything.

He passes through the doorway. Iralene said that he was allowed to walk through the house. Is it part of the secret within the secret within the secret where he now lives?

Fitting the piece of plastic into the lock to keep it from latching, he closes the door behind him.

The hallway is wide. The floor is terra-cotta. Partridge tiptoes to the stairwell and stares down into darkness. The music is coming from the lower level. As he descends, barefoot, the stairs lose the feel of terra-cotta. They're rougher, more like cement.

At the foot of the stairs, he walks into a beautiful room of overstuffed sofas and armchairs, paintings of colorful squares, dots of color. On the white wool carpet, there's a little white dog – the size that would fit in a handbag. It pants and stares at nothing. It doesn't seem to know Partridge is there. People were allowed to bring their pets with them into the Dome, but most of those animals have died off by now. Miniature-size dogs are the only kind allowed to breed.

The living room opens to a kitchen, where Mimi is at the stove pulling out a tray of muffins. 'Take that from the top again, Iralene, will you? There was a misstep – a flat that should be a sharp.'

The piano music stops. Partridge turns and sees Iralene sitting at a piano, a dark mahogany upright, on the other side of the room. She straightens her shoulders, and the song starts at the beginning again. Iralene said she didn't play the piano. Was she just being modest?

'Good morning,' Partridge says to Mimi, who hasn't yet noticed him standing there. 'Or is it still night?'

Mimi doesn't respond. She's icing the muffins. He's pretty sure that she doesn't like him.

He walks over to Iralene, and that's when he steps on the woolly white rug. He's barefoot, but the rug feels no different from the cement flooring.

This isn't real.

He reaches out and touches the sofa. But his hand simply cuts through air. In his bedroom the images must be overlaid on top of real things. But here, there's nothing.

'Iralene,' he says and touches her shoulder, but there is no shoulder. No Iralene. She wanted him to follow the music – to see this for himself.

He presses one finger to a piano key, and it resists then lets out a note that mixes with Iralene's song. The piano is real. He hammers the keys with his fist.

He shouts, 'Is anyone here?'

Mimi pulls out another tray of muffins and says, 'Take that from the top again, Iralene, will you? There was a misstep – a flat that should be a sharp.'

It isn't a new tray of muffins. It's the same tray. They're stuck in a short loop. Did his father create this fake world? Is it for Partridge's benefit? Does his father think that he'd believe this? Be comforted by it? While Partridge was locked away in the academy, was this a world that his father retreated into? What makes Partridge angriest is how shoddy the work is. Maybe it exists just so his father can walk through the room and pretend for a moment that he's part of a family – since, obviously, Partridge wasn't enough – and then move on.

'Home sweet home,' Partridge says to no one. He walks to one of the walls, puts his hand on it, and follows it to the edges of the image. The walls are buttery yellow and occasionally decorated with a wall sconce or painting, except that those things don't exist at all. What lies beyond this? Maybe a way out. Finally he comes to a corner that isn't a corner. He runs his hands along the wall and continues on until he's on the other side of the image.

He finds himself in a dimly lit hall, lined with doors close together on either side; a strange bass hum emanates from each door.

The doors are marked with placards. They read, SPECIMEN ONE AND TWO, SPECIMEN THREE AND FOUR . . . all the way to SPECIMEN NINE AND TEN. And then, on the rest of the doors, there are names etched on small, silver placards. Partridge reads name after name – all women, from what he can tell.

IRALENE WILLUX. The placard is new, maybe because the last name is new. Iralene is now his stepsister, another Willux. Why is her name here? What does she have in common with specimens?

Below her name is another placard: MIMI WILLUX. It too is new, freshly polished, shiny, no spots of rust or tarnish.

This is what Iralene wanted him to find. The secret within the secret within the secret – what layer of secrets is he in now? He doesn't want to know what's inside these small rooms.

He knocks lightly.

There's no answer.

He knocks again. 'Iralene? It's me, Partridge.'

Again, no answer.

He turns the knob and opens the door.

There's a gust of cold from the room; in fact, the air is the coldest he's ever felt it in the Dome. He touches the wall with the flat of his palm, looking for a switch. His hand hits a button. The room lights up.

And there are two six-foot-tall capsules in a bare room. The capsules are fogged, their glass grayed with crystalline patterns of ice. Partridge walks up to one. He rubs the glass with his hand. A face frozen, completely still.

Mimi Willux.

Suspended. That's the word she used.

He staggers backward, running into the door. Ageless. This is how. She saves time by preservation. Why is Mimi suspended? Is this how she stays young looking? Some cryogenic state, some self-induced hypothermia?

Iralene. He walks up to the other capsule. He lifts his hand, gathers his courage, and then wipes away the iciness. The capsule is empty. He presses his hand to the glass and realizes there is no humming motor keeping it cool.

Where is she? Why would they do this to her? She's just a teenager. Or is she? Partridge remembers the way she looked at him when he guessed her to be only sixteen. Are Iralene and Mimi both much older than they seem?

He runs out of the small room, shutting the door behind him. There's no exit down this hall. He runs back the way he came, his legs still weak. As he finds the brightly lit edge of the living room and starts to enter it, the room crackles. There's a pop of light. A bright flash. And then the room darkens. It's a basement. Nothing more. He sprints halfway across the empty room. No doors. No windows. But now he sees a piano shoved under the stairs. A real piano with real keys and pedals and everything. A dream version of the one that had been stripped bare at the warden's house, where he last saw Lyda.

Lyda. He's glad she isn't here. What would they do to her?

He takes the stairs two at a time. The terra-cotta is gone. His door is open. Hadn't he closed it behind him?

He walks into the room, which is bare except for a few stark furnishings – a plain bed, a bedside table, an old lamp, a wardrobe.

Iralene is there by the window, which is open, but there's nothing beyond it – no ocean, no moonlight.

On the bed, there's a metal key – the key to his collar.

'I saw it, Iralene,' he says. 'I saw what they're doing.'

'You don't even really know,' she says. She turns and looks at him. 'You can't really understand it all.'

'Who's down there? How many?'

She looks at the window casement, rubs it with one hand. 'I can't even begin to explain. There are so many things I'm not supposed to understand.'

He walks over to her and takes her hand. He needs to know that she's real. Her hand is trembling. 'Why do you do it?'

She looks at him as if he should know the answer to this question. 'We exist only when needed. The cold slows any damage to our cells. My mother and I can both stay young.'

'For my father?'

She rips her hand away from him. 'For our own self-esteem! This is for us! Not your father, not you. It's so we can feel good about who we are – inside and out.' Her voice is high and ragged in her throat.

'I'm sorry,' he says. 'I didn't mean to upset you.'

She walks to the wardrobe, opens it, and pulls out a suit on a hanger and then two shiny black shoes by their heels. 'You'll need to fit in.' She walks back to him and shoves the suit and shoes at his chest. She turns her back, and he starts to undress quickly. 'I overloaded the system with requests – India, China, Morocco, Paris, the Nile. It will repair itself quickly. You need to hurry.'

He puts on the pants and zips them, pulls on the shirt and

jacket without buttoning them. He loops the tie around his shirt collar. 'Socks?' he says.

She walks back to the wardrobe, searches the single drawer at its base. 'There aren't any.' She looks like she's going to cry. 'An oversight! I can't believe it!'

'It's okay. It's okay.' He buttons his shirt now, and shoves on the shoes. He goes to the bed, picks up the key, feels the iron collar for the lock, fits the key in, and turns.

The collar pops open. He throws it on the bed, the key still in it, and rubs his chafed neck.

'You can walk the ledge outside of the window to the fire escape,' she says as she walks over to him. She lifts the ends of the necktie and starts looping it into a knot. 'Then you can run.'

'Come with me,' Partridge says. 'You don't have to stay here.'

'I can't go.'

'Of course you can. You don't even have a collar.'

'I don't have one because they know I'd never leave.' She tightens the knot around his neck.

'Iralene, they'll know you arranged for the system to go down. They'll know you helped me out of here.'

'I was being honest when I hit all those buttons. I really want to go to India, China, Morocco . . .' Her voice trails off.

'I don't trust my father. I don't know what he'll do to you.'

'Go, Partridge. Just go.'

'I won't forget this, Iralene.' Partridge goes to the window, climbs out onto the ledge, and, still gripping the frame, says, 'Thank you.'

'It was our secret,' she says. 'We shared it. It was ours.'

'That's right,' he says.

'Go.'

He walks down the ledge, foot over foot. The Caribbean

breezes are gone. The air is static again. He climbs onto the fire escape in his shiny, thin-soled shoes and looks down to the cement below.

He looks up and sees a building of windows. None of them are lit.

PRESSIA

STARS

PRESSIA WALKS QUICKLY UPHILL toward the dormitory lights. The night is blustery. She pulls her collar up, crosses her arms, tucking the doll-head fist out of sight, the way she used to in the market. She can feel the burn on one side of her face like it's fresh. Brigid – half beautiful, half ugly. It's as if Willux ordained it, and he *did* ordain it, in a way, by burning and mutating them all. He was forged by fire – what did that mean? He was made new. The survivors weren't.

She walks along the side of the building and glances quickly into lit windows, not wanting to pry but needing to find Wilda. In one, a soldier's studying some papers. In another, there's a kitchen with people working in a steam so thick that some of the windows are opaque.

Finally she comes to a dimly lit window with only one small bed and a chair. The door to the hall is open. A guard paces back and forth. A nurse dozes in a chair. And there is Wilda. She's in bed. Her skin still looks creamy and clear.

She's asleep, but even so, Pressia sees the trembling bedsheet.

Pressia pushes away from the window and slides down the wall onto the cold ground. Pressia knows what DNA is. It's why she has her mother's freckles and her father's dark, almond-shaped eyes and shiny hair. The survivors are changed, marked, down to their very DNA. It's why babies who've been born post-Detonations aren't born Pure. The double helix of snakes and DNA – how are the two related?

She looks up at the sky. The stars are lost in the cover of ash. The constellation Cygnus is up there somewhere. She wishes she could see it. She imagines what it was like to see stars every night, to take them for granted. She knows that sailors never took them for granted. They used them to navigate. Stars, with their fixed constellations in the sky. Her grandfather told her that they used to wish on them, and that the brightest ones were often not stars at all but planets. 'Twenty point sixty-two, forty-two point oh three, NQ-four,' she whispers into the air.

And then she stands up, abruptly. Navigation. The stars were used to help people find their way. The coordinates 20.62, 42.03, NQ4 don't exist just in the sky. They could direct someone on earth too. The constellation of Cygnus – is there a dome on earth that is connected to those coordinates? These are things she barely grasps, but Bradwell might understand them.

She starts walking quickly downhill, back toward the stone cottage. Her feet naturally start to run. She runs so fast that her coat kicks open. It flaps on either side of her like wings. Brigid, the swan, searching for Cygnus, the swan. For a moment, she hopes to take flight.

She sees the orchard and light streaming from the windows of the cottage.

As she gets close, she hears voices coming from the other side of the door. She wonders at first if they're from one of Fignan's videos, but they're too loud and crisp. She hears El Capitan and then Helmud's echo.

She opens the door and steps inside. Bradwell is standing by the bed, holding Fignan under one arm. El Capitan and Helmud are beside him. Their backs turned to her, they're talking urgently.

On the table, there's a pile of the robotic spiders sent down from the Dome – some whole, some in parts.

'What's going on here?' Pressia asks.

'We got one,' El Capitan says.

'One what?'

'Have a look,' Bradwell says and backs away from the cot.

Pressia approaches slowly.

El Capitan steps out of her way. 'Consider it a gift.'

Pressia sees one of the Special Forces soldiers, lying on the bed, his head wound in gauze. His eyes are open but he looks hazy. He's long and lean, too big for the cot, his feet stretching far beyond the end of the mattress. Both arms are heavy with machinery and guns. His jaw is so large that he's like a different species. And maybe he is. He looks at Pressia and smiles.

She says, 'Hi.'

He struggles to sit up, leaving a fresh splotch of blood on Bradwell's pillow. It's too much effort and he falls backward.

'What happened to him?' Pressia whispers.

'He's Hastings, Partridge's buddy. And he's all good now,' El Capitan says. 'We just had to debug him and take out the ticker. One of the nurses up at the dormitory did it. She was a little nervous, but nothing exploded, so it was worth it, right? I mean, here he is. He wanted out! He's ours now!'

'*Ours*,' Helmud coos as if talking about a newborn.

Hastings closes his eyes and seems to drift to sleep.

'What in the hell are we going to do with him?' Pressia whispers.

'I won't mind having his muscle and guns on our side,' Bradwell says, 'but I hope he's got some information in that huge head too.'

El Capitan shrugs. 'I'm just kind of proud. He's like a trophy or something, isn't he?' He crosses his arms on his chest.

'You came in breathless,' Bradwell says. 'What's going on?'

'I had this thought while I was out there,' Pressia says.

'About what?' Bradwell asks.

'The formula – where it might be hidden. A long shot, but . . .' She walks to the table and picks up a spider and holds it in her hand. 'Stars are used for navigation. Twenty point sixty-two, forty-two point oh three, NQ-four could be directions meant for someone on earth. Is there a dome – and not just any dome, but an ancient one, an important, *holy* one – that is connected to the coordinates of Cygnus?'

Bradwell joins her at the table and sets Fignan down on it. He asks him to show the constellation. Fignan brightens. Stars twinkle in the dusty air.

'It's not enough,' El Capitan says.

'How would you know anything about star coordinates?' Bradwell says.

'I was raised among some hard-core survivalists, remember? When other kids were getting their pictures taken with oversize puppets on theme-park vacations, me and Helmud were being taught how to bury guns, for shit's sake. I know how to track and hunt, start a fire, ward off predators. I know how to record what's edible and what'll kill you. We were all back to basics. Prepared for the world's end. And survivalists know something about stars.

'Cygnus is an important constellation. It's also called the

Northern Cross, and it's huge.' El Capitan points at Fignan's display of the swan.

'Every day the constellation cuts a huge shape across the sky. It covers too much ground. You'd need to know coordinates on a specific day at a specific time.' El Capitan reaches behind his back, grabbing Helmud's whittling knife and digging dirt out from under his thumbnail. 'Or you'd need to really pinpoint it – down to one star, something that cuts a smaller path. It would help narrow the hunt for holy domes.'

Fignan shows a flurry of shifting domes and constellations; they pass quickly through the cone of light like a sheath of papers being gusted by the wind.

Hastings moans and kicks a little but doesn't come to.

Pressia sinks to a chair pulled to the table, which is covered in the robotic spiders' various wires, small ball-bearing joints, metal casings, spokes, and the blank digital displays. 'Why did you bring all of this here?' Pressia asks El Capitan.

'You used to make things, right? Thought you might like to try your hand at something new.'

Pressia thinks of her prosthetics and her handmade creatures – butterflies, turtles, inchworms. 'What'd you have in mind?'

'How about turning those suckers back into weapons, of your own design,' El Capitan says.

Pressia looks at all the ghostly girls' faces lining the walls. *Willux. Will-ux. Will-ux.* 'It's in Willux's notes,' she says. 'I know it. All those doodled birds and spirals and blubbering stupid poems. It's in the messed-up parts that make no sense.'

El Capitan laughs. 'Willux doodled birds and wrote poems? The greatest mass murderer in history? This I've got to see. Fignan!'

'Seriously, Cap,' Bradwell says. 'We don't have time to make fun of Willux now.'

'No,' Pressia says, and she stands up slowly. She's trying to remember the poem – high in the sky, the truth written, a wing, something *holy*? 'Fignan, I want to see the poem. The love poem about his voice going shy and her beautiful face . . .'

Fignan searches his databases. He flips to the image of a notebook page. And there it is.

She reads it aloud: '*She rises every day to the top of the sky, / Brushing over the holy mound with the tip of a wing. / I'd tell you this but my voice is shy / Because your beauty is, too, a sacred thing.*'

'What a sweetie,' El Capitan says.

'Sweetie,' Helmud says.

'*She rises every day*, like the constellations, *to the top of the sky,*' Bradwell says.

'*The holy mound,*' Pressia says. 'That's our spot!'

'And what's that written beneath it?' Bradwell asks.

'Another version of the line *I'd tell you this but my voice is shy* that reads, *The truth is written up there on high,*' Pressia says. 'Fignan, show us Cygnus again.'

The notebook fades and the constellation reappears. Pressia looks at the tips of the swan's wings. 'This one protrudes. It has more of a tip than the other wing,' she says, pointing to one of the wings marked with a *K*. 'What's this one called, Fignan?'

Fignan launches into a description of a star known as Kappa Cygni, which runs on the fifty-third degree of the north latitude. It cuts a sixty-nine-mile-wide belt around the world, passing over Dublin in Ireland, Liverpool-Manchester-Leeds in England, Hamburg in Germany, Minsk in Belarus, and a number of Russian cities.

'Fignan, let's run the fifty-third-degree latitude through the World Heritage Sites,' Bradwell says. 'See what kinds of *holy mounds* pop up.'

Fignan starts whirring through the data. A map lights up and sites start popping up on it as green lights – four in the United Kingdom, two in Germany, one in Poland, one in Ireland, and two in Belarus.

'Ten?' Pressia says. 'That's about nine more than I wanted.'

'Fignan,' Bradwell says, 'screen the ones that aren't really ancient – nothing medieval even – and then search only for domes. No castles, no important battlefields or towns.'

The green lights in Germany disappear, then Poland, then the two in Belarus. One by one, the lights in the United Kingdom fade out until there's only one left – in Ireland. Fignan zooms in on a place called Newgrange. They all lean in. A grassy mound encased in white stone appears.

A dome.

And then, just as he did when they fed him each correct name of the Seven, Fignan shines a bright green light – confirmation.

'Are we right, Fignan?' Pressia asks. 'Did Walrond program you to give us that green light? Is that what it means?'

He flashes the green light again.

'That's it!' Pressia says. 'Newgrange!'

'But it's an ocean away,' Bradwell says. 'What the hell was Walrond thinking?'

'Maybe he was thinking he didn't have many options,' Pressia says.

'We'd need a ship or a plane to get that far,' El Capitan says.

'That far,' Helmud repeats.

Pressia looks at all the faces lining the walls. This can't be a dead end. The faces stare at her. They're telling her to keep going, not to give up. 'What can we do?' Pressia asks. 'There has to be something.'

'What? Build a plane or a ship tough enough to cross the Atlantic?' Bradwell says.

El Capitan rubs the back of his neck and sighs. Helmud sighs.

'But one airship already exists,' Pressia says.

'What's that?' Bradwell says.

Pressia stares at the dome frozen in midair. 'Remember how the Message first found us?' she says. 'A few days after the Detonations, pieces of paper came flitting down from the sky. We heard the distant rumble of an airship. My grandfather always said that he saw the bulk of its body dip down from the dark sky, just once. A hull. He saw it. It exists.'

'Okay,' Bradwell says. 'But where would we find it? How in the hell would we ever get our hands on that airship?'

The room is quiet for a moment, and then there's a voice – a voice that's deep as a bass drum. 'My head,' Hastings says, and he sits up in the small bed. He puts his heavy boots on the floor, leans over with his elbows on his knees. 'I have maps in my head.'

PARTRIDGE

PAPER SNOWFLAKES

THE STREETS ARE EMPTY. Partridge is running along the narrow sidewalks under the low lights of Mitchard Theater, past the Good Morning Coffee Shop and elite housing complexes – the Oakes, Hawks Rise, the Wenderly. This is the second level, called Upper Two, far superior to Upper One. From here, he sees Betton West, where he and his father and Sedge once lived. They had a balcony and private access to the roof garden.

There are curfews and guards making security rounds. The only allowable reason to be out at this hour is an emergency, someone headed straight for the medical center on Level Zero, which is also home to the academy, where Partridge needs to be. The levels above Zero don't reach all the way to the outer edges of the Dome. For purposes of light and circulation of air, Upper One, Two, and Three are encircled by thick, glass walls running the circumference. He can see the edge of this tier, the curved glass where it ends up ahead of him. To get to Zero, he has to make it to the Dome's center to a set of elevators. But cameras are mounted in the corners of each elevator. Should he wait until the morning rush so he can blend in, or would that be worse? There's one private elevator, used by his father and other higher-ups. He's ridden it a few times with his father, once to Sedge's small memorial service. But that one is heavily guarded.

Partridge turns quickly down a dimly lit path – just wide enough for an electrical cart. He stays in the shadow of an apartment building, listening for the whir of a security cart's electrical motor. The only sounds are his breath, his shoes on the cement, and the occasional circuitous hiss of the monorail in its spiral through each of the Dome's tiers.

He passes a restaurant called Smokey's. He's eaten there at least a hundred times. Supposedly real food, it always tasted fabricated – soy processed to feel like meat in your teeth, even manufactured bits of gristle. Better than soytex pills, though. The masses living on the first level might never get the chance to eat there – except on a honeymoon. Its decor never changes; neither does the waitstaff, nor the menus.

He hears a strange ticking noise behind him. He turns and looks but nothing's there except a streetlight, a moth flitting by the bulb. A moth? Birds sometimes escape the aviary. Sometimes you see a darting of wings, even a real nest propped in a fake tree. But insects are dealt with harshly. The grounds are laced with pesticides. Workers in white suits with tanks of poison on their backs make endless rounds. A moth is a rarity and it unnerves him, maybe simply because he's not as completely alone as he thought he was.

He starts running again, passes a Laundromat, a drugstore, a gym. And then he comes to a bank of windows rippling with white – an elementary school with paper snowflakes taped to the glass. Some are intricate and almost lacy. Others are bulky and awkwardly cut. But they all quiver from the air circulation like they're alive, breathing.

This was the gift he was going to give Lyda. He said, 'Paper snowflakes. Is that all it would take to make you happy?' And she whispered, 'Yes. And you.' She kissed him. He remembers the softness of her lips. 'This.' He misses her. The pain is sharp, like taking a blow. He's already breathless and now feels unsteady.

He steps off the path and cuts across Bellevue Park. Its Astroturf is perfectly manicured. He reminds himself that the ground doesn't have eyes or teeth or claws. It's fake, harmless grass. This is the ground he grew up on. The trees never grow; leaves never change color. They're exactly the same as they were when he and Sedge played war games, taking turns as wretch and soldier. Sedge was a good kid, did what he was told, never whined or refused to go to bed on time. He never unwrapped a gift and said, 'That's not what I asked for,' as Partridge had a couple of times. Partridge was sullen. He thought he was tough but cried easily. He asked too many questions, stared at strangers. If someone offered him candy, he took as many as he could get away with. Petty crimes, but they add up. Sedge told Partridge to be tougher, tried to help Partridge fit in, not get in trouble, and just grow up, endure childhood. It doesn't make sense that Partridge has survived and Sedge didn't.

He hadn't realized how hard it would be to come back into the Dome after losing Sedge and his mother, after leaving Pressia and the others, especially Lyda.

He hears the soft whir of a motor behind him – an electrical cart outfitted with a searchlight. He slips behind a stand of poplars as the searchlight glances through the trees and roves on. He can see the driver. His belly is wedged in, almost touching the wheel. He wonders who this guy knew to earn a spot in the

Dome. Had he once had some powerful job, which secured his family a small apartment and a job in a golf cart?

Partridge loosens his tie. Was tying men's neckties part of Iralene's training? He wishes he could have persuaded her to come with him. He doesn't trust his father or Mimi. The rows of doors – he sees them in his mind. Specimens. What kind? And for what purpose?

He feels something tickling his bare ankle. He scratches and a large black beetle lands on its back in the dirt, its legs wheeling in midair. Another insect? He flips it over with his shoe. The beetle gives off a low, dull red glow and then scurries off. Was it partially robotic – like the spiders sent down from the Dome? Partridge isn't sure what the moth and the beetle mean. Maybe they're part of his father's latest spying devices to collect information and maintain obedience.

Now he hears voices. Partridge dips behind a hedge lining the chainlink fence enclosing the tennis courts. Two guards are waddling up the path. One rests a hand on his flashlight. Their keys jingle.

'He can throw a perfect spiral. Five years old. Perfect. You know, I played.'

'We all know.' The guards are so close Partridge can see the shine of their shoes.

'Seriously, the kid could have been good. Now what? No competition, no training. I tell you we're all just—'

'Shut it,' the other guard says, stopping in his tracks. Partridge holds his breath. The guard looks around. Partridge feels the blood pumping in his head. But then the guard says, 'Anyone could hear you out here. Say whatever you want to yourself in the shower. But not out here. Not to me.'

The guards then walk on in silence.

Partridge lets out his breath. How the hell is he going to get to the academy unseen? He feels something on his shoulder – another beetle? No – a hand, pale with long, delicate fingers.

'Partridge.' A face seems to almost float into view – a boy's face, skinny and freckled.

'Who are you?'

'Vinty Firth.'

'Vinty Firth?' Algrin Firth was a friend of Vic Wellingsly's and always hated Partridge, but his father's name was on his mother's Cygnus list. Partridge remembers Algrin talking about Vinty. His parents were distressed because they thought Vinty was too much of a runt to get into the academy.

'Yep, that's me,' Vinty says. 'I knew we'd find you!'

'Are you in the academy now?' Partridge asks, as if this kind of thing even matters anymore.

'First year.'

'What are you doing out here?'

Vinty looks around quickly. 'You've got to come with me – now.' Whose side is Vinty on? He wonders if the moth and beetle have already pointed out his location to some system run by his father. If so, why send a runt like Vinty Firth?

'Look, I'm not going to be dragged in by my father. You can tell him—'

'Not your father,' Vinty says. 'This is Cygnus. We are Cygnus. We've been waiting for you.'

PARTRIDGE

UNDER

VINTY SEEMS TO KNOW that the guard riding the cart is coming long before Partridge hears it. He pushes Partridge down an alley between two shops, and the cart whizzes by. Vinty holds his hand up, meaning *wait, wait, wait*. The sound fades and they keep on going.

Partridge starts to ask questions, but Vinty puts his finger to his mouth and they press on. He tries a few more times – forming different questions, bending low to whisper – but Vinty always shakes his head.

Vinty leads him to the center of the Dome's elevators, guards his face, dips toward the elevators, and pushes the closest call button.

A few come and go. Their doors open, but Vinty doesn't make a move. The elevators are empty. Vinty hits the button again. 'When the right one comes, crouch low.'

Finally, one of the middle elevators opens. Vinty nudges Partridge.

Inside, there's a large, wheezy man and a small woman. Their elbows are hooked together in such a way that Partridge imagines them fused like that. The man's cheeks are flushed and his chest is racked with coughs. He's obviously on his way to the medical center on Zero. Vinty pushes Partridge to step into the elevator. He doesn't want to – possible contagion in the Dome is feared above all else, and that old fear kicks in. Plus, why take the one elevator with people in it?

But Partridge quickly realizes that this has been arranged. The man pretends to be annoyed that the doors are opening on this level, complains to his wife between coughs – all while his broad body and long coat are blocking the camera from picking up on Vinty and Partridge, who crouch and step inside just before the doors close. They're wedged in so tightly with the man that Partridge can smell his aftershave and medicinal talcum.

They don't stop at Upper One, home to the masses – large apartment buildings, schools, some recreation spots, shopping, as well as the rehab center for psych patients, where Lyda was locked up.

But when they get to Zero, the man and his wife walk out slowly, blocking Vinty and Partridge expertly all the way out of the sleek row of elevators. When they turn right, heading toward the medical center, Partridge and Vinty peel left, toward the academy.

The academy is only a few short blocks. In addition to the academy and medical center, Zero is also home to farms and pastures, lowest-level workers' housing, equipment, food processing, health and science labs, drug manufacturing, security's headquarters, and the zoo – the Cage's Cage. If you were allowed to follow the agricultural fields all the way out, you'd eventually run into the Dome's actual wall – the one shared with the outside.

It's exam season, right before Christmas break, and so the academy is quiet – no music after seven p.m., hushed voices in the halls, no sports, no games. The place still feels alive, though, charged with memory. The strangest thing is how, when they walk into the first hall, Partridge can feel his old self transported back to him through the smell – sweaty, rambunctious bodies, the rubber pellets brought in from the turf fields, the wood polish rubbed into the floors and the banisters, an astringent cleanser. He breathes it in.

Does it feel like home?

No, but it's part of him. It's his childhood, in a way. He showed up at the academy when he was still twelve – early admittance. He was about the size of Vinty Firth, who's leading Partridge down one hall and then the next. Partridge showed up in these halls innocent – a kid who still told himself his mother's fairy tale of the swan wife at night. And now?

The halls glow dimly with security lighting. They walk quickly down the hallway lined with oil portraits of the headmasters. He sees the one who was in place when Sedge had supposedly died, who called Partridge into his office and gave him the news. 'It's going to be okay, son. He won't make it with us on our journey to New Eden, but he is in God's paradise now.' *God's paradise* – as opposed to his father's reinvention? That was before Partridge knew his father liked to play God.

Partridge has the urge to throw open the doors to his old dormitory, sprint down the hall, jump up and tap the exit sign attached to the ceiling – an old habit – swing his head into Weed's room and shout, *Mind if I look at your notes later?* then walk into his own room to find Hastings combing his wet hair in the mirror. He'd flop on his bunk bed, talking Hastings into playing ball on the quad later even though Hastings just took a shower. No use thinking about any of that now. It's all gone.

'Where are we going, Vinty?'

Vinty says, 'Under,' as if this is any help.

They pass the teachers' offices, their windows blocked by closed blinds. Partridge sees Mr Glassings' door, its metal nameplate, and he's awash with relief. It gives him some hope that Glassings isn't gone.

Vinty passes the science labs too. Finally, they're near the theater. Vinty opens a door leading backstage and walks up a short set of stairs. Partridge has never been backstage before. He wasn't in any shows or chorus or band. He never won any awards. Lyda was part of the chorus. In fact, her singing at the spring concert was the first time he'd ever noticed her. There were two dozen girls or more, but she was different. She tilted her head when she sang and closed her eyes like she was feeling the music in a way the other girls couldn't.

With the curtains drawn, the space feels muffled and small. A bit of light seeps up from below the stage through the fine cracks between the floorboards. He tries to remember the song that Lyda's group sang. It was an old song about wanting a piece of the American dream. Was it feminist? Was it the girls' way of saying they wanted more? He'd have never thought of these kinds of things back then, but Lyda would have, in some way, wouldn't she have? He's still surprised that she didn't follow him back in. She's changed outside the Dome.

'This way,' Vinty whispers.

Partridge follows Vinty through a cardboard set of a cottage and past some lights.

Vinty squats and opens a trapdoor. Partridge follows him down a ladder under the stage, which is what Vinty meant by *under*. Partridge is suddenly worried that he's been led into a trap. He mentioned Glassings to Iralene. Did she rat him out?

Damn it. Vinty knew the word *Cygnus*, and Partridge just followed him trustingly.

There's light in one corner of the room, which explains the glow between the cracks of the stage's floorboards. Although it makes no sense, Partridge is afraid that he's going to find his father here amid boxes, folding chairs, small tables, paint cans and brushes, candlesticks, a random assortment of hats – the wreck of what could have been a home.

Sitting before him are two wingback chairs. The one facing Partridge is empty, but he's sure that the other isn't. He senses someone's presence. Sitting between the two chairs is an upright wooden barrel. A lamp and a small glass terrarium filled with beetles sit on it. The kind of beetle Partridge swatted off his ankle.

Partridge looks questioningly at Vinty.

'It's okay,' Vinty says.

Partridge moves forward, his heart kicking in his chest, and calmly takes a seat as if he isn't afraid at all.

And there, facing him, is Durand Glassings, his old World History teacher.

'Professor Glassings,' Partridge says. 'Thank God it's you.'

Glassings smiles broadly, leans forward, and grabs Partridge's hand, but only to pull him back to his feet and into a hug. 'Jesus, Partridge, I thought I'd never see you again.' He holds him tight. 'I'm so sorry about your mother and Sedge.'

It's the strangest thing, but Partridge feels like he's been waiting for this moment – without knowing it. He starts to cry. He wishes that he could pretend he wasn't, but his breath jerks in his lungs. He's been waiting for someone to say he's sorry – someone *like* a father. And he realizes that's what Glassings is to him in this moment. Maybe that's what he always was to him – like a father.

'Here, take a seat,' Glassings says quietly as he releases Partridge.

Partridge sits down and wipes his eyes.

Glassings' eyes are shiny with tears too, though he's smiling. 'Goddamn it, Partridge. I'm glad you're here. Look at you. What was it like out there? Tell me.'

It strikes Partridge that this is the first time anyone has asked. It shouldn't surprise him. The people of the Dome don't want to ever really think about those on the outside, but the question does take him by surprise. 'It's dirty, dark, sooty, dangerous, but, I don't know, the wretches aren't wretches. They are some great people who survive, day in and day out, under brutal circumstances.' He thinks for another second, and Glassings waits patiently. 'It's real,' he finally says. 'And real is good.'

'Well, you made it out of the Dome and back in again,' Glassings says, 'in one piece.'

'Not quite,' Partridge says. He pulls the cap off his pinky and shows Glassings where it was chopped off.

'How'd that happen?'

'A payment I had to make, I guess you could say.' Partridge replaces the cap. 'My father would like to see it grow back.'

'Your father.' Glassings' expression darkens. 'Well, he's the man to get it done.' He then says to Vinty, 'You can go, Vinty. Thanks for getting him.'

Vinty starts to scurry back up the ladder, but he stops and says to Partridge, 'I always wondered what you'd be like in person.'

'Me?'

'Of course! Who else?'

'And am I what you expected?'

Vinty cocks his head and says, 'I wasn't sure you could do it, but now I am.'

'Do what?' Partridge says, glancing at Glassings.

But Vinty scurries up the stairs, shutting the trap door behind him. 'My mother told me some things before she died, that you were planning for me to take over from within. Is that what Vinty means? All that time, you were waiting for a sign that I was ready? I had no idea.'

'Are you ready now, Partridge?'

'How am I supposed to lead from within?'

'It won't be easy.' Glassings looks down at his hands, and Partridge feels like Glassings has something to tell him but can't quite bear saying it.

'How can we start a revolution in the Dome?' Partridge asks, hopeful that Glassings has a plan.

'A revolution?' Glassings wags his head and looks up at him. 'Did you listen to any of my lectures, Partridge?'

'No offense, but you were always going on and on about ancient cultures. None of it seemed to apply to my life.'

'Without setting off any alarms, I was trying to prepare you. I chose my words carefully. I wrote lectures specifically for you.'

'What did I miss about revolutions? Tell me that.'

'Revolutions are usually started by people who are hungry. Sure, there are ideological revolutions, but, again, people rise up because they feel that the alternative is no longer livable. They have to be desperate.'

'Are you saying that the people here aren't desperate? I think you're wrong.' Iralene is one of the most quietly desperate people he's ever met. 'I think they are and they just don't know it.'

'Oh, they're desperate, all right, but so desperate that they're clinging to what they have.'

'If they knew the truth,' Partridge says, thinking of Bradwell. He wishes Bradwell were here with him now. 'If they could see what I've seen out there, if they really knew all of what my father did to the world, they'd rise up against him. They would. I know they would.'

Glassings sits back in the chair. Now that Partridge looks at it, he can tell that it's not just a wingback. It's a prop of a throne. 'You don't get it, do you?' Glassings says.

'What?'

'All the adults in the Dome already know the truth,' Glassings says. 'The things we teach in the academy are bedtime stories. We all know the truth, Partridge. We all carry it with us.'

PRESSIA

DREAM

BRADWELL IS ASLEEP and Fignan is resting by the small heater, soaking up energy, but Pressia is working on the spiders. Each was created with incredible explosives. She's taken them apart and reworked them into small hand grenades. She's written instructions on a new stone and has built three prototypes.

In the morning they'll head out, following the maps in Hastings' head, to find the airship. But she wanted to leave these instructions behind. The lawn of what used to be the boarding school is crammed with tents, filled with people who, with proper education, can take all the robotic spiders dislodged from survivors' bodies and produce a lot of these munitions. Why not put them to work? Plus, she was having trouble sleeping, so she put herself to work too.

Bradwell thought El Capitan and Helmud should stay, and El Capitan thought Bradwell should. Just before El Capitan and Helmud left with Hastings for the night, they fought about it.

'They need you to be here in charge,' Bradwell told him.

'You could play that role. You're not healthy enough for this trip.'

'I'm not sitting this out.'

'Neither am I,' El Capitan said.

'Neither am I,' Helmud echoed.

'If you find that airship, you're going to need a pilot,' El Capitan told Bradwell.

'A pilot,' Helmud said, some surprise in his voice.

'My father got a psych discharge from the air force and disappeared,' El Capitan said, 'but I spent my childhood learning everything I could about flight and playing those simulators. I don't have a single memory of my father, but I know we've got two things in common. Flying and being crazy.'

'Crazy,' Helmud said.

'A crazy pilot? That's not exactly optimal,' Bradwell muttered.

'Seriously,' Pressia said, 'what are the chances that the airship is going to work like an old flight simulator you played as a kid anyway?'

But El Capitan refused to listen. 'Better to have someone who knows *something* about flying. It'd be a shame to find the airship and not know the starboard from the aft. Maybe Fignan will help too. As copilot.' Fignan whirled his lights proudly.

As El Capitan said good night and started walking Hastings up to the dormitories, Bradwell yelled to him from the cottage door, 'So we all head out together! See you in the morning!'

El Capitan just waved a surrender without looking back, and that was that.

Pressia stands up, stretches her back, and runs over the things in her bag again. She unwraps the swaddled vials, lays them on the table, and holds each of them up, one by one, catching the light. They swirl, bright and amber. She can't help but think of her mother – a scientist, a brilliant one. But what good did her mother's logical mind do her? Ivan Novikov kissed her. They were likely dating when he died. Somehow, maybe playing on her grief, Willux – Ivan's murderer – won her over and she married him. Did she figure out, as Walrond eventually did, that Willux killed Ivan? Maybe that's what led her to Imanaka, Pressia's father. Pressia is sure of one thing: Her mother didn't always do what was rational and logical. She was driven to make choices because she listened to her heart, not her head. Eventually, those decisions killed her.

Pressia refuses to make the same mistakes – no matter what it felt like to lie with Bradwell in the forest.

Right now, she has to protect her mother's legacy. Without these three vials, there will be no cure – for anyone.

The cloth Partridge gave her to bind the vials doesn't seem thick enough for a journey as dangerous and possibly deadly as this one. She cuts a rectangle of wool from a blanket and uses it as extra padding before rewrapping them in the cloth.

'You're up,' Bradwell says, his voice rough with sleep.

'Did I wake you? Sorry.'

'No, no.' He sits up and rubs his head.

'What should we do with Partridge and Lyda's maps of the Dome?' she asks.

'We should leave them here, I guess, where they'll be safe.'

'I guess so.'

Bradwell looks out the window. 'Do you ever think about Partridge?'

'I hope he's not getting too comfortable,' Pressia says.

'He's a Pure. I can look past that, but still there's a gulf between us. I don't know if we could ever be able to really read each other.'

'And what about me?' Pressia picks up the vials and gently secures them to her body.

'I trust you.'

'But do you think you can read me?'

He smiles. 'No.'

'What's funny?'

He plumps his pillow and rests his head on it. 'This dream I just had. You were in it.'

'What was it about?'

'A flying dream. I used to have them all the time when I was little, during the Before.' He thinks for a moment. 'I guess I haven't had a flying dream since I had birds in my back, actual wings.'

'How did you fly in the dreams when you were little?'

'I could hold my breath and levitate, little by little, and then eventually I was high enough that I could open my arms so the wind would catch them and I'd just sail.'

'And in this dream?'

'I didn't have any birds in my back, but I wasn't a boy either. I was myself now but . . .'

'Pure?'

'I guess so. Maybe that's why I woke up thinking of Partridge in the Dome . . .'

'How did it feel?' Pressia's never dreamed she could fly.

'I felt . . . younger. I was my age, but I didn't feel the way I do now. It was like I could fly because I wasn't weighted down with everything. I knew, in the way you know things in dreams, that my parents were alive. And there were fields beneath me and streams, and it was lush. Like the Detonations had never happened.'

'And I was in the dream?'

'I saw the river, the one we crossed, and you were in it. I could see you, struggling.'

'You mean drowning.'

'That's what I thought. And as I went down to save you, it was that night again. That cold night.' She nods quickly, blushing at the thought of it. 'And I knew that to get to you, I had to remember that my parents were dead and that the world was an ash pit. And once I did that, I started to fall. I landed in the river. I plunged down deep, and I saw you there underwater. And I was myself again – birds in my back, my scars. And . . .'

'Did you save me?'

He shakes his head. 'I started to tell you the dream because it's an example of how I *can't* read you.'

'Right.'

'You were with all these girls – all these faces lining the walls – and you could breathe underwater. In fact, you could sing. You were all singing. The song moved through the water. I could feel the song on my skin; the notes vibrated.'

She thinks of his skin on hers, the snow coming down like bits of lace. 'And?'

'You didn't need saving at all. I thought you were drowning but you were fine. You looked at me in this way I can't describe.'

'What way?'

'Kind of ferocious. I couldn't tell if you were angry at me or . . .'

'Or what?'

'Nothing. I can't read you, even in my dreams. That's the point.'

She looks inside her bag as if she doesn't have its contents memorized. 'There's a dream reader in the market. Have you ever seen her?'

'I don't believe in that kind of thing.'

'I do. Sometimes at least.'

'Are you going to read my dream?' He sits up and puts his feet on the floor.

Pressia already has read the dream. Bradwell is coming on this trip to watch over her, to protect her. But maybe there's some part of him, deep down, that doubts she needs his protection. She picks up her bag and sets it by the front door. 'You're still holding on to your promise to my grandfather. Even in your dreams, you're being good to your word. And you're willing to sacrifice a lot to do it – even the idea that your parents could be alive.'

'Maybe you can read me better than I can read you.' As soon as he says it, she realizes that she wishes he'd argued with her. She doesn't want him to still be carrying that old debt. She doesn't want to still feel like a burden. It's quiet a moment. Pressia isn't sure what to say. She looks at the girls' faces – in particular the one who looks like Fandra, her old friend.

Pressia turns and stares at him. 'Why are you coming on this trip?' she asks him. 'No survivors have ever really made it far away and back again.'

'Why are you?'

'For Wilda. If we can find the formula, there's a chance we can save her.' This is true, but it's only part of the answer. Pressia can feel the truth itching inside her, clawing, wanting out. 'And I want to see if there are others out there. Maybe they made it out and didn't want to come back.' She walks to the table and picks up the kitchen knife she used to cut the wool. She touches the edge of the knife – still sharp. 'My father. The tattoo of his pulse was still beating on my mother's chest. He's still alive. Out there, somewhere.'

'But Pressia . . .' Bradwell stands up and walks to the table that sits between them.

She carries the knife to the chopping block. 'I know, I know. The chances of finding him are almost nothing. But you wanted an answer, and that's what I've got.' She's surprised that she's said all this aloud. It's been lodged in the back of her mind – for how long? She couldn't admit it, even to herself, because it sounded too selfish and childish. She sets the knife down.

He puts his knuckles on the table and leans closer. His eyes are still tired, but he seems to be squinting through the fatigue as if he's trying to see her clearly, and as if he's trying to read her right now.

'You're wrong about the dream,' Bradwell says.

'Really? How?'

'I'm not going because I still want to protect you. Because of some old promise.'

'Then why?' Pressia asks.

'I'm coming on this trip because . . .' He leans toward her. 'Pressia, because I—'

'Stop,' she says. 'It's suicidal to care about someone out here.'

'Then maybe I'm suicidal.'

Her heart is pounding so loudly in her chest that she presses her hand to it in the hope of steadying it. She stares at him, not sure what to say.

And then Bradwell's expression softens. He raises his finger and whispers, 'There it is. Right there.'

'What?'

'The look you gave me in the dream. The one I can't read.'

PARTRIDGE

BEAUTIFUL BARBARISM

THE ROOM IS QUIET except for the beetles clicking in the glass terrarium. Partridge can't speak, stunned by the enormity of the betrayal. All those years, he believed the bedtime story. And then outside the Dome, he thought his father and a few high-level types had duped them all. But they'd always known – all the people who were old enough before the Detonations to weasel their way into the Dome: his teachers, coaches, barber, the women who came to clean the apartment every week, the lab technicians, the dormitory monitors. 'All of them?' Partridge utters.

'All of them.'

He shakes his head. His plan to tell people the truth and let them choose a better way of living – it won't work. 'It's not possible. How could they live with themselves?'

'Many can't live with themselves. That's why we've had to accept suicide as socially acceptable, which turned out to be convenient. It keeps the populations in check, and each suicide opens a space for someone to have a baby – a baby who doesn't have to ever know the truth, someone to feed the new story to.'

Partridge squeezes his eyes shut. 'They knew . . . all along . . .'

'There will be no revolution, Partridge. The ones who were capable of leading a revolt were murdered before the Detonations or died in them.' Partridge thinks of Bradwell's parents. 'Except for a few.'

'Cygnus,' Partridge says, opening his eyes.

'We were led by your mother. We're not the toughest or the bravest. We're the ones who could live double lives, who could know the truth and keep moving on. We're the ones left. There are few of us, but we're growing stronger, bolder.' Glassings props his elbows on his knees. 'Partridge,' he says in a voice so solemn that Partridge knows this is the moment he's going to tell him something awful, something that will change his life forever. He can feel the enormity of the unsaid in the air. He can see the darkness of it clouding Glassings' face. 'There's something I have to—'

'Wait.'

All Partridge wants is a few more minutes with Glassings, just the two of them sitting in this room like father and son. He just wants to stall. He says quietly, 'First, just tell me about the beetles. Just . . .' His hands are shaking. He clasps them together. 'The beetles,' he says. 'One thing at a time.'

'Okay,' Glassings says. 'We sent out thousands of them. Other insects too. They're cyborgs really. They give us information, and we can control them from afar.'

'Are they traceable?'

'Nope. That's the beauty. Of course, Willux's people have brought him a few. He knows there are people against him. He feeds off it, in fact. But he doesn't know where they're coming from or what they're looking for.'

'You're crazy!' Partridge blurts out, and then he remembers Glassings was once his teacher and he apologizes. 'Sorry, sir, but really, my father would find a way to trace them. He'd never knowingly allow forces against him to have their own surveillance.'

'He hasn't gotten us yet,' Glassings says. 'We're careful. People like us have to be to survive.'

'And the man and his wife who got me into and out of the elevator?'

'There's your proof. Our network is solid, and we can help you do what you need to do.'

Partridge sits back in the chair. This is it.

Glassings' eyes look suddenly soft and weary. He's older than Partridge remembers him. He says, 'You need to assassinate your father.'

Partridge shakes his head. 'No.'

'Listen,' Glassings says quickly. 'We'd set it up. We have a pill. It works fast. The poisons are untraceable. And you could get in close enough. You're his son.'

'I won't do it.' He feels sick.

Glassings doesn't say a word. His expression is grave, unmoving.

'I'm not killing my father. If I become a murderer, then I become my father. Don't you see that?'

'What if it's self-defense?' Glassings looks at him angrily. 'You've done some damage out there, haven't you?'

'You have to do things you wish you didn't have to out there. It's filled with Beasts and Dusts and Groupies and now Special Forces.'

Glassings stands up and walks to the back of the chair. He holds it tightly with both hands and says, 'This isn't about retribution. We want to stop your father. He's still a very dangerous man.'

'You think I don't know that?'

'Wouldn't you kill someone if you knew that they were just going to keep on killing others?'

Partridge wants to end this once and for all – his father's brutality, the legacy of death. He could get in close, all right. He'd want his father to know just a split second before he died that Partridge had done it. Partridge imagines that momentary flash of terror in his father's eyes. He can't give in to it. 'I have to try to lead from within the right way.'

Glassings sits down again. He presses his knuckles together. He doesn't look at Partridge. 'He has big plans for you.'

'What plans?'

'I've been told that he wants you to settle down, to prove your stability.'

'He remarried. Did you know that?'

'It was a quiet affair.'

'Iralene is my stepsister. He wants me to settle down with her.'

Glassings jerks his head back. 'That's a little incestuous, isn't it?'

'Not technically, but yeah, it's crazy.'

'He likes to keep everything very closely knit.' Glassings looks at Partridge keenly. 'What about Lyda? . . . Is she still alive . . . out there?'

How could he know about Lyda? 'You know she was taken out of the Dome?'

'As a lure to pull you in. Yeah, we had people in the rehab center. Even the guard who escorted her out is one of ours. Is she okay?'

'I hope so.' He thinks of her singing on the stage – this stage, the one just above their heads – the music coming from deep within her.

'Maybe you can just play along with Iralene.'

'What? I'm not using her like that.'

'What if it worked to her advantage as well? It wouldn't be good if you ignored her, would it?' He knows Glassings is right. 'The word is that your father is going to show you how he runs things and then hand over the reins. Next in line in the Dome, right now, is Foresteed.'

'Foresteed, right. I'd forgotten about him.'

'He's become the face of the Dome's ruling body since your father's gotten older, weaker. But your father would prefer you.'

'Why me?'

'You want the truth?'

Partridge nods.

'He thinks he can manipulate you.'

'But haven't I proven that he can't really . . .'

Glassings tilts his head, raises his eyebrows. 'Review the facts,' he says. It's one of his catchphrases as a World History teacher.

Partridge thought he'd escaped the Dome, only to find out that's what his father wanted and planned. Willux wanted Partridge to lead him to his mother, and he did. And now Partridge is back because his father threatened to kill people until he returned. 'Shit,' Partridge says.

'You have to think long and hard about your father, Partridge, and what's best for the greater good.'

'Murder?'

'Just tell me you'll think about it.'

Partridge grips the arms of the chair. 'Where do I go from here?'

'You've got to find your father, get in close with him. You can't do anything if you don't have his trust and get information.'

'Are you going to turn me in?' Partridge asks.

'If I'm the one who brings you into your father, it'll shine a spotlight on our relationship.'

'But it would prove that you're loyal to my father.'

'I don't want any kind of spotlight whatsoever.'

'What, then?'

'One of the other teachers here maybe. Did you have a bond with any of them?'

'Hollenback.' Partridge's science teacher. 'I stayed with him and his family over some of the Christmas breaks.'

'Hollenback is perfect. He toes the line. He'll make the call as soon as he sees you. He's the one who handed Arvin Weed over to them so they could get at Weed's scientific genius.'

'I saw Arvin,' Partridge says, 'when they were *Purifying* me.'

'Arvin is crucial, Partridge. He's the one Willux has pinned his hopes on. He thinks that he can come up with a cure. He's working that kid to death.'

'Isn't Arvin on our side?'

'He was. But Willux has great pull. I'm sure he's made him promises. Who knows if Arvin will be strong enough?' Glassings looks at Partridge. 'It's why you have to be careful.'

'I'm not going to get pulled in by my father and I'm not going to kill him. So where does that leave us?'

'If you change your mind . . .'

'But we can't even communicate.'

'We're around.'

'I guess I should go.' Partridge stands up and walks to the ladder.

Glassings rises too. 'You know,' Glassings says, 'I don't have a son, Partridge. I probably never will have a child, what with the regulations. But if I did, I'd want him to be like you.'

Partridge's throat is too tight to speak. He looks down at his shoes and then his eyes catch Glassings', who smiles at him – a smile tinged with both sadness and pride.

Partridge smiles. '*Beautiful barbarism* – you said that once during a lecture about ancient cultures. It still applies to us now, doesn't it?'

Glassings nods.

'See, I was listening to your lectures. Some of it stuck.'

'Be careful out there.'

Though it makes no sense, Partridge gives him a salute.

Glassings salutes back.

Partridge climbs the ladder, opens the trapdoor, and climbs back up onto the stage, closing the trapdoor behind him. He walks quickly farther backstage, following exit signs. He finds a door, pushes it open, ready to breathe the cold air.

And then he's outside.

But that's just it. No one's ever really outside here.

PRESSIA

TEACUP

In THE BLACK SEDAN that once belonged to Ingership, courtesy of the Dome, they've made their way through the Deadlands teeming with Dusts. El Capitan is driving, hunched toward the wheel, Helmud perched on his back, busy whittling a bit of wood. Hastings, as navigator, sits beside El Capitan, his long legs crammed in tightly against the glove box. It turns out that Willux owns a fleet of airships built to survive the Detonations. Hastings is taking them to one that doesn't have high levels of security. Hastings didn't say why it isn't highly protected; maybe he doesn't know.

Dusts fan cobra-like hoods, arch spiny backs, lift claws and teeth from the earth itself. El Capitan plows into them. It pains him to kill the Dusts this way but only because he loves the car so damn much. He groans every time it takes a hit, which makes him an emotional and erratic driver. Pressia and Bradwell, in the backseat, grip the headrests, the doors, the seats. Twice, their elbows brush each other when the car jerks to one side. She can't stop wondering what would have happened if she'd let him finish telling her why he was going on the trip. What if she'd walked around the table to meet him on the other side? Would he have kissed her? She let the moment go. At the time, it felt like a relief, but now she wants the moment back; and at the same time she wants this gnawing in her stomach to stop. What is this gnawing? Love or fear or both?

Pressia has placed Fignan between her boots. He's now sampled the DNA of El Capitan, Helmud, and Hastings – stealthy pinpricks. He didn't share the results; they weren't anyone he was looking for.

Bradwell and Pressia keep their guns pointed toward the shut windows, ready to use them. The cracking of the Dusts' bodies and the sand, dirt, and soot that then explode and pelt the car are deafening.

The car's body is rutted with long scars, deep pocks, dings, a few old bullet holes. The front fender was already kinked from ramming Ingership's porch and pummeling through Dusts, and now it's mangled. The back bumper is gone, the front grille corroded. Each Dust they hit scours the chrome and the paint job. Pressia says, 'Maybe if you didn't slam into every Dust, the car would have a better shot of holding up.'

'If this car dies, each dead Dust is one less that'll kill us,' El Capitan says defensively. 'You want to drive?'

'Up ahead!' Hastings shouts. 'See them?'

'Yeah,' El Capitan says. He smashes through a small herd of Beasts with lean faces, dark eyes, and gaping maws. The creatures are stronger and stranger the farther they get from the Dome.

The car hits a bump and the tires find a remnant of highway – gravel pinging the undercarriage. It's enough of a road to cut off the Dusts. A few snap at the edges and then slowly retreat into the earth.

'Where are we headed?' El Capitan asks Hastings.

'Northwest.'

'Can you get a little more specific than that?' Bradwell asks.

El Capitan shakes his head. 'There's a little problem with our navigator . . .'

'What's that?' Pressia asks, leaning forward.

'Hastings and I sat down last night to work out the route and we hit a snag. He's got full programming – a knowledge of maps, internal compass, highly developed sensory perception, full automatic weaponry – but also behavioral coding. His strand of loyalty coding will allow him to give us only so much.'

'Loyalty,' Helmud says.

'Do you mean that Hastings can't tell us the actual location of the airship?' Bradwell says.

'I can't give you everything you need,' Hastings says. 'I can fight my coding only so much and lead as far as I can.'

'No offense, Hastings' – Bradwell leans over the front seat, and Pressia knows that he's about to say something offensive – 'but how do we know that your loyalties aren't still with the Dome and you won't turn on us?'

'Turn on us?' Helmud says.

'You don't know,' Hastings says.

'Your coding is strong,' Bradwell says. 'It's probably drilled into your cortex, the stem of your brain, imprinted on your cells.'

'Easy now,' El Capitan says.

'Cap, if he decided suddenly to open fire on all of us out here, who could blame him? He's been programmed to hate us, to see us as the enemy, right?'

'He's going to get us there, one step at a time. He's fighting for it. It takes willpower to overcome that coding,' El Capitan says. 'We should be thanking him, taking what we can get.'

'What we can get,' Helmud says.

'I think it's smart to admit that there's a risk,' Bradwell says. 'I'm not saying I don't trust him. It's just—'

'That you don't trust him,' Pressia says.

'I don't trust the Dome. I think it's stupid to underestimate them.'

'Maybe it's stupid to *overestimate* them too,' Pressia says. 'Maybe that's how they get away with so much. Hastings might be a good example of why we shouldn't overestimate them.'

Hastings shoots her a look, as if insulted.

'I mean, it could be that the human part of him is stronger than the Dome thought. Maybe emotions are a real force. Maybe there are some things you can't alter.'

Bradwell looks like he wants to say something, but then Hastings says, 'Don't trust me. Will it change anything?'

Hastings is right. They're already about six miles into the Deadlands. They need him.

'I can tell you,' Hastings says, squinting in concentration, 'for one thing, this airship works in some ways like old-world airships.'

Bradwell lifts Fignan, asking him to fill them in. Fignan explains how old-world airships worked on the principle of filling a balloon, or something like it, with a gas, usually hydrogen or helium, that's lighter than air. The crafts, in fact, floated.

'Airships,' Helmud says wistfully.

El Capitan scratches his head. 'But Willux must have known that after the Detonations no one would have access to those gases for fill-ups. It can't work that way.'

'It doesn't,' Hastings says. 'They created an extremely thin, lightweight material that was rigid and strong enough to hold something approaching a one hundred percent vacuum without being crushed by the air pressure around it.'

Fignan searches his data. 'Endohedral fullerenes.'

'What are those?' Bradwell asks.

Fignan lights up a quick video. 'Fullerenes,' a narrator explains, 'are complex, variously shaped molecules of carbon, sometimes called buckyballs. Both terms were named in tribute to Buckminster Fuller, scientist, inventor, futurist.'

'Good ole Buck!' Pressia says quietly, remembering that's exactly what Willux wrote on one of his notebook pages.

'And how does that relate to us?' El Capitan asks.

Hastings tells him that under Willux's watch, the small molecules had been grown large and combined with other molecules to make the thin, strong, rigid skin of the airship's vacuum tanks. 'To rise up, it simply pumps air out. To descend, it lets some back in, weighing down the airship.'

'Wow,' Bradwell says, clearly impressed.

Pressia stares out over the Deadlands. 'They were so smart, and look at what they did with all that intelligence.'

Hastings gives El Capitan his limited understanding of instrumentation and navigation. And Bradwell asks Fignan for a map of the area. The map is an old one of highways, churches, office complexes. Fignan gives facts about the geological makeup, weather patterns in this region, the population per square mile – all of it pre-Detonations.

Out the window, there's the barren landscape. That world is long gone. Pressia's tired of his pre-Detonations facts. They seem only to illustrate all that's been lost.

Bradwell interrogates Fignan about Cygnus – the constellation, various swan species classified under the term, mythology. Fignan's voice drones on, soft and low.

They pass old fast-food-chain signs on tall poles, now fallen, one after the next, like trees felled in a storm. Some of the signs shattered. Others cracked like eggs. Whatever was within them – tubes of light? electrical wires? – has been destroyed or stolen. The wind has pushed the dust into drifts that seem to be eating the rubble of hotels, restaurants, and discount outlets. Still, Pressia sees small signs of human life – an occasional house made of a roof blasted loose from a gas station, primitive lean-tos on the wind-protected side of a partially demolished Hardee's.

And as Pressia keeps her eyes on the passing landscape, Fignan is retelling a Greek myth about two close friends, Cygnus and Phaeton, who were always in competition. They challenged each other to a chariot race across the sky. But they both flew too close to the sun. Their chariots burned and they fell to earth, unconscious. When Cygnus woke up, he searched for Phaeton and found his body trapped by the roots of a tree at the bottom of a river. Bradwell touches her arm. 'Did you hear that?'

She knows what he's thinking – Novikov and Willux, the accidental drowning that might not have been an accident at all. She nods.

Fignan goes on. 'Cygnus dived into the water to retrieve Phaeton's body for a proper burial. Without it, his spirit wouldn't be able to travel to the afterlife. But Cygnus couldn't reach him. He sat on the bank and cried, pleading with Zeus to help him. Zeus answered, saying that he could give Cygnus the body of a swan, allowing him to dive deeply enough to pull Phaeton from the river. But if Cygnus chose the body of a swan, he would no longer be immortal. He would live only as long as a swan lives. Cygnus became a swan, dived into the water, pulled up Phaeton's body, and gave him a proper burial so Phaeton's spirit could make it into the afterlife. Zeus was so moved by this selflessness, he created a constellation in the image of Cygnus – a swan – in the night sky.'

'Willux would have been Cygnus. Novikov was Phaeton.' Pressia turns to Bradwell. 'Do you think Willux was really trying to save him?'

'The myth is weirdly prophetic,' Bradwell says. 'If Novikov had the formula, if he was really already experimenting with reversal – successfully – on his own body, and if Willux killed him, then he did become mortal. He sealed his fate. Like Walrond said . . .'

'*He killed the one person who could have saved him,*' Pressia says. 'Even if he didn't fully understand this myth, he must have heard it. I mean, he chose the swan as a symbol for the Seven. He had to have researched what the swan means – it's not crazy to imagine that he came across this stuff.'

'I think Walrond was right about Willux's obsessive mind, the importance of Cygnus – the constellation – the tip of its wing passing over Newgrange,' Bradwell says. 'I wasn't sure before, but, I don't know – I feel like I'm starting to see the patterns of Willux's mind.'

Pressia looks out at the remains of large factories hulking to the west. Corrugated roofs peeled loose, the factories look both airy and gutted. 'I wonder who survives out here.'

'I don't know, but they must be tough.'

'No more road,' El Capitan says.

The road crumbles away. The Dusts are rippling on the horizon. Pressia tightens her grip on her gun, holds it to her chest.

In the distance, there's a large, skeletal, serpentine structure – a tall neck that ends abruptly, a backbone that dips toward the earth, and then a loop, like the old-fashioned letters her grandfather taught her, cursive. 'What's that?'

'It's an amusement park,' Hastings says. 'We'll have to pass it to the east.'

Bradwell leans forward over the front seat. 'Jesus. I know that place. I went there as a kid. It was brand new, but really retro. You know how the Return to Civility loved anything that felt old-world. It was called Crazy John-Johns. There was a clown – a huge clown with a bobbing head – a Tilt-A-Whirl, and old-style roller coasters. Not just the simulators in theaters, but the real thing. Real wind in your hair, filling up your lungs. My father took me there. We rode Rolling Thunder and the Avalanche.'

'Crazy John-Johns,' El Capitan says. 'I remember advertisements. My mother never could scrape together enough money.'

'Mother,' Helmud says, tucking away his knife.

Pressia thinks of her grandfather, Odwald Belze, who told her, again and again, about a trip to Disney World that she took during the Before – a story he invented to give her a life, one he knew nothing about.

'It's inhabited,' Hastings says. 'The roller coaster is a lookout tower. Can you see them?'

'Who?' Pressia asks, but then, at the top of the roller coaster, she sees a few small figures sitting on the vertical tracks, probably having scaled them like a ladder.

'The last time I was here,' Hastings continues, 'they proved to be dangerous. They have a power source and gunpowder left over from fireworks displays and—'

The sedan suddenly jerks sideways and spins a tight circle. The back tires churn dust. The car jerks to a stop.

'And traps,' Hastings says.

'What the hell?' El Capitan shouts. He pulls the rifle strap over his and Helmud's head, reaches for the handle.

'Don't go out,' Hastings warns.

'Go out,' Helmud whispers.

'I've got to see the damage.' El Capitan opens the door and steps out. He crouches by the front tire then rises and rubs the frame. 'Damn it!' he shouts. 'Why would someone do this to my baby?'

'My baby!' Helmud shouts.

'What's wrong?' Bradwell calls.

The Dusts are not far off. The air is still.

'Someone dug some kind of something right into the ground,' El Capitan says. 'A pink hole with teeth! Some giant freakish mouth!'

Pressia slides across the backseat. 'This I have to see.'

'Me too,' Bradwell says.

'Be careful and quick,' Hastings warns as the two of them get out of the car.

The punctured tire sits in what is, in fact, a perfectly round large pink hole, maybe made of fiberglass. Inside it, there's a set of large, sharp spikes, a few of which are dug deeply into the dead tire. A tarp, now loose, flutters from it like a wild veil. 'Smart,' Pressia says. 'They covered it with a tarp, let the sand and ash cover it, and waited.'

Hastings steps out of the car. He stands a few feet from them, his eyes scanning the horizon.

El Capitan kicks the ground, cursing loudly.

Bradwell knocks on the heavy-duty fiberglass with his knuckles. 'It's a teacup,' Bradwell says. 'From a teacup ride.'

'A teacup ride?' El Capitan says. 'My car was taken down by a teacup from a Crazy John-Johns teacup ride?'

Pressia thinks of her grandfather's stories of his childhood – the Italian festivals, the goldfish in plastic bags given as prizes, the cannoli, the games and rides. She looks across the terrain between them and the amusement park's chain-link fence. The Dusts are huddling nearby. 'Do you think there are more traps?'

'Yes,' Hastings says. 'Get back in.' He locks his vision on the amusement park now. 'On this route, we lost three Special Forces soldiers – heavily armed and combat-ready.'

'Three of them? Dead?' El Capitan says, stunned.

'What's the plan?' Bradwell says.

'The plan was not letting my car get eaten by a teacup,' El Capitan says.

'How many more miles, Hastings? Can you tell us that much?' Pressia asks.

'Thirty-five point seven two miles.'

'We won't make it all in one day now,' El Capitan says. 'We'll have to try to get around this and find a place to sleep for the night on the other side.'

'*If* we make it to the other side,' Bradwell says.

'If there is an *other* side,' Pressia says.

'If,' Helmud says.

'Do you hear it?' Hastings says.

'What?' El Capitan asks. His anger has shifted to fear.

But there's no need for an answer. They all feel it, up through the soles of their boots – the earth rumbling under their feet.

PARTRIDGE

CHRISTMAS TREE

PARTRIDGE WAKES UP to the face of Hollenback's five-year-old daughter – Julby Hollenback. This was the room he used to wake up in during the winter holidays he spent with the Hollenbacks. He can hear Mrs Hollenback singing in the kitchen; she always did love songs about snowmen and sleigh rides. Julby's older now. Her two bottom front teeth are missing.

He came here last night just after leaving Glassings. He walked up to Hollenback's apartment and saw the small knocker in the shape of a lion's face, the academy's mascot, draped in curlicue ribbon – something Mrs Hollenback teaches the girls to make in the History of Domesticity as an Art Form. Below the ribbon were two snowflakes – paper ones, like those taped to the school's plate-glass windows. It's as if Lyda were here with him all the time. And for a moment he imagined the family asleep, cocooned in their sheets. He didn't want to wake them up.

But he raised the knocker and tapped it hard.

After a few minutes he heard shuffling and Hollenback's voice saying, 'Who is it? Who's there? What on earth?' And then the clicking of the lock. Hollenback flung the door wide.

And there he was, agitated, fine hairs floating on top of his nearly bald head, cinching the belt of his robe. His shoulders seemed frailer, or maybe it was just that he wasn't wearing his sport coat. He was expecting a prank or an overblown emergency.

He stared at Partridge. One moment Hollenback thought he knew what the world would bring, and in the next moment, it all changed. Partridge could see the shock in his eyes, and he liked that Hollenback seemed kicked off balance. In that moment, he hated Hollenback for knowing the truth, for swallowing it every day, passing down the lie.

You awake now, Hollenback? Partridge wanted to say. *This is how life is. This is how it goes.*

Hollenback shuttled him inside. 'Partridge Willux,' he kept saying to himself, 'how about it?' – and then made a call from the house phone. When he came back, he looked pale. He said, 'Stay the night. Everything is okay. Someone will come for you in the morning.'

And now Julby is in Partridge's face. 'You can't sleep all day.'

'How are you doing, Julby? You seem all grown up.'

She's wearing a sweater with a Christmas tree design. 'I'm in kindergarten, group three, with Mrs Verk. My mother told me to tell you that we're going to eat.'

'Eat?'

'It's our Saturday meal,' she says proudly. Partridge remembers that the Hollenbacks eat at noon on Saturdays: a sit-down meal, spare food, but real – not soytex pills or chalky power drinks. Real food. It's a perk of the senior faculty. 'You're invited.'

'Are you sure?' He knows that there's only so much to go around.

'Uh-huh. And some other person is eating with us.'

'Who?' It couldn't be his father – not Glassings either.

'A *girl!*' Lyda. This is his first thought, but it's quickly replaced by a more logical assumption. Iralene. 'She has shiny hair and she's already here. And she smells like bubbles.'

'That sounds like Iralene.'

Julby shrugs and picks at the balls that decorate the Christmas tree on her sweater. 'She's here to take you home.'

'I don't have a home.'

Julby looks at him and laughs. 'You're funny.'

'I wasn't trying to be.'

Her face becomes solemn. 'Jarv doesn't have a home anymore.'

Mrs Hollenback was always making excuses for Jarv. *He's just small now because he spits up a lot. Delicate digestive system. He'll outgrow it!* Children who don't develop well are often taken away for treatment. Had Jarv been flagged? 'How's Jarv these days?' Partridge says as he sits up and gets out of the bed. He is still dressed in his suit pants and shirt, rumpled now.

He finds his necktie on the back of a chair. Julby taps on the window like there might be something on the other side. 'Jarv is stupid,' Julby says.

'Jarv isn't stupid. He's just little still, that's all. Is he eating better?'

'How do I know? He's gone to get unstupid.'

Jarv is gone. He thinks about Mr Hollenback again – the way he seemed older to him, shrunken. Maybe the loss of Jarv aged him. Partridge doesn't want to tell Julby that he's sorry, because that might make her think there's something to be sorry about. There is, of course. Sometimes these kids don't ever come back. 'But he'll be home soon.'

'Maybe,' Julby says. 'He was just gone one day, so maybe

that's how he'll come back. A surprise.' She looks at the open door then picks at the balls on her sweater again. 'I think you should stay for Christmas. We like it when you're here.' Julby runs out of the room and down the hall shouting, 'He's awake! He's awake! He's awake!'

Partridge walks out of the bedroom and dips quickly into the bathroom. As he's washing his hands, he takes the cap off his pinky. The skin looks more layered, firmer. He worries that the pinky growing back is a sign that he's turning back into his old self. His father wants the pinky fully formed, wants the past erased, wants him cleansed. When will he see the old man? Partridge splashes water on his face, stares at himself in the mirror. *I'm still me*, he says. *I'm still me.*

Walking out of the bathroom, he hears laughter from the kitchen. He walks past the small living room, the walls filled with shelves of antique books and, in the center of the room, a fake Christmas tree with its medicinal scent of pine spray. There is only one stocking hanging from a hook on a bookcase. It reads julby in swirling scroll. No stocking for Jarv. A few months after Sedge had supposedly died, no one mentioned his name in Partridge's presence. It was as if he'd never existed.

As Partridge walks into the kitchen, he bumps into Mrs Hollenback, wearing a white apron stitched with the baby Jesus in a manger just over her chest. She looks gaunt too – older, like Mr Hollenback – but she still has that restless, chipper energy. She has white flour on her hands and hugs him without really touching him. 'Partridge! So good to see you. You didn't tell us that you had this beautiful friend!'

As Mrs Hollenback backs away, Partridge sees Iralene, with a guard standing behind her chair. Although the guard has no weapons fused to his arms like Special Forces, he's undergone enhancements. Maybe he's mid-transformation. He's wearing a military uniform, with a gun in his holster. Partridge feels like a prisoner again. It's not Iralene's fault, of course, but for some reason, it makes him angry at her.

'Hello, Iralene.'

'Hi.'

'So did my father send you?'

Iralene smiles. 'There's going to be a party.'

'What kind of party?' Mrs Hollenback says, distracted by Mr Hollenback and Julby arguing about something in the foyer. 'I said no, Julby,' Partridge hears Mr Hollenback say. 'This is very important. I need you to be on your best behavior or else.' Or else what? You'll be taken away like Jarv? You'll disappear?

'It's just something small,' Iralene says. 'Elegant but casual.'

'It sounds lovely,' Mrs Hollenback says. 'What's the occasion?'

'Well,' Iralene says, glancing at Partridge nervously and then turning her attention to Mrs Hollenback. 'It's an engagement party!'

Mrs Hollenback claps her hands, the flour creating small bursts of cloud. 'Oh, Partridge! I'm so happy for you two!' She jogs from the room and yells down the hall. 'Ilvander! Julby! There's news!'

Partridge sits down next to Iralene. 'What are you talking about?'

'Your father has skipped forward. He wants to see how far you're willing to go to meet him.' Her eyes flick to the guard and back to Partridge again.

'So we're engaged. Just like that?'

Mrs Hollenback is calling out, 'An engagement! Our Partridge and Iralene! Come quick!'

Iralene reaches out and grabs his shirtsleeve. She whispers, 'If you don't do it, there's no more need for me. I've betrayed them. If I can't get you to come back . . .'

He's furious at his father for puppeteering this twisted setup. Iralene looks anguished. 'I'll talk to him,' he says. 'We'll work this out.'

Mr and Mrs Hollenback are both there now, and before Partridge has a chance to clarify the situation, there's a flurry of excitement, congratulations, handshakes, hugs, claps on the back.

'Well, Julby, what do you think? There's going to be a wedding!' Mrs Hollenback says.

Wedding. The word makes him sick. He thinks of Lyda and being with her in the warden's house, open to the sky. He'd been ready to spend the rest of his life with her. Forever. And now this?

Julby is the only one who's quiet. Her cheeks are red as if she's been crying. 'That's nice,' she says.

'Tell them congratulations!' Mrs Hollenback says.

'Congratulations!' Julby shouts angrily. 'Lucky us! Lucky us! Lucky us!' She turns and pulls down some drawings taped to the walls – flowers, horses, and rainbows.

'Not now, Julby!' Mr Hollenback says. 'Not in front of guests!'

'Lucky us!' Julby screams and then she runs out of the kitchen.

Mrs Hollenback covers her hand with her mouth. Her eyes tear up. She then reaches for Partridge and Iralene. She grips their hands. 'Don't tell anyone she was just like that. They'll get the wrong impression. She's fine. She's a good girl. She's normal! Not like Jarv. Julby will grow up fine. Don't tell them about this. Okay? Please.'

Mr Hollenback says, 'Helenia, stop. Don't make more of it than it was.'

'We won't tell anyone, Mrs Hollenback,' Partridge says. 'We won't. We promise.'

Iralene smiles. 'I heard the girl say, "Lucky us," and she's right. We're all lucky. We have much to be thankful for.'

Mr Hollenback touches his wife's shoulder. 'See, dear?'

'We're not talking about Jarv,' Mrs Hollenback says.

'That's right,' Mr Hollenback whispers. 'We're moving forward, not looking back. We've already made that decision.'

Mrs Hollenback nods and walks to the sink. 'Yes, yes, of course. Lucky us. Lucky us. Lucky *us*.'

LYDA

DWARF DEER

Lyda has learned the forest. At this time in the afternoon the animals move to water, taking a break from a day of hiding. The light through the trees begins to take on a slant, and it catches the dust that swirls in the air. There is the constant and irregular ticking of the forest, the birds with their warped squawking from the treetops, water trickling to find more water to join with, and the scent of earth and dust.

Mother Hestra is on Lyda's left, a few yards away. She walks unevenly because of Syden, but almost silently too. Lyda knows the words etched in reverse, darkening Mother Hestra's face: . . . THE DOGS BARKED LOUDLY. IT WAS ALMOST DARK. She's never asked what they mean or why they exist. It seems impolite to bring it up. Mother Hestra has never talked about what she was doing during the Detonations or much about her life in the Before.

The underbrush in the forest is thick, which is why they hunt here. They've become excellent at harvesting the smaller animals – dwarf deer, rats, the two-legged weasels that drag their bodies along after themselves, lizard-like. They let the dangerous predators hunt in the night. But they're never far from danger. The mothers have been hunted while hunting, and killed by Groupies and Beasts.

Lyda can smell the day nest of a dwarf deer close by. They rest in groups and have a sharp, musky odor, not a thin scent like the little dogs, regularly bathed in scented shampoos, in the Dome. Lyda loves the smell of the nests. It makes her feel alive. The grip of the bow is polished by her sweaty palm. She made the arrow by hand with Mother Hestra's help. The bow is made of fiberglass borrowed from something the mothers dismantled and cut into strips. The string is fine and shiny. Whenever Lyda releases it, it plays a note in her right ear, as if the strings were taken from a musical instrument.

Lyda checks that the guide feathers are true, that the arrow fits snug in the bowstring, ready to be drawn.

She senses rustling ahead. She stops, raises her hand. Mother Hestra freezes. Lyda kneels to get sight lines through the underbrush. Mother Hestra also takes a knee, remaining silent and still.

Lyda finds her target: a chubby dwarf deer tipping forward on its shortened front legs to nuzzle something on the forest floor. If Lyda hits it right behind the shoulders, snapping its spinal cord and continuing on into the skull, the preoccupied animal should never feel the sting of the arrow. A poor shot will mean tracking the injured animal through the undergrowth, and most likely losing her arrow. She rarely misses.

Lyda draws back the string and sights down the shaft. She's learned that the first move of dwarf deer is backward, off their shortened front legs and onto strong haunches. She takes aim. She's ready and her breathing is still, but as she's imagining the arrow's flight into the deer, she feels buzziness in her chest and throat, as if her stomach has flipped from nerves, and now she's nauseous. It's the way she feels sometimes when thinking about Partridge, a flushed heat of remembering what it was like to kiss him, to be alone with him. Lovesick. That's what it's called and that's how it feels. Still, she lets the arrow fly, and she knows right away that she wasn't steady, that the arrow will drift.

And she's right. The arrow rips straight through the lower ribs of the deer. It squeals, piglike, and topples, but it's up quickly and moving for cover.

Mother Hestra starts running, bracing her son's head against her tightly, and is out in front of Lyda before she's even to her feet.

Lyda runs after her through the trees. She wants to apologize, not only to Mother Hestra, but to the animal. She knows it's suffering. Hopefully, the wound will cause bleeding that Mother Hestra can track easily and quickly put the deer out of its misery. Lyda doesn't want the scent of blood to draw the more vicious hybrids from the brush, though.

Lyda follows in Mother Hestra's wake. Mother Hestra is fast and light, even with the weight of the child; she's learned to compensate for the imbalance.

Lyda readies another arrow just in case other animals start circling. Mother Hestra has a gun robbed from a cache that the Basement Boys had stripped from Special Forces, but she will use it only as a last resort, if attacked.

What made Lyda miss? She may have eaten something bad, or she might just be hungry. Partridge comes into her mind again, just briefly, but she shoves him out. She has to be alert and present in the forest. She tightens her grip on the bow, takes a few more steps, and sees Mother Hestra standing over the furred lump. The deer is panting, blood soaked into its fur, pooling near its muzzle. It jerks its head as if still trying to get up.

Mother Hestra takes out her gun. She rubs the words burned into her face – ... THE DOGS BARKED LOUDLY. IT WAS ALMOST DARK – quick and rough. She doesn't hide her child's eyes; this is all part of life. But Lyda looks away and then hears a muffled crack. She knows that it's the butt of the gun on the deer's skull. Why waste a bullet? The deer is at peace now, Lyda thinks, but as she rounds a tree and sees Mother Hestra and the deer, she knows that something is wrong. Mother Hestra turns to her. 'She was with child. They do this sometimes. In death, the body expels the fetus, giving it a chance of survival.' There is a wet, slick, hairless, four-legged body. Its eyes are puffed and sealed shut. Lyda knows that she will remember this image. She'll see it tonight when she closes her eyes. It will haunt her.

Lyda turns away, unable to watch. She crouches, puts one hand on the dirt, and vomits. She's completely surprised. She's gotten used to blood. This has never happened before. She's even more surprised when she vomits again.

Mother Hestra touches her shoulder. Lyda gets to her feet, wipes sweat from her brow – sweating even though it's cold outside.

Mother Hestra looks at her very strangely. *The dogs barked loudly. It was almost dark*, Lyda thinks to herself. Why those words? Why? She doesn't like the way Mother Hestra's eyes look so intense, so anxious. Finally, Mother Hestra says, 'You've stopped bleeding, haven't you?'

'Bleeding?'

'Your periods.'

Lyda blushes. This isn't talked about in the Dome. There's a small cabinet in every bathroom in the girls' academy with all the necessities. No need to talk about it. But she hasn't had a period in a while. She assumed it was because of so much physical change – hard work and strange, spare meals. 'You're right.'

'Did you lie with that boy?'

'Excuse me?' Lyda backs away and brushes the dirt from the knees of her pants.

'We guarded you all that time. We kept you separated. We were trying to save you, and this is what happened? Did he hurt you?'

Lyda shakes her head.

'Did he make you do this thing?'

'What thing?'

'Don't you even know what I'm saying to you?'

Lyda knows what she's saying. She's known the truth in some small voice in the back of her mind. She knew it when she saw the dwarf deer's fetus, didn't she? Isn't that part of why she turned away and got sick? She knows it now, but she can't say a word.

'You're pregnant. That's what. We have to tell Our Good Mother.'

'I can't be pregnant.' There was a misunderstanding. He'd asked if she was sure, but she thought he was talking about something else. The pregnancy is just a misunderstanding. The woods look suddenly dangerous now. The afternoon light is fading.

'You are,' Mother Hestra says. 'I know this is the truth.'

'But we aren't married.' They were only pretending to be husband and wife.

'Don't you know how it works? Hasn't anyone ever told you?'

Lyda thinks of her lessons in infant care – how to apply ointment to rashes, how to pick crust from the infant's scalp, how to rub teething serum into the gums. They didn't teach her about pregnancy. The girls whispered. 'No, I don't know how it works.'

'Well, you've learned by experience then.'

She thinks about the brass bed frame, her body and Partridge's body on the floor under the coat. Pregnant. There's a child growing inside of her. How small is it? She wants to see her mother. She has to tell her. But she may never see her mother again.

'Mother Hestra!' Lyda reaches out her hands. 'What will happen to me?'

Mother Hestra opens her arms and embraces Lyda. 'Our Good Mother will make a ruling. She will know what's best.'

'A ruling?' She grips Mother Hestra more tightly.

'She is the judge in all matters.'

She pulls back and searches Mother Hestra's face. 'What will she do to me? Punish me? Banish me?'

'I'll think of the right way to tell her. It will be okay,' she whispers. The forest makes its soft ticking noises all around them. 'Hush now. Hush.'

EL CAPITAN

EYES

EL CAPITAN SHOUTS AT HASTINGS to get in the car. Everyone else is running back to the car, but Hastings stands his ground, his weapons poised to fire. Jesus, what could possibly make the earth vibrate like this? Dusts, yes. But what kind? And how many would it take to rattle El Capitan so violently that he feels the vibrations deep in his own rib cage and Helmud's ribs too – reverberating on his back? 'Hastings!' he shouts again.

'Leave him!' Bradwell says. 'Get in the car.'

'You can't reason with Hastings, Cap!' Pressia shouts.

She's right. He's probably programmed to be brave like this; he has no choice but to stand his ground and fight. El Capitan would love to be able to override his own instincts and emotions, mainly fear. Fear claws in his chest like a trapped animal.

The dust and earth and sand whip around them. He stares at Pressia, her cheeks red from being stung by the ashen dirt in the air. He wants Bradwell to stop being so protective of Pressia. Why does he have to grab her hand like that? She can stand on her own two feet. She doesn't need him.

'Take cover!' Hastings shouts.

'Fine!' El Capitan shouts.

Pressia and Bradwell pile into the backseat together. El Capitan and Helmud get behind the wheel. They slam the doors, lock them, tighten the windows. The car teeters in the teacup trap. Helmud has buried his head behind El Capitan's back.

'Why won't they show themselves?' Pressia says. 'We know they're there, underground. Why won't they come up?'

'They're toying with us,' Bradwell says. 'We just have to sit tight and see what we're dealing with.'

'We can't stay in here!' Pressia says loudly over the howling winds and rumbling earth.

'Hastings isn't going to be able to hold them off by himself,' El Capitan says. Could he go out there and stand by Hastings? Does he have the guts? He checks the rifle's ammo and thinks of his father – his psych discharge. Was it because he wasn't tough enough – or was he considered crazy because he took big risks? What's El Capitan's legacy? He wishes he knew.

'Even if the car holds up, they can wait us out. We'll die of dehydration,' Bradwell says.

'I won't let that happen,' El Capitan says.

'Let that happen?' Helmud whispers nervously into the back of El Capitan's neck.

Bradwell grabs the back of El Capitan's seat and pulls himself forward. 'If we go out there, they'll devour us.'

'Damned if we do and damned if we don't,' El Capitan says. 'I'd rather go out fighting them than hiding out like I'm weak!'

'Are you calling me weak?' Bradwell says.

'If you're just going to sit in here and die, then yes. I'm calling you weak.'

'Weak, weak,' Helmud says, as if confessing.

'Listen here, Cap, you're just some—'

'Just some what?' El Capitan says. 'Lowlife whose mommy and daddy weren't professor types?'

'That's not—'

'Look!' Pressia shouts, staring out the window.

The ground shivers in small, coin-size spots, each quivering independently of the others until, one by one, eyes erupt from the ground. Hundreds of them. Maybe thousands. It's as if something planted here has suddenly bloomed, but instead of flowers, there are eyes, each one beating back the dirt with jerking blinks. Wet, batting eyes, encrusted at the edges with dust and ash, they squint and shine like strange kinds of clams or oysters that have muscled up from sand in droves.

Bradwell pushes off the driver's seat and says, 'Damn. These aren't ordinary Dusts. What are they?'

El Capitan has seen an eye or two before, out in the Drylands. They're usually just the smallest vestige of a human – fused to the earth, lost forever. But Hastings, still trying to stand his ground, is startled by them, so much so that he staggers backward, knocking into the car, his weaponry clanging against the hood.

Pressia reaches forward and grabs El Capitan's arm on the back of the seat, surprising El Capitan so much that he almost jerks his arm away. He's not used to people touching him like that. He's an officer. He tries not to move at all. 'They aren't just eyes, are they?' Pressia says.

His voice has gone rough in his throat. 'No. I don't think they are.'

Pressia tightens her grip and El Capitan feels a flush in his cheeks. 'What should we do?'

'We should stick together,' he says.

'Together,' Helmud says, drawing attention to the fact that they are forever stuck together. El Capitan hates his brother with a quick flash of anger.

'What do you mean they aren't only eyes?' Bradwell says.

Pressia's hand is still there. 'That rumbling,' she says. 'What if that's their bodies beneath them – big ones?'

'We should make a run for it before they start to rise up, if, in fact, that's what they're going to do,' Bradwell says.

Pressia's hand slips from El Capitan's arm. 'We don't have a choice. This is only going to get worse.'

Hastings rips off a round from one of his automatics. He's aiming at the eyes themselves, which disappear underground as the bullets pop across the dirt, sending up thin trails of dust that spiral off in the wind.

But the ground only starts rumbling louder than before, more violently.

'He shouldn't have done that,' Pressia says.

As if responding to the threat, dusty bulbous heads, cheek-bones, gaping mouths, small rounded nubs for ears emerge from the earth. They draw up their shoulders and scrawny arms. Their bodies are so heavy with the earth, they seem like they're pulling themselves up from tar. They climb up from the earth – torsos, haunches, legs.

Human?

They're emaciated, their ribs slatted, their shoulders and backs bony. But some also seem to have been fatter. Their middles are draped in what seems like a mesh dirt fabric that used to be skin. Their eyes are still batting furiously, but the rest of their faces seem almost dead – slack and loose-jawed. They move as if their arms and legs are swollen and their joints are stiff.

Hastings turns and fires, but unlike the Dusts closer to the Dome, they don't break loose or rip apart. No. The bullets form dark holes. A bead of blood will appear but then coagulate, dark and scabbed, almost immediately.

'Why aren't they dying?' Pressia says.

El Capitan instinctively turns the key, revving the engine. He pumps the gas.

'What are you doing?' Bradwell shouts.

'Getting us out of here.' El Capitan throws the car into reverse, but the tire is in too deep. The back wheels just churn up dirt and dust and rocks. He jams the car into drive, trying to urge the car out of the hole. 'Come on! Come on!'

Helmud is clawing his brother's back, as if he could dig a hole and hide. Hastings keeps shooting.

Pressia shouts, 'It's not working, Cap!'

A heavy fist strikes the windshield. The face moves into view – the furiously beating eyelids, the hollow-looking dark pit of a mouth. Another Dust paws at the side windows.

Hastings is trying to fend them off. Each bullet momentarily stuns them. He's firing frantically now – not only at the ones by the car, but also at those who are surfacing around him.

The car is quickly covered in hands, pounding and clawing. El Capitan can hear Hastings firing but can no longer see him. It's their eyes that El Capitan can't take – alive and crazed. It would be better if they were deadened eyes, laconic and glassy like those of zombies. He hasn't thought of the word *zombies* for a long time. He used to download pirated movies that weren't on the sanctioned list – terrifying ones. And after the Detonations, he saw those dead eyes, charred faces, and bodies walking – leaden, slow, and steady. He saw one of them grip the bark of a tree and when he pulled his hand away, the skin of his arm pulled loose, smoothly, like a long black glove.

One of the Dusts bucks from the window, howling and spinning. One of its eyes is a bloody mess – just a socket. It falls to its knees. Why has this one fallen? Why now? The other Dusts are drawn to the writhing Dust – maybe by the scent of its blood or by its high-pitched human cry – and, on their heavy legs, they move in on it. The bleeding Dust is flipped to its back. Its one socket bleeding over into its good eye, which is blinking away the blood, the Dust stares up at the other ones and slowly spreads its arms wide in surrender.

Hastings shouts, 'Move! Now!'

While the Dusts feed on the downed one, Bradwell and El Capitan get out of the car, but Pressia's frozen. She's staring at the Dusts feeding on their own kind.

'Pressia!' Bradwell shouts, leaning back into the car, Fignan locked under one arm. 'Let's go! Now! Move!'

But it's as if she can't hear him. She's stuck on the horror of this image. El Capitan pushes past Bradwell and says, 'Listen to me, Pressia. Can you hear me?'

She nods.

'Just close your eyes,' El Capitan tells her. 'Just close them and turn your head and look at me.'

She blinks and then closes her eyes.

'And turn to me.'

She turns her head and opens her eyes. For a second, El Capitan can't speak. There's something in the way she's looking at him that makes him breathless. She's looking to him with hope. She needs him.

'Now just come on and don't look back, okay?' She grips his arm and gets out of the car.

Helmud's skinny arm pops out over El Capitan's shoulder. He has something in his fist. He opens it. And there is a . . . bird?

Pressia takes it. 'A swan,' she says. 'Thank you, Helmud.'

'Yeah, he's quite the artist, right, Helmud?' El Capitan says, furious that his brother – his idiot brother – just stole this moment from him. He's been back there whittling a swan? 'Quite the gift giver.'

They all start running, guns on their backs, downhill toward the amusement park.

'Is she okay?' Bradwell asks El Capitan.

'Fine!' he says.

'Thank you for that back there,' Bradwell says.

El Capitan refuses to answer. If he did, he'd be agreeing that Pressia is somehow Bradwell's responsibility. And as far as El Capitan can tell, she isn't.

The ground is trembling so violently that El Capitan loses his balance and falls hard, scraping his palms. There, in front of his face, is an eye. It blinks so hard that he can hear it clicking. El Capitan gets up and keeps running.

The amusement park looms in front of them. It's wrapped in a chain-link fence topped with barbed wire. Through it, El Capitan can see some of the park: a great ship lying on its side, a giant clown head – Crazy John-Johns himself – his skull cracked but still poised on a neck made of a massive rusted spring, and the Ferris wheel that must have broken loose from its dock, rolled, and snagged on a set of guy wires. The bottom of the Ferris wheel and its multicolored cars have been lost in drifts of windswept dirt. All the colors are faded, but it's still one of the most beautiful things El Capitan has seen in a long time. He thinks of how many times his mother had promised to take them. 'Next year, when times aren't so tight,' she'd say. Just before she was taken away to the asylum, she told him she'd take him to the amusement park when she got home again. He told her that it didn't matter. 'It's just stupid Crazy John-Johns. Like I care about a stupid clown.' But now he wishes they had come, just once. Breathless and terrified, he can't help but say to Helmud, 'Will you look at that!'

'Look at that,' Helmud says. Maybe it stirs a memory in Helmud too.

'Which way?' Pressia shouts.

'Go left!' Hastings shouts. 'Follow me.' He's strong and long-legged. He could go a lot faster, but he's sticking by them, scanning the terrain at their feet and the horizon in all directions.

'It was their eyes, wasn't it?' Bradwell shouts. 'That's the most human thing about them. The part that's vulnerable. If we can get at their eyes . . .'

El Capitan thinks of the Beasts in the Rubble Fields and how you have to find that one exposed slip of living, breathing tissue, under what seems like an armored stone shell, and dig your knife in deep to kill it. The eyes, he thinks – of course. He whips his gun around front and fires at more eyes peering up in the distance.

'No!' Pressia shouts. 'It draws their attention!'

El Capitan looks back over his shoulder, and Pressia's right. A few of the Dusts have looked up from the devoured Dust and are looking in their direction now.

Pressia pulls out her knife and, while running, jabs it into the center of an eye that suddenly appeared nearby. It bursts with blood that soaks the dirt. The ground heaves and then goes still. This quieter death doesn't draw the other Dusts' attention.

'Here,' Bradwell says, holding out his hand. 'Give me the knife. I'll do it.'

'No, I'll do it,' El Capitan says.

But Pressia sprints out in front of them. She pierces one eye and then the next, clearing a path with quick jabs.

'Helmud!' El Capitan says, realizing his brother is armed. 'Give me your whittling knife.'

Helmud shakes his head. No, no, no.

'Hand it over now!'

No, no, no.

El Capitan reaches over his shoulder and whaps his brother on the head, one side and then the other. 'Give it!'

No.

'Maybe he wants to do it himself,' Bradwell says.

'Are you crazy?'

'Crazy!' Helmud says.

Pressia looks over; her knife is bloody. 'Cap!' she says. Does she mean stop beating up Helmud? Does she want him to let Helmud try to kill some Dusts?

It's clear now that it's a losing battle anyway. Dusts pull themselves up from the ground on either side. The ones that devoured the bloody-eyed Dust are now filling in from behind. There are too many of them closing in. So why not let Helmud have at it? Helmud doesn't have it in him anyway. He doesn't have the muscularity, the timing. El Capitan would actually like to see Helmud fail. After he made that swan and gave it to Pressia, this'll remind Helmud of his weakness, his dependency, and that he should stay in his place. 'You ready, Helmud?'

'Ready Helmud!' Helmud says.

And so El Capitan spots a Dust close by. He lowers himself to the ground, tilting to his right. Helmud raises his whittling knife high in the air. He drives it down into the dirt, almost half a foot off the mark.

'Not even close! Give me the goddamn knife!'

Helmud shakes his head violently.

El Capitan lets him try again. This time Helmud nails it. The eye pops with blood and disappears. El Capitan says, 'This one, here.' Again Helmud hits the eye dead-on. El Capitan keeps going, letting Helmud get in shot after shot. As much as he hates Helmud for getting the hang of this, he's suddenly proud of him too. El Capitan keeps them steady. Helmud drives in the knife. They make a good team, get in a rhythm, and move quickly. Maybe Pressia will see what a good brother El Capitan is. Bradwell sticks by Pressia, and El Capitan moves in close to her too.

Hastings is now behind them, the ground saturated with a dotted path, vibrating with the deaths of Dusts, quick convulsions.

Pressia looks up. She understands now that there are too many of them. 'It's over,' she says. 'We're outnumbered.'

They stop and turn slow circles as the Dusts move in.

The chain-link fence surrounding the amusement park is only fifty yards away to their right. But would that be a safe haven? People are keeping watch from their lookout atop the roller coaster. It's possible that they could be working with the Dusts or using them to draw in prey. They set up the teacup trap. Maybe this is all part of their plan.

'There's nothing we can do,' Pressia says.

His heart twinges. Her gaze is so intense, it's as if she's trying to memorize his face. No one has ever looked at El Capitan like that.

Hastings says, 'Aim for the eyes and open fire.'

'It'll just call more of them in,' Pressia says, but then she shakes her head. 'I guess it doesn't matter if you're killed by a hundred Dusts or a thousand.'

'It's all math at a certain point,' Bradwell says.

'Do what you want. I'm going out shooting,' El Capitan says.

'Shooting,' Helmud says.

PRESSIA

CRAZY JOHNJOHNS

As EL CAPITAN, BRADWELL, and Hastings open fire, Pressia's ears are ringing. Her vision blurs with sand and grit. She holds her knife tightly and is ready to keep fighting when she's struck on the back so hard she falls forward, landing hard. Her knife flies from her grip. Her palm skids across the ground, burning.

She can hear the Dust – its labored grunting.

As she whips around to face it, she feels the binding that keeps the vials in place twist and unravel, loosened by the Dust's sharp claw-strike across her back. Before she can pull the vials to her body, they tumble and roll in three different directions. She calls out, 'Bradwell! Cap! Hastings!' The Dust lurches toward her. Hastings fires a shot, obliterating the Dust's head, and it falls to the ground.

In the distance, the dirt starts to convulse. The quivering earth lets loose a cloud of dust. A fine crack splinters the dirt, running jaggedly toward Bradwell. He's oblivious. His head is up, his eyes scanning in every direction.

El Capitan shouts, 'Bradwell! Move!'

The noise of the rumbling is so loud that Bradwell can't hear. As Pressia scrambles away from the Dust, she wants to run to him, to pull him to safety. But the vials – she can't abandon them. She reaches and grabs one vial, then the next.

But the third is out of reach. She can't lose it. It's too precious. She pushes herself forward, lunging, but the ground starts to crack close to the vial. Its amber fluid trembles.

A dirt-caked hand emerges from the crack, pulling itself from the ground. A mangled Dust, hunched and battered. The vial teeters near its thick, mud-caked body as it heaves itself up. The Dust's left hand knocks into the vial at first and then crushes it beneath its palm.

'No!' Pressia cries out. The liquid soaks into the Dust's hand. And immediately the hard-packed dirt and sand breaks up. Its joints become bulky and thick. The skin turns ruddy and human looking – a large, swollen human hand. It's an astonishing hand – human and massive and strong.

The Dust stares at its hand, rubs it on its chest, holds it up, and gapes at it. Then the Dust just looks at Pressia. Clutching the two remaining vials, she crawls backward, quickly, getting to her feet and running.

El Capitan shouts to Pressia, 'Duck down!'

She kneels and tightens to a ball. El Capitan takes the Dust out with one shot.

When Pressia lifts her head, she sees that the ground all around Bradwell is still cracking; fine dark fissures zigzag all around his boots. He sees it now too. He's surrounded by widening cracks.

'Bradwell!' she shouts, but she can't help him. She grips the vials. Could she have helped if she hadn't gone back for them? She feels sick. 'Bradwell!' she calls again, uselessly.

Hastings, with his hyper-fast reflexes, runs toward him, pitches Bradwell's body into the air. Bradwell lands on his shoulder and looks up at Hastings astonished just as a hole cracks open under Hastings' boots. He falls into it and tries to climb out. But the hole isn't a hole. It's another trap, and it snaps shut. It has him by one leg. Hastings panics and fires at the ground itself, perforating the dirt. His eyes are wild. Pressia recognizes this look. She's seen it before in Special Forces – part terror and part determination. Hastings goes into overdrive to save what's left of him. He wrenches his upper body back and forth as if it's been fishhooked, and he uses his one leg on solid ground to push himself away from the locked trap.

Bradwell scrambles to his feet, sees what he's doing, and staggers backward.

El Capitan shouts, 'No!' Helmud shouts it too.

Pressia knows it's the only thing Hastings can do. She turns her back, not wanting to see it.

And then she looks at the Dust, the dead one whose hand had absorbed the contents of her mother's vial. Its muscles have flared and bulged – thick and strong, running up the forearm. She thinks about what her mother told Partridge – that the bionanotechnological medicine in the vials *can't disengage tissue*. *It adheres and builds it*. The human cells of the Dust's hand seem to have rebuilt themselves at a fevered rate. This medicine is a kind of cure that can't be trusted to know when to stop. It can't undo fusings. What would the vials do to the human cells lost inside her doll-head fist? She's amazed by the beautiful transformation, the sudden humanity of the Dust's hand – the taut elasticity of the skin over bone, muscle tissue. And then she hears the sickening snap behind her. Hastings lets out a hoarse scream – loud and seemingly unending. She turns.

He has ripped himself loose. His leg, from the knee down, is gone. There's only a bloody tangle of flesh and tendons, muscles.

Hastings hops twice and falls. His blood is pouring into the dirt.

'We need a tourniquet!' Bradwell shouts.

Pressia presses the vials to her chest with the doll head and, with her other hand, pulls off her belt. She runs to Hastings and Bradwell, kneeling beside him. 'I'll go as close to the wound as possible,' Pressia says. 'There's an artery, the femoral, that runs along the back of the knee. It's got to be cut off or he'll bleed out.'

Bradwell looks at her, impressed.

'I'm the granddaughter of a flesh-tailor. I've held down patients getting amputations.'

Bradwell pushes on Hastings' thigh while Pressia loops the belt around the meat of his leg and ratchets the belt, pulling on it with all her strength. El Capitan gives a hand. Together, they force a new hole through the belt's leather to keep it in place.

'Hastings,' Bradwell says, gripping the fabric of his uniform. 'Stay with us. Okay? Just hold on.'

El Capitan looks around. 'We're going to die out here.'

'Die out here,' Helmud says.

Pressia can feel it too. The Dusts are being drawn by the scent of blood. 'Bradwell,' she says.

He looks at her. 'Don't say it. I know. I should have had more faith in Hastings, maybe more faith in people in general.'

'It's not that.' She wants to tell him something. But what? They could die out here, and last time they were in this situation, she couldn't think straight, couldn't speak. Does she want to tell him that he makes her feel like she's falling? That she wants him to feel the same way about her?

'What is it, Pressia?'

She feels like her chest is going to explode. The wind and dirt are flying all around them. She grabs his sleeve. And then there's music somewhere overhead – plinking notes of some jaunty tune playing loudly over an ancient PA system, the shrill ring of feedback. The song is so worn out, it warbles.

'Like an ice-cream truck,' Bradwell says, but Pressia doesn't know what that would sound like. Ice cream came in trucks that played music?

Hastings tries to lift his head. 'Stay down,' Bradwell warns.

The Dusts know this song. By the looks of their contorted faces and their frantic blinking, this song means something awful to them. They lift their heads to the sky. They beat their ears with their arms. They kneel down, bow their heads. Some moan and cry out.

Then something whistles through the air. One of the Dusts' heads pitches back. It cries out, and when it pulls its chin to its chest, it's clawing at its eye. A bullet. Blood pours from the wound, soaks into the dirt-skin of the Dust's face. Another bullet pops next to Bradwell. He reaches out and pulls Pressia down to Hastings' chest and covers her. El Capitan and Helmud also cover their heads.

The Dusts start to push themselves into the ground. They're capable only of slow movements, but Pressia can tell that they're panic-stricken. More bullets strike the Dusts. One bullet hits and rolls in front of Pressia – a small, hard ball. She picks it up. Bradwell sees it. 'A beebee?' he says.

'What's a beebee?'

They look up at the amusement park, searching for the attackers. 'Where are they coming from?' Bradwell says.

Then a dart flies through the air, piercing a Dust's temple. The

Dust's eyes freeze, lock. It makes a gurgling noise in its throat and falls to its chest, limp.

Pressia looks at the long, knotted neck of the roller coaster. 'Whoever it is, they're protecting us.'

As the music keeps playing, the Dusts shrink back into the ground until, finally, the last few remaining eyes blink – once, twice – and they're gone.

The fence surrounding the amusement park is lined with spikes, which must be buried deep as Dusts can travel underground. She can see the top of the clown's hard plastic head, the split running along the bald pate, as if he's about to crack in two and reveal something else inside. His mouth is a bright red semicircle, his nose a red ball, and his eyes are bugged out. She feels watched.

Not far from the Crazy John-Johns clown head, there's a tall pole. Dented and bent in the middle, it's still managing to stand. Attached to the top are two bullhorn speakers that fan out like metal lilies. That's where the music is coming from.

Bradwell is on his feet, walking in the direction of the chain-link fence.

El Capitan and Helmud stand up and move slowly toward the fence, but Pressia stays at Hastings' side.

'Are the Dusts gone?' Hastings asks her.

'For now.'

Pressia feels dazed. The slow, exhausted chinkle of notes floats in the air. The wind is still strong, the air cold. Pressia says, 'Someone in there saved us. We need their help. We have to get Hastings somewhere safe.'

'You can leave me here,' Hastings says. 'I'll only slow you down.'

'Not an option,' Bradwell says. 'You saved me. I'll never forget it.'

'It's going to get dark fast,' Pressia says. 'And now that the car's dead—'

'Don't say the car's dead,' El Capitan says. 'It's just . . . resting.'

'Resting,' Helmud says.

'Fine then, with the car *resting*, we're live targets.'

'Pressia's right,' Bradwell says. 'We need to know who's in that amusement park. We need their help.'

Pressia spots a bloody dart on the ground, one that a Dust pulled from its eye and dropped. She gets up, walks to it, and nudges it with her boot. The handle is held together with duct tape. 'Look.'

El Capitan walks over. 'Duct tape? Jesus. I miss duct tape.'

Pressia runs the distance to the amusement park's chain-link fence. She peers in at the small, boxy lean-tos and imagines that they were once game booths, places where people could win a goldfish in a plastic bag, the way her grandfather had as a boy at the Italian Festival. Hadn't he said he'd thrown darts at balloons attached to a corkboard?

A shadow scurries from one small lean-to to another. Pressia walks quickly down the fence, hoping for another glimpse. And she gets one.

It's a girl, her gold hair long and ragged. Her left arm is shriveled, a stump just below her elbow.

It's Fandra.

After all this time, Pressia's dear friend is alive. It's like a piece of herself has been returned – and there is the wrecked barbershop, Freedle in his swaying cage, her grandfather with his stumped leg and whirring throat fan. She and Fandra used to play house, using blankets propped by the table and chair. It hits Pressia now that home, the kind made by her childhood imagination with Fandra, was the safest, truest home of all.

'Fandra!' she says.

Fandra runs up to the chain-link fence, hooking it with one hand. She's wearing a long skirt and sneakers, an old green windbreaker, partially melted at the collar. Pressia grabs Fandra's good hand with hers, their fingers latching through the metal wires. 'It's you!' Pressia says. She feels almost light-headed with happiness.

'Pressia! How did you get here?'

'Fandra?' It's Bradwell's voice. 'Fandra? Is that you?'

Fandra looks beyond Pressia. She smiles broadly. 'Hello, Bradwell.'

Pressia looks behind her to see Bradwell standing there, bruised and dusty, barely able to speak. 'I thought . . . and it was my fault . . .' He takes a few steps forward, but tentatively, as if she's a mirage.

'I'm not the only one who made it out, Bradwell,' Fandra says. 'The underground . . . it worked! We just couldn't send word back.'

Tears streak down Bradwell's dirty, ash-covered cheeks.

'You're part of New History,' she tells him.

'New History?' he says.

Pressia looks back through the fence. A few heads peer out from behind the lean-tos, a miniature train seared to a set of circular tracks and the upended disk of what was once a Tilt-A-Whirl.

'Fennelly?' Bradwell says, staggering toward the fence. 'Stanton? That you?'

'Yes, sir!'

'I can't believe it. Verden, you made it!' Bradwell says. 'I was sure you were gone. I was sure it was my fault.'

'We're here,' Fandra says. 'And we're alive, because of *you*.'

PARTRIDGE

HUMANITY

THE ACADEMY BOYS are now awake. They're playing their radios softly behind their shut doors. Partridge knows all the songs on the sanctioned list. This one is about the beach, which seems kind of cruel, as they'll likely never see a beach again in their lives.

'Where are we headed?' Partridge asks Iralene.

She glances at the guard, maybe asking permission to tell him. The guard nods. Iralene has introduced him. His name is Beckley.

She says, 'Your father is ready to see you.'

'Really?' Partridge says, feeling a sick jolt in his stomach. 'A little quality time with the old man. Where is he?'

Iralene looks at Beckley again.

'His office,' Beckley says.

It's in the medical center where Partridge was tortured. He doesn't want to go back.

A door at the far end of the hall flies open. A few boys pile out. They're younger than Partridge, and he knows only two by name – Wilcox Brenner and Foley Banks. They notice the guard first and then they look at Partridge and Iralene. They recognize Partridge. Everyone has always recognized him. But their reactions are charged in a new way. He can't read their expressions – fear, excitement, or, more simply, alarm?

They seem to know who Iralene is too. She nods to them, almost regally.

One of the boys shouts, 'Partridge! Hi!' like he's a fan or something. Beckley takes a quick step forward so he's out in front of Partridge, as if the kid is going to charge him.

The others knock the kid around. 'Shut up,' they mutter.

Obviously, a story about him has been passed around. Partridge wishes he'd thought to ask Glassings what that story might be.

The boys turn the corner and Partridge asks, 'What have they been told about me?'

'Your story has been leaked to the press,' Beckley says. There's only one newspaper, *The Update*. 'Cleaned up a little.'

'You can't call that propaganda a newspaper. It's just Dome press releases and society stories.'

'That would make you a society story,' Beckley says.

The guard opens one of the heavy doors to the courtyard. Iralene's eyes dart around its fake trees and boxy shrubs, like she can't drink in enough of what's around her. She's looking at the world the way a prisoner does when given a short reprieve.

'What's the story say about me?' Partridge whispers to Iralene.

She ignores him, raises her chin, and looks straight ahead. 'Beckley, aren't we taking a car?'

'The orders were to take you in by way of monorail.'

'They'll be packed this time of day,' Iralene says nervously.

'Yes,' Beckley says.

'I don't like all those people staring at me,' she says under her breath.

'Why will they be staring at you, Iralene? Why won't you tell me what's in the paper?'

'Don't you remember?' Iralene asks coyly.

'How can I remember what didn't happen?' Partridge says. 'How about Beckley here tells me?' They walk up the stone path to the school buildings that connect to the monorail on the lower floor. Beckley opens the door wide.

'You and Iralene met after a dance and fell in love. And then you were showing off for her and there was an accident and you went into a coma. She's stayed by your side all this time. Devoted to you. Rumor has it you're secretly engaged.'

'Huh. So I never escaped?'

'No.'

'I never risked my life or found my mother or watched my brother get killed or—'

'Hush!' Iralene hisses. The school building is empty, as it's a Saturday. The hushed halls echo with their footfalls and then Iralene's low voice. 'Your father told me the truth about that girl who dared you to escape to prove your love for her.'

'Lyda?' His father set her up as the scapegoat?

'Yes, her.' Iralene seems irritated by the mention of Lyda's name. She unsnaps her pocketbook, finds a tissue, and covers her nose with it.

'Is that the secret story my father fed you?'

She doesn't answer.

'Well, that's not what happened.'

'You regretted it, of course,' Iralene says. 'You were wrecked out there, ruined, nearly killed because of her!' She glances at the cap on his finger. 'Your father had mercy on you. People sacrificed their lives to save you!'

He can't tell if Iralene believes what she's saying or not. 'Seriously, Iralene. You can't really think that.'

'You could be a little thankful,' Beckley says with a shaming tone. 'My cousin is now in Special Forces because of the fallout.'

'The fallout?'

'The secret search to save you and then finding those poor wretches in such dire conditions,' Iralene says. 'Special Forces were built up, immediately, to try to help those poor lost souls.'

They head down a flight of stairs. 'Special Forces were there to hunt me down. And was it also broadcast that my father ordered robotic spiders that would explode those poor lost souls until I was returned?'

Iralene stops on a landing. 'Please, Partridge.' She reaches out and squeezes his arm. 'Don't say things like that.' She means it. She's begging him.

'Why are you so upset, Iralene? Because you know I'm telling the truth or because you think I should just go with the lie? But which lie, Iralene? There are so many to choose from.'

Iralene says nothing.

'And don't ever say anything like that about Lyda again,' Partridge warns her.

Iralene pulls her hand away quickly. The stairs rumble with the noise of an approaching monorail. They all hurry down the rest of the stairs, making it to the tracks just as it's pulling up.

She presses the tissue to her nose more tightly. 'I hate the smell of this place. Don't you, Beckley?'

'What smell?' Partridge says.

She looks at Partridge, tilts her head. 'Don't you smell it?'

The doors glide open.

'No, what smell?'

They step inside. The monorail car is packed with people, all chattering. Then, as they turn and stare, the car goes silent. A mother and her two children jump up from their seats, offering them.

'That's okay,' Partridge says.

But the woman says, 'Please! It's okay! My honor!' If he says no again, he worries she'll panic. They sit down, Partridge between Iralene and Beckley. The train hitches forward then glides.

Iralene whispers to Partridge, 'It's the scent of humanity, Partridge. It smells like mortality. Death.'

Partridge remembers the stench of ash and death shuttled around on the wind. Blood. The iron-scented air after his brother and mother were killed. That's death.

People smile and nod, but not just at him – at Iralene too. The tissue is still blocking part of her face, but he can tell she's smiling back.

'We're a couple,' Iralene says. 'I'm the one who stayed with you through that coma, the first name on your lips when you woke up.'

'Iralene—'

She shakes her head. Her eyes are brimming with tears, but she manages to smile. 'You were right. There are many truths. I can pick and choose anytime I want to. That's how it can work, if you want it to, Partridge.' And then she slips her fingers into his hand, the one with the capped pinky.

Partridge feels the eyes on him. He can't pull his hand away. It would be seen as a rejection. Rumors would start flying. It would hurt Iralene deeply. It might even put her in danger. This is her role in life, her mission. And since he's refused to kill his father, this is the truth that has to stand – for now. What will he say to his father when he sees him?

The monorail glides through the tunnels, stopping at brightly lit platforms. People nod as they leave, and the new passengers are surprised by Partridge and Iralene's presence. Partridge looks out the window. When the train hits a tunnel, all he sees is his own stunned expression blinking into the glass. He can pretend, for a moment, that Lyda is out there, on the other side of the glass somewhere. He wants to tell her that he's not betraying her. This will pass. He'll come back for her.

The train jerks to a stop. Beckley gets up first, as if they need a human shield to get them to the door. Partridge takes his hand away from Iralene. He doesn't want to have to hold it everywhere he goes from now on.

They walk onto the brightly lit platform and into the fluorescence of the medical center itself. This is the smell that makes him feel sick – not humanity at all, but the astringent antiseptic smell of covering up sickness and the sharp, sulfuric scent of enhancements. He remembers the academy boys escorted to their rooms, where they'd strip down and get into their mummy molds, that feeling of near suffocation, the enhancements coursing through your cells. Afterward, Partridge felt slack with exhaustion, but also filled with a jagged, nervous energy, as if all his organs, tissues, and muscles were spent except for his nervous system, which was charged like a battery.

As they make their way to the elevators, they get the same reaction as in the train. Fortunately, the elevator is empty. Beckley hits the fourth-floor button.

'Why the fourth floor? That's not where my father's office is.'

'He's in a special ward now,' Iralene says.

His father has been moved to the part of the hospital reserved for the seriously ill. The last time Partridge saw his father was on a screen in the communications room of the farmhouse. He looked weak, palsied, his chest was sunken, but his father, Willux, on the contagion floor? It seemed impossible. 'He's that sick?'

'He's in a weakened state – temporarily, of course,' Iralene says. Beckley radios ahead that they're coming.

The elevator is quiet except for a small tune leaking from an unseen speaker. It sounds computer-generated to produce a calming effect, but the fakeness has the opposite effect on Partridge. The manufactured music agitates him.

When the elevator doors open, they're met by techs holding white coats, paper slippers, masks, plastic caps, and gloves.

Iralene and Beckley stretch out their arms for the white coats, raise their hands for the gloves, and bow their heads for the caps, obviously used to the drill.

But Partridge says, 'Don't touch me. What's your problem?' The techs stand by stiffly as he dresses himself. He can't reach the ties in the back of the white coat, so one of the techs steps forward and does it for him. For some reason this is incredibly embarrassing, like he can't tie his own shoes. He feels stupid in the puffy plastic shower cap. The gloves cut into his wrists. He starts to walk but the slippers are, in fact, slippery. He feels emasculated, childlike. His father is so deeply manipulative that Partridge wonders if this is part of his plan.

Herded by half a dozen techs, they walk through automatic doors, passing two heavily armed guards. They turn onto a wing of empty rooms. Only the nurses' station buzzes with activity. This wing obviously has only one patient – Ellery Willux.

The technicians stop before they get to the door at the end of the hall. One says, 'There's a guard inside, but otherwise he's requested to see you alone.'

Everyone is watching now – the technicians, the doctors, the nurses, Iralene and Beckley, even the two heavily armed guards on the other side of the glass doors.

Partridge nods. 'Fine by me.' He starts to walk into the room, but Iralene touches his elbow. He turns and she kisses him on the cheek. Everyone sighs as if this is the sweetest thing they've ever seen. Iralene doesn't seem to notice that he's bristled. Instead she reaches up and touches his nose – ever so lightly – like it's a playful secret sign. He looks around at all the staring faces.

Iralene whispers, 'Good luck!'

He puts his hand on the door, but before he opens it, he suddenly has this incredibly optimistic hope – he'll open the door and there won't be a hospital room at all, but instead a little living room. His father will be healthy and sitting next to Partridge's mother, and Sedge will be standing by a window. They'll tell him it was all just a test, some kind of coming-of-age ritual that's been passed down for generations. 'We're a family again,' his mother will say. And Lyda will pop out of a side door.

But he knows that this is jaggedly insane.

He pushes the door open and steps inside.

The guard is there, as the tech said. He stands at attention beside the bed, which is covered by a clear, rectangular tent. The plastic tent shivers inward then puffs a little as if the tent itself is breathing. There are various pumps, chuffing and hissing. Machines chirp and beep; the only one he recognizes shows the rhythm of his father's heart.

These machines are trying to stall death, but it's here in this room.

For a minute, he thinks of his father, the man who held him as a baby, who tucked him in some nights, who's always been in his life. No matter how evil he might be, even if he's a mass murderer – on the greatest scale in all of history – some part of Partridge will never forget that he's his father. Your father can be the person you most hate and most fear, yes, but deep down you expect that he'll be the one to save you. Partridge feels weak. He remembers what Lyda told him – he still wants his father to love him.

And then Partridge hears his father's voice. 'Partridge.' And Partridge's cheeks burn, his heart beats hard. This is the man who killed his mother and his brother. Partridge won't ever forget that either. He steps closer to the tent. He sees the red oval of his father's face, the raw skin. But now his neck and one hand are blackened, as if the skin is completely dead. The hand has atrophied and looks like a claw, curled on his chest as if guarding his heart.

His father presses a button on the side of his bed. The plastic tent retracts on one side. His father's eyes are closed, but his chin is crimped, as if he's about to talk. His chest is enclosed in a large metal contraption, which is making the chuffing and hissing noises. The box must contain some instrument pumping his lungs. Oxygen tubes are screwed into the box on either side and run up into his nostrils. Partridge imagines pinching the tubes. It's a floating image. But he can't deny picturing it in sudden and vivid detail – his father gasping like a fish, his mouth gaping, stretching his cheeks until they're taut and ready to rupture.

'Partridge,' his father whispers as the box on his chest draws air. 'I knew you'd come back.'

'I wouldn't exactly say I volunteered,' Partridge says.

'You came back . . .' His lungs compress and expand in the box. 'Because you don't hate me. Tell me that you don't hate me.'

'Are you going soft on me after all these years?'

His father opens his eyes, blinking under the fluorescent

lights. His eyes are slightly clouded. The skin on his clawed hand and neck is shiny, as if it's wrapped in another coating of skin – clear and almost polished looking. 'I set up a world for you here. A world where you could travel. A girl. Have you noticed that?'

'You gave me a girl?' Partridge grips his father's bed rails.

The guard leans forward. 'Sir?' he says to Willux.

'It's okay,' Willux says. 'He's fiery. Just young.'

'Congratulations, by the way,' Partridge says, 'on the wedding.'

'Don't be sullen.'

'You're a sick man.'

'I'm dying.'

'That's not how I meant it.'

'Are you going to take' – the machine gurgles – 'what's being offered? You're a hero here.'

'I don't want to be a hero.'

'What do you want?'

'I want to be a leader.'

His father pushes another button on the bed rails, and the head of the bed rises. 'I've been waiting . . . to hear you say these words.'

'You have?'

'Who else would I want to replace me? Who else but you, my son.' He reaches out his good hand and holds it to Partridge's cheek. His eyes are wet and shining. Partridge has never seen his father cry. Sedge was his father's favorite, the one destined to do great things.

'Is that possible?' Partridge asks.

'You can be the one to lead them – out.'

'Out of the Dome? Into the New Eden?'

'I won't make it.'

'You really think I can do it?' Maybe he doesn't have to kill his father or even wait for him to die. Maybe his father will give it all to him.

Partridge's father pulls his hand from Partridge's cheek. 'You'll have to prove your willingness to leave the past behind, to move forward, with us, here in the Dome. Prove it not just to me but also to those in my inner circle, who know the truth of your departure.'

Partridge doesn't like the sound of this. 'How can I prove my loyalty?'

'We don't have much time.'

'What do you have in mind?'

The metal box around his father's lungs chugs and then releases a long hiss of air. 'Your mind.'

'My mind?' Partridge feels sick. 'What do you mean?'

'I want the part that remembers leaving us, that blue-eyed girl, those wretches you were with out there – everything outside this Dome – gone.'

'What?' Partridge says. 'No.'

'Aren't you haunted by the vision of death?'

He rears away from his father's decaying body. He walks to the far wall and spreads his hands on the cool tile; the cast on his pinky makes a sharp click. 'You mean visions of murder.'

'They would be erased too. The bad, the ugly, the dark.'

He sees Sedge's bloody body, his mother's face shattering as his brother's skull explodes. Blood. A thin spray of it like a bursting cloud. For a moment, he wishes it were gone – that memory – but he can't give it up, and he refuses to lose everything that means something to him. 'No,' he says.

'It's the only way,' his father says. 'It's the only way I'll let you in. You want in, don't you?'

'Think of something, *anything* else.' He looks at his father. He imagines cuffing his throat, bearing down with his thumbs.

'This is the only way,' his father says. 'You'll marry the girl.'

'Iralene?'

'You'll marry her and prove your loyalty by letting go of those memories, that slim section of your past – and that's it.' His father closes his eyes.

'And what if I say no?'

His father smiles, some skin on his face cracking. 'I'm not a forgiving man.'

Partridge shakes his head. 'It's not even possible. You couldn't erase memories that specific even if you wanted to. You're bluffing.'

'Arvin Weed is a boy genius,' his father says quietly, as if he's almost drifting off to sleep. 'He can do almost anything. *Almost* anything.'

Arvin Weed can erase Partridge's memories of his escape, of meeting Pressia, his sister, of Bradwell and the mothers, of El Capitan and the Dusts, of his mother and his brother, of being with Lyda in the brass bed frame on the roofless house.

But he can't save Ellery Willux from degenerating, cell by cell. He can't save his father from death. Not yet, at least. But as these machines hum and hiss to keep him alive, isn't the race on? If his father dies, he wants Partridge in charge. But the unspoken here is that if Arvin discovers the cure, his father won't need Partridge to lead. So if his father is willing to hand over the reins, Partridge needs to grab them, quickly.

PRESSIA

DUCT TAPE

THROUGH THE FENCE, Pressia spots an old merry-go-round, off-kilter but still sound. Its roof of bare spokes attaches to the horses' poles. The circular parade of horses is frozen and warped, their bodies partially melted, their muzzles contorted. A white horse bares its teeth, but its neck and mane are lank and twisted. There are torqued hooves and chopped tails. But worst of all are their eyes: still and wide, some melted down the slopes of their faces. Once upon a time, this merry-go-round was pristine – innocent and whimsical – which makes it all the worse now.

'You can't come in,' Fandra says. 'They've seen *him*.' She nods at El Capitan and Helmud, who's resting his chin on his brother's shoulder.

El Capitan is standing next to Hastings, whose bleeding has slowed but whose face is contorted with pain. 'Me? What's wrong with me?' El Capitan says.

'Me?' Helmud says, clearly insulted.

'You rule the OSR,' Fandra says to El Capitan, suddenly overtaken by rage. 'You've killed people we've loved. Do you think we could ever forget it?'

'Oh.' What could he say, really? He was a vicious and cruel leader.

Pressia tries to step in. 'He's changed,' she says, but she knows it will do no good. She sees the set of Fandra's jaw. 'He saves lives now. He helps people.'

'It doesn't matter. The only reason he hasn't already been shot' – she glances over her shoulder at the top of the roller coaster's broken neck – 'is because he's with a prophet.'

'A prophet?' Pressia asks.

'Bradwell,' Fandra says.

Bradwell looks a little stunned. 'Well, I'm no prophet—'

El Capitan interrupts. 'Look, hate me if you want and love him, but we've got a soldier who needs help.' Hastings.

'They'll take the dying one,' Fandra says. 'They take in the dying. It's how I came to live here.'

This small mention fills Pressia with hope. The survivors who live here aren't just those who escaped the OSR in the city. There were people already in place who survived the Detonations. Maybe there are more groups like them – and her father could be among them.

Just then, there's an electrical buzz. The gate opens. A few scrawny survivors appear, carrying a handmade stretcher constructed from a sheet wrapped around two metal poles.

'I need to know about my brother,' Fandra says, looking at Pressia and Bradwell. 'The last time I saw Gorse was during a bloody battle. Did he make it back?'

'He did. He's fine,' Bradwell assures her.

'I knew he'd make it. I *knew* it.'

It takes all the survivors who've stepped out of the gate to lift Hastings onto the stretcher. The plinking music is still blasting through the PA system to ward off the Dusts. The survivors keep their eyes peeled, and they all steal glances at Bradwell, obviously awed by him. A prophet.

'Wait,' Hastings mutters. 'You need the destination.'

'And your behavioral coding won't let you give it to us,' Bradwell says. 'What the hell are we going to do?'

Hastings shakes his head. 'No.'

'Put him down a minute,' El Capitan says. The survivors ease him to the ground.

'No, what?' Bradwell says.

'You were right not to trust me. It wasn't the behavioral coding that wouldn't let me give it to you. I've got the strength to override it.'

'Then why didn't you?' El Capitan asks.

'If I told you, it'd be one less reason to keep me around. I don't want to be expendable.'

'Tell us now,' Pressia says.

'Fignan,' he says. 'I want to tell Fignan. He'll understand the information I have.'

Bradwell unstraps the box from his back. Fignan lights up.

'Thirty-eight degrees, fifty-three minutes, twenty-three seconds North, seventy-seven degrees, zero minutes, thirty-two seconds West,' Hastings says.

Fignan whirs while accepting the data and blinks a green light when he's got it.

'Wait – tell us why this airship is different. Why isn't it with the others and heavily guarded?' Pressia says.

'All I know is what I heard,' Hastings says. 'It has sentimental value for Willux. I don't know how or why. And it's not guarded because Willux doesn't think a wretch could ever make it there alive.'

'Oh,' Pressia says.

'Sorry,' Hastings says. 'You wanted the truth.'

They lift the stretcher again and start to carry Hastings into the amusement park.

'You're going to take good care of him?' El Capitan calls to Fandra. 'We've got some medical supplies and an EMT who was here the day of the Detonations with his kids. He knows what he's doing.' The fence closes behind Hastings' stretcher with that same electrical hum.

Pressia is trying to remember her grandfather's explanations about amputations – the angles the sawing should take, how best to keep the bone shavings away from the wound, the best dressings and the uses of certain oils to keep the wound from adhering to the dressings, the elasticity of woolen socks, even pressure. 'Tell him that you don't want to let up on the arteries. Every drop of blood is a great loss. If they add up, that's how you'll lose him.' Her grandfather lost one once. A young girl with a crushed leg who bucked on the table, loosening the tourniquet. Her grandfather tried to get it back on, but the girl's thrashing and the slickness of the blood made the tourniquet hard to grip.

'I'll tell him,' Fandra says, and then she lowers her voice and whispers to Pressia, 'I'm so glad you two are together. You found someone to love who loves you back.'

'What?' Pressia says. 'Who are you talking about?'

'You and Bradwell,' Fandra whispers, surprised Pressia doesn't know.

Pressia shakes her head. 'No, we aren't together.'

Fandra smiles. 'I see how he looks at you.'

'It's going to get dark,' Bradwell calls to Fandra. 'Is there any place safe enough for the night?'

Fandra points into the distance. 'There's a stone underpass from an elevated train track. You'll be okay if you take turns standing guard.'

'Thanks for helping us out there,' Bradwell says. 'Without it, we'd be dead and buried.'

'We owe you,' Fandra says. 'You know that, Bradwell. So many of us here owe our lives to your lessons in Shadow History, the underground, and you. Thank you!'

'You're welcome,' Bradwell says, obviously choked up.

'I imagine you all have set out to do something important?' Fandra says.

'Or maybe just crazy,' El Capitan says.

'Go on, then,' Fandra says. 'And keep going!' She steps away from the fence.

Pressia misses her already, and not only Fandra but her childhood, the tents of sheets – *pup* tents – called home.

'We'll see each other again,' Pressia says.

Fandra nods and then runs off back into the depths of the amusement park, and she's gone.

Set against the sky in one direction, there's the bare stalk of a tower, with the charred frames of chairs dangling from it. Pressia imagines for a moment what it would have been like to be there when the Detonations hit – the air filled with light, the force of the heat, and, if you survived at all, to be suspended in midair, dangling above the earth, seeing the hysteria and destruction in every direction. She looks at Bradwell. Fandra thinks they're together, that they found each other – *someone to love who loves you back*. And then it's as if she is being spun by one of these rides. Her stomach flips. Bradwell, his clothes ripped in places, dotted with blood, his muscles riding beneath his shirt. His ruddy cheeks and dark lashes. Bradwell.

They start walking, but she has to look back at the roller coaster, black and bony against the darkening sky.

PRESSIA

FIREFLIES

AFTER WALKING FOR AN HOUR or so, they find the stone underpass. It's beaten but standing. They sit on the ground, eat from the provisions El Capitan has brought – heavily salted meats. When they're finished, El Capitan offers to take the first watch. He walks up the incline and sits on the tracks.

Bradwell says, 'We should snug up, backs to the wind.'

Pressia nods. They lie down together, him curled around her, his arm wrapped around her waist. Her heart is thudding in her chest, but it's countered by this gnawing in her stomach – that same old gnawing that she's named fear.

'What do you think Hastings meant about the airship having sentimental value?' Pressia asks him.

'Willux is a romantic, according to Walrond. Aren't romantics sentimental?' Is Bradwell a romantic, deep down? Isn't his footlocker, filled with memorabilia of the past, sentimental?

'You know what I'm sentimental about?' Pressia says.

'What?'

'The things I don't remember – stuff I've only heard about.'

'Like what?'

'Like fireflies,' Pressia says. 'During the Before. Do you remember them?'

'The yards had too many chemicals for lightning bugs to survive, but farther out, in the unmown fields, they used to crawl up the grass at dusk and flash a little yellow light. My father took me out to the country once to see them. They blinked off and on and we chased them, caught them, and put them in glass jars, poking holes in the lids.' She can feel his warm breath touching the edge of her ear. 'But I thought you wanted to know about the Detonations, not the Before.'

'I've remembered things now. A few.'

'There were other kinds of insects just after the Detonations.'

'What kind?'

'They were fatter than lightning bugs, more like glowing blue butterflies that flashed and then disappeared into thin air. They were beautiful. After I left my aunt and uncle's house, people were dying everywhere, but some of the ones who could still walk tried to catch these phosphorescent things – little flames, that's what they were like, these quick little darting flames. I almost went with them, remembering my father and the unmown fields, but this woman grabbed my arm. 'Don't follow them,' she said. 'They are drawn to death.' She shouted warnings too, but they didn't listen.'

'And what happened to the people who tried to catch them?'

'The people who touched those little flames – even if they only held one for a second, trying to bring it back for their dying kid to see – didn't last long. They were sick within a few hours and dead from the radiation poisoning within a few days – quick, violent deaths.'

Pressia shudders. 'I have a feeling that won't go away.'

'What is it?'

'It's a feeling in my stomach. I've thought it was fear, but maybe it's guilt.'

'What do you feel guilty about?'

'Being alive.' She tries to imagine the glowing butterflies darting and disappearing and the people, out there, sickly and staggering and trying to catch some beauty. And then she thinks of her mother in the forest, sickly and staggering, kneeling next to her dying son, her eldest, Sedge. Pressia feels the weight of the gun again. Her ears start ringing and suddenly she's crying.

'Pressia,' Bradwell says, holding her more tightly. 'What is it?' His voice is somber, almost scared.

'No,' she says. 'I can't tell you.' She hears the rustling wings of the birds embedded in his back, brushing the cloth of his shirt. She can't look at him. She can't say a word. The bloody mist is a cloud around her.

He sits up a little and tilts his head so it's touching hers. 'Tell me. Tell me what it is.'

She says, 'I killed her. I thought it was the right thing to do, but now . . . I'm not sure. I don't know.'

'No,' he says, 'I was there. It was a mercy.'

She can't catch her breath.

'I felt that way for a long time, Pressia. I hauled all of this guilt around for years.'

'What did you feel guilty about?'

'I was asleep in bed when my parents were shot, Pressia. I slept through their murders.'

'You were just a little boy.' Pressia turns and faces him. 'It wasn't your fault.'

'And it's not your fault that your mother is dead. It was a mercy. I was there.'

'I know why they didn't listen to the woman's warning about the blue butterflies,' Pressia says.

'Why?' Bradwell says.

'They needed something to catch and hold. They needed beauty. I can't explain it. They needed to believe that something beautiful might come from all the terror. I understand the impulse to want to believe in something beautiful again – and hold it in your hands like that.' It's dark but she can see the shine of Bradwell's eyes. He's staring at her intently. He cups her face in his hands, which are warm, strong, and rough. He kisses her. She closes her eyes and kisses him back, feeling his chest pressed against hers. His lips are hot. She grips his shirt. Everything around her seems to fade.

When he pulls away, they're both breathless. 'What were you going to say to me out there when the Dusts were circling us?'

'Something about falling . . . how you make me feel like . . . I'm falling and crashing.'

He kisses her, quick kisses – her mouth, her jaw, along her neck. 'When I first met you, I thought we were made for each other even though we seemed like opposites in some ways and we fought. But now . . .'

'What?'

'Now I feel like we weren't *made* for each other. We're *making* each other – into the people we should become. Do you know what I mean?' She does, immediately. It feels like the truest thing she's ever heard.

'Yes,' she says, kissing him. 'I know what you mean.'

PARTRIDGE

CAKE

Pᴀʀᴛʀɪᴅɢᴇ ɪs sᴛᴀɴᴅɪɴɢ in a bathroom in someone's upscale, topfloor, roof-access apartment in the Wenderly, back on Upper Two. The Crowley family? He's not even sure who's hosting the party, only that it's in honor of his engagement to Iralene. It dawns on him that he doesn't have a ring. Isn't he supposed to propose first? He thinks of Lyda. He gave her the music box. It meant more than a ring. It was the truth. This is all fake, temporary.

Partridge can hear the murmur of conversation, the occasional laugh rippling above it. These people know he escaped, although they think he did it on a dare, to impress a girl from a bad crowd. But they can't know his father wants him to hand over his memory of it all. Then what? They'll all pretend the story of the girl from the bad crowd also disappears? These people are good at denial. They practice it daily, like a religion.

Arvin Weed – this is his hope. Glassings might have his doubts, but Partridge has to hold out hope that Arvin is going to get him through this – hopefully he can fake the damn operation. He's a boy genius after all, right? He hopes Arvin's here somewhere in the small crowd and that he can get a minute alone with him.

Partridge strips down and takes a brand-new suit off its hook. He puts on the pants, buttons the cuffs of the shirt, knots the light blue tie, and pulls on the dark blue suit jacket. It fits so perfectly – even the smooth contours of the leather shoes – that he wonders if they got his measurements from his old mummy mold. It's disturbing how much they know about him – not just his shoe size but down to his DNA.

He doesn't want to smile and shake hands. Will Iralene's mother, Mimi, be here? He wonders if she comes out of her capsule for these kinds of things.

There's a knock at the door. 'Do you need anything?' It's Beckley.

'I'm fine.'

'People are asking for you. Are you ready?'

'Just a minute.' He pops off the cast on his pinky. One day, will there be any sign that it was chopped off? If his memory gets erased, will there even be the tiniest scar left over to tell what happened? His mother's research made this possible. She could have rebuilt her own limbs with bionanotechnology, but she refused. Her body was the truth and she wasn't going to cover it up. Partridge wonders what the hell he's doing here.

Beckley knocks again. 'Sir?'

Partridge replaces the cast, opens the door, and strides out ahead of Beckley, toward the voices. 'Let's get it over with.' He walks through the living room, which is white and fluffed, and out onto the terrace.

Everyone turns. Some start clapping. Someone clinks a fork against a wineglass. He sees faces he recognizes – all smiling and laughing and calling his name. There are neighbors from Betton West, where Partridge grew up, the Belleweathers, the Georges, the Winthrops, and high-ranking officials – Collins, Bertson, Holt, and some he recognizes only from public announcements, including Foresteed himself, who's become the face of Dome leadership. More people are chiming in with their forks against wineglasses. Even the help, young men and women in white shirts and navy-blue vests and bow ties, have frozen in place and are smiling at Partridge. They're serving real food – puffed pastries, cubed chicken skewered with toothpicks. What do they expect from him?

Beckley leans forward. 'You could wave.'

'What?' Partridge says, baffled.

'Nod or something.'

Partridge gives a small wave then tucks his hands in his pockets, not sure what else to do. He's actually relieved when he sees Mimi in the crowd. She is leading Iralene to him, beaming. Her skin shimmers with makeup. Her hair is piled up in a loose network of curls on top of her head, like a tiered cake.

Iralene's dress and corsage of dyed-blue flowers match Partridge's tie. She's holding a boutonniere, with the same dyed-blue flowers. The flowers look real, fleshy, not plastic at all.

'Hello, Partridge,' Mimi says. 'It's so nice to see you again. How lovely that this has all worked out.'

Iralene lifts herself on her tiptoes and kisses Partridge's cheek. The crowd gives a collective *awww* and finally the clinking stops. Partridge can feel the heat in his cheeks, but it's not because he's embarrassed by the public display of affection. No. He's furious. How far does this have to go? Why do they have to be paraded like this? Iralene pins the boutonniere to the lapel of Partridge's suit. When he thinks she's done, he backs away, but it was too soon, and Iralene pokes herself with the needle. A dot of blood beads on her finger.

'Sorry,' Partridge says.

'It's okay!' Iralene says.

'Just finish the job,' Mimi says angrily, handing her a cocktail napkin.

Iralene pushes the pin all the way in. 'There,' she says.

The couple then turn around and face the crowd. Mimi says, 'Please eat, drink, mingle! We'll have some dancing later!'

Dancing would only make him think of Lyda. He'll have to get out of it.

'It wasn't my idea,' Iralene whispers. 'Don't blame me, Partridge.'

'Of course not,' he says. He reaches down and holds her hand. 'We still have our secret, Iralene, to help each other. Don't we?'

'Yes.'

She's wearing an engagement ring. He lifts her hand. 'Where did this come from?'

'You,' she says. 'You gave it to me before the accident!'

'You can't do this, Iralene.'

'But you agreed to your father's plan. Your memories are going to be gone. I'll fill them in for you. This is how you help me.'

'Is that what he's got planned? My memories will be erased and then I'll be force-fed the story from the society pages?'

'You can choose the truth—'

'Stop.'

'Neither of us can stop this, Partridge. It's bigger than both of us.'

'Weed can stop this,' Partridge says. 'I need some air.'

'We're already outside,' Iralene tells him.

They're outside on the roof deck. But the air here is no different from inside the apartment. Partridge feels claustrophobic. He scans the crowd. That's when he sees Arvin Weed wearing a red tie, lifting a puffed pastry off one of the waitress' trays.

Partridge thinks of all those train rides with Weed's head bowed to his screen, reading, the way that made him invisible. The last time Partridge saw him, the day Partridge had planned his escape, just before Vic Wellingsly offered to beat Partridge's ass, Arvin had given Partridge a look as if, for a second, he might stick up for Partridge. But then he didn't. When it comes right down to it, does Weed have enough courage to be on Partridge's side? Partridge has seen him tested, watched him tuck his chin to his chest and let his eyes glide back to a screen. Weed's got to help him this time. It's his only chance.

'I see an old friend of mine,' Partridge says. 'I'm going to catch up with him.'

'You don't want to introduce me to him?'

'I just need a little time, okay?'

Iralene nods. 'There's cake. I'll see if it's going to be brought out soon. I'll meet you back here.'

'Fine.' Making his way through the crowd is harder than he expected. His father's friends stop him, shake his hand, clap him on the back. They make jokes about marriage using prison terms, and Partridge hates them for it. *This* is a prison sentence, more than they'll ever know, he'd like to say.

Across the room, Arvin is being congratulated too. Partridge can hear little bits of praise, sees the telltale handshakes and back-claps. What did Arvin win now? Partridge catches Arvin's eye. Arvin looks around nervously, downs his glass of punch, excuses himself from his admirers, and walks toward the punch bowl for a refill.

'We need some fresh blood,' Holt says. 'We're glad your father's bringing you in.'

'I'm looking forward to it,' Partridge says, keeping an eye on Arvin, who's now being lauded by Mr Winthrop, one of Partridge's neighbors, a top adviser of his father's and an avid tennis player.

'What's Arvin Weed's latest accomplishment?' Partridge asks the group.

They all start talking at once. 'A team effort and a real breakthrough!' 'Great work!' 'A true feat of scientific achievement!'

Partridge feels sick. Has Weed figured out the cure? The men keep prattling on and finally Partridge cuts them off. 'You have no idea what the breakthrough is, do you?'

They look at one another. Holt finally says, 'Message from on high told us that it was truly praiseworthy.'

'But you don't know *what* you're praising him for?' Partridge is exasperated, but also filled with dread.

'Not really,' Holt says.

'Not at all?'

'No,' Holt confesses. 'But it's truly great, Partridge. Truly.'

And then Foresteed himself appears – broad-chested, lightly tanned, his hair a little stiff. 'Partridge! How good to see you safe and sound. You had us worried.' He pats Partridge's shoulder in a fatherly way, but then glances at Holt and smiles. He leans in. 'We've all had our heads turned by a pretty face, though. Right, Holt? Happens to the best of us. I got the chance to sow a few wild seeds myself.'

'Excuse me?' Partridge says. Is Foresteed talking about Lyda? Is that what this is about? Lyda corrupted him and he had wild seeds to sow?

'That's right,' Holt says. 'We're men, after all.'

'Boys will be boys,' Foresteed says. He grabs the back of Partridge's neck now and rattles it a little, as if he's being playful, but Partridge has always been suspicious of chummy people. As his father's son, he's had to be.

He sees Arvin edging away from Mr Winthrop. 'Excuse me. There's someone I've got to talk to.' But Foresteed grabs him by the arm and pulls him in close. He whispers, 'You know, I've heard that the operation erases everything right up until the moment you were put under and only as far back as they pinpoint it.'

'Interesting,' Partridge says.

'Which means I could say anything right now and it'll be washed clean away.'

Partridge looks up at Foresteed's square jaw, his narrowed eyes. 'Go ahead, then. Say what you want to say.'

'You're just a little shit, Partridge. That's all you are and all you'll ever be. And if you think I'm going to let you take over because your daddy says so, you're wrong.'

Partridge stares at Foresteed, refuses to look away. 'Nice to know that you're a coward. Why don't you tell me that again when I can remember it, huh?'

'I'd prefer it take you by surprise.'

Partridge twists his arm and Foresteed releases his grip. 'Happy engagement!' Foresteed says loudly.

Partridge tries to head Arvin off before he makes it to the door. 'Weed!' he shouts.

Arvin keeps moving.

Partridge shoves through a small circle of women. 'Sorry. Excuse me.' He cuts Arvin off just as he's about to slip out. 'Are you ducking me?'

'Partridge!' Arvin says. 'Hey, I was hoping to see you but figured you'd be swamped. I gave up trying.'

'Really? Because it seemed like you were trying to sprint out.'

'No, no,' Arvin says. 'Not at all.'

Partridge grabs him by the elbow and walks him into a corner of the living room. 'Don't screw with me, Arvin.'

'Hey, that hurts,' Arvin says. 'Not all of us got the same enhancements, you know. Can you lighten up a little?'

Partridge lets go of Arvin's elbow. 'What enhancements have you gotten? Brain and . . .'

'Behavioral? I oversaw my own enhancements, Partridge. I've been given incredible resources and power. You can't imagine.'

'No,' Partridge says. 'I can't. I'm a pawn here, Arvin. So tell me, what's all this congratulatory buzz for? What's your breakthrough?'

'I'm not at liberty to say.'

Partridge lowers his voice. 'Is it the cure?'

Arvin looks at the ground, shakes his head ever so slightly. 'No? It's not the cure? What is it?'

'I can't say!' Arvin's flustered. He looks back up at Partridge.

'Don't get irate, Weed. Listen, I'm relying on you.'

'Well, you've got that right. I'm completely in charge of the next phase,' he says, suddenly cocky.

'What's going to happen to me, Arvin?'

Arvin tugs at his necktie. 'How's the pinky progressing?'

'Fine. Don't change the subject.'

'It's really amazing what we can do these days. Regrow a pinky? I mean, as a kid, did you think we'd ever be able to do that?'

'I never thought I'd *need* to regrow a pinky.' A waitress walks by with a platter of cheeses. 'No, thank you,' Partridge says and then, once she's passed, he whispers, 'Don't dodge the question. I want to know what's going to happen to my memories, Weed.'

'Memory's a tricky thing. It isn't infinite. It's a net. Your mind is an ocean. We can dredge only so far.'

'What's that mean?'

'There are things you consciously remember and then there are things that have settled down into the deepest silt on the ocean floor of your memory. Your subconscious. If something is down that deep, we can't touch it. We can try to damage pathways, but that's about it. Then, after a short time when there's limited access to the damaged pathways, they get sealed off forever.'

'But I'm not going to have to worry about that. Am I, Arvin? You're in charge. You're going to take care of it.'

Arvin winks again – the same kind of nervous, almost undetectable winks that he gave Partridge when he was going through his cleansing. Arvin's on his side; Partridge is almost sure of it! 'Your pinky is being regrown, Partridge. It's amazing. You should be happy with that science.'

'Yeah, I guess so.'

'Be happy about it,' Weed says, like a command.

'I'm happy, okay? I'm very, *very* happy that I'll get my pinky back. All right?'

'Some elemental part of your pinky still existed. That's why it could be brought back.' Is Arvin telling him that his memory will be able to be brought back too because some elemental part of it exists deep down?

'It's dark outside,' Arvin says.

Partridge glances over the crowd of guests on the roof deck. 'It's gotten late.'

'It's only going to get darker,' Arvin says.

This sends an icy shiver through Partridge's body. It's a warning. Whatever Partridge thinks he knows, Arvin Weed knows more.

Arvin looks at a vase of flowers. He touches the center of a flower. 'It's not the cure,' he whispers. 'It's worse than that, Partridge.' *What can be worse than the cure?* Arvin shows Partridge his finger, dusted with pollen. 'Nice touch,' he says. 'Real flowers. Wonder where they got 'em.'

Partridge wants to ask him more questions – so many he's not sure where to start – but Iralene arrives. She glides her hand along Partridge's arm.

'You found me,' he says.

She turns her mouth to Partridge's ear and whispers, 'They've brought out the cake,' as if sharing an intimate secret.

'Good to know,' Partridge says, and then he introduces Iralene and Arvin.

'I know Arvin,' Iralene says. 'Nice to see you again.'

Arvin shakes her hand awkwardly, pumping it too hard then looking at his shoes. He was always nervous around girls. It's kind of comforting that some things don't change.

'How do you two know each other?'

'Lessons,' Iralene says. 'I've been taking private tutorials over at the academy. Brushing up. It'd be a shame if I couldn't enter into intelligent conversations with you, Partridge. Wouldn't it?'

'We ran into each other a few times in the academy halls,' Arvin says, looking up, 'when I was there visiting friends.'

'Who have you taken lessons from?' Partridge says. 'Which teachers?'

'A few here and there. It was so boring I could barely stand it.'

'Glassings? Welch? Hollenback? Who?'

She shrugs. 'What's the difference between any of them, really?'

'I should be going,' Arvin says.

'Do you want some cake?' she asks. 'It's lemon cake!'

'Thank you,' Arvin says, 'but I'm full and I've got to take off.'

'Oh,' Iralene says, pouting. 'Sorry to see you go.'

He smiles at Iralene but doesn't seem to have anything to say. He turns to leave, then doubles back. 'I'll see you tomorrow, Partridge.'

'Tomorrow?'

'Your father's a great man but not known for his patience. The procedure is scheduled for tomorrow.'

'But . . . no. It's too soon.'

'What can we do about it? Right? All you can do is prepare yourself. Mentally.'

Mentally, Partridge thinks. How do you mentally prepare yourself to lose a chunk of your mind?

And then Arvin pauses for a moment. He wants to say something, but he looks at Iralene and her presence stops him. Partridge can tell that instead of saying what he wanted to, Arvin is trying to put it another way.

'What is it?' Iralene asks.

'Nothing,' Arvin says. 'I'm just glad Partridge is back. That's all.' He looks at Partridge. 'Glad you're back. You're here.'

'What do you mean?' Iralene says and she pokes Partridge with her elbow.

'Back? Here? Ha, ha!' Partridge says. 'I never left.'

LYDA

CAIRNS

IN THE MIDDLE OF THE NIGHT, Lyda slips her hand under her cold pillow. She finds the metal edge of the music box that she keeps hidden against the plaster wall. She pulls it to her chest. Usually, she'll open it – for a brief second – to let a few notes out as if the music itself might suffocate in the box and die. But this time she doesn't. She sits up and slips her bare feet into her cold boots. She doesn't lace them. She doesn't get dressed. She simply puts on her coat over her sleeping dress – given to her by the mothers. Freedle lets out a mechanized chirp. He wants to come too? She lets him perch on her shoulder, close to her neck, where her long hair once draped. She walks as quietly as she can past the sleeping mothers and their children. It's winter, so they're congested, a little wheezy, and restless.

They're living now in an old storage room beneath what was once a factory that manufactured some kind of candy – something gummy that required animal parts. Almost a decade later, the air still smells sickeningly sweet with a dark undercurrent of death. The smell of the factory makes Lyda feel sick. Mother Hestra spent the day telling Lyda about pregnancy – how she will continue to feel sick and light-headed for a while, but that this will pass as she swells, how her breasts will feel tender – they already do – and how she needs to eat more. Lyda asked about labor and birth, but Mother Hestra said they would talk about that later. 'Only so much we need to get to now.'

Lyda's mind is drawn to the future. When new babies are born of survivors, they're also altered in some way. Their parents have been so deeply affected by the Detonations that their genetic coding is altered. And the changes may be also environmental. Radiation has been drummed and sealed into the earth, air, water. It rides on the ash and is breathed into lungs. Lyda was taught this in the Dome. Will her child be altered too? She's had dreams where she gives birth to something furred, mangled, fanged, its ribs glittering with glass.

Partridge isn't worrying about this. He doesn't know a thing. She feels more alone than she ever has in her life. It's been a month since she's seen him. Sometimes she pictures his face and the image breaks apart in her mind.

Holding the box, Lyda walks out of the storage room and into the airy factory itself. There's only one light – a dim one. It guides her down rows of old conveyor belts, machinery, exposed pipes. The mothers have gutted this place, per usual. They've stripped away gears, chains, rubber handles, levers, everything of value, giving the space a hollow feel. Lyda knows that Mother Hestra wants to tell Our Good Mother about the pregnancy soon, and Lyda is afraid of what judgment she might dole out. Our Good Mother terrifies her.

She grips the box tightly to her chest and walks as fast as she can. There is no door on the other side of the factory's large room – only a rectangle where one used to stand. She steps out into the cold night air. Freedle chirps lightly, perhaps happy to be outside.

As alone as she feels, she doesn't want Partridge to hear anything about the pregnancy. It would distract him from his mission. And now his mission has become more personal. She thinks of the girl she saw, Wilda – not born Pure, but made Pure. If Lyda's child is marked, will she want the baby to be made Pure? She'd like to think she wouldn't, that, instead, she would be proud of her child, in any form. But sometimes she thinks that the child would want to be Pure; it's natural. If the others find a way to reverse Rapid Cell Degeneration, the child might be able to be made whole.

She also doesn't want Partridge to know she's pregnant because she wants him to come back for her out of love, not obligation. She hates herself for thinking like this. He isn't coming back. She must keep telling herself this. Some part of her feels like he doesn't deserve to know about her pregnancy. This is hers. He is gone. She has to learn to rely solely on herself.

The ground is hard-packed cement and icy dirt. Lyda walks around the corner of the factory, and there's a graveyard. It's makeshift and small, surrounded by metal spikes that have been driven into the ground and roped with barbed wire. The spikes go deep so that the Dusts can't infiltrate.

Lyda unlatches the gate and locks it behind her. Instead of tombstones, there are cairns, pale rocks neatly piled over each grave. Two of the graves are fresh – a mother buried alone and a mother and child buried together. The mother and child used to sleep on cot number nine. Lyda stops by their cairn. The stones are so white they seem to glow. She places a hand on the stones. It seems, for a moment, that everyone in the world is replaceable.

This mother and child are gone. But Lyda and her child are coming. One day they'll be gone too – buried under a pile of rocks or left like Sedge and Partridge's mother in the woods. Bodies. Is that all we are? Is there also the wick of soul stirring inside Lyda, inside the baby too? Is she doubly souled now?

The metal box.

She walks to the corner of the graveyard and picks up a trowel by its rough wooden handle. She kneels, sets the music box on the ground, and lifts the trowel with both hands, stabbing the cold dirt as hard as she can. It breaks a little. She strikes the ground again and again, her breath coming out in huffs, then she wedges the trowel in deeply enough that she can upend one chunk of dirt, then another.

Eventually there's a small hole. She picks up the music box. Freedle opens his wings in anticipation; he's always loved the tune it plays. She winds the tab, her fingers so numb that it's hard to get them to work. She remembers the warmth of being with Partridge under his coat in the middle of the four-poster bed frame. She needs him right now. Tears slip down her cheeks. She opens the music box one more time. The notes pop up. Freedle flits in the air over her head. She lets the music float in the cold. The music box winds down, slower and slower, until it's done.

She starts to wedge the box into the hole, but then she stops. She winds it up one more time, but she doesn't open the lid. One day, if someone digs it up, she wants it to play for them. It's what the music box was meant to do. It may be too corroded to work by then, but she wants it to have that chance.

Freedle lands on the ground beside her. Is she trying to bury Partridge in some way too? No. That's not possible. He's still with her, no matter what. She'll always hold on to some part of him.

Burying the music box means that she's stopped hoping he will come back for her. She can't live that way anymore. She has to get used to the idea that she'll fend for herself and her child. She'll make it, alone.

She pushes it deep into the hole, covers it with the clods of dirt, and presses the dirt down, tamping it with the trowel.

PARTRIDGE

SEVEN SIMPLE TRUTHS

I'M SUPPOSED TO WALK YOU to *your* door,' Partridge says, 'if we're going to be traditional about this.'

'And kiss me under a porch light,' Iralene says. They're back in the hallway, standing in front of the locked door to Partridge's room. Iralene holds the key and looks at Partridge expectantly.

He sticks his hands in his pockets, sending the message that he's not making a move. 'I wonder what the room is set for. Do you know?'

She slips the key into the lock. 'If you don't like it, I can change it to anything you want.' She opens the door, but before Partridge walks inside, Iralene says, 'That goes for me too, Partridge. I can change. I can be the person you want me to be.'

'Iralene,' Partridge says.

'Thank you,' Iralene says, looking down at her hands, 'for saying yes to all of this. For pretending in front of all those people that you actually want to marry me. Thank you for all of it, Partridge. I know that this night didn't mean much to you, but for me . . .' She looks up at him and smiles, but the smile is fragile.

'Where do you go, Iralene, to sleep?'

She says, 'Downstairs, silly.'

'Iralene,' he says. 'Downstairs is a mirage. It doesn't exist. Where do you go?'

'You know where I go,' she says. 'Don't make me say it.' And then she laughs as if she's kidding around, as if this is all fun and games.

'It's not good for you,' Partridge says. 'It can't be good for you.'

'Preservation,' Iralene says. 'There's nothing better for your longevity.'

'Do you have dreams in those capsules? You can't. Your brain is too slowed down, like all of your other cells. You can't dream in there.'

'Are you inviting me in?' Iralene says. 'They'd like that, even if you took advantage.'

'I wouldn't take advantage.'

'If you don't think I should be in a capsule,' Iralene says, 'then invite me to stay with you tonight.'

He's not sure what to say.

'It's okay, Partridge. I'm used to suspension. I'm one of the lucky ones!' He thinks of Mrs Hollenback in the kitchen. *Lucky us*. If Iralene is lucky, who's unlucky?

'Stay,' he says.

She smiles and bows her head shyly. 'Thank you.'

They walk into the bedroom. It's rustic, with a patchwork quilt on the bed, faded flower-print curtains, a view of a moonlit prairie.

'I can turn off the cameras, you know,' Iralene says, 'for the right reason.'

Partridge glances up at the cameras perched in the corners of the room and then back at Iralene. She's pretty. That's the honest truth. But he can think only of Lyda and feels an ache every time. His fingers remember the feel of her skin. He has to have faith that Arvin has a plan that will save him from the operation tomorrow. He can't lose Lyda. But also he wants the cameras off. He wants to think, even for a short while, that his life is his own. Maybe if he's not being watched, he can think more clearly. 'Okay,' he says. 'Let's turn 'em off.'

Iralene walks up close to Partridge. She leans in so close that he can feel the heat of her body. She whispers, 'For the right reasons,' her lips brushing his ear.

He nods for the sake of the cameras.

Iralene reaches into her pocketbook and pulls out the orb. She touches the screen and each of the cameras clicks off, one by one. Partridge sighs and sits down on the edge of the bed. Arvin told him to prepare himself mentally, but how? He looks at Iralene. 'I have to ask you something, Iralene.'

She sits down beside him and draws a crazy eight on his leg. 'Anything.'

He lifts her hand and puts it back in her own lap. 'What did you mean when you said you were the lucky ones?' There's something about it his mind won't let go.

'Willux suspends us for the right reasons. You know, the way he's put in orders to suspend those who are stricken with various ailments, hoping for science to catch up and be able to cure them.'

'Those stricken? Like who?'

'People think that we have the resources to take care of all those people in rehab centers who can't be released back into society and the babies who are born not quite right. Well, don't waste resources, right? Not when you can suspend them.'

Partridge thinks of baby Jarv. Is he in the hospital, or is he suspended in a cold capsule somewhere? 'Who told you this?'

'No one tells me anything,' she says. 'They talk in front of me like I'm an imbecile, and things sink in.'

'Are you saying that . . .'

'We have no neighbors, Partridge, only icy compartments that keep people from aging – or at least slow it all down.'

Does Glassings know this? My God.

'It's all for the best,' Iralene says. 'Daddy's helping people.'

'Don't call him that.'

'But your father is my stepfather and he's going to be my father-in-law one day too. Right, Partridge?'

'One step at a time, okay? Just tell me how my father is helping people.'

'I've grown up down there, on ice and not, wandering the halls.'

'Iralene,' he says. 'No, don't say that.'

'It's the truth and I'm not sad about it, because I don't know much else, do I?'

'Iralene, I'm sorry.' Maybe he's apologizing for his father.

'It's okay. What I'm telling you is that there are some I've found, some capsules on this one corridor on the floor below us, that are different.'

'How?'

'They're Daddy's little relics.' *Little relics.* He's heard the expression before. Ingership said it to Bradwell just before he died. He said that Willux wouldn't mind adding Bradwell to his collection, his *little relics.* 'I think they're a collection of people he doesn't want to kill but doesn't want alive either. He simply wants to keep them.'

'Iralene, you're not lucky. This is no way to live.'

She puts her hands on Partridge's face. 'Save me from it, then. Save me.' She kisses him. Her lips are soft, but he pulls away. He holds each of her wrists gently.

'We're going to get through this,' he says. 'But not the way they want us to. We're not falling in love.'

She stares at him for a moment.

'I'm not going to fall in love with you, but I'm not going to abandon you either. I'll see us both through. Are you listening?'

She nods, but her eyes are fixed and distant, as if looking through Partridge.

He picks up a few extra pillows and sets them down in the middle of the bed, making a divider. He says, 'Here. Sleep on this side.'

Iralene lies back, stiffly. She gently rests her head on the pillow.

'Go ahead and dream tonight,' Partridge says.

She closes her eyes. 'But I think I've forgotten how.'

Partridge gets up and walks to the other side of the bed. He imagines Jarv in a child-size capsule – his face frozen stiff. Partridge has to remember Jarv after he undergoes the operation, that Jarv needs him. He has to remember everything.

Prepare yourself. Mentally. What did Arvin mean?

The wink. Partridge realizes how much he's relying on Weed's stupid wink. He was sure it meant that Weed would save him, but what if Weed's turned into a tricky bastard? Or what if he's got some damn eye disorder? Jesus, Partridge thinks. He's got to go in and risk it, believing in Weed, but he also has to come up with a contingency plan. If his father gets his way, is there someone he could trust to tell him the truth of his life? If Glassings told him that he'd broken out of the Dome, found his mother and his brother, and watched his father kill them, that he has a half sister out there and a girlfriend he's promised to go back to, he'd think

Glassings was drunk. And it wouldn't be in Iralene's best interest to tell him that he's in love with Lyda and that his engagement to her is a fake.

He can trust only himself. He has to find a way for his current self to tell his future self the truth. Iralene's asleep already, breathing heavily.

Partridge spots her pocketbook on the bedside table next to her. He walks quietly back around the bed, picks it up, and pokes through her tissues, lipstick, a few folded bills. He feels the hard edges of Iralene's identification card – a picture of her, updated per usual at sixteen. She looks the same, down to the gentle waves in her hair. He's about to slip it back in, but then his eyes catch on the issue date – eight years ago. It's not possible. Eight years ago, Iralene wasn't sixteen yet. How long has she been suspended? She was chosen for him, and then her aging was slowed so that he could catch up? Did his father choose her when he was just a kid? Earlier even? Did his father put Mimi and Iralene on the list because he was already seeing Mimi before the Detonations?

He looks over at Iralene, half expecting her face to have suddenly aged. She's twenty-four years old. Iralene doesn't just look young. She seems young. But what makes people grow up? Experience. She's been robbed of that incrementally for his sake. He's immediately stunned by guilt. But he didn't ask his father to do this for him. How dare his father do that to Iralene?

He puts her identification card back in her pocketbook. He pushes his fingers to the bottom of the purse and feels the ridges of a pencil. He pulls it out, along with a square receipt. Before the party, Iralene bought breath mints.

Partridge has to write in small letters. He's so overwhelmed, he numbers his thoughts.

1. *You escaped the Dome. You found your half sister, Pressia, and your mom. Your mom and Sedge are dead. Your father killed them.*

2. *You're in love with Lyda Mertz. She's outside the Dome. You have to save her one day.*

3. *You've promised Iralene to pretend to be engaged. Take care of her.*

4. *In this apartment building, there are living people, suspended in frozen capsules. Save them. Baby Jarv might be among them.*

5. *Trust Glassings. Don't trust Foresteed.*

6. *You don't remember this because your father made you have your memory of your escape erased. He caused the Detonations. People in the Dome know this. He must be taken down.*

7. *Take over. Lead from within. Start over again.*

These are seven simple truths. From there, he can figure out the rest. And now he has to hide the list. Where?

He walks around the bedroom and then into the bathroom. Because this is supposed to be a rustic farmhouse, the bathroom is outdated. There's no shower, just an old claw-foot tub. The sink is a basin with two spouts – hot and cold. And the toilet is the old kind with a worn seat and a box attached to the wall. Instead of a handle to push to flush, there's a cord to pull.

There's a simple problem: If he hides it, how will he know to look for it?

He looks at the box attached to the wall again, the pull string.

He flips the lid down on the toilet and stands on top of it. He looks inside the box. It's half filled with water. A chain leads to a rubber bobber. Pulling the string moves the bobber, lifting a stopper that allows all the water to rush down the pipes and into the toilet below.

If he unhooks the chain, the toilet won't flush. He'd have to figure out how to fix it and he'd find himself back here again, standing on the toilet lid. If he wedges the note in between the box and the wall but fitted under the box's lid, the note would flip to the floor when he opens the lid the next time.

He quickly folds the note into an accordion. He writes on the top fold *To: Partridge. From: Partridge. Read me.*

He shoves it in and realizes that he'll need to devise a plan to get back to this room. What kind of plan? He has no idea.

And then he hears a scream. He runs into the bedroom and over to the bed. Iralene is kicking and thrashing.

'Iralene!' he shouts. 'Wake up!' He holds her shoulders. She claws his chest. 'Iralene!' he shouts again.

She opens her eyes, gasping for breath, and looks around the room, like a caged animal, and then she looks at Partridge. 'What happened to us?'

'Nothing,' he says quietly. 'It was just a bad dream. A nightmare.' She throws her arms around his neck and holds him tight. 'We were so small. We'd become so small, and they'd forgotten about us. I tried to call to them. I tried to fight to get help, but there was nowhere to go. And we were so tiny, Partridge, like dolls in little plastic containers.'

'It didn't happen. You were just dreaming. Shhh,' he says, stroking her hair. 'Shhh. It's okay. You need to fall back to sleep.'

'Is it really okay? Are you sure?'

'Just a dream. Everything's fine. It's going to be all right.' He tries to believe what he's saying. 'I promise.'

'Please hold me,' she says.

He lies down and she puts her head on his chest, fitting

her hand in between the buttons of his shirt.

'I want you to remember this,' she says. 'That you were good to me. Tomorrow, after your operation, I'm going to tell you about this moment. How sweet you were.'

'This is my favorite version of this room, Iralene,' he says. 'Tomorrow, when you remind me of this moment, make sure it's this room – not a vacation spot or a big city. This room feels like home. Promise me you'll keep it on this one. I want to live in this one. No matter what I say tomorrow, make sure this is the one we come back to. Okay?'

'This one. I'll make sure. I promise.' She smoothes the wrinkles of his shirt. Her head on his chest, he imagines she hears his thudding heart. They're awake and alive in a building filled with suspended bodies – the living dead.

'Can I turn the cameras back on, Partridge? I feel safer with them on. Watched over. And I want them to see us together like this. Can I?'

'I don't like them, but, for now, okay.'

She reaches over to the bedside table and presses the screen on the orb. The corner cameras' lens covers retract with the familiar clicking. And once again, the eyes are on him.

PRESSIA

SOLSTICE

Pressia SLEEPS FITFULLY and finally wakes up. Beneath the layers of her coat and two wool sweaters, she feels the curve of her back snug to another warm body. She turns quickly.

Bradwell, fast asleep; she's shocked by the bulk of him, like finding a beautiful bear in her bed – but she's not in bed. She's in a stone underpass. She remembers that there are fairy tales about bears and beds, but she can't remember how they go. The flank of his ribs rises and falls. Both of them fully dressed, his legs crisscross hers. They kissed and kissed until her lips felt raw and, finally, they had to fall asleep.

The birds embedded in Bradwell's back stir beneath his shirt. It's night but she can make out his face in the ash-dimmed moonlight – his features are so peaceful that he looks young. He *is* young, she reminds herself. They both are. And he looks so vulnerable that she can almost imagine what he'd have been like if none of this had happened – the murder of his parents, the loss of Walrond, the Detonations . . . Is it possible that Bradwell could have been the sweet, tenderhearted type? Maybe some part of him is still tenderhearted and that's why it's taken them so long to find each other again like this. He's afraid of getting bruised just as she is.

She instinctively touches the two vials, now wrapped around her stomach. They're safe.

She won't be able to fall back to sleep, and it's probably time to relieve El Capitan and take her shift. She slips away, pulls her rifle over her back, and picks up her knife.

As she makes her way out of the underpass, she hears singing – a rough, low voice singing a love song about a man whose lover died in the Detonations. Pressia's heard it many times before.

Ash and water, ash and water makes the perfect stone.
I'll stand right here and wait forever 'til I've turned to stone.

It has to be El Capitan's voice. She puts her back to the side of the hill, stays quiet, and listens. His voice is sad, mournful, heartsick. She didn't know that he had this in him. She wonders if El Capitan is in love with someone or if he's lost someone he loves. There's no other explanation for the depth of longing in his scratchy voice.

She doesn't want to embarrass him by getting caught listening, so she walks back into the underpass and steps out again, coughing loudly.

He stops singing – mid-note.

She calls his name. 'Cap?'

'What is it?' he says gruffly.

She climbs the hill and finds him sitting between the dented mangled tracks, cradling his gun. Helmud is on his back and El Capitan is rocking a little, as if he's trying to keep a baby asleep – Helmud or the gun? He doesn't seem to know he's doing it. Fignan is there beside him, silent and unlit. 'Why don't you head in and get some sleep. I'll take my turn.'

'Where's Bradwell?'

'Asleep.'

'Really?' he says, as if he's accusing her of something. Does he know that they kissed?

'Yeah, really. He'll take his turn next. I couldn't sleep.'

'I see.'

'What's wrong with you?'

'Nothing.' He stands up. 'You want Fignan here or should I take him with me?'

'Leave him,' Pressia says. 'If it's quiet enough, I can do some research.'

'So far, it's been quiet – more or less.' He starts toward the hill. 'We're really just starting out, and we're already a man down. We need to focus. All of us.'

'I know that.'

He raises his eyebrows at her as if doubtful. She doesn't like the suspicious look in his eyes. Helmud lifts his head sleepily. He sees Pressia and smiles. Pressia says, 'Go back to sleep, Helmud.' El Capitan looks over his shoulder at his brother. 'Yeah, go to sleep.' He turns and jogs down the hill.

It's cold. Pressia wraps her arms around herself. She hums the song for a few minutes, thinking of Bradwell. The song is about waiting for someone who isn't coming back. Her fears creep back in.

The terrain is desolate and quiet, so she says to Fignan, 'Wake up. Let's work.'

Fignan's lights blink on. His legs buzz out from his body and he perches on them.

'I want more information about Ireland, and about New-grange,' she says.

Fignan shows her a dizzying array of information – a history of wars, topography, weather, geology, even a few mentions of Irish mythology, poetry, storytelling. The air around her is lit as if she's warming herself by a campfire.

Eventually, he homes in on Newgrange, which is older than Stonehenge and the Pyramids, and was built by an advanced ancient culture. Inside its dome, there's a passage that reaches about sixty feet to the center of the mound. Once a year, during the winter solstice, the sunrise shines light directly into that passageway into the heart of the dome through some kind of special opening, called a roof box, just above the entranceway. This now happens four minutes after sunrise, but five thousand years ago, it would have happened exactly at sunrise.

There's something about it that makes her mind itch. She asks Fignan to tell her about the winter solstice – the shortest day and longest night of the year. 'When is it this year?' she asks.

'December twenty-first,' Fignan says in his slightly metallic voice. 'Sunrise is at eight thirty-nine a.m.'

'Why were they obsessed with the winter solstice?'

Fignan takes her to another page of information about how some researchers thought it had been a burial mound, but others thought it had been a place of worship for an astrologically based faith.

'Which brings us back to Cygnus,' Pressia whispers. 'The constellation.' She feels strange all of a sudden. She has a sharp twinge in her chest and she's breathless. It's as if her body has figured something out that her mind hasn't yet understood. Astrologically based faith. Sunrise. December twenty-first. Eight thirty-nine a.m.

'How long does the sun shine in the chamber?' she asks Fignan.

'Seventeen minutes,' he reports.

'And it illuminates the floor, right? The floor of the chamber?'

Fignan lights up, as if confirming this information.

Pressia lifts Fignan and scrambles down the hill beside the underpass. She shouts, 'Bradwell! Cap! Helmud! Wake up!'

Bradwell lifts himself to one elbow. 'What is it?'

El Capitan, who's sleeping just beyond him, says, 'What the hell?'

Helmud asks fearfully, 'Hell?'

'Walrond,' Pressia says. 'Remember what he said?'

'What? Can I get a little context?' Bradwell rubs his eyes with his beautiful hands, the hands that were on her body, the hands she loves.

'Walrond said *Time is of the essence* in the message. Remember? You wondered why he'd say something like that, didn't you?'

He sits up. 'Yeah. I mean, time was only of the essence when they had a shot at stopping Willux before he detonated the world – not now.'

'What's this about?' El Capitan says.

'I was just researching Newgrange, and there, time is of the essence only once a year,' Pressia says. 'On a certain day at a certain time.' She explains the mound, the passage, and the light that illuminates the chamber. 'For only seventeen minutes.'

'Do you think that's where Walrond might have hidden the formula?' El Capitan says.

'If Walrond knew there was a good chance Willux would spare the dome in Newgrange, he'd have hidden it there and maybe this is how he pinpointed it,' Bradwell says. 'This could be his X marking the spot.'

'We have to go now,' Pressia says. 'We have to collect our

things and go. December twenty-first is only three days away. We need the light on the floor. We need those seventeen minutes.'

'The box is a key,' Bradwell says.

'A key,' Helmud says. 'A key.'

———

The terrain is flat, windswept, dusty, ashen. The sun edges up on the horizon. Fignan has Hastings' coordinates and has set a course. Dusts rise up here and there. They take turns shooting them – in most cases a single bullet from a rifle suffices. Aside from that, they're all quiet.

Bradwell glances at Pressia. She wants to believe they share a secret, but El Capitan is suspicious. Did he see them kissing?

El Capitan eventually breaks the silence. 'It's like the pulsing tattoos on your mother's chest, Pressia. Those survivors at Crazy John-Johns must be proof that there are little clans of survivors like this, maybe all over the world. Anybody wondering who else is out there?'

Pressia thinks of her father. 'Yes,' she says.

'It's possible,' Bradwell says, glancing at Pressia again. 'But we can't get our hopes up.'

'If it's possible that people have survived,' she says, 'it's also possible that, somewhere, some of them have thrived.'

El Capitan says, 'It's theoretically possible.'

Helmud nods, thoughtfully.

'We can't be thinking theoretically right now. Okay?' Bradwell stops dead in his tracks. 'Listen. We're all hounded by the same thought, aren't we?'

El Capitan and Pressia stop too.

'What's that?' El Capitan says.

'We can be as optimistic as we want, but we're all afraid we won't make it. Chances are we'll die out on this trip.'

'We can't afford to think like that,' Pressia says. 'We can't afford not to,' Bradwell says.

She looks down at her doll-head fist, its eyelids, clotted with ash, fluttering in the wind. It's as dangerous to fall for someone as it is to be optimistic. Is that what he means? She told him she was falling, but he said they were making each other. Is he backpedaling now?

'Let's just all shut up and keep moving,' El Capitan says. 'Let's not think at all, just take the next step and the next.'

'Not think at all,' Helmud says.

'Fine,' Bradwell says.

The terrain eventually opens to hills, scrub pine, stalks of barren trees. They follow a road that's been blasted to gravel. Some of the bits of rock still hold on to the yellow paint of the old dividing line.

They come to a river. Upstream there's a dilapidated dam. The top of the dam is still intact but it's covered with cracks and fissures, one of which leads to a hole that seems punched out of the middle of the dam, forming a spout. The river has reasserted itself below, churning and rushing, and Pressia can't help but think of almost drowning, the deep chill of being locked underwater.

When they reach the dam, El Capitan climbs to the top of it, bends to one knee, and inspects the ground. 'It's passable,' he shouts. 'There are animal tracks running across it, both ways.'

Bradwell says to Pressia, 'We get to stay dry this time.' There's something about the shine of his dark eyes that makes her want to dive into the water and almost drown just to lie down with him again – that feeling of being close to him.

'I guess we do.'

She climbs to the top of the dam. From there, she sees small clumps of rubble, collapsed buildings, ripped roads, a few charred husks of cars, a bus fallen to one side, disintegrating into the ground.

Bradwell follows her, and Fignan claws up next. 'Quaint Americana,' he says.

'How much farther, Fignan?' El Capitan asks.

'Farther?' Helmud says.

Fignan calculates and says, 'Eighteen point two miles.'

Bradwell stops. 'Eighteen point two miles? That might put us close to DC. Can you put those coordinates up on a map from the Before, Fignan?'

El Capitan walks over.

Fignan shows a map, a wide angle of where they are and where they're going.

'Close up on the destination,' Bradwell says.

Fignan tightens the screen.

'Is that DC?' Pressia asks.

Fignan's screen freezes.

'That can't be right,' Bradwell says.

'What is it?' Pressia asks.

'A dome,' Bradwell says. 'Well, I'll be damned!'

'What dome?' El Capitan says.

'It's DC, all right,' Bradwell says. 'Didn't anyone ever take you on a field trip, Cap?'

'I went to a colonial village once,' he says. 'We watched people make wax candles.'

'Is it a famous dome in DC?' Pressia asks.

Bradwell shakes his head. 'It can't still be standing.'

'*What* can't be standing?' Pressia shouts. 'Tell us!'

'The Capitol.'

'The capital of what?' Pressia asks.

Bradwell shoves his hands in his pockets and stares out into the distance. 'The Capitol of the United States of America,' Bradwell says. 'In other words, the Capitol Building. It was a dome. It was a beautiful dome.'

'Jesus,' El Capitan says. 'The US Capitol Building? *That* dome? Is *that* where the airship is?'

Bradwell nods. 'What's left of it, I guess. Can't be much.'

'Willux parked an airship at the US Capitol Building?' El Capitan says. 'Now, *that* is sentimental!'

'Willux,' Helmud says, amazed.

The wind whips around them. Bradwell says, 'You're going to get your field trip after all, Cap.'

Pressia starts walking across the top of the dam. The wind is strong and when it gusts, she's afraid it will kick her off. She hunkers lower. The wind lifts her hair, billows her pants and coat. She tries to imagine an airship inside a massive dome. What would that look like?

She makes the mistake of glancing over the steep edge, the water shooting from the hole, pounding and foaming below, and immediately wishes she hadn't. When she looks up, she sees something dart out – a small, bristly-haired Beast. Its back is up, arched almost catlike. But it's more like a large rat with sharp teeth, bared. It emits a sharp, high squeal. Its feet are thickly clawed, perhaps retractable. 'We've got a friend here,' she says.

'I'll take it out,' El Capitan says.

The Beast's eyes are slightly rubied. 'It's going to pounce,' Pressia says. 'You better have good aim.'

El Capitan raises his rifle very slowly. Helmud covers his ears.

When the Beast hears El Capitan cock the gun, however, it leaps at Pressia. She crouches and rolls. El Capitan fires, but the Beast is in motion and he misses. Its narrow, fanged muzzle is now in Pressia's face. She punches and rolls too close to the edge. Her legs slip off, just over the gaping hole spouting water. She's holding on to the edge with her one hand and the elbow of her arm with the doll-head fist, her cheek skinned by the cement. The Beast is snarling in her face.

El Capitan lunges at the Beast this time, gripping the skin at the back of its neck as it bites and claws. Bradwell grabs Pressia's arms. She holds tight to Bradwell's coat sleeve, her knuckles against his muscled shoulder. He pulls her in close. She keeps a hold of his coat, steadying herself, catching her breath – soaking up the feeling of being close to him.

Helmud hits the Beast, trying to get it away from his brother. El Capitan finally wrestles loose. The Beast has drawn blood, but it caterwauls and limps away.

Hands on his knees, El Capitan is breathless. He looks up at Pressia and seems to notice the way she's still holding on to the sleeve of Bradwell's coat. If he thought there was a deeper allegiance between Bradwell and Pressia, it might not sit right with him. El Capitan is unpredictable. She lets go of Bradwell, brushes dirt from her pants.

Bradwell says, 'What the hell *was* that?'

'Some kind of weasel,' El Capitan says.

'I was almost killed by a weasel?' Pressia says.

'But you weren't,' Bradwell says. 'We saved you. Some would even call that romantic.'

'Not my definition of romantic,' El Capitan says.

'You've got a definition of romantic?' Bradwell says, surprised.

'What? I can't be romantic?' El Capitan says. 'So happens I

believe in that kind of thing. But not just saving a girl. That's only chivalry.'

Pressia remembers El Capitan's voice, mournful and rough. Maybe the idea of Pressia and Bradwell together reminds El Capitan of the love he lost, the one he was singing about. It's hard to imagine El Capitan in love, but of course he's capable of love. He's human, no matter how tough he pretends to be.

'Everyone gets to be romantic,' she says. 'If that's what they're after.'

LYDA

VOW

LYDA IS SITTING ON A STOOL in the factory in a row of mothers, peeling the dry, rough skin of tubers. They're pocked with nubs, some of which have grown little strings, almost like tentacles. Others have been kept in storage so long that they've grown what look to be purplish claws, as if they intend to turn into Beasts and crawl off. Lyda doesn't mind the work, though. Once the skin is gone, they are bright white and slick. They slip like fish from her grip into the bucket to be filled; then they'll be hauled off and steamed. The soft ticks and scrapes of paring knives are the only noises.

When she sees Mother Hestra walk through the factory's empty door frame, her stomach knots. Mother Hestra has spent the morning waiting to make a request of Our Good Mother – to allow Mother Hestra and Lyda to speak to her alone about a private but urgent matter. Our Good Mother doesn't usually accept requests for individual appointments. She believes in solidarity and that any piece of news is better absorbed by the group all at once. *A wave could crash down on an individual and sweep them out to sea. But if we stand together, we buoy up and then down. It's but a ripple.*

Our Good Mother terrifies Lyda. She'd rather not talk to her at all.

And yet, Mother Hestra's expression is one of muted triumph; even Syden looks like he's happy. She says to Mother Egan, 'Lyda has to come with me. This is a request of the highest order.'

Mother Egan says, 'Highest order, huh?'

Mother Hestra nods.

'Fine, then. Lyda? You heard. Go on now.' Mother Egan is in charge of the tuber peeling and looks like a tuber herself – dry, dark skin, a few pocks. She doesn't have a child attached to her. She lost her children during the Detonations. Lyda stands up, holding the hem of her apron, catching the peelings. She stands over the garbage and brushes the skins into the can and puts her stool back against the wall.

All the mothers are looking at Lyda now – their children too. They watch Lyda in a way she's gotten used to. They're proud to claim a Pure as one of their own, but they despise her too. They assume Lyda knows no suffering. Some whisper to her, 'Aren't you pretty?' and 'You have very fair skin' – compliments, except their tone is hostile. Once she found a note on her pillow that read, *Go back. We don't need your kind here.* And when Mother Egan first gave her a paring knife, she said, 'Be careful with that. Wouldn't want to scar that creamy Pure skin.'

It's these times when Lyda misses Pressia. She didn't know her well, but they went through a lot together, quickly, and Pressia never seemed to hold Lyda's background against her. She's sure that if she could tell Pressia about the pregnancy, she would have a real friend, a confidante. Where is Pressia now?

She misses Illia too; her stories, though strange and dark, were transporting, and they seemed to have lessons in them, the kind mothers hand down to daughters.

As she walks out of the cavernous room, she feels their eyes on her back. She wonders what they will think of her when word gets out that she's pregnant. They'll hate her even more, won't they? For being careless and stupid. For giving herself over to a boy so thoughtlessly. They'll think she's a slut. She's heard the word before. Three girls were whispered about like that at the girls' academy. They wound up in the rehabilitation center. They stayed a long time and came back somber, wearing shiny wigs until their hair grew back. What punishment will be doled out here?

The day is overcast, the sky a darker gray. The clouds look more ashen at their edges.

'Did you tell her?' Lyda asks Mother Hestra.

'That's for you to do. She knows there's something to tell.'

'Will she kick me out? She wouldn't do that to a young mother, would she?'

Mother Hestra doesn't say anything for a moment. Finally she sighs. 'She's unknowable. But it's good that we're telling her alone first.'

They pass the graveyard. Part of her suddenly wants the music box back. But she knows she shouldn't want this. Partridge is gone.

They walk to another building – the vat room, where Our Good Mother has been living. Two women stand guard at the door, heavily armed. They don't have just spears and darts and knives – these are old weapons of choice; they now have guns stolen from the Basement Boys.

Mother Hestra says, 'I've brought her back with me. Highest orders.'

They allow Lyda and Mother Hestra to step inside.

The vat itself sits in the center of the high-ceilinged room like a huge metal caldron. Our Good Mother's throne is behind it. But today she's not there. She's lying on her back on a cot while one of the mothers pulls on her neck. The mother says, 'Deep breath in and hold it. Ready?'

Our Good Mother closes her eyes lightly and nods.

The mother twists her head with a quick jerk. Our Good Mother's neck pops. She sighs. 'Thank you.'

The mother stands. She has a child sitting on one of her hips, resting her head on her mother's chest. The mother sees Lyda and Mother Hestra. 'Someone's here for you.'

Our Good Mother looks over. 'Yes, they have an appointment.' Lyda expects her to sit up but she doesn't. Though it's cold, Our Good Mother's arms are bare, and Lyda can see the baby mouth in her biceps clearly. It's wet with spittle and makes a little pursing motion with its lips. 'Speak to me,' Our Good Mother says.

Mother Hestra says, 'Lyda's news is very—'

'Not you,' Our Good Mother says. Her eyes are closed again and she's lying perfectly still. Lyda can see the hard metal of the window frame embedded in her chest, its light rise and fall in sync with her breathing. 'Lyda, tell me this urgent news.'

Lyda takes a small step forward. 'I'm not sure . . .'

'Is it news from the Dome? Has he contacted you?'

'Partridge?'

'Who else?'

'No,' Lyda says. 'I don't think he can.'

'So he's abandoned you altogether?'

Lyda pauses. 'I guess you could say that.'

'Well, that's not news. A Death is a Death. This is what Deaths do. They leave.'

She looks back at Mother Hestra. *Tell her*, Mother Hestra urges. *Do it.*

'But before . . . ,' Lyda says, turning back to Our Good Mother. 'Before he left . . .'

Our Good Mother opens her eyes.

Lyda takes a deep breath. 'Before he left when we were running, Special Forces were everywhere and—'

Our Good Mother pushes herself up to a sitting position. She looks at Lyda, her eyes tightening, her face covered with the small fissures of wrinkles.

'We were alone when we were running. And there was the warden's house. It had no roof and—'

'Tell me what happened in the warden's house.'

'The top floor,' Lyda says. 'There was nothing over our heads. And there was an old bed frame. Four posters. Brass—'

'What did he do to you in the warden's house, Lyda?'

Lyda shakes her head. She can tell she's about to cry. She knits her fingers together. 'He didn't do anything to me. It wasn't like that.'

'Are you trying to tell me that he raped you?'

'No!'

Our Good Mother stands up. 'You're saying that he abducted you from Mother Hestra, dragged you to the warden's house, where no one would hear you scream.' She moves in close to Lyda's face. 'And he raped you?'

'That's not how it happened! He didn't rape me. It wasn't like that.'

Our Good Mother slaps Lyda so hard and fast that it doesn't even hurt at first. It only burns and then the stinging rises, hotly, to her cheek. She reaches out, and Mother Hestra's hand is there to steady her.

'Don't ever defend a Death,' Our Good Mother says. 'Not here. Not to me.' She whips away from Lyda, walks to the wall, raises her fists, and pounds them on the wall until she whimpers from the pain. She stops and seems to be frozen there, her head swung low.

'She's pregnant,' Mother Hestra says softly.

'I know,' Our Good Mother says.

The room is completely quiet for a long time. Finally, Lyda can't take it anymore. 'What are you going to do to me?' she asks.

'I'm not going to do anything to you,' Our Good Mother says. 'It's what I'm going to do *for* you.' Our Good Mother's voice is a rough whisper. It scares Lyda more than her fists on the wall.

'What do you mean?'

'I'm going to kill him,' she says matter-of-factly.

'What?' Still shaken and unsteady from the slap, Lyda's knees almost give out beneath her. 'No, please.'

'It's the truth,' Our Good Mother says. 'I will kill him, and to get to him, I will have to kill others along the way. It's inevitable, but it's time we planned an attack on the Dome. Time to fight.' She walks to Lyda.

Lyda can't fathom that something so fleeting and quick and innocent could start a war. Others are going to die because of those few moments in the warden's roofless house. 'Don't,' Lyda whispers, crying. 'Not for me.'

Our Good Mother puts a gentle hand on Lyda's stomach. She looks at Mother Hestra and says, 'A baby we can all hold. The first since the Detonations.'

'The first,' Mother Hestra says. 'It will be beloved.'

Our Good Mother sighs and puts a finger to the baby mouth

in her arm. She fits the finger into it and rubs the lower gums. 'Two baby teeth,' she says. 'Did I tell you that? After all these years, two small white buds.'

PARTRIDGE

FIBERS

WHEN HE WAKES UP, Iralene is gone. Her side of the bed is perfectly made and she's reset the room to the beach, which gives him a surge of panic in his gut. Will Iralene be good to her word and switch it back to the farmhouse when he comes back? If not, he's screwed.

Breakfast is set out for him – again, real food: oatmeal and pink juice. The cameras watch him with their glassy eyes. He stares into them, as if to tell those watching that he's not afraid. It's a lie. He's so scared he can barely eat. He walks to the window and sees the old man combing the beach with his metal detector. He leans out the window and shouts, 'Hey, stupid fake old man! You're doomed! You'll never find a damn thing!'

The man turns, smiles, and tips his hat.

There's a knock at the door.

'Come in.'

He assumes it'll be Iralene, as she seems to be with him at all times. But it's Beckley's voice behind the door. 'Here to take you in,' he says.

'Already?' Partridge says. 'Can't you give me a minute?' He's not sure what he needs a minute for. He'd like to turn the room into the farmhouse and check to see if the note's still in the toilet box. Without Iralene, he can't.

'They need you to come in now,' Beckley says.

'Goddamn it,' Partridge says. He hears the rattle of the key in the lock.

Beckley swings the door open. 'Ready?'

Within an hour, Partridge is back in the medical center, scrubbed and dressed in a hospital gown, lying on an examination table in an operating room, alone.

He hears the familiar click and hum of the air-filtration system. Straight up in the ceiling there's an air vent. The air pours down on him and he wishes it were more like the feel of wind. The air vent was his escape route before. But now he has to stay. He has to have faith in Arvin Weed.

A technician walks in. 'Here to put on the straps.'

'Straps?' Partridge sits up – an instinct. He tries to laugh. 'Come on, now. Do I look like I need to be strapped down?'

The tech is expressionless. 'Dr Weed said it was necessary.'

Weed ordering straps seems like a really bad sign. 'Doctor? Weed's no doctor.'

'He is a doctor now.'

'Look, I don't need straps.' Partridge puts his hand on the technician's chest. The technician stares down at it and back at Partridge. And Partridge realizes that this is no regular tech. He's been through enhancements, and before Partridge knows it, the tech has flipped Partridge's arm across his body, paralyzing him with pain. His breath comes in short grunts.

With a few more quick motions, the tech has him strapped in. He stands at the foot of the gurney until Arvin walks in, wearing full scrubs, even a mask, so Partridge can see only his eyes. 'Give us a minute,' Weed says. 'I want to talk the patient through the process, answer any questions.'

The technician walks out.

Partridge and Arvin are alone, though there are still cameras. Partridge is desperate for some reassurance, even if it is coded.

'Why'd you have him strap me down? I don't need to be strapped down.'

'We have to restrain you when we put you under anyway,' he says, glancing at one of the cameras in the corner of the room.

'Tell me this is going to work out all right,' Partridge says. 'Can you do that?'

'This is really groundbreaking work here, Partridge, and we will be recording it for posterity.'

'All of it?'

'Of course.'

'Can't I have a *real* moment alone with you?'

'Why would you want that?'

Does this mean Weed won't be able to give him any reassurances or that he never intended to in the first place? 'You know why I'd want that, Weed.'

'Well, how about I explain the science of memory and this process?' He doesn't care about science right now. But he's afraid that if he says a word, his voice will crack. He could break down, right here – and it would be recorded for all posterity. He decides to let Weed talk while he steels himself.

'Short-term memory is chemical. But beyond that quick recall, memory gets lodged in your brain. It's anatomical. Basically, we've learned how to turn on and off specific neurons and neuron patterns in the brain. When memories form, they create these patterns. So if we turn off the right ones, we can deaden those memories. It's called optogenetics. We talked about it once, when new advances were unveiled, remember?'

'Um, it rings a bell. Kind of.' In fact, Partridge was good at tuning Weed out when he got on a scientific jag. Now might not be the best time to confess to this.

'First we select and then genetically alter the chosen neurons by using viruses bearing certain kinds of DNA. You know, microbiology, and, in your case, we will then introduce into the neuron a susceptibility to be deactivated by specific colored lights. We'll go in with extremely fine optical fibers, which we will thread – very carefully – into your brain. And we'll hit one of those patterns. In this way, we can then deactivate the neuron and its circuit by sending light signals through the fibers. And voilà!'

The idea of someone entering his brain with fibers makes him sick. 'Voilà. You go into my brain and flash some lights.'

'That's the short version.'

He swallows hard. 'Lovely.' Arvin told him at the party that once the damaged pathways cut off access to the deep memories – the silt at the ocean floor – there's a short period of time when you can still get at them before they're sealed off forever. How long will he have? 'Tell me something, Dr Weed. How long do I have to swim down deep?'

'Swim? What are you talking about?' Arvin pulls out a needle. 'I'm going to hook you up to an IV here, Partridge. So just relax.'

'How long, Weed?' Partridge begs, turning his head, not wanting to see the needle go into the soft skin in the crook of his elbow. Arvin uses some tape to hold it in place.

'Quiet now.'

Partridge looks at the stent in his arm, his skin, red and pinched from the tape, bulging around it. Arvin is tapping the tube that connects the stent to a bag of clear liquids hanging from a metal post. Soon, the room will go dark. Partridge will be gone, under, out. 'How long to swim to the ocean floor?'

'Ha!' Arvin calls out to anyone who might be listening. 'He's starting to hallucinate a bit. He'll be under soon enough.'

'How long?' Partridge says again. 'Tell me!'

Arvin's masked face begins to blur. He taps Partridge's pinky cast. 'How long do you think it'll take to grow back the rest of the way? A week or so, right? Amazing. It'll just come back – an entire pinky,' Weed says, almost singingly. 'An entire pinky. An *entire* pinky.'

An *entire* pinky, an *entire* pinky, an *entire* pinky, Partridge thinks. Is Weed telling him he'll have one week to dredge up the memories? Just a week or so? He'll have to find the list of seven simple truths by then. But even if he believes them, he'll have no clue that he has only seven days to remember what was lost. The lights sway and flicker overhead. The room jerks and dips. Arvin's face is so blurred now that Partridge isn't sure that it's him at all. A few more people in masks walk in, shifting around him.

Partridge can't go under. He can't let them put fibers in his brain. He arches his back, fighting the straps. He shouts to Weed, but he's not sure if any sound is coming from his mouth at all. The people in masks keep working, stoically, methodically.

He bucks and thrashes, thinking about the old man with the metal detector on the beach. Will he forget about him completely? He called him stupid, fake, doomed. What if the old man is real and he walks that beach every day and he thinks that Partridge is fake? Would it make a difference?

He is going limp. He closes his eyes, hears beeping. Is it the metal detector? He sees the man on the beach again, looking up at Partridge in the window. When he smiles and tips his hat, Partridge sees that it isn't an old man. It's a young man. It's Partridge himself, happy to wave to a fake stranger from a real beach – with real things buried beneath real sand – and beyond him, an endless stretch of ocean.

PRESSIA

AIRSHIP

To AVOID HEAPS OF RUBBLE, they move south into Washington, down Rock Creek Valley. More than once they hear low moans, sharp cries, some of which sound human. Birds wheel overhead and perch heavily on limbs. Some have an oily sheen. A few have reptilian heads, and one is more like a bat, but large, with a swiveling head and quick jaws, snapping air. Its wings, tufted with light patches of downy fur, chop the wind. It caws like a crow.

After a little over two miles, Pressia sees a chopped tower, its top half fallen and shattered. There are piles of brick and stone, some arches still intact.

'What was this place?'

Fignan states their coordinates. 'Thirty-eight degrees, fifty-five minutes, fifty seconds North. Seventy-seven degrees, four minutes, fifteen seconds West.'

'Enough with the coordinates,' El Capitan says. 'What was it?'

'The Washington National Cathedral.' Fignan flashes an

image of a beautiful structure with arches, flying buttresses, and spires.

'A church,' Pressia says.

'Only much bigger,' Bradwell says. Pressia knows that he's drawn to churches. He owes his survival in part to the crypt of Saint Wi. 'It was massive. People must have come from everywhere.'

'Let's go see it,' Bradwell says.

El Capitan stares at him. 'Why?'

'It's elevated. We need a better view to see the best route in.'

They start to climb. The mound of rubble is enormous.

'Your parents didn't believe in God, did they?' Pressia remembers that they didn't go to church, refused to be card-carrying, but God?

'They believed in facts; they had faith in the truth. In that way, they were devout.'

'And what do you believe in?' Pressia asks. She'd like to believe in God. She almost does. Sometimes she can feel something beyond all of this. She likes to look up at the sky, the one thing people in the Dome don't have, which makes her feel sorry for them.

'What if God and the truth are the same thing?' Bradwell says. 'What if the truth is at the center of everything? If you believe in that, you believe that the truth will win out in the end. It will reveal itself . . .'

'Like God?' Pressia asks.

'I don't know.'

'During the Before, the box we stored God in kept getting smaller and smaller. On the one hand there was science. And with all that science, Willux thought he could play God. And then on the other hand, there was the church invented for their own purposes – where the rich knew they were blessed because they were rich. Once one person's better than another, it lets people get away with all kinds of cruelty.' Bradwell shrugs.

'The box we put God in blew up in the Detonations like everything else,' Pressia says. 'Or maybe it just kept getting smaller until only a speck of God still exists, maybe only an atom of God.'

'Maybe that's enough for God to survive.'

El Capitan has gone ahead and calls to them. 'We've got a view! Come and look!'

Pressia and Bradwell scramble up the rubble. Mixed in with it are pieces of multicolored stained glass. Even dusted with ash, the colors are still vivid. Pressia picks up a shard. It's sharp-edged but its surface is smooth. It once was part of something beautiful, she's sure, something to inspire people.

Once they're at the top of the cathedral's rubble, Pressia looks down into its sunken top. And there, lost down the deep hole of the airy cathedral itself, is what once was a green copper roof, collapsed in on itself. Shining up from gritty layers of ash and dirt are some yellows, some reds, and shattered, senseless, patternless stained glass. But Pressia's heard that art is supposed to reflect the world, which means these broken panes are still art.

'So this is what's left of the city,' Bradwell says, staring out at the view.

Pressia turns and looks down at the flattened landscape ahead of them. The city has been overtaken by a swampy, cold marshland. Beasts and birds scuttle through the wet underbrush. Huge tracts of rubble lead to the spectral remains of a severed obelisk. It's a nub and a line of cracked stone – maybe marble, now blackened.

'The Washington Monument,' Bradwell says. 'The pencil.'

'Where's the White House?' Pressia asks.

'It would be out there,' Bradwell says, pointing just north of the fallen obelisk. 'It's gone.'

'And the museums?' El Capitan says, Helmud gazing excitedly over his shoulder. 'You promised me a field trip.'

'There they are. Archives, National Gallery, American History, Natural History, Righteous Red Wave Museum . . . See all that blasted stone in a line to the east of the pencil?' Bradwell points to heaps of rock. 'The Declaration of Independence could still exist. It's supposed to drop, at a moment's notice, into an underground vault. Supposedly it could have survived a direct hit.'

'Look there,' El Capitan says, pointing a little farther east. 'Isn't that what we're looking for?'

The US Capitol sits up against the horizon like a delicate soap bubble. It's rickety, yes, but it's there, on a small hill that rises up from the marshland. It's a broken dome made of pale stone, now gray. Its roof is mostly gone, fissured and cracked. It's missing chunks from its walls and therefore seems airy and, from a distance, almost lacy. Pressia thinks of the way moths eat wool, leaving thin, gauzy holes.

And through those holes, Pressia can see that the dome isn't empty at all. Something sits inside of it, glints of metal. The airship – its bulky frame, its hull. Could it really be in there?

'Look, Helmud,' El Capitan whispers to his brother. 'There it is.' Pressia wishes her grandfather could see this. He told her many times about that day after the Detonations when the airship skimmed through the clouds, droning in the sky, and how all those white pieces of paper fluttered down, each printed with the Message. They thought it was something to give them hope – the Dome, from which their brothers and sisters were watching benevolently. They were going to join them again one day in peace.

And now, as beautiful as the Capitol Building is and the promise it holds – that airship – it feels like a betrayal, a deep and hateful wrong. It's not even surrounded by chain-link fence like Crazy John-Johns. It's just sitting there, unprotected, proof of Willux's arrogance. He never believed a wretch would make it this far alive, and if they did, he probably didn't believe they'd have the courage to steal it.

Even though El Capitan is close, he stands on the other side of Bradwell, and so Pressia slips her hand into Bradwell's. Their fingers weave together as if they've done this a million times, as if it's already a familiar habit.

'It was here all this time,' Bradwell mutters.

'Damn,' El Capitan says.

'Willux didn't build that with his own goddamn hands,' Bradwell says. 'The people built it. People he thought of as expendable.'

'People like us,' El Capitan says.

'It's ours,' Pressia says. She squeezes Bradwell's hand and he squeezes back. 'It belongs to us.'

'Hell yes,' El Capitan says.

'Hell yes,' Helmud says.

'So,' Bradwell says, 'let's take what's ours.'

They move quickly back into the creek valley and, within half an hour, their boots are wet from tromping through marshes.

They've had to wade through some swamps, thigh-deep on Pressia. The water is icy. Pressia's feet ache from the cold.

'They used to call this area Foggy Bottom,' Bradwell says. 'Somewhere around here.' True to its name, the air is misty. 'Let's stick to the high ground.'

This will mean climbing the rubble around them. El Capitan, weighted by his brother, looks worn out already. 'You sure?'

'I like being able to see what's in the water,' Pressia says.

This is the deciding vote. They climb, but the rubble holds its own dangers as they don't know if Dusts and Beasts have survived out here. They veer east toward the Capitol.

It starts to rain a little. Pressia hunches her shoulders against the damp. Bradwell's hair beads with droplets. He shakes it roughly. Soon they're surrounded by thin saplings. The water, cold and dark, covers their boots again.

Pressia is the first to hear the growling. She stops and crouches.

'What is it?' El Capitan whispers.

A roar rips through the air. It's louder and deeper than any other growl Pressia's ever heard. 'I don't know what that is, but it's big.'

'I just thought of something,' Bradwell says, 'about that field trip, Cap.'

'What?' El Capitan says.

'The National Zoo.'

Something glides over Pressia's boot. She sees a large, blunt, gnarled, lizard-like head, crusted in dulled glass – maybe Plexiglas. She freezes. The Beast is probably three feet long. Its tail swishes as it swims on. Pressia knows what were once caged in zoos – exotic animals, both beautiful and ferocious. 'This isn't good,' she says.

The Beast roars again, and then lets out a series of sharp,

high-pitched yaps. Small, slippery Beasts start paddling madly away from the noise. Some have giant ears and rodent-like faces. Others have rubbery coats and are snakish but also otter-like in shape. The birds take flight. The air is alive with wings – small, slick birds with darty eyes. One is massive and pink. Its broad wings are magnificent, its beak askew. Deer – or *are* they deer? – spring up and dart. They're hooved and swift. Some are black, others striped. Some have antlers – flat, sharp, entwined, or coiled. They have various hides – furred, woolly, slick and reptilian, burned and scarred, dotted with shards of glass and rock. They're light on their feet, bounding over rubble, then disappearing.

'It's coming,' El Capitan says. 'I say we run too.'

And so they take off, splashing through the marsh, guns held tightly to their chests.

Up ahead, Pressia sees a shape lumbering toward them. They all stop. El Capitan points his rifle out and takes aim.

'Wait,' Pressia says. She can't help but think that if you were once caged here, it's your right to reclaim the land. 'We're the trespassers.' She lowers herself to the underbrush.

The mist is so thick that, at first, the Beast is only a dim shape, but slowly, from between the trees, the shape defines itself – a hulking gorilla. It limps; its left leg is splinted by a kind of metal rod. It has rubber covering its entire chest, something deeply grooved, and is holding a baby gorilla, but the baby is limp and partially decayed. Not fused to it, no. The baby was born and now has died. The stench is strong. Pressia assumes that the infant died of dehydration. How could the mother nurse with a chest fused to rubber?

The gorilla cries out angrily.

And Helmud lets out a cry in response.

'Shut it,' El Capitan says over his shoulder.

'She'll get violent, protecting her baby,' Pressia says.

'What's left of it,' El Capitan says.

'She hasn't given up,' Pressia says.

They hear another roar now – this one is catlike, far off.

'Were there lions at this zoo?' El Capitan asks. 'Do I even want to know?'

Bradwell sighs. 'Unfortunately, they had just about everything. Well stocked.'

'This way,' Pressia says. 'There's a clearing. I can see it through the trees.'

They move slowly at first, backing away from the gorilla. The gorilla looks at them mournfully, as if she'd been looking for help. She grips the baby to her chest and squats on a rock. She lifts the baby to her neck to nuzzle it, and that's when Pressia sees the gorilla's hand – hairless, pale, and delicate. The vestige of something human.

Pressia looks away. Was the human consumed completely?

El Capitan and Bradwell have already started running. She feels queasy, hot to her core, but she runs after them, continuing east. On the other side of the trees, there's a stretch of swamp and more trees. Pressia is out in front now, and as she sprints, the ground abruptly disappears beneath her foot, and she drops forward. Her foot catches the ground again over a foot and a half down. She staggers but doesn't fall.

Bradwell and El Capitan both take the same tumble. Bradwell looks off east – where the pencil and Capitol Building loom – and west, where the Lincoln Memorial looks like it was chopped down. 'The Reflecting Pool,' Bradwell says, searching the water with his boot. 'This could be it.'

'The Reflecting Pool?'

'They used to demonstrate here, back when those kinds of things were allowed,' Bradwell says. 'They rallied and gave speeches, hoping for change. Right here.'

They push on through the water, which gets deeper for a while. When Pressia is hip-deep, she feels things moving through the dark water. Fish? Snakes? Muskrats? Hybrids of all three? She's glad the water is dark. She doesn't want to know. She closes her eyes and keeps going. The water recedes as they step up on the other side of the pool. The obelisk isn't far off now, and the Capitol is just beyond it.

They run over a small hill, faster now because their goal is in sight. They climb a final hill and it's there, right in front of them – a massive building. Pressia presses her hand to its cold stone facade.

'It's just so cocky to leave the airship out here,' Bradwell says, 'as if Willux was so damn sure no one would ever have the strength to make it this far.'

'Without Special Forces, we probably wouldn't have,' Pressia says. 'It's called irony,' El Capitan says. 'We got here because of Willux's own creation.'

'Own creation,' Helmud says.

They round the building and find the entrance. There's a large melted glob of iron – what used to be a statue.

'What was it?' El Capitan asks.

'A Righteous Red Wave statue,' Fignan says. 'Dedicated to the movement two months before the Detonations.'

They step inside and move through corridors, find an unblocked staircase, and then an upper-floor opening onto a large, airy expanse. The dome is tall and open overhead. The wind pushes through the holes, creating funnels of brisk air.

And there, just as Hastings said it would be, is a large, hard, elliptical shell, propped by metal beams and leashed to the ground by thick wire. Beneath it, there's a gondola with two propellers attached behind it. The propellers point at a rudder that's connected to the back of the shell. The gondola has doors with small silver handles. The back of the gondola is a solid material with portholes. But the front third, its nose, is a cabin with wide windows that curve with the conical nose of the airship.

Though gritty with dust, it's still a thing of sheer beauty.

The airship.

They circle it, awestruck.

El Capitan is the first to lay a hand on it. He spreads his fingers wide on the body of the cabin as if it's the flank of a horse. He's talking to himself. 'Starboard propeller, port propeller.' He looks behind the rudder and sees a plank running perpendicular to it. 'Aft planes.'

Pressia's grandfather talked about the airship as if it might not be real, as if it were myth or legend. He'd spotted it himself, but still its existence seemed to require an act of faith.

'You sure you can man this thing?' Bradwell asks El Capitan.

'Never so sure of anything in my life!' El Capitan says, but his voice is too loud for the hollow, echoing space, too forced. He's trying to convince himself that he's telling the truth. Isn't that what they're all doing, on some level – lying to themselves that this trip is possible at all?

Then there's a grunt. It's coming from outside the Capitol. Distant, but clear. A grunt and then three sharp, staccato cries.

EL CAPITAN

CLOUDS

IN THE COCKPIT, El Capitan touches every switch, every throttle, every knob. 'Look at all this,' he says to Helmud. 'Did you think it would be this beautiful?' He's a little breathless, shocked by the sheer reality of it all.

'*This* beautiful,' Helmud says, hunkered low on his brother's back in the tight space.

Fignan buzzes in. 'It's all here,' El Capitan says to him. 'You know how these things work, right, Fignan? All retro, throwbacks from the old dirigibles. What's the name of that famous one that blew up?'

'The *Hindenburg*,' Fignan says, projecting an image of the fiery crash accompanied by an audio clip of a reporter saying, 'Oh, the humanity.'

'Thanks, Fignan,' El Capitan says caustically. 'That was *just* what I needed.'

He can hear Bradwell and Pressia talking in the cabin. He doesn't like the way their voices are lowered, as if swapping secrets. He saw them last night on the cold ground, kissing. He'd come down from his lookout on the train tracks just to report that all seemed clear then stumbled out quickly, trying to catch his breath in the cold air. 'What the hell,' he'd muttered. 'What? What?' Helmud had kept asking until he told him to shut up.

He can't think about that now. He unlatches a compartment, finding a checklist and manual. He hands these to Fignan. 'You can learn these pretty quickly, right?'

Fignan clamps the two items in his pincers and starts scanning the pages.

El Capitan reaches overhead and grips the control stick for the rudder and planes. The grooves fit his hand perfectly. He touches the gauges on the console, each dial cleanly labeled: FORE-BUCKY, MAIN-BUCKY, AFT-BUCKY. 'Talk to me, Fignan. How does this baby really work?'

Fignan explains the tanks overhead, made of extremely strong, extremely lightweight, but relatively new molecular structures. A voice narrates an explanation: 'The more air is pumped from them, the more lift they will give until they reach a near-perfect vacuum.'

'So it rises by pumping air out. How long until it's ready to take off?'

Fignan recites the manual in an automated voice of his own: 'The process will take approximately one half hour before reaching flight buoyancy.'

'What about throttles?' El Capitan asks, anxious to get in the air.

'The throttles control the propeller speeds to push the airship forward. There are two sets of throttles for the propellers on either side of the console.'

'And down here?' El Capitan says, pointing below the simple compass with its needle to some kind of screen.

'The navigation display table.'

'Maps?'

'Maps are from before the Detonations.'

'They'll help some, but not for landings. Who knows what shape the terrain will be in. What about GPS and satellites? They've all been knocked out, so how's it going to navigate?'

'This craft does not rely on GPS satellites or control towers.'

'Willux knew all of that would be wiped away by the Detonations, so what would have been the point? What I'm a little worried about,' El Capitan says, wedging himself into the captain's chair with Helmud shoved up against his back, 'is navigation over the ocean. No reference points out there. Even celestial navigation like sailors once used wouldn't work, especially without any way to tell time and have star charts and all that. Not that I'd be able to figure that stuff out anyway.'

'There was a new transocean navigation system developed with this issue in mind. It involves craft-launched laser-reflecting tracking buoys coupled with a Dead-Reckoning Integrated Visual, or DRIV, that shows up on a navigation display,' Fignan says. 'The ship has a series of gyroscopes and accelerometers that track its position, orientation, and velocity, and from this the DRIV system calculates the change in our location since the last buoy was launched.'

'Sweet.' El Capitan is impressed. 'Like medieval and smart-bomb technology mixed.'

'The navigation display table has launch buttons for the laser-reflecting tracking buoys. The pilot engages the first one when the aircraft reaches the flying altitude you will maintain, then repeats it every two hours.'

Fignan explains that the energy source for the pumps, the cabin heat, and the propellers relies on cold fusion. And there are masks that will drop from overhead if they get over ten thousand feet.

El Capitan pulls forward a pair of binoculars attached to a seemingly old-world hinged arm connected to the wall. He looks through them and finds that they've got a night-vision setting. The airship seems complex, a feat of science, but science applied to a simple machine.

El Capitan scratches his chin and says to himself more than to Fignan and Helmud, 'Thing is that the days are so short over there now. It's winter. The chances of a daylight landing are next to nothing. We have only two days to find the dome at Newgrange, hitting the solstice, and only with short windows of daylight. We have to go now.' El Capitan's stomach is fluttering with nerves. There's a silver button to start the energy source.

'Okay then,' El Capitan says. 'I'm going to push the power-source button, right? Okay?'

'Right? Okay?' Helmud says, which makes El Capitan self-conscious about sounding so unsure of himself.

'Just tell me if I'm going to do something wrong, Fignan. Got it?'

Fignan flashes a green light.

El Capitan puts his finger on the silver button and then pushes it. His hand poised to lift the three switches, which will start pumping air from the bucky tanks, he looks at Fignan, who flashes another green light.

El Capitan flips the switches.

Bradwell pokes his head through the cockpit door. 'How long before we can get in the air?'

'Half an hour or so. The air in the tanks has to be low enough for the airship to rise.' He feels smarter than Bradwell, for once. 'Why?'

'I heard more noises.'

'Beasts?'

'Not sure. It was a light scratching sound, but from below.'

'Keep listening,' El Capitan says.

As Bradwell heads back into the cabin, Pressia squeezes past him, so closely their bodies touch. 'Everything making sense?' she asks El Capitan.

'It's straightforward.' This bravado makes him panic. He wants to tell her he's in over his head, but it's too late. He's already lied.

'Really?' Pressia says, staring at the console. 'Straightforward?'

'Yeah,' he says. 'Don't you think I can do it?'

'I didn't mean to doubt you,' she says. 'It just looks . . . complicated.'

El Capitan doesn't say anything for a minute. He looks up through the glass ceiling of the cockpit, at the gaping roof of the US Capitol, opening to the gray, windswept sky. He thinks of how he felt about the sky after his father left them for good. 'When I was a kid I stared out windows, lay in fields, stumbled around because I kept my eyes up instead of in front of me. *You've got your head in the clouds!* my mother used to say. But she knew I was looking for planes. My father knew how to fly, and sooner or later his plane was going to fly by up there, and I wanted to see it. Each plane offered that possibility. I noticed planes everywhere – books, magazines, toys.' He looks at Pressia. 'Maybe that's how it was for Willux and his domes when he was a kid. When you're in the world looking for only one thing, you find it or it finds you. The obsession can be mutual.'

Pressia looks at him as if he's surprised her. But there's real respect in her expression, maybe even admiration. It sends a charge through him. He's used to a kind of respect based on fear, but this is different. He's glad that Helmud has stayed quiet and let him have his say. For a second, he can almost imagine that they're alone, that it's just the two of them.

And then there's a thud on the hull.

Pressia whips her head around.

Bradwell calls out from the cabin, 'I see three Beasts. Maybe more. They're big.'

The floor of the airship shifts, tilting slowly one way and then the other.

'Holy shit, are they moving this thing?' Bradwell says.

And that's what it feels like – Beasts beneath the airship, lifting it upward.

But then El Capitan says, 'No, maybe not. It's rising! Isn't it? Do we have a little lift?'

'Lift!' Helmud cries.

They aren't off the ground yet, though. The Beasts are now pounding on the hull.

'You should probably sit down back there,' El Capitan says to Pressia. 'Buckle up.'

There's a very loud thud, grunts, and high-pitched cries.

'Hurry, Cap!' Pressia shouts, and she runs back into the cabin.

El Capitan closes the door, quickly lifts Fignan and sets him in the copilot's chair. He pulls the seat belt around the Black Box, clicks it, and tightens it with a jerk. He sits in the captain's chair, but he can't strap himself in. He's too bulky with Helmud on his back.

The airship is still lifting slowly, losing the rough hold of gravity, rising, but not quite fully airborne.

El Capitan lays his hands on the navigation display, which has flickered to life with a screen. There's a crude map and, in the center of the screen, a green blip, which is the airship itself.

'What do I do?' he says to Fignan.

'Turn on the port and starboard engines.'

He scans the console. The pounding on the hull becomes rhythmic. The cries have become yowls that sound more like incantations. He finds the right labels, flips the switches.

'Come on, Fignan! Now what?'

The airship feels like it's no longer bound to the earth. 'We're up! Right?'

And then the airship jerks to a stop, the wire tethers taut on either side. El Capitan forgot the moorings and now he panics.

'What's wrong?' Bradwell calls out. 'What's happening?'

The yowls grow louder, hungrier.

'Release the mooring, fore and aft,' Fignan says.

'Yeah, and how do I do that?' The airship bobbles again. Is it possible that the Beasts are tugging at the moorings?

'Why did we stop?' Pressia shouts. 'El Capitan?'

'It's okay!' he calls out, and he hopes that it is, but he's not sure. 'Fignan!'

Fignan illuminates a reference page, showing El Capitan a picture of a red button under the display.

El Capitan runs his hand along the underside of the display, finds the button, hits it. The wires unhook and recoil, making a loud zipping sound as they retract. The airship lurches upward so quickly that El Capitan grabs the console in front of him so he's not pitched to the floor. He accidentally flips a switch and a loud siren sounds out.

'Jesus!' he says.

'Jesus!' Helmud shouts.

He hits the switch again and the siren winds down. But this might have been a good thing. The Beasts are crying now, as if the siren frightened them.

'You need help in there?' Bradwell shouts.

'Help!' Helmud cries.

'We're fine,' El Capitan shouts. The airship has started to rise quickly – too quickly. It's edging closely to the lip of the broken dome. 'Fignan!' El Capitan shouts.

'The propellers control the direction of the airship,' Fignan says, with unsettling calm.

El Capitan grips the propeller levers and jerks them to the left, away from the interior of the dome. But it was too fast. The airship dips. El Capitan loosens his grip. The controls are more sensitive than he'd thought.

He compensates in the other direction, more lightly this time. The airship bobs left and right, teetering close to the edges on either side. El Capitan draws in his breath, an instinct, as if this could make the ship thinner.

They keep rising and he jostles the controls a little left and a little right until he almost finds the center of the lever and the airship steadies and lifts . . .

And then finally they're out. He hears Bradwell and Pressia hoot and clap. He remembers the look that Pressia gave him after he'd made that comment about obsession, the charge it gave him. She thought he'd said something smart. She respected him for it. He feels that charge again, like a lit fuse in his chest. The low, dark clouds scuttle by. El Capitan is in the air. He isn't a little boy, abandoned by his father, craning his neck to find a distant airplane buzzing across the sky.

No, he's the one in the sky. It's not the first time in his life he's felt like a man. El Capitan has always had to be more of a man than he should've had to. Instead, it's like he's no longer that lonesome little boy, afraid to show any weakness, too afraid to cry even though he felt desperate and sad and lost, the one who's sure his father left because he couldn't stand to look at his worthless son ever again.

For the first time in his life, he's not worthless at all.

PART III

PARTRIDGE

IRALENE

PARTRIDGE OPENS HIS EYES. The back of his skull aches. A ceiling fan swirls overhead. He isn't in Glassings' World History class. He isn't in his dorm room.

And then a girl's face appears, a little blurry at first but it snaps into focus. The girl says, 'Oh my gosh! You're awake!' She calls out, 'He's awake!' She fiddles with a pocket-size handheld. 'I'll send word to your father! He'll be so relieved.' And then she looks at him and touches his arm. '*Everyone* will be relieved, Partridge. All of us!'

He's trying to remember how he got here. Is it after curfew? He's never been inside the dormitory at the girls' academy, but he's pretty sure they're nothing like this – spacious with billowy curtains. He blinks at the girl and, for no reason he understands, there's only one phrase in his head and so he says it aloud, hoping that it will make sense to her. 'Beautiful barbarism.'

'What's that?' the girl says.

'Glassings' lecture on ancient cultures. He was giving a speech on . . .' He remembers Glassings' blazer.

'Aren't you glad that's over with? Lectures, classes, teachers. That's one upside to an injury like yours. You're free!'

'Free?' He wonders what she means. He'd like to believe her, but he can't. He tries to lift his head but feels the sharp headache again. He touches two shaved patches close to the base of his skull where the pain, deep in his brain, is the sharpest. 'Where am I?'

'This is our place, Partridge. Don't you remember that part?' She holds up her hand and wiggles her fingers, showing off an engagement ring with a large diamond. 'They said you wouldn't remember things, amnesia, what with the blow to the head. But I told them you'd remember *me*.'

So he took a blow. That's why his head hurts. Amnesia. He stares at the girl, trying to place her. 'Uh, yeah,' he says. 'You're . . .'

'I'm your fiancée. We're engaged. Your father's set us up here in this place. We met at the dance.'

'The fall dance?'

'None other!'

'I asked you to the fall dance?' He doesn't remember seeing this girl before. He remembers girls doing calisthenics and singing in a chorus on stage.

'You went with someone else, but later that night, you met me, and the other girl flew out of your head.' She reaches for his hand, lifts it for him, holds it to her cheek.

That's when he sees that part of his pinky is gone – severed at the top. 'Jesus! What happened to my hand?'

'Hush, Partridge. You shouldn't get excited like that.'

'What happened to me?' His voice sounds loud and off-kilter in his own head, as if he's hearing it broadcast.

'A coma. You've been surfacing from it. In and out. It's winter now. Almost Christmas!'

'Was I in an accident? Jesus, tell me!' He touches the nub where the top of his pinky once was. He imagines a knife coming down on it and a strange pop. The knife makes him think of old kitchens. There's a Domesticity Display set up now in Founders Hall, or is there?

'The accident was horrible. Don't you remember the ice rink?'

He shakes his head. The room swirls behind her. Panic seizes his chest and yet he's exhausted. 'The ice rink?' He can almost feel a spot in his mind that's vacant – a blind spot. He tries to look at it but as soon as he looks, it shifts out of view. 'What ice rink?'

'They set one up for fun – a plastic sheet that they froze in the gym. You and Hastings went in after hours. You weren't supposed to be there. You laced up skates and were racing on the ice and you got tangled somehow. You fell, knocking your head on the ice. Hastings accidentally ran over your pinky, slicing it clean off.'

That vacancy, that erasure in his mind, feels like a sheet of white ice. 'Where's Hastings?' He has to hear Hastings' version. 'Back at the dorm?'

'Special Forces.'

'Hastings? He's not Special Forces material.' Was Partridge going to be taken in too but then left behind because of the accident? He thinks of Sedge. He almost wants to ask if he's really dead, but then the truth is there: Sedge has been dead for a couple of years. He killed himself. The end.

'They had to recruit a number of boys quickly. Vic Wellingsly is gone, the Elmsford twins, Hastings, and more. The wretches,' she whispers. 'There have been uprisings. They needed more soldiers.'

'Out there? Outside the Dome?' He thinks of dusty wind, can almost feel it on his skin.

'Shhh,' she says. 'Not everyone knows that, but yes.'

Partridge's head feels impossibly heavy. 'My coding sessions,' he says. 'They're all messed up now. I've missed a ton of them. And school. Where's my father?'

'It's okay,' the girl says. 'Your father has a plan for you. A very good plan!'

He feels a pang in his chest. Is it fear? 'Me? Why? He doesn't even like me.'

'Your father loves you, Partridge. Never forget that!'

'What kind of plan?'

'Not just for you, but for both of us!'

'I don't even know your name.'

'You *do* know my name. It's Iralene. You knew that. It was tucked away in there, kept forever. Don't you remember it?'

Iralene. Secrets. Promises. 'I do remember it now,' he says. *Iralene. Piano. Iralene. In the cold. In the dark.* 'Yeah. I do.' Does he love Iralene? Do they have secrets and promises? Have they been together in the cold and dark? He stares at her. She leans in and kisses him softly on the lips. He feels like he remembers kissing in the cold, undressed. Cold? Where would they have cold like that? The gym, chilled for the ice rink?

'Tell me more about you. Fill in some details.'

'Well, my mother was a widow. She's known your father for years and, just recently, they married. But we're not blood-related, Partridge, so it's okay.'

'My father remarried? He's not the type . . .' Not the type to fall in love, Partridge thinks. His father doesn't understand love. 'Your father died? My mother's dead too. She was a martyr. She died during the Detonations trying to save people.' This doesn't seem right but Iralene accepts it.

'Yes, I know,' Iralene says. 'My father . . . well, he got in trouble for fraud and was sent to jail before the Detonations. Luckily my mother already knew your father when this happened and so he helped us, financially. We wouldn't have made it without him, much less have gotten into the Dome.' The story churns inside Partridge. It makes him feel sick. Why? His father was helping someone. He fell in love again. These are good things, aren't they?

Iralene picks up the handheld from her lap. 'There's a voice message from your father.'

He straightens up – a habit when his father's involved.

Iralene pushes a button and his father says, 'Partridge, I'm so glad that you're awake and well enough to receive this message.'

Partridge hates his father so suddenly and with such a powerful rage that he feels like his chest might explode. 'Wait!' he says to Iralene. 'Press stop.'

The room goes quiet.

He covers his mouth, trying to steady his breathing.

'Are you okay?'

'Play it,' he mutters. 'Get it over with.'

'Now I want you to take it easy,' his father goes on. 'You should ease back into your life. Enjoy yourself.' Partridge's heart is still pounding. His father has never told him to enjoy himself. Not once, ever. And there's something about his voice – it sounds strained, maybe even older than he remembers and not just a few months older but years, maybe decades. He wonders if his father isn't feeling well. Is that why he isn't here in person?

'In a few days,' his father says, 'you'll be called back into the hospital. There will be more they can do to try to salvage and renew some of your' – he hesitates here but then must decide to remain clinical – 'your brain's synaptic firings. After that's done, my son, I will be calling on you. I will be asking great things of you as a leader. I'm making it official now.' He pauses the way he did in public addresses. A dramatic pause. His father is about to announce something. Partridge's stomach tightens as if he's expecting a punch. 'You will be my successor. I can't lead forever. I need to start handing over some power. Who better to give it to than you?'

Partridge is stunned. He still feels the fiery burn of hatred, but now he also feels disoriented, as if the room isn't fixed in time or space. His father wants him to be his successor, to lead? Nothing makes sense – not his father, not this room of billowy curtains, not the girl who's staring at him now, wide-eyed.

His father says, 'I imagine Iralene is by your side at this very moment. Listen to me – these next few days, you two have fun. That's an order. The future is coming and it's coming quickly.'

And that's the end of it. Iralene is gazing at Partridge, the handheld gripped tightly in her hands. 'Partridge?' she says softly.

He punches the mattress as hard as he can and he's surprised by his own strength. She startles, her back going rigid for a second.

'It makes no sense!' he says, the pain surging through his skull. 'My father's ashamed of me. *That's* something I know and have always known.'

'He *loves* you,' Iralene whispers.

'You don't know anything about me and my father,' Partridge says.

'But I do,' she says, moving to the edge of his bed. 'Maybe he never wanted to admit that he needed you before. Maybe he wanted to spare you the burden of your future. But he needs you now. He's been—'

'He's sick, isn't he? Is he dying?'

'No, no, not dying,' Iralene says quickly. 'He's been unwell. He'll get better soon, but I think he is mortal. Who else does he have?'

Partridge lets his eyes drift around the room. He's not sure how to argue with Iralene. His father has never made sense to him. Maybe she's right. Sedge is gone. His father is left with Partridge.

'It's important that you rest,' Iralene says, 'so we can start enjoying ourselves. That part was an order, right?'

'I guess so.'

Iralene stands up and walks to the door. Partridge glances at the fan overhead. *Fan blades*. For a second, he imagines them as sharp metal knives, able to chop him to pieces. Where did that thought come from?

He looks at Iralene, who's standing in a shaft of sunlight coming in from the window – like real afternoon sun. He hears waves rolling in and out.

'Is that the ocean?'

'Think of it as a night-light,' Iralene says, 'that your father made just for you.'

His father wouldn't make anything just for him. That was something his mother would have done. He thinks of her at the beach, wrapped in a wind-whipped towel. It's an old memory and he's relieved that it's still in his head. He thinks of her the way he always has: She died a saint. But as soon as the thought appears in his mind, he comes back to the last words he remembers hearing before he woke up – nothing about racing Hastings on a man-made ice rink in the chilled gym. No. It's Glassings' voice, lecturing in a stuffy classroom about ancient cultures, rituals for the dead. *Beautiful barbarism*.

LYDA

KNOWING

MOTHER EGAN WALKS IN, holding a plate of leeks, tubers, tender meats, and a glass of pink-tinged liquid. 'Up, up,' she says gently.

Lyda is confined to cot number nine, a prison-like confinement, which is fine with her. She feels sick with guilt. She can't stop thinking of Our Good Mother telling her that she intends to kill Partridge, that she's going to attack the Dome and people will die in the process. Our Good Mother has announced that the mothers are to prepare for war, that Lyda is the cause, and that she represents all of them – ruined, abandoned, left to fend for herself.

Lyda lifts herself and Mother Egan plumps a pillow behind her back. She hands Lyda the plate with its fork. 'Some red, thick-skinned fruits were found this fall. We've thawed and pressed some for you. Mother Hestra wants you strong.'

Lyda sips the drink, salty and sour. She still feels nauseous from time to time, but mostly she's equal parts tired and restless. 'Thank you.'

Mother Egan smiles. 'Anything for you.' All the mothers are nicer to her now, but not out of sympathy – more like fear. They sense she has power. 'I can't wait for the baby to come!'

Lyda forces a smile. But she wraps a protective arm around her belly. Just whose baby will this be? Another reason the mothers are nice to her – they covet the baby.

'A baby will be a joy for all of us.' Mother Egan looks at her, hungrily.

'Thank you for the food,' Lyda says again and she's relieved when she hears someone walking into the room – a distraction. Mother Hestra. She's been hunting. Her sack is freshly bloodstained but empty. She's already delivered her catch. 'Mother Egan!' Mother Hestra says. 'Mind if I visit with the patient?'

Mother Egan doesn't want to leave, Lyda can tell. She's brought food and has an excuse to be with Lyda. But she can't raise a fuss. 'Of course I don't mind,' she says. 'Enjoy your meal.' This is a subtle reminder that Lyda owes Mother Egan this meal, this kindness.

'I will,' Lyda says.

Once Mother Egan is gone, Mother Hestra sits down heavily on the bed. Syden looks sleepy and red-cheeked from the cold air. 'How are you?'

Lyda chews the soft meat. 'I'm thinking of leaving.' She's surprised that she's said this aloud. It's only a dim thought in the back of her mind. The idea of trying to survive out there alone terrifies her.

'You won't make it,' Mother Hestra says. 'Listen, you were the incident. If it wasn't you, it would have been something else. It's time.'

Lyda glances at Syden, peeking around his mother's stomach. 'He didn't hurt me. You know that.'

Mother Hestra drops her sack. She rubs her hands together, trying to warm them up. 'But did you really understand, Lyda? Did you really know what it might mean?'

'Did *he*?' Lyda can't even say his name.

'Didn't he?' Mother Hestra says.

Lyda isn't sure. Did he really know that she could get pregnant? Lyda had never heard of a baby being born to someone not married. So there was no living, breathing proof that it could happen to someone like her, so young. She remembers the warm skin of Partridge's chest, their hot breath trapped in the coat. He asked her if she was sure. He had to know. Why else would he ask her that question? And she didn't even understand what he was asking, that he wanted permission, much less what granting it might mean. But she could have stopped him. She didn't want to stop.

Lyda puts her plate and glass on the floor. She lies down in the bed, presses her hands together, and tucks them under her pillow. 'It doesn't matter whether he knew or not,' Lyda says, although it does matter. It's the difference between the two of them being sucker-punched together or her alone. 'Mother Hestra,' Lyda whispers urgently, 'I need to get word to Bradwell, Pressia, and El Capitan. Is that possible? They might be able to help. This attack can't happen.'

Mother Hestra says, 'I don't know about that.'

Lyda needs to tell them what's happening. Maybe they'll have an idea how to make all this crazy talk of war and death end. She feels like crying. 'The Dome . . . you don't know them. You don't understand how well equipped they are, how powerful. All of you walk around without any idea . . . It'll be a bloodbath. Don't you understand that?'

Mother Hestra shakes her head and smiles. 'We're not

attacking the Dome. We're attacking *Deaths*, the men who made us suffer for years before the Detonations ever rained down on us, the ones who ruined and abandoned us all. You stand for abandonment, whether you want to or not. You are all of us and your child is all of our children.'

'I don't want to stand for anything.'

'Sometimes you don't have a choice.'

'Promise me you'll *try* to find my friends. Please,' Lyda begs her. 'Just try.'

Mother Hestra strokes Syden's hair. 'We'll see,' she says. 'But no promises.'

PRESSIA

LIT

THE SKY IS DARK. Every once in a while, El Capitan tells them where they are, calling through the open door to the cockpit, his voice confident and, strangest of all, happy. Pressia's never heard El Capitan sound happy like this before. He's told them the total distance of the trip – 2,910 nautical miles – and depending on the winds and speed the ship can manage, it'll probably take somewhere between thirty-five and fifty-six hours.

They've passed Baltimore, the upper Chesapeake Bay, Philadelphia, New York City, Cape Ann, the Gulf of Maine, Prince Edward Island, the Gulf of St. Lawrence. She wishes it were daylight, so she could see them; instead she imagines toppled cities, wrecked highways and ports, plus roaming Beasts and Dusts.

The airship's engine room is noisy. The pumps hiss and thrum. 'What was in each of those cities during the Before?' she asks Bradwell, who's sitting next to her.

'In Baltimore there was a big harbor, an aquarium and ships, a huge Domino Sugar sign that was always lit up. In Philadelphia, there was the statue of a man on top of a building and an enormous bell that stood for liberty. In New York City, well . . .' His voice trails off. 'My parents would say that you had to be there before the Righteous Red Wave settled in. You had to be in it to believe it. It was alive.'

Pressia knows that any number of things could go wrong. They might not make it over the ocean. El Capitan might not be able to land this thing. Ireland may be a dusky crater or filled with Beasts and Dusts more vicious than the ones they've known. If they're lucky enough to get to Newgrange in time for the solstice, the sun might illuminate a spot on the floor, and they might dig to find . . . an empty pocket of air, dirt, nothing at all. And she still doesn't know how Fignan will somehow act as a key.

But knowing all of that, there's still this moment – up in the air with Bradwell, going somewhere, trying to get out, acting on hope. The joy is there, sitting solidly within her. They hold hands.

El Capitan calls out, 'We're over Horse Island, Newfoundland. Last landmass before the Atlantic.'

Pressia looks out of the porthole, beading with moisture that streaks the glass like tears pushed from your eyes in a strong wind, and she imagines Horse Island overrun with teams of wild horses. But all she can see is the billowy shift of sooty clouds.

'I'll be releasing the first buoy in thirty seconds,' El Capitan says. 'It's going to be loud. Hold tight.'

Bradwell squeezes her hand. 'I'm holding tight.'

The release of the buoy is so thunderous that the airship vibrates. A flash passes the window, filling the cabin for a moment with a brilliant glow. And suddenly she remembers the

Detonations sharply. Light blasting through everything. Glowing windows and walls and bodies and bones.

Lit.

Lit up.

Like an explosion of the sun.

And then the light fades. The small porthole is dark again. She breathes out, leans her head against Bradwell's shoulder. She says, 'For a moment, it was like . . .'

'I know.'

It's night and this is a small miracle – holding Bradwell's hand as they're skimming the clouds, careening over the dark ocean, sailing through the sky.

PARTRIDGE

WHALES

THE SWIMMING POOL has been closed to the public so Partridge and Iralene can swim alone. He isn't supposed to get his head wet because of his injury, but he's allowed to wade around.

Iralene wears a yellow swimsuit with a short skirt wrapped around her waist. She floats on her back, dips underwater and comes up again. Her makeup doesn't smear.

There's a guard named Beckley, standing on the cement, fully dressed and armed. When he's out of earshot, Partridge asks Iralene, 'What's with Beckley?'

'He's watching out for you, if you have symptoms or something,' she says. 'Just in case something goes wrong.'

'Really?' Partridge says, pushing his arms through the water. 'He doesn't look like medical personnel.'

She seems to change her mind. 'Well, if you're going to be the leader, you need to get used to being protected.'

'So the guard isn't really a doctor's suggestion, but my father's idea?'

'Yes,' she says. 'See how much he loves you?' It's also a way for his father to keep tabs on him at all times.

Partridge feels weak – but it's more mental than physical. His body is weirdly restless. He wonders if it's because while in the coma, he stored energy, pacing the cage of his body, waiting to be let loose. He'd like to shoot hoops. 'Aren't there some academy kids around who I could play a pickup basketball game with?'

'The doctors would never let you do something so dangerous!'

'I'd like to just see who's around, maybe even some of my teachers.' He'd like to see Glassings and ask him about his last memory – the lecture on beautiful barbarism. 'Did they send me cards? We always did that when kids went into quarantine.'

'Of course they did! But they were . . . destroyed. The doctors didn't want to risk germs coming in with them.'

'Really? You just destroyed them all?'

'Yes, but there were tons of them. People really like you.'

'They're *supposed* to like me,' Partridge says. 'I'm Willux's son.'

She swims around his waist and bobs back up. '*I* like you,' she says. 'I'd like you no matter what.'

Although he couldn't swear to it, she seems honest. She dips underwater and swims through his legs. When she breaks the surface behind him, she says, 'It's hard to believe it's winter. Isn't it?'

'Maybe it isn't,' Partridge says. 'Who knows what it's like on the outside.'

Iralene laughs. 'You're so funny. It's one of the things I love about you.'

But Partridge wasn't joking. 'Do I think you're funny?' he asks Iralene.

She swims in close, touches her wet nose to his. He feels an ache – is it love? It feels more like homesickness or lovesickness. Iralene says, 'You think I'm pretty.'

'But do I think you're *funny*?'

She looks away. 'You think I'm everything you've ever wanted!'

Partridge nods. She's got to be. Why else would he have proposed?

Beckley is driving them in a small enclosed motorized cart. They sit in the backseat. They're being kept out of sight. Iralene's hair is perfectly puffed. How she managed it so quickly after the swim Partridge isn't sure. Was there a pit crew in the ladies' locker room?

'Where to now?' Partridge asks.

'The zoo,' she says, looking out the foggy plastic window. 'The butterflies and the aquarium are my favorite, remember?'

He doesn't remember, so he doesn't answer. He notices a small beetle on the back of Beckley's seat. He almost reaches out to touch it. But something in him tells him not to point it out to Iralene.

They go to the butterfly house first. It's kept warm and moist. They're surrounded by dense foliage. The butterflies dip and sputter all around them. Beckley keeps a respectful distance. He looks uncomfortable among all the flitting wings.

This section has been cleared just for them too, but some parts must be open to the public; Partridge can hear children not too far off. This trip reminds him of Christmases when he used to stay with the Hollenbacks, Julby and Jarv, stockings and little presents, lonesome holidays when his father was too swamped with work to take Partridge for even a few days.

Sometimes they came to the zoo and walked around.

Iralene holds Partridge's hand tightly, as if she's afraid of butterflies.

'I wonder if my father will want me to spend the holidays with him? Will we suddenly bond while he prepares me for my new future?' He can't even say the words without sounding a little sarcastic.

A bright blue butterfly alights on Partridge's shoulder. Iralene points it out. 'Look! It's so delicate and perfect!'

The butterfly really is beautiful. This close up he can see the black, velvety edges of its wings. But he looks past it, at Iralene – her brilliantly green eyes, her perfect features, her shining hair. 'Does my father love me now all of a sudden?' Partridge says, the butterflies batting all around their heads.

Iralene slips her arms around his waist. 'Maybe it's been hard for him to show his love, what with the losses you two have suffered.'

'You mean with my mother dead and Sedge having killed himself.' He's not sure why he says it so bluntly. Maybe he's testing her.

'Sad,' she says, 'but we really shouldn't talk about them. The past is gone!'

Partridge has the desire to defend his mother and Sedge, as if they've been pushed aside. He's suddenly angry. He reaches around and unhooks Iralene's hands. 'Don't say that.'

'What?'

'Don't talk about them like that. The past isn't the past.' He walks away from her.

'Now that we're engaged, there's hope for a beginning. A new start. That's what we can be for your father, for each other.'

'Something's not right,' he says, rubbing his temple.

'What do you mean?' She walks toward him, but he takes another step away.

'I don't know,' he says. He makes a fist. 'My body,' he says, and he stares at himself.

'What about it?'

His body doesn't feel like it's been bedridden. His muscles are the strongest and leanest they've ever been. He doesn't trust Iralene, even though there's something about her that's sincere, innocent.

'Partridge,' she says, 'talk to me.'

He says, 'Nothing. It's nothing.'

A sprinkler goes off overhead, puffing out mist.

Partridge thinks of blood. A misty veil of blood. The image stains his mind. The butterflies become frantic. He looks over his shoulder for Iralene, but he can see only bits of her dress, her hair, as if all the wings have chopped her into small fragments of herself.

———

Even the halls that connect the butterfly house and the aquarium have been cleared. They walk through a glass tunnel, fish swimming on either side and overhead. The jellyfish puff and glide, puff and glide. Iralene presses her hand to the glass.

'I wish we had a camera,' she says. 'I'd love to have a picture of this.'

'Don't you have a million of them from when you were a kid?' There are only so many places in the Dome to take memorable childhood pictures.

'Of course I do!' She hurries away from the glass and grabs his hand.

They walk along quietly for a while, and then there's a

commotion up ahead, some quickly scurrying footsteps.

Beckley lifts his hand and tells Partridge and Lyda to stop. He walks ahead of them, toward a blind turn. 'Who's there?' he calls out.

A man's voice calls out nervously, 'Just me! I got lost on my way to the restroom!' Glassings rounds the corner. He's flushed like he's been running.

'Please turn back the way you came,' Beckley says authoritatively.

'Wait!' Partridge says, and he starts to jog toward Glassings but slows down because his head's throbbing. 'Glassings!' he says, reaching out his hand.

Glassings shakes it with great vigor. 'Partridge!'

Iralene moves in between them. 'We can't talk now!' she says. 'Partridge can't have any visitors. His immune system is very weak! Right, Beckley?'

Beckley puts a firm hand on Glassings' chest. 'We need you to back off now, sir.'

'No, no,' Partridge says. 'It's just Glassings.' Iralene pulls on Partridge's arm. 'Let go of me!' he says to Iralene. 'Leave him alone, Beckley! For shit's sake, he's my World History teacher!'

Beckley ignores Partridge. He draws his weapon, and although he keeps it pointed at the floor, he says, 'I'm going to need you to walk away, Glassings.'

'Whoa, now,' Glassings says.

'What the hell is the matter with you, Beckley?'

'Everything's okay,' Glassings says. 'I was just saying hi. I hadn't seen Partridge since he made it back.'

'Made it back?' Partridge says.

'Shut up!' Beckley says, and he raises the gun.

'Holy shit, Beckley!' Partridge shouts. 'Back the hell off!'

Glassings doesn't say a word now. He walks backward very slowly, his hands in the air.

Beckley says, 'Keep moving, Partridge, and everything's going to be okay.'

Glassings nods to Partridge. *This is serious*, Glassings' expression reads. *Do as he says*.

'Come on,' Iralene says.

He lets her pull him around the corner. Once there, he rips his arm loose. 'Quiet.'

There's no gunshot. No scuffling. No noise at all.

In a minute or two, Beckley returns, as if nothing happened. He mutters, 'Let's move,' and walks on down the hall.

Partridge strides up to him. 'What the hell was that back there?'

'Following orders. No contact with anyone other than Iralene. Period.'

'Glassings is just a teacher of mine from the academy, and you drew a gun on him!'

'Nothing personal. Orders.' He keeps walking, shoulders stiff, no expression.

Partridge doesn't know what to say. He turns to Iralene. 'Orders,' she says, 'that's all!' She tries to reach out to him, but Partridge shrugs her off. He's so angry that he can't even speak.

When they get to the small aquatic theater, Partridge takes a seat in the back and stares straight ahead at a wall made of super-strength glass. On the other side the beluga whales, beautiful and strong, pulse their thick tails through the water.

Iralene sits next to him. He can tell she's gazing at him but refuses to look at her. 'Why the hell did my father give the order not to talk to anyone but you?' Partridge asks, watching Beckley out of the corner of his eye.

'For your own safety, for your own good.'

'Stop it, Iralene. Something's wrong. I know it.'

'Of course something's wrong! You're just coming back to your life. It's a great shock, Partridge.'

'What did Glassings mean? He said that he hadn't seen me since I'd been back. Back from where?'

'I don't know!' Iralene says, jerking her shoulders up and down. 'Maybe back from the brink. That's the way I think of it. You were gone and now you're back!'

'That's not what it sounded like, though. It sounded different.'

'I'm going to ask the doctor if it's normal for patients like you to be suspicious of the gap in their memory. I bet it is.'

'You think so?'

'I'm sure of it.'

The belugas glide by, two of them, side by side. Partridge is deeply tired. He rubs his eyes and lets them blur as he stares into the water. 'Why are we doing all these things, Iralene?'

'We have to rebuild,' she says. 'We fell in love this way. I can't sacrifice all our past. It would break my heart if we couldn't remake the memories.'

It surprises Partridge that a girl like Iralene *loves* him. She seems so normal, so perfected, and he's never felt normal and has always been far from perfect. It seems cruel that he's doomed to not remember any of it. He wonders how intimate they've been. It's a fair question. Not one that he's comfortable asking. What if they've acted like a married couple already and he doesn't remember it? He'd love to know and, at the same time, he wouldn't, because even though she's attractive, he's not attracted to her. He knows Iralene but he doesn't; that's the strange thing. They're close and also strangers.

'Are we supposed to rebuild the memories or remake them?' he asks.

'What's the difference?'

'Do you believe that memories can be rebuilt? I mean, will I ever remember the first time we were here together? Or do we just have to redo everything? *Remake* the memories.'

'I don't know,' she says. She seems to stiffen up a little. 'Your father told us to have fun. It was an order.'

'Maybe I don't like to be told what to do.'

'Don't be like that,' Iralene says, and it's the first time he's heard an angry edge in her voice. It surprises him, in a good way. He'd like to think she has some fight in her. She glances at Beckley as if he weren't just a guard but also an informant, a tattle. She points to the belugas. 'They have belly buttons, you know. They're a lot like us.'

The belugas swish their tales so powerfully it's as if he can imagine human legs like a mermaid's beneath their skin. 'Maybe we're like them,' he says.

Iralene smiles at him. 'This is the happiest I've ever been.' She's telling the truth. He can feel it in the way she's gazing at him. And, too, she's waiting for him to agree. Her eyes are brimming with tears. 'You still love me, don't you?'

The question makes Partridge panic. Beckley shifts his weight, glances at them and then away. He's too far away to hear, but still Partridge hates that he's here at all. It's like he has an audience – a grudging one that sometimes pulls a gun.

How can Partridge tell Iralene that he's not sure? He feels an ache of love. He feels it when he looks into her eyes. If he's not in love, he once was. Still, he can't honestly say that he loves her and he couldn't possibly tell her that he's not sure. He doesn't even have a memory of having first kissed her, much less having loved her.

Her lashes are dark, her lips full. She's there, waiting, and so he leans in and kisses her. She's surprised by the kiss at first. She stiffens for a moment and then relaxes into it. He waits for the rush – something passionate or at least familiar. But the kiss doesn't bring anything back. It's as if this is their first kiss, except it doesn't have the tingling of a first kiss. It feels hollow, empty.

When he pulls away, she says, 'It's okay, Partridge.'

'What's okay?'

'I understand.' Does she understand that he can't tell her he loves her? He wishes the memories would flood back to him. She deserves that much.

'You're beautiful,' he says. 'You really are.'

She puts her hand on his cheek.

He says, 'I could . . .' What? *Try* to fall back in love with her? 'We have time,' he says. 'We don't have to rush it.'

She shakes her head, puts her mouth to his ear. 'But we don't have time, Partridge. We don't.'

LYDA

WEAKNESS

THE NOISES OUTSIDE are drumming loudly in Lyda's ears. They've been at it all day – the mothers calling names from rosters, organizing the women into groups, hammering, sawing, children squalling. The place is a hive.

They're preparing for their attack on the Dome. Lyda can do nothing to stop them. She sits cross-legged on top of her blanket, feeling useless. She resists the urge to slam her hands over her ears and pound the floor with her feet. The mothers haven't explained their plan to Lyda, but she knows it's doomed.

Mother Hestra walks into the room. She stands like a pillar beside cot number nine, staring down at Lyda. Syden coughs as if to get her attention, but she can't look at them. She's too distraught. 'Were you true to your word?' Lyda finally says. 'Did you look for them?' Pressia, Bradwell, El Capitan and Helmud – that's who she needs now.

Mother Hestra says, 'They're gone.'

'Gone?' Lyda looks up at Mother Hestra. 'Gone where?'

'None of our spies within the outpost know, but they've gone far. Past our own boundaries. Farther than we've known anyone to go.'

'They'll get killed out there.'

'Whatever drove them must be important and worth the risk.' Lyda's tired of people risking their lives for what's *important*. Partridge is gone. Illia is dead. And now the others have left. She's alone. 'What about Wilda?'

'Who?'

'A girl. Just a little girl. The one they made Pure.'

'There are many like her now.'

'Did she go with them?'

'No.'

'Is she okay?'

'None of the Purified children are okay, Lyda. And Deaths did this to them. They're shutting down. It's only more reason for us to fight.'

Lyda shakes her head. 'What were you like during the Before?' she asks Mother Hestra. 'Do you remember being that person?'

'I was a writer.'

'A writer? What did you write?'

'I wrote two kinds of things: those the government allowed and those the government did not allow.'

'". . . The dogs barked loudly. It was almost dark . . ." Did you write that?'

Mother Hestra nods. 'It was about my sister who tried to run. She lived out past the Meltlands. She didn't live a double life like I did – one for the government, one hidden away for myself. She was part of the resistance. They found her. They set dogs after her.'

'I'm sorry,' Lyda says. 'How . . .'

'How did it get burned onto my face?'

Lyda nods.

'I was holding the page I'd written up to the light of the window. The white of the paper reflected the light. The black of the ink absorbed it and burned the words into my skin. I was living a lie. I wasn't ever going to tell anyone about my sister. I was going to write it and put it in a drawer. And now I live with that sin of cowardice on my face forever.'

Lyda looks down at her hands. They now have calluses and nicks. She doesn't want to be Pure anymore, and now, because of this baby, she isn't and that feels right.

'Your friends,' Mother Hestra says, 'led us to important things. The outpost has been working hard. We found what they've been making and then went in and took them. Do you want to see?'

Lyda sighs and looks up. Part of her wants to stare at this wall – in particular a water stain that looks a little like the head of a bear – until all the noise fades and it's over. Done. But she can't. 'Show me.'

Mother Hestra reaches into her hunting sack, browned with dried blood, and pulls out a hunk of hard, black metal.

'What is it?'

'Well, it was a robotic spider sent from the Dome to kill us. But now it's a grenade that we will use to kill them.'

'The Dome has withstood the Detonations. Do they really think that handmade grenades are going to make a difference?'

'There's one more thing that we found,' Mother Hestra says. 'The very thing that we need the most, tactically. These will make all the difference.'

'What?' Lyda can't imagine what would make any difference in a battle against the Dome.

Syden reaches into his mother's hunting sack this time. He

pulls out two flattened, ashen pieces of thick paper. One of them is colorized on one side with the faded print of an advertisement. She recognizes it immediately. The SPRUCE UP YOUR HOME! poster that she took from the broken Plexiglas on the metro train. Syden offers them to Lyda. She takes them and unfolds them on the cot, running her hands over her own drawings of the girls' academy, the rehabilitation center, and Partridge's of the Dome's interior, floor upon floor, in exquisite detail.

'Our maps.' She thinks of lying on her stomach in the train car across from Partridge, the way he edged across the maps on his elbows and kissed her. She lifts her hand to her lips. 'Partridge.'

'Yes, Partridge – the Death,' Mother Hestra says. 'He did good work.'

Lyda and Partridge were talking about Christmas. She told him about her father, who once gave her a snow globe, and she realized that she was a girl trapped in the globe. He told her about his Christmases at the Hollenbacks' apartment. He promised her a gift: a paper snowflake. He asked her if that was all it took to make her happy and she'd said *Yes*, but added *this* and *you*.

'Partridge marked how he got out and perhaps where you were forced out as well – the points of weakness,' Mother Hestra says.

Weakness, like not being able to bury the past. Weakness, like not giving up hope when you know you should. Lyda blinks tears onto one of the maps then wipes her eyes.

'The grenades,' Mother Hestra says, 'should be launched at the points of *weakness*.'

Lyda looks up. 'No,' she says. With the maps and the grenades, could the mothers actually be able to do some real damage? The Dome is a fortress, yes, but when Partridge escaped, he proved that even fortresses have holes. The maps aren't enough to bring down the Dome, but they may be enough to get inside – armed – to hunt down Partridge, as Our Good Mother has vowed, and kill him.

Frantically, she folds the maps and gathers them in her arms. 'They're wrong. They're fakes. He was tricking you.'

'Really?' Mother Hestra says.

'He's a Death. You can't trust him.'

Mother Hestra grabs Lyda's wrist. 'Don't do this. I know what you're up to.'

'You taught me never to trust a Death!'

Mother Hestra says emphatically, 'I know what Deaths do when they work their way into a woman's mind. Stop trying to save him. These are the points of weakness!'

Mother Hestra's grip is steely. She pulls sharply on Lyda's arm, and the maps fall to the floor. The maps that she helped Partridge make could allow them to get at him – to murder him. 'Points of weakness,' Lyda whispers.

EL CAPITAN

BLURRED

THEY'VE FLOWN THROUGH two days and one night, and now it's getting dark again. El Capitan's eyes are blurry with exhaustion and his nerves jaggedly charged with adrenaline. Helmud has slept and woken and slept again. El Capitan jerks him awake. They're getting closer. He briefly opens the near-airtight vacuum seals on all three tanks, allowing for an intake of air to lower their altitude. No longer the endless glassy ocean below, a spotlight under the nose reveals they're gliding over the dark outlines of hills, valleys, rocky crests, dark lakes, and wrecked cities, tracts of hobbled houses and buildings.

'See that, Helmud? A different country. Never thought you'd see a different country, did you?'

'Did you?' Helmud asks.

'No, I did not,' El Capitan says.

The navigation console offers a topographic map, but it's useless. The Detonations altered the land. El Capitan will have to land the airship soon. 'How much farther?' he asks Fignan.

Fignan lights up. 'Seventeen point two miles. Due east.'

'Okay,' El Capitan says. 'Let's start looking for a flat stretch of land.' The airship bucks, jerking El Capitan backward, as if Helmud were tugging on him sharply. 'What the hell was that?' he says, his heart starting to race.

Fignan beeps, unsure what to do. 'Sixteen point one miles!' he blurts, as if this is going to help.

The airship smoothes out, and so he sighs. 'Okay. Just a glitch. It's fine now.'

But it isn't. It happens again, more sharply. El Capitan gets on his feet. The back of the airship lolls; the nose tips upward. Helmud hunches low on El Capitan's back.

'Jesus, find the part of the manual about emergencies! Do you think it's something in the aft-bucky?' El Capitan asks Fignan.

'In case of emergency,' Fignan says, 'in case of emergency. In case of engine failure in the aft-bucky . . .' Is he flipping pages of the manual? Fignan's lights are all on. 'Check the navigational display.'

El Capitan sits back down and runs his eyes over his console. A red light flickers on an outline of the airship's basic structure, indicating a hairline leak. He turns up the pumps in the failing tank, getting rid of the air as fast as it's being taken on. The red light is still flashing, but the fracture is small, contained. As long as he monitors it, keeping the balance of air, the airship should hold on until he can land it.

'I have to bring it down.'

'Bring it down!' Helmud says.

The airship slows again. The aft-bucky is taking on even more air. The airship is dragging. It lurches backward.

'What the hell is going on in there?' Bradwell shouts.

'Small leak. Taking on air!'

And then suddenly Bradwell is hulking in the door frame. 'Small leak? What does that mean?'

'We're fine. Go sit down. Buckle up.' The fact that El Capitan couldn't strap himself in – what with Helmud on his back – hadn't worried him during takeoff, but he wouldn't mind having a buckle in place now.

'You need help!' Bradwell says. 'You need a copilot.'

'I've got Fignan, plus a copilot permanently installed.' He points to Helmud on his back.

'Cap,' Bradwell says. 'Let me do something—'

'You can't!' El Capitan says. 'Go back to your seat. That's an order.'

Bradwell staggers back to the cabin. El Capitan can hear him talking to Pressia. Is Bradwell undercutting him while his back is turned?

El Capitan doesn't want to bring it down any farther from his mark than he has to. They're less than fifteen miles out, but every mile they have to make on foot could be overrun with deadly creatures – impassable. He's got to bring them in tight.

The spotlight hits a strange herd of loping creatures – Beasts, Groupies, Dusts, or something else altogether? They disappear into a small stand of trees.

The airship rolls to one side. El Capitan pulls hard in the opposite direction to straighten it out. A whistling sound is coming from the aft-bucky, and the navigation display shows a new, longer fissure.

'What? Why? Fignan!' El Capitan shouts. 'Maybe I'm over-working the pumps and it's too much pressure!'

'Too much pressure on the pumps can result in cracking, especially if the airship has been cruising at high altitudes for durations exceeding forty hours,' Fignan reports.

'Damn it! Why didn't you tell me this before?'

Fignan doesn't say anything. His lights dim, as if he's expressing some measure of guilt.

'Stay with me here, Fignan! You're all I got!'

'You're all I got!' Helmud says.

'Don't get all jealous, Helmud!' El Capitan shouts at his brother.

There's a cracking sound – loud and sharp. Something has broken and come loose. The airship jerks again, more sharply this time, sending El Capitan and Helmud rocketing back in their chair.

'Cap!' Pressia shouts. 'What's going on?'

God, he doesn't want to fail, not with Pressia here – not with her life in his hands. 'I'm going to land her! We're taking on too much air.'

He has no choice but to crank the pumps on the good tanks, hoping not to lose altitude too quickly and end up in a tailspin. He pulls himself to his feet and stares down at the topographic map and at the large, bulky land slipping underneath the ship.

Up ahead there's a ring of greenery and verdant woodland, but on the other side it seems relatively flat. He doesn't think he can clear it; there's a meadow, though, on this side of the greenery that he's set his sights on. It's only nine miles off target. 'The wind is coming from the northwest!' he tells Fignan. 'How do I land this sucker?'

'It is best to steer the airship into the wind before touchdown.'

'Right, okay.' El Capitan noses closer into the wind and angles toward the center of a field. 'It'd be nice to have a landing crew on hand.' He crests a hill, and, once over the flat land, he starts to hover, nose straight into the wind, with the propellers pushing against it to keep the ship steady.

Still, the tail is weighing them down. He eases up on the

pumps on the other two tanks. The airship starts to sink, quickly. 'Not too fast! Not too fast!' he urges. He extends the pronged feet that they'll land on. 'Easy does it.'

'Easy does it!' Helmud says.

But the back of the airship is too heavy. They're going down too fast now. He applies pressure to the pumps of the intact tanks, but it comes as a burst, popping the nose up. 'Hold on!' he shouts. 'Brace for landing!'

Helmud grips his brother's shoulders, but El Capitan can't brace. He's still trying to soften the blow of the landing, kicking in the propellers, cutting the front tank, and riding the middle tank hard. 'Brace for landing,' Helmud whispers hoarsely. 'Brace for landing!'

When they hit the ground, El Capitan's head slams into the throttles. He's knocked to the floor. He's dazed, one eye immediately blurred by blood. The middle tank is still pumping, which makes the airship still somewhat buoyant. It gets kicked by the wind, sending the whole ship to its side. The windshield hits something, cracks, and splinters. Capsizing, El Capitan thinks.

He's shoved against the glass side of the cockpit. He struggles to stand since the airship still has life.

'Brace for landing!' Helmud shrieks. 'Brace for landing!'

'It's okay, Helmud! It's okay, brother!' He reaches over his head and slams the final working pump and the propellers with his fist. The airship breathes a sigh of relief and bobbles as if it's on the ocean floor. The navigation console is a blank screen.

Blinking blood from one eye, El Capitan drags himself on his elbows to the windshield. The world on the other side of the glass is dark. He notices the silence. He calls out, 'Pressia!' but his voice is weak.

And then everything is blackness.

PRESSIA

BLOW TO THE HEAD

Pressia is tilted, almost upside down, secured to her seat by her lap belt, which now cuts sharply into one of her thighs. Her face is poised by the porthole. She can see only thick, sharp blades of grass. The airship has rolled to its side by gravity, no longer buoyant.

She runs her hand under her sweater and checks the vials. Unbroken.

'What the hell happened?' Bradwell says. He's held in place by his seat belt too, but he's tall enough to reach out a hand and support himself by pushing against the side of the curved wall above the porthole.

'Crash landing.' She finds the smooth handle of the belt buckle, but if she releases it, she could land hard.

Bradwell pushes both of his hands against the ceiling. 'Unhook my belt, then I'll help you with yours.'

She fits her hand into the flexible silver handle of his seat belt and pulls it up. His arm strength cushions the fall. He stands on the side wall, hooks his one arm around Pressia's waist as she wraps her arms around his neck. She loves that he's broad and strong, his muscles toughened by years of brute survival. He pops her seat belt loose and helps her down.

They clamber to the cockpit, the airship rocking under their shifting weight.

El Capitan is sprawled out, unconscious, his arms spread wide, a gash on his head, his blood pooling like a dark halo. He's out cold.

Helmud lifts his head from over El Capitan's shoulder. 'Brace for landing,' he says quietly. 'Brace for landing. Brace for landing.' His cheek is red and wet with his brother's blood.

'Jesus,' Bradwell says, 'what do we do?'

Fignan sits beside them. 'Apply ice to reduce swelling. Apply pressure to stem the flow of blood.'

Pressia kneels beside El Capitan. She pulls her sweater sleeve down over the heel of her hand and holds it to the wound. 'Get a blanket,' she tells Bradwell.

He climbs back through the door quickly.

'Where's the medical kit?' she asks Helmud.

'Brace for landing,' Helmud says again, his eyes wide and skittish.

'It's going to be okay, Helmud,' Pressia tells him.

Bradwell re-emerges and hands her a blanket. She folds it and holds it to the wound. A navy-blue blanket, it quickly takes on blood, turning a shade darker.

'Check his eyes,' Pressia says to Bradwell.

Bradwell lifts one of El Capitan's lids. 'What am I looking for? Dilation?'

'Yes,' Pressia says. 'And hopefully they're dilating in sync.'

Bradwell lifts both lids together. He moves back and forth, blocking Fignan's light and letting it in. 'No such luck.'

'He has a concussion,' Pressia says. 'We can't leave him behind.'

'We can't abandon the mission,' Bradwell says.

'Brace for landing,' Helmud says.

El Capitan's eyes flutter.

'Cap?' Pressia says. 'Are you okay?' She touches his cheek with her doll head.

He blinks up into her eyes. He squints. His eyes swim away and float back to her face and then he locks onto her eyes. He tries to whisper something, but at first his voice is too hoarse.

Pressia bends closer. 'What is it, Cap?'

He lifts his hands and cups her face gently. 'Pressia,' he whispers, and then he kisses her. It's a brief kiss – soft and gentle on her lips.

Pressia is stunned. She's not sure what to say. She's holding her breath. Her eyes are wide open. She remembers El Capitan singing the love song, and then later, on the dam, how they were all fighting over the definition of romantic.

She's still holding the blanket to his head wound. She shakes her head. 'Cap,' she says. 'You just . . .' *Kissed me*. El Capitan just kissed her. It must have been a mistake.

Then he says, 'I love you, Pressia Belze.'

And there is no mistaking that.

He drops his hands and his eyes glide away from her face. His lids close. Just like that, he's out again.

Helmud looks at her and says, 'Pressia?' as if he'd like to know if she loves El Capitan in return.

She feels like crying. That love song he sang. Was he thinking of her? She's stunned. She wonders how long he's felt this way, how long he's walked around bearing this secret. Now she understands the look he gave her when she was holding on to Bradwell so tightly on the bridge.

Bradwell stands up and walks to the cockpit door. He says, 'I didn't know.'

'What do you mean?' She feels a surge of panic. Is he talking about her and El Capitan? Does he think that there's been something going on between them? 'There's nothing to know.'

Bradwell punches something. Pressia hears the sudden crack. The airship wobbles for a second. Is he jealous? Or just mad that he didn't know something — even though there was nothing to know?

'We're not thinking straight!' Pressia says. 'None of us! He didn't mean it. He's—'

'He meant it,' Bradwell says. 'I should know. I've been wanting to say those words for so long. And he comes along and says them?'

'He's taken a blow to the head!' Pressia says and then she stops, her mind running over what Bradwell's just said. 'You've been wanting to say those words?'

His back to her, he freezes. He draws in a breath. 'Yes.'

'Yes,' Helmud says, as if he's known all along.

She looks at Helmud, truly looks at him for the first time in a long while. She wants to ask him if he's known about this secret. Helmud understands much more than he lets on. He scrapes his small row of upper teeth against his bottom lip anxiously.

'What are we going to do?' Pressia says to Bradwell. 'One of us has to keep going. One of us has to stay.'

Bradwell doesn't answer.

She lifts the blanket. The bleeding has slowed. The wound is swollen but not gushing. 'Helmud,' she says. 'Put your hand where my hand is.' She offers him a fresh section of blanket. He takes hold and she pushes on his hand. 'Apply steady pressure.'

He says, 'Pressure.'

She gets up and walks toward Bradwell. She can see only his back, the birds shifting beneath his shirt. He's looking at his knuckles, probably having cut them. There's a dent in the wall – a spiderwebbed shatter in the lining. She passes him and climbs through the doorway and gets a bag of supplies – food and water. She carries them back into the cockpit.

'I'm going to keep going,' she says. 'You're staying.'

He turns around, shaking his head. 'No, no, no. That's not happening.'

She pushes the supplies into his arms. 'Yes, it is.'

'There's no way you should head out on your own.'

'You forgot that I'm here, on some level, for selfish reasons.'

'You're not going to find your father, Pressia.'

'If you go out there and you find him or some clue – one measly clue – about his existence, instead of me, I'll never forgive you. This is my trip to make.'

'It's not just yours, Pressia. Walrond left that message for my parents before he killed himself, before I found my parents shot to death in their beds.'

Of course he found them. She'd just never realized it. 'You *found* them?'

He looks at Helmud holding the blanket to his brother's head.

'Bradwell,' she whispers.

'It was morning. I went down for breakfast. They weren't in the kitchen. I walked through the house, calling their names. Then I started running . . . I opened their door. And there they were.'

'I'm so sorry . . .'

'I didn't know they were dead at first. The blood didn't look like blood. It'd dried. But when I got close and touched my mother's arm, it was stiff and cold. And I could see the blue tinge of her skin.'

'Why didn't you tell me?'

'I've had years to get over it.'

'You can't get over something like that.'

'So I'm selfish too. I'm doing this because my parents are dead. Willux had them killed. I'm not just along for the ride. I'm not doing this just for the greater good.'

'Bradwell,' she whispers. 'I'm the one who's going to keep going. And you're the one who's going to stay, because my father might still be alive.' It's cruel, but it's the truth.

Fignan maneuvers his way over the cockpit door.

'You can't leave me here with Cap after he *kissed* you, after what he *said* to you!'

Is he blaming her? Does he think she led on El Capitan or was having a relationship with him at the same time as Bradwell? She turns and walks, unsteadily, along the walls of the airship, to the door in the cabin, now almost overhead, that leads outside.

'Wait!' Bradwell says. 'No! You can't . . .'

She uses the seats as a kind of ladder to climb up to the door. She turns the large wheel that locks the door into place and then lets it fall open.

'You're really doing this.'

'Hand me Fignan. I'll need him to help navigate.' She props herself on her elbows, pulling herself the rest of the way up then sitting on the side of the airship's gondola. It's dark, even with the glow of the airship's light coming up from the door, the glass cockpit, the portholes.

Bradwell runs his hands through his hair and rubs the scars on his cheek roughly.

'I'll go without Fignan. Is that what you want?'

Bradwell sighs. He picks up Fignan and hands him to her through the cabin door. Fignan lights up a narrow spotlight that flits through the surrounding field, the distant trees.

She slides off the gondola to the ground.

Bradwell scrambles up after her. She looks at Bradwell, his hair sticking up messily on his head, his muscled shoulders, his eyes dark and wet. What does he think of her? What does he think of the two of them together? He's a black box, unknowable.

She can still feel El Capitan's kiss on her lips. It surprised her maybe most of all because it was so tender. El Capitan isn't the type to do anything tenderly. She doesn't love El Capitan – not the way he loves her. But she does love him in *some* way. They've been through so much. When she had no one, he helped her. He saved her. And she's pretty sure that in some elemental way she's changed him. There's so much between them now. It's not a simple or easy relationship. How could it be? When she first met him, she was afraid he was going to shoot her.

Bradwell looks at her expectantly.

She listens, for a moment, for what might be out there. It's quiet and for some reason that scares her even more.

She says to Bradwell. 'I feel it right now.'

'What?'

An airy sensation in her stomach, her heart drumming in her chest like she's falling, falling. 'I don't understand what we mean to each other or everything we've been through together. But . . .' She rubs a tear from her cheek. 'I know that one day I'll miss it – even the brutal parts, even the awfulness. I'll miss you,' she says, looking up at him, 'this moment, right now.'

He looks at her like he's memorizing her face.

'I'll make it there,' she says.

'I want you to make it back.'

PARTRIDGE

NEBRASKA

Partridge AND IRALENE'S DAYS are rigorously scheduled – a picnic by the soy fields, a visit to the planetarium, private dance lessons with Mirth and DeWitt Standing, from whom they learn the cha-cha, the rumba, the fox-trot. DeWitt counts loudly over the scratchy music. Mirth says, 'Chins up! Chins up!' while Beckley stands by, smirking.

And the polite chatter is relentless. Sometimes he's furious for no reason. Maybe it's just that his father supposedly wants him to be a leader and *this* is how he's using his time?

What's worse is that he has no control. If he asks to do something else – catch up with friends or find Glassings so that he can apologize for Beckley pulling a gun on him – Iralene tells him that he's too fragile. 'You can have contact only with those fully screened for disease and illness.'

Sometimes he wonders if it would be better to be unconscious than to be shuffled through one stupid little date after the next. And there's never even a tiny spark of memory. The one thing that returns to him again and again is what Iralene said in the aquarium: *But we don't have time, Partridge. We don't.*

While Iralene is changing shoes after a dance lesson, he asks her what she meant by it.

'I don't even remember saying that, Partridge. You know me. Sometimes I say silly things!'

'I don't know you,' he says. 'That's the problem.'

She looks up at him, startled, and then lets out a quick peal of laughter, but as the laughter fades, it sounds like she might cry.

'Sorry, Iralene. I didn't mean to hurt your feelings.'

'Hurt my feelings? What are you talking about?'

Since the kiss in the aquarium, she's been a little more keyed up. Maybe she's waiting for him to fall in love with her again. He's trying. God knows, he's trying. I mean, what kind of a jerk would take a blow to the head and tell a girl that he didn't love her anymore? He couldn't do that to her.

Still, he feels manipulated and powerless. Later in the backseat of the motorized cart, he leans forward and tells Beckley that he wants to see his father. He's said this many times and Beckley always makes up excuses. This time Partridge adds, 'Let me guess, Beckley. I can't see my father because of back-to-back meetings or a long dinner with other leaders or a presentation he has to prepare for?'

Beckley doesn't answer. Iralene pats his knee. 'I'm sure he'll call you in for a visit soon!' As if Partridge is hurt by his father's lack of attention.

He's not hurt. He's suspicious.

And he's exhausted. His head still aches. Sometimes when people ask him questions, he feels like he's trying to read their lips because he can't quite hear them; it's like he's inside the tanks with the belugas, staring out from behind the thick pane of glass. 'Excuse me? Sorry. What was that?'

His exhaustion is bone-deep. He remembers this feeling just after the Detonations, after his mother died. He walked around waterlogged, too heavy to move. *Blessed, blessed.* That's when the word became so prevalent. *We're blessed to have gotten in.* If you're blessed, it's hardly your fault that you got in and others didn't. Being *blessed* is beyond your control. It was no one's fault – the blessed and the unblessed had been, before the Detonations, a hidden quality, something buried in the soul. But it had been made plain who was and who wasn't blessed. It was so clear, in fact, there was a list.

This meant you weren't allowed to feel guilty. Guilty of what? God's love? His blessings?

Partridge was supposed to be joyful. They all were. If they weren't, they were squandering God's blessings. He tried, but the grief – unspoken, unexpressed – only got heavier. The grief was physical. That's what this postcoma feeling reminds him of – the physicality of grief.

But he's got nothing to grieve. His life is better than he even remembers it. He confesses to Iralene one night, looking out over the beach scene, that his life feels so much better that it's almost uncomfortable. 'It's like I've been stuffed into a body that's not quite mine.'

'The wrong body? That sounds awful!' Iralene stares at him. He's trying to get used to the fact that she takes everything he says literally.

'Okay, fine, not the wrong body. It's more like when I'd sometimes accidentally pick up someone else's blazer at the boys' academy and it was too tight across the back, too short in the sleeves. Just wrong.'

'That's just because you have to catch up to this moment.

You're still back there and you have to work to get to the future, which is right now.'

'Huh.'

'It's not wrong. It'll start to feel right when it's familiar, that's all. What do you have to complain about now anyway?' It reminds him of the blessed and the unblessed, the wretches out there, living their doomed existences. What are their lives really like? He rubs the back of his neck and imagines the taste of dirt, ash. And the imagining is so real it almost feels like a memory.

Once the academy has closed for the Christmas holiday, Partridge suggests that they walk the grounds. 'Come on!' he says. 'Can we do just one thing that I want to do?'

'Okay!' Iralene says. 'If it'll make you happy, let's do it!'

The doors to the dormitories have already been locked, but Beckley lets them slip into an open window on the bottom floor.

Partridge shows Iralene his old room, cleaned out, empty. He tells her about Hastings, the old nag, the way he always said, 'I won't take it personally,' but he always did. He misses Hastings. 'He was this big lanky lug of a guy. He just wanted to have fun, shoot the shit. He lived for that kind of thing.'

Iralene wanders around the room, bounces on the lower bunk bed. 'Was this one yours?'

'No,' he says, pointing up the ladder.

Iralene smiles then climbs the ladder and lies down on the mattress, stripped bare, crossing her arms behind her head. 'What did you dream about up here?'

He dreamed about girls like Iralene walking into his dorm room and climbing the ladder to his bed, but just then he hears the click of the air-ventilation system. They regulate the temperatures even when no one's here. He walks to the window. 'What did I dream about?' He imagines the girls lined up on the field below, doing their morning exercises. That one girl turns her head. She looks straight at him. Who is she again? What's her name? Doesn't her mother work in the rehabilitation center? Does she sing in the choir? 'Mertz,' he says.

'What's that?' she says nervously.

'Nothing,' he says, looking up at her. 'I was just trying to remember someone's name and it came to me. You know how that is.'

She nods.

'I just can't picture Hastings toeing the line in Special Forces.' He walks to the mirror where Hastings used to fuss over his hair. He remembers Hastings standing there, in that very spot, dressed in a suit. 'The dance, right?'

'What about it?'

'Hastings – I just remember him giving me a hard time for not being ready to go.' He looks up at Iralene. 'And I met you after the dance?'

'I was there meeting a friend. Not everyone goes to the academy, you know.'

'I know, I know,' he says gently. He doesn't want to hurt her feelings again. The academy is reserved for the kids of the elite. 'Didn't I have a date? Wasn't I with someone?'

Iralene looks at him sadly. In fact, it's almost as if she's going to start crying. This is how it goes with Iralene. Partridge can't tell what's going to set her off.

Beckley whistles. Partridge walks over to the window and looks out. Beckley's there waving them down. 'Beckley,' Partridge says. 'He's like a mother hen.'

Iralene climbs halfway down the ladder and then says, 'Catch me!'

Partridge walks over. She reaches out and wraps her arms around his neck. He holds her up off the ground for a moment and then dips her to the floor, but she doesn't let go. It's the kind of hug you'd give someone you were saying goodbye to, someone you might never see again.

'Iralene?' he whispers. 'You okay?'

'We need to be alone. We have to. I can ditch him,' Iralene whispers. 'I know how to ditch everybody. I've got a plan.'

And she does.

Later that night, Iralene and Partridge are in his bedroom. He's wondering what might happen next. They haven't kissed since the aquarium. It hadn't sparked any memories and it hadn't been the most exciting kiss in the world, but, hey, shouldn't he at least try again? Iralene is beautiful. He was in love with her at some point.

But as soon as he thinks about the possibilities, he feels a wave of exhaustion. Honestly, he'd like to get in bed, alone, close his eyes, and let this entire day blur to the background of his mind. He almost says, *I want to go home.* Why does he feel so homesick?

But Iralene has a sense of urgency now. This is the one place they can get away from Beckley, but it seems strange. Partridge is well aware of the cameras eyeing them from the corners of the room, but still, he was never left alone with a girl before. All coed academy interactions were hawked by dowdy chaperones lurking in corners. Cameras are fine, but there's nothing quite like the physical presence of a wheezy calculus teacher to break the mood.

Iralene opens the orb. She presses in a code, and, as the handheld glows through the cracks in her cupped fingers, the room starts to change. The billowing curtains kicked by the automated ocean breeze turn to a dusky yellow print with blue flowers. They hang, thick and lank, in the windows, which are closed up tight. The bed turns into an old four-poster, a patchwork quilt folded at the foot of it. There's also an old tilted wardrobe and a rickety bedside table.

'What happened to the beach house?' Partridge says.

'You made me promise to take you back to this place.'

'Really? What is this place?'

'An old farmhouse. Somewhere in Nebraska, I think.'

'I wanted to come back to *Nebraska*?' Partridge says. It doesn't make sense. 'Are you sure I said this place? Was I joking? When did I make you promise that?'

Still holding the orb, she crosses her arms as if she's cold and turns a slow circle. 'You just did, okay?' She's agitated. She walks up to him, puts her hand on his shirt, runs it up under his collar. 'I think we should be alone.' She flits her eyes to the corners of the room where the cameras are perched.

He puts his hand on hers. She grips his hand, holds it tightly. 'I don't know.'

'Do you trust me?' she says.

It's a loaded question. There's something in Iralene's voice that makes it clear she wants him to consider his answer very carefully. He looks into her eyes – a bright vibrant green. He hasn't really had a lot of interaction with many girls – not even his own mother. But still, Iralene's not like other girls. She's sweet and demure, but steely. Is she following his lead or secretly leading? She's capable of much more than she lets on, and yet he's sure that she's good. 'Yes,' he says, 'I trust you.'

Iralene starts working the orb again. She's pressing the screen madly. The room shifts and churns. The lights sputter. Finally, it returns to the farmhouse, but the lights dim and the cameras make little defeated clicking noises, and the orb sighs. 'I've overloaded the system. You have a little time. Does this place mean anything to you?' Iralene asks.

'No.'

'Think about it.'

'Okay,' he says, nodding at the room in all of its plainness. 'I'm *thinking* and . . . nope. It doesn't mean a thing.'

She sighs. 'You have to find what you hid here!'

'What I *hid* here?'

'I'm sure you hid something for yourself to find later. Why else would you ask me to return to this place?'

'You're not making any sense.'

She rips back the covers, then gets down on her hands and knees, and looks under the bed. 'Do you think this is easy for me? I've been waiting almost all my life for the possibility of you falling in love with me. But I can't do it, not like this.' She gets to her feet, crying now, throws the pillows, runs her hands along the windowsill.

He walks over to her and holds her by her shoulders. 'Iralene, calm down. Talk to me.'

She swallows and blinks, clearing tears from her eyes. 'The last night before they swiped your memory . . . you hid something here so that you would know the truth.'

'*Swiped* my memory?' Partridge feels sick. 'I thought you said that . . .'

'No, there was no accident.'

He thinks of their kiss. He looks around the room. 'Were we ever . . .'

She shakes her head. 'You were never in love with me.'

He rubs the back of his neck, feeling the hard plastic of his cast. He holds his hand out in front of his face. 'But what about my pinky?'

'Partridge,' she says, 'if you were going to hide something here, where would you put it?'

'Well, I wouldn't have known that I was going to be looking for it. Would I?' He's confused but also angry. 'All this time, you've been lying to me!'

'I'm telling the truth now. You have to think! There isn't time!'

He walks around the room, feeling dizzy. 'Nothing makes sense. I don't know what's true and what's . . .' He looks at Iralene. 'What did you mean you've been waiting all your life for me to fall in love with you?'

Iralene grips the bedpost, the bright blue veins standing out on her thin inner wrist. She's sobbing.

Partridge walks up to her. 'Tell me what's going on.'

'I'm giving it all up,' she says. 'You have a chance, Partridge. You have a chance to stop it from happening.'

'What?'

'He's going to kill you.'

'Who's going to kill me?'

'Your father.'

'Why would you say that? He's just actually started to like me . . .'

She grabs the front of Partridge's shirt. 'You can stop him,' she says. 'I'm giving you this chance. You have to take it.'

'Iralene . . .'

She walks away from him to the far wall. She leans against it. 'I'm giving up everything for you, Partridge.'

'Why?'

She looks at him and smiles through her tears. 'With you,' she says, 'I really have felt the happiest I've ever felt in my life. I'd always wanted to know what that was like. Happiness. And I've felt it with you.'

'Iralene.' There's so much more he wants to ask her.

She slides down the wall and sits on the floor, her dress ruffling around her. She pulls her knees to her chest and hides her eyes. 'Find it,' she says, her voice muffled and hoarse. 'You don't have much time.'

PRESSIA

BREEDING

PRESSIA STARTED OUT RUNNING, but there was no way to keep the pace. So she begins running only on downhill slopes when the momentum is with her, like it is now. It's dark. She holds Fignan under one arm. He sends out a cone of light that tours the trees – stunted, gnarled, and hunched – and then bounces back to the path in front of her. The ground is covered in dense ivy. It blankets rocks, the trunks of trees, the forest floor. She hits a patch and her boots lose their grip. She slips then staggers, steadies herself by grabbing hold of a branch. But she starts running again, dodging branches, jumping ruts, and jutting roots. She knows that she's running out of time. The mud suctions the tread of her boots, slowing her down.

Fignan keeps her on track, lighting up a map with old roads and landmarks. And he's counting down the hours to the solstice. Seven hours and forty-two minutes left. There's a chance she'll make it, but she doesn't think of the destination – only each step to the next.

She misses Bradwell, El Capitan, and Helmud. She still thinks about El Capitan's kiss, his *I love you, Pressia Belze*, and Bradwell, watching her leave. The more she thinks of them, the more certain she is that she needs to be here, without them, on her own.

She's seen a few glimpses of birds – or are they bats? They seem shrunken, and they dart more than glide. Small rodents skitter through the underbrush. They're twisted creatures – deformed in ways she's come to expect: fusings, scalded skin, hybrids.

But the air here isn't as blurred and darkened by ash, which makes it seem like the world is bigger, simply because she can see more of what lies around her. The greenery has rebounded more quickly too.

A thorned twig hooks Pressia's pant leg so hard that she falls. She catches herself on one elbow, but the jolt knocks Fignan into her ribs, kicking the air from her lungs.

She pulls her leg free, ripping her pant leg. A spot on her skin feels stung. She touches it and finds a welt. When she pulls her hand back, her fingers are smeared with blood.

'You okay?' she asks Fignan.

He bobs his lights.

'Nasty thorn,' she says.

She stands, the welt throbbing, and tightens her hold on Fignan. She starts to run again, but the ground feels even more slippery. She has to slow down, reaching from tree to tree to stay on her feet.

The dirt feels like it's shifting beneath her – as if the ivy is alive. She pushes on as fast as she can, but then something wraps around her ankle. She falls again. A vine curls over her arm. She tries to rip free, but there are more thorns. They quickly puncture her skin. Blood rises then drips over her arm. Another vine entwines her leg. 'Fignan!'

One vine circles her biceps, snakes up her shoulder, then behind the back of her neck across her cheek and toward her mouth. She shakes her head then thrashes, ripping up some of the vines. They simply pop from the dirt, their loose root tendrils dangling, but the cord of the vines holds strong. She and Fignan are lashed to the ground. She's stuck. She panics. 'Fignan! I can't move!' Only her eyes are wild. She doesn't want to die out here. She'd rot into the ground. Bradwell and El Capitan and Helmud would wait for her, never knowing what happened.

She hears Fignan buzzing and then a piney scent fills the air. 'Do you have a knife?' she shouts.

He beeps.

She can feel him sawing away vines. He severs one and it goes slack, spiraling off her leg.

Fignan moves to the vine twisted around her good arm, saws through it. She can then pull the knife from her own belt, and they're both working. She feels a new vine loop the ankle of her boot and quickly constrict the leather. She turns and slices it.

She gets to her knees, then she's almost standing. A quick vine whips through the air and circles her wrist where the doll head meets her skin. She imagines the vine choking the doll, and the image freezes her for a moment. But then she slips the knife between the doll head and the vine and cuts herself out. Fignan pops loose the last vine tethering her to the ground and she stumbles free.

The ivy recoils, hissing away from her.

She grabs Fignan and starts running as fast as she can. His light bounces along the terrain in front of them until she sees the end of the woods. She sprints toward it as fast as she can. Once out of the trees, she keeps running until she finds herself in the middle of a field.

There's a stretch of land and the hulking remains of a building in the distance, walls on either side that crumble to nothing. The ivy has inched up the remains of the walls and the building, cloaking all that's left – perhaps devouring it.

Her lungs heaving for air, she sets Fignan on the ground, rests her hands on her knees, and tries to catch her breath.

'We've lost time,' she says. 'How much do we have left?'

'Five hours and twelve minutes.'

'We can still make it,' she says, but she feels weak. Her clothes are lashed with small rips and dotted with blood seeping up from her skin. Each nick of a thorn feels like a bruised welt. 'I just need a second,' she says.

She starts shaking; her head feels like it's filled with bees. Her vision blurs and as she tries to focus it, she stares at a small clutch of clover with waxy leaves. She turns Fignan so that his light shines on the leaves. The ash that's settled on the greenery is fine and silky, so light that the green of the leaves still shines through. The leaves are dotted with tiny insects, like little ticks but with bright red, hardened shells.

The insects seem to have front pincers that work as arms shoveling ash as they click across the leaves on their delicate legs. 'Are they cleaning the ash away, clearing little paths?' she asks Fignan. But then, no – it seems like they're eating the ash. They're streamlined and purposeful. Their bodies are symmetrical, each one like the other. She says, 'What if they were bred for this purpose?' She stands upright, feeling chilled and sick.

Fignan beeps.

'If it's true, some of the Irish survived. They're here, some-where, and they're smart.'

EL CAPITAN

BROTHERS

THERE'S SOMETHING AT HIS MOUTH – nudging his lips, harder and harder, insistent. He slaps it away. Flecks of cold water spray his face. The clang of metal against metal.

He opens his eyes. He's on his side, curled.

His head. He reaches up and touches a gauzy pad over what feels like a gaping wound in his skull. The pain is sharp and deep – has his head been splintered open with an ax?

He hears Helmud's nervous breathing in his ear – faint and rapid. He's not alone. He's never alone.

They're in the airship.

The airship is down.

They're lying in the conical nose of the cockpit. His blurred vision focuses on grass and ivy, flattened on the other side of the wide window – like flowers pressed in a book. He remembers his grandmother's old books; pick one up and a purple flower would slip out – flat, dry – and wisp its way to the floor like a little gift, like a little secret love note.

He kissed Pressia.

The thought of it rockets him forward. He lifts his hands – his rough, callused palms up – and stares at them. He held her face in these hands. His lips touched hers. Why did he kiss her? Jesus. Why in the hell did he do that?

'Helmud,' he says, his voice rough and dry. 'Where is she?'

'Where is she?' Helmud says.

'Stop it!' he shouts. 'This is not the goddamn time for that shit, Helmud.' He tries to stand up.

'Stop it!' Helmud yells, wrapping his arms around his shoulders and jerking him backward. 'Stop it!'

El Capitan looks around the cockpit. Helmud has been trying to feed him. A metal cup, packets of dried meats. Helmud's knife.

El Capitan feels dizzy. His hand slides along the glass. Just as he gets to his feet, his boots skid out from under him and he's down again. He can't even stand. His face goes hot with shame. Bradwell was here when he kissed Pressia. He's sure of it. El Capitan slams the heel of his boot into the glass wall. What does she think of him now?

She's gone. Not that she could stay. How could she? The clock's winding down. She had to go. But did Bradwell go too?

'Did they leave us here to die?' El Capitan says. 'Goddamn it, Helmud. Did they think you were going to take care of me?'

'Take care of me,' Helmud says.

He knows that he should be wondering if they've gotten to Newgrange, if they've found the formula, but instead he's thinking that they could say anything to each other behind his back. They could make fun of him. Of course she didn't want him to kiss her. He's a guy with his brother on his back, a freak among freaks.

He knows why he kissed her. He was proud of himself for

flying this airship, even proud of himself for the emergency landing. And when he saw her face, he was glad she was alive. He loves her. He said it aloud. He's sure he did. And there's no going back now.

'Maybe we'll die here, Helmud. Maybe that'd be for the best.'

Helmud twists to one side. He's rummaging through a sack. 'For the best.'

'I'm glad that Dad gave up on me before he saw us like this. You know, Helmud? You know what I mean? I'm glad he left before he saw how sick we are. We're *sick*. Look at us.'

He feels Helmud's hand slip under his chin, pulling him up from the ground. El Capitan sits up, but not straight. He doesn't have enough energy. He slouches, leaning against Helmud, who has a spoon in one hand and a little tin of rice in the other. Helmud loops his arms around El Capitan. He moves the spoon to his brother's mouth. Helmud says, 'Look at us.'

El Capitan feels like crying. Helmud, after all these years, is going to take care of him. It's the two of them, bound.

'Look at us,' Helmud says again, and then he adds one more word: 'Cap.'

He isn't repeating a word. He isn't just an echo. He said something. El Capitan doesn't know when he last heard Helmud say his name – before the Detonations? El Capitan looks over his shoulder. He stares into his brother's face. It's like he hasn't seen it up close in years. Helmud isn't just a kid anymore. His face is warped but sturdy. His eyes are sunken and now they fill sweetly with tears. 'Look at us,' El Capitan says. 'Look at us.'

'Look at us,' Helmud says.

And then, overhead, El Capitan hears footfalls – heavy ones. A Beast? He sees his gun shoved up against the wall. He reaches for it. The pain in his head shoots down his spine. The gun is just out of reach. He plants his boot and shoves himself and Helmud forward.

The footfalls land hard inside the airship, which rocks a little. He hears someone coming toward the cockpit door.

His fingers brush the butt of the gun. He pushes off once more, wincing with pain, grabs the gun, swings it around, cocking it, and points it at the door – a large, shadowed figure.

'Jesus, Cap! Put that down.'

Bradwell.

'You're here,' El Capitan says.

'Yeah, I'm here and Pressia isn't. She went out, alone,' Bradwell says as he stands up.

'You let her?'

Bradwell glares at him, chin tucked to his chest. 'Are you criticizing me? I don't think that's in your best interest right now.'

'That sounds like a threat.'

'A threat,' Helmud whispers.

'Take it as a friendly warning.'

El Capitan doesn't like threats or warnings, but he likes the fact that Bradwell seems rattled. Maybe the kiss had more effect than he thought. 'How long has she been gone?' he asks, sitting up as much as he can.

'It'll be dawn soon. Maybe she's there. Maybe not. I couldn't go with her and leave you two here alone, could I?'

'You didn't go with her . . . because of me?'

'Because of me?' Helmud says, putting down the tin.

Bradwell nods. 'She told me I had to stay with you and Helmud, and she was the one who had to go.'

'You should've gone,' El Capitan says angrily. 'The last thing I want is Pressia out there alone! Anything could happen to her out there! We don't know this terrain, its Beasts and Dusts!'

'You wanted me to leave you here to die?' Bradwell says.

'Wouldn't you have made the same sacrifice?' El Capitan says. 'For her!' And, in this moment, El Capitan feels like he's said the unsayable – that they're both in love with her, that they'd die for her.

Bradwell crosses his arms on his chest. The birds rattle angrily on his back. 'I guess we've got that in common.'

El Capitan isn't sure what to say. His arms are weak. He rests the gun on the floor.

'We also both know that she wouldn't let either of us sacrifice the other on her account,' Bradwell says.

'Right,' El Capitan says.

'But also,' Bradwell continues, 'I couldn't leave you here to die . . . because you're like a brother to me. Both of you.'

'Both of you,' Helmud says.

El Capitan is stunned. He feels guilty. He kissed Pressia. Bradwell was standing right there. He told her he loved her. Brothers don't do that to each other. 'Sorry,' El Capitan says.

'For what?'

'I'm sorry about Pressia. I didn't mean to—' El Capitan says.

'Shut up,' Bradwell says and he walks over to El Capitan, stands over his body. El Capitan braces himself. There's a chance Bradwell might kick him in the ribs. 'You need to eat something.' He squats down, picks up the tin. 'And we've got to think of how to repair the damages. We've got to find a way to get this ship home.'

'Home,' Helmud says.

'Home,' El Capitan says, as if he's now the one who echoes his brother.

'I'm going back out,' Bradwell says, handing Helmud the tin. 'I think I know where the crack in the tank is. I'm going to get a closer look.'

'Is it safe out there?' El Capitan asks.

'Don't know for sure. So far, it's been quiet.'

'I don't like quiet,' El Capitan says. 'Puts me on edge.'

'On edge,' Helmud says.

Bradwell stands up. 'When I get back, I want you to have eaten all of it.' He nods at Helmud. 'You hear that, Helmud? Make sure he gets it all down.'

El Capitan feels Helmud jerk his head. A nod.

As Bradwell starts to leave, El Capitan says, 'I'd have stayed behind to save you.'

Bradwell stops. 'Thanks.'

'Thanks,' Helmud says.

Bradwell crawls out of the cockpit, into the cabin, and up out of its side. El Capitan listens to the scrape of his boots, feels the airship shift a little with his weight. He hears his footsteps overhead and then gone – Bradwell on the ground.

Helmud pushes the spoon to El Capitan's lips. 'Wait,' El Capitan says, but as soon as his mouth is open, Helmud shoves the food in. El Capitan chews obediently. Helmud's hand appears again, holding the spoon, ready to shovel it in. El Capitan's the weak one now. Helmud is the strong one. And, for a minute, El Capitan lets his weight sag against his brother. He lets his brother hold him up, feed him, take care of him. When was the last time anyone took care of El Capitan? Not since his mother was still at home. When he got headaches, she'd take a cool rag and lay it over his eyes, and let him eat gummy candies. El Capitan closes his eyes for a minute. He gives in.

And that's when he hears the shout – Bradwell's voice. 'Cap!' The call is loud and short, as if his mouth has been muffled. El Capitan bolts forward, his skull struck by sharp, searing pain. 'Bradwell!' he shouts. 'Bradwell!'

Nothing.

Quiet.

'Bradwell!' He hears only his breath and Helmud's, both coming hard and fast. 'Bradwell!' he says to Helmud. 'He's gone. Has he been taken?'

'Taken,' Helmud says.

El Capitan lurches forward. 'We can't just let him go.'

'Let him go,' Helmud says. 'Let him go.'

'No!' El Capitan says, getting onto his hands and knees and beginning to crawl to the door. His elbows buckle. He falls to his chest.

'Let him go,' Helmud says.

'No!' El Capitan whispers. 'No.'

LYDA

CHIRRUPS AND GRUNTS

GROUPS OF MOTHERS are causing distractions in the Rubble Fields and the Meltlands, drawing Special Forces to them. Meanwhile Lyda and a troop are winding through the trees in a long, snakish line in the middle of the night with lanterns on sticks, bobbing over their heads. Groups of four carry small catapults on their shoulders like child-size coffins. Lyda is in the middle. She looks at the women's faces, distorted by shadows, and wonders if some of them have been chosen to gain entrance into the Dome through the points of weakness. Are they to kill Partridge with a knife, a gunshot, an explosive? Even though she believes that the Dome will not be breached, the mothers scare her. They're strong, crafty, and violent.

She'd like to at least try to warn Partridge. At the same time, her instinct to run is undeniably strong. Maybe it's the baby growing inside of her that makes her want to turn back the way they came, or maybe it's her own cowardice. When she was escorted out of the Dome, she was sure she'd be raped, beaten, devoured; when no one was there at first, she pounded on the sealed door, hoping to be let back in.

Now being inside the Dome scares her more than being on the outside. She loves the sooty air, the damp woodlands, the sharp breezes. It's *alive*, and she's alive in it.

No one has explained to her why she's here, and she hasn't asked Mother Hestra, who walks in front of her in the line. Maybe Our Good Mother wants her to see this violence – a punishment for trusting Partridge and defending him in her presence. She worries she'll be a sacrifice – like Wilda was – as a warning. But no. She represents the mothers – their abandonment – and carries the most precious thing of all to them: a baby. She's not sure how or why, but she's a pawn. That's how she got out of the Dome and maybe that's how she'll wind up back inside of it.

The mothers' commands are chirrups and grunts. Some signal has been given. The line stops in unison. The lanterns are lowered. The mothers break from the line and move into the underbrush.

Mother Hestra grabs Lyda's hand. They move quietly toward the edge of the forest that opens to the Drylands. They crouch behind a thorned bush with waxy leaves.

Through the stunted trees, Lyda sees the Dome on the hill, cold and sterile, brilliantly aglow. Will the grenades have any impact? In the Dome's shadow, the grenades seem more like mosquitoes than weapons. 'This is only going to make the Dome angry,' Lyda says, pulling her hand from Mother Hestra's. 'Doesn't Our Good Mother understand how much firepower they have?'

'What are we supposed to do? Wait forever? Be good and quiet?' Mother Hestra says.

'This isn't the right thing to do.'

'I no longer rely on right or wrong,' Mother Hestra whispers.

'I know doing and not doing. Sometimes you must do.'

Lyda feels Freedle stirring in her pocket. She's supposed to protect him for Pressia. She should have left him behind, but Freedle is her small, wing-beating protector.

The leader is searching the Drylands. Lyda assumes they will head out into them, to get as close to the Dome as they can with the catapults.

At this very moment, Partridge could be back at the academy, walking the halls to his room. Maybe he's woken up in the middle of the night because he can't sleep. Maybe he's thinking of her. She squeezes her hands together, closes her eyes, and thinks of Partridge, as if she can warn him. If they're connected, truly connected, maybe he'll be able to sense her warning.

And then the mothers roll the catapults uphill into the Drylands. Quickly and quietly, they load the grenades into the catapults – like what? Simple apples. Amputated fists. And then they dislodge the safeties.

When they step back, they say, 'Clear,' and another set of mothers releases the locks on the springs. The arms of the catapults eject the grenades.

As they land, the sound is like a smattering of footfalls. Puffs of dust rise near the outer ridge of the Dome. A few hit the Dome's hard outer shell.

And then they begin to detonate. Powerful and concise explosions. Syden covers his ears and cries.

'Yes, yes, yes,' Mother Hestra whispers proudly.

Once they start, they don't stop. At first the Dome doesn't shudder. They're hitting the air-filtration system dead-on, but it's sealed.

And then a door opens – the one Lyda was sent out of, what seems like years ago now.

A line of Special Forces soldiers pours out in a row – long, sleek, muscled – at high speed and starts tearing downhill toward them.

'Why aren't they firing?' Mother Hestra says.

Lyda's heart chugs in her chest. 'They'd rather get in close and find out who we are.'

'We want them to get in close.'

'What's that supposed to mean?'

'We want some of us to be captured. We can cause real damage only from the inside. You know this.'

Lyda shakes her head. 'That's crazy!'

The mothers continue to load the catapults. They aim at Special Forces. The grenades land, thudding the ground around the soldiers, and then almost immediately explode. Most of the Special Forces scatter, but some stay in formation – as if they're programmed and can't react to the new situation. Their bodies are blown up – but not all at once. The grenades aren't that powerful. They shatter chests, splinter legs, jaggedly tear off an arm.

Lyda can't stomach it. This is her fault. She grabs Mother Hestra and begs, 'Make them stop! They're just academy boys! They're just kids!'

'They're Deaths, Lyda. Deaths!'

Lyda realizes that no one is going to stop this. The mothers will continue to kill the soldiers except for those who broke formation, and those soldiers who have taken cover in the woods will return fire. She hears a shot from a sniper rifle. One of the mothers working a catapult goes limp and falls to the ground.

Lyda has to stop this. If she runs to the Dome now, the mothers would stop firing. She's pregnant. She might get shot by Special Forces or captured, but if someone has to get captured, it should be her. She has to get to Partridge and warn him. The baby – she worries about the baby, but she can't let this go on, knowing that it's her fault.

It's not logical. She doesn't have it all sorted in her head. She just knows she has to do something, as Mother Hestra said. And so she edges away from Mother Hestra, stands, and starts running.

Mother Hestra screams, 'No, Lyda! Come back!' She then shouts, 'Hold your fire! Hold your fire!'

Lyda remembers running down this hill when she first left the Dome – that feeling of not having run since she was little, the freedom of it – and now she's running back again. She pumps her legs as fast as she can. She keeps her eyes on the Dome.

A few more grenades go off. She can hear gunshots in the woods.

She knows that, if she's lucky enough to avoid getting shot, she could end up back in her old cell with its narrow bed, white walls, untrustworthy clock, trays of food, little pills, and the image of the window, set on automatic to imitate changes of light throughout the day. Her head will be buzzed again, so close they'll nick her scalp.

Her mother will be there, her cheeks burning with shame. And Partridge – he'll be there too, won't he?

Finally, there are no more explosions, no more gunshots. In fact, it seems deathly quiet. The only sound is the wind tunneling in her ears. Her throat is dry, her lungs cold. Is it bad to run when you're pregnant? Women didn't ever run in the academy.

She can't hear much of anything over the pounding of her feet and her loud, hammering heart, but then she sees something out of the corner of her eye – a quick blur of motion.

Don't look, she tells herself. *Don't look.*

She hears a click and the echo of a ping. She feels a sharp sting in the side of her thigh. She looks down and sees a fine metal prong, much smaller than the robotic spiders. It's locked onto her leg, piercing her thick wool pants. She manages to take a few more strides, but then her knee buckles. Her leg feels numb. She falls to the ground and rolls to her back. She sees the ashen limbs of spindly trees, the black sky, and then a face – heavy jaw, sunken eyes, nostrils that pulse like gills.

She lifts her head and looks down at the prong in her leg, her woolens wet with blood around the wound. They could have killed her, but they didn't. She remembers the pregnant dwarf deer in the woods, her fur soaked with blood, panting, the way she still tried to stand up as she was dying. Mother Hestra told her that they sometimes give birth when attacked. Will she lose the pregnancy?

'Don't,' she whispers and lays her head back.

She's suddenly very tired. Her eyes drift lazily back up to the sky then close. She feels someone lift her up, cradling her, then running. They're taking her back . . . home.

PARTRIDGE

BROKEN

NOTHING'S WHAT HE THOUGHT it was and, for some reason he can't explain, he feels better knowing that this life that he woke up into – which was supposedly his *own* life – is a lie, as fake as this Nebraska farmhouse. Partridge's father doesn't love him. That's the honest truth. He's known it all along. He knows that he should reject the idea that his father wants to kill him. That alone should be proof that Iralene is having some kind of nervous breakdown – she's gone silent and still, sitting with her back against the wall – but, deep down, he believes her.

His father says he just wants him to enjoy these few days before he starts to hand him vast amounts of power. But his father hasn't ever wanted Partridge to enjoy himself. And Ellery Willux has never handed power over to anyone in his entire life.

Ellery Willux – the full name, just thinking it, turns Partridge's stomach. 'My father met your mother before your father was put in jail,' Partridge says to Iralene. 'Did you ever have a problem with that? A suspicion?'

'Are you suggesting your father had a hand in my father's incarceration?' She shakes her head. 'No! You can't think like that! Your father was *married* then, Partridge. I'm sure my mother would never, ever get involved with a *married* man. Your father is your father, Partridge. But my mother is good, deep down. She is good.'

'Okay, okay!' He knows that Iralene's no fool. She's thought it through thousands of times. She knows. Why else would she respond so angrily? There's no time for that line of thought anyway. Iralene might be right about all of it. If his memory has been swiped, then he knows some truths – on a gut level. And this gives him confidence that he didn't have before. Something is kicking in. He doesn't have much time.

He wonders, How can you hide something to find later if you know you won't even know to look for it? You'd have to hide it someplace where you know you'd find it – by accident.

He walks quickly around the room, his eyes ticking across the floorboards, the headboard, the cross on the wall. He flings open the wardrobe, hoping that he created a note that might fall to the floor. He pulls open the small drawer in the bedside table then slams it shut. He runs into the bathroom, turns on the faucet in the sink and the tub. He pulls the cord on the old-fashioned toilet. It pops. There's no rush of water.

It's broken.

He closes the lid on the toilet, steps up on it, opens the box attached to the wall. A piece of tightly folded paper falls to the floor.

'I found something,' he calls to Iralene. He jumps down, picks it up. He sees the words *To: Partridge. From: Partridge* written in his own handwriting, which strikes him as some joke. He unfolds the paper and finds a list.

1. *You escaped the Dome. You found your half sister, Pressia, and your mom. Your mom and Sedge are dead. Your father killed them.*

2. *You're in love with Lyda Mertz. She's outside the Dome. You have to save her one day.*

3. *You've promised Iralene to pretend to be engaged. Take care of her.*

4. *In this apartment building, there are living people, suspended in frozen capsules. Save them. Baby Jarv might be among them.*

5. *Trust Glassings. Don't trust Foresteed.*

6. *You don't remember this because your father made you have your memory of your escape erased. He caused the Detonations. People in the Dome know this. He must be taken down.*

7. *Take over. Lead from within. Start over again.*

He walks out of the bathroom and into the farmhouse bedroom in fake Nebraska. He lifts the paper in the air. His hand is shaking. He looks at Iralene. She says nothing. He takes the cast off and stares at his stub.

'That happened to you outside the Dome,' Iralene tells him. 'Weed fixed it so it'll grow back.' He puts the cast back on his trembling finger.

Glassings. He can trust Glassings. With what? World History? Everything is too huge to process.

Iralene stands up and takes a step toward him.

Partridge thinks about the idea of having a half sister. He thinks of his mother, Sedge – alive, dead, alive, dead. 'Lyda,' he whispers, remembering her singing in the choir. That was the face he saw earlier in his mind, looking at him from the rows of girls. He feels that ache again. He was right – not love, lovesickness. 'Lyda Mertz.' He stares at Iralene.

She nods.

His chest feels like its breaking wide open – an ache, a release. His father, murdering his mother and his brother? Murdering the world? 'My father isn't perfect, but he didn't cause the Detonations. I can tell you that much. That's almost as crazy as me escaping the Dome.'

'It's not crazy,' Iralene says. 'And you know it.'

He feels suddenly furious. 'You don't expect me to believe . . .'

'You can stop him. Glassings told you how.'

'Glassings. I'm supposed to trust him.'

'And I wasn't supposed to trust him.'

'What do you mean?'

She whispers, 'I've played both sides.'

'What? Why?'

'I had no choice. You think survival is something only wretches have to think about, Partridge? Don't be so naive.'

'What? Iralene, I thought—'

'I am who I am at any given moment, Partridge. That's the only way you can know me.'

He doesn't know what to say. 'But I trust you, Iralene. I do. You're good. I know you are. I can feel it.'

She closes her eyes, as if she's very weary. She smiles. 'You might be the only person I've ever really known,' she says. 'Do you understand what I mean?'

'I do know what you mean.' To know someone, to be known. That matters more than he'd have ever thought it would. 'Listen, Iralene. Tell me. How do you know Glassings?'

'I was taken for lessons. I'm not an academy girl but I had to be educated if I was going to be worthy of you. But they took me to lessons with all the ones they didn't quite trust. I was there to test them, to listen. And I did.'

'Did you report?'

'I reported that I was bored. That my education was pointless. Glassings gave me something to give to you.' She hands him a small, plain white envelope. He opens it. There's nothing but a capsule inside.

'What is it?'

'Poison – deadly and untraceable. You have to give it to your father. The capsule will dissolve within forty seconds and the poison will leach into his system quickly. He will die within three minutes.'

'I can't kill my father. If you murder a murderer, you're just as bad.'

'That's what you said the last time you were asked.'

'Well, at least I'm consistent.'

'You might change your mind. I can prove your father's darkness,' she says, 'if that's what you need. It's here. It's in this building.'

The bodies, suspended.

'Jarv,' he says.

'Yes,' she says, 'Jarv.'

Iralene leads Partridge quickly out of the room and through the hallway, down a set of stairs, across a large, empty cement room with cracks in the walls, exposed pipes, and, oddly enough, an upright piano. It all feels eerily familiar. He's been here before. His mind might not remember but his body does. A chill shoots through his spine.

He doesn't want to see his father's darkness, but he has to. He can't believe anything else on the list unless he can prove at least one thing – see it with his own eyes.

She holds his hand and leads him down a hallway lined with doors. Each door has a placard with a name on it.

They pass door after door and with each one, he feels sicker inside. 'What is this place?'

'I've spent much of my life here, suspended. So that I stay fresh and age almost imperceptibly over time.'

'You've spent much of your life here? How old are you?'

'I won't tell you.'

'The Detonations hit only nine years ago. How old can you be?'

'This technology predates the Detonations, Partridge. My mother and I aren't bound by years like others are. We started early.'

'How early?'

'I started doing sessions when I was four years old.'

Her face is clean. No lines, no wrinkles. Her eyes are clear and bright. 'Jesus, Iralene. How old are you? Just tell me.'

'I'm your age, Partridge. I've been your age longer than you, that's all. And I'll be your age for as long as I can.'

'Iralene,' he whispers. 'What have they done to you?'

She shakes her head. She doesn't want to talk about it.

Partridge walks slowly down the row of placards: PETRYN SUR, ETTERIDGE HESS, MORG WILSON. 'But preservation isn't why all these people are here. It's not why Jarv is here. His parents – I know them. They're good people. They wouldn't try to preserve him.'

'What was wrong with him?' Iralene says flatly.

'Nothing,' he says defensively, but then he looks at Iralene sharply, because of course there was something wrong with Jarv. 'What do you mean?'

'The little ones come in sometimes because there's something not quite right. Why waste resources on them? But on the other hand, we'll need more people when we're in New Eden. Once there, we'll have enough for everyone. He can grow up when we get there. They didn't euthanize him, Partridge. That's the good news.'

'*That's* the good news? That they didn't kill him for being a little slow to develop?'

'So he was slow.'

'I guess. His parents were worried. There were some issues. I don't remember what exactly. It was last winter.'

HIGBY NEWSOME, VYRRA TRENT, WRENNA SIMMS.

'His little collection of relics,' Iralene says. 'Some of them are people who should have been executed for wrongs, for treason. But he kept them out of sentimentality.'

They take another turn and there's a bank of windows instead of the doors. It's like some twisted version of a nursery you'd find in the labor and delivery wing of a hospital. There are glass-enclosed, egg-shaped beds. The children are inside them. All are outfitted with tubes in their mouths to provide oxygen. He can hear a hum of electricity.

He jogs down the row, looking for Jarv, and finally he finds him – fourth from the end. His name is clearly marked on the pod. There's an infant in the pod beside him, but the last two are empty – waiting. Jarv's cheeks are pale, and his lips around the tube have a bluish tint, as do his eyelids. But his arms and legs are still pink and fleshy – though that flesh is probably turgid. There are crystals on his kneecaps; one foot is covered in a silvery skin of ice, as if he's wearing one lace sock.

'How do we turn it off ?' He walks down the row of glass. 'Jesus! How do we get them out?' He finds a metal door. He yanks on it. It's locked. 'We've got to get him out of there.'

'Even if you could get in, it would be too dangerous for

you to bring him out of his suspension. It can be done only by a doctor.'

'Where's a doctor? I can talk him into it. I can get him to reverse this!'

'There's no need for doctors to be here around the clock. The doctors show up when necessary. Those in suspension have their vitals monitored by computers. And if one fails, well, it's never a tragedy, is it? The tragedy has already come.'

Partridge leans his forehead against the window. 'So his parents don't know?' He starts to cry. He should have earlier, probably, when he read the note, but this is when it hits him.

'They don't know where he is exactly, but they probably have an inkling.'

'They can't know.'

'Sometimes the young ones are released for a while, brought over to the medical center. The parents come in for visits. It's rare. They have to have special ties to secure such permissions.'

'This has to end.' He pushes away from the glass. 'This can't go on.'

'He has plans for you too, Partridge. Worse than this.'

Partridge looks at her. 'It doesn't make sense. You told me that he wants to kill me, but why would he be setting me up as a leader, as his successor, if he's just going to off me?'

'I don't know.' She turns away.

'You're lying – you're holding something back, aren't you?'

'You can end this. You know how.'

'He's the killer. You want me to become one too?'

'I want you alive,' she says. 'Keep the capsule on you. Forty seconds and its shell will dissolve and then within three minutes it will be over. Only you can get close enough to him to make it happen.'

The capsule is in the envelope. It's folded in his pocket. 'I'll keep it, but I don't intend to use it.'

'There's someone else I want you to see,' she says. Partridge follows her to the end of the hall and around another turn. 'I haunt this place when I can. I don't want them to all feel completely alone. It's not like you think in there, really. The researchers don't think that we're capable of knowing anything when we're in that state. But I think we know when someone is with us, when someone visits.'

They turn down another hall – more names on placards. FENNERY WILKES, BARRETT FLYNN, HELINGA PETRY.

'I know when new people arrive, and when the circumstances are strange, I pay attention.'

'Who is it?' Partridge says. He knows that his mother and brother are dead, a fact he made clear to himself.

'It happened while you were out of the Dome. He was in from the medical center. I remember him because he's different from the others. For one thing, he's older than most people in the Dome. As you well know, the elderly aren't worthy of resources and aren't likely to even make it to New Eden anyway. But the other thing' – she slows her steps, looking closely at the names – 'that caught my eye was that they didn't put the oxygen tube in his mouth. They sealed his lips and, instead, put the tube directly into his throat.' She stops at a door and points to the placard. 'Odwald Belze,' she says. 'Do you know the name? Belze?'

He feels the name stir some ill-lit portion of his brain, a spark of recognition. Belze. Belze. He wants to remember something more. He touches the placard with his hand. The cast on his pinky clicks. And, for a split second, he thinks of one eye – small and glassy. It's open. Click. It's closed. Click. It's open again.

The small eye of a doll.

Iralene walks to the end of the hall. She puts her hand on a large metal door – locked and barred, an alarm system mounted on the wall. 'And this one, heavily secured, unmarked. Who knows what's on the other side of this door.'

PRESSIA

LIGHT

F<small>IGNAN</small> COUNTS DOWN the miles and then the yards and
then Pressia sees it, atop a grassy hill. Newgrange. The large
mound hasn't been obliterated, wiped off the face of the earth.
It remains.

'How much longer?' she asks.

'Six minutes and thirty-seven seconds,' Fignan says.

The sky is already beginning to turn a hazy shade of pink. She
runs as fast as she can. The bruised welts from the thorns ache
with each step. Fignan's light jostles in front of her, bouncing
along the ruts and ivy. The cold wind stings her cheeks. Her lungs
burn from pumping the chilled air – cleaner and clearer here.

She sprints to the side of the mound, puts her hand on the
massive, mossy stones, touching the spirals carved into the
rock, then runs her hand along the cold quartz wall. She climbs
a set of steps. Nearly lost in a curtain of ivy, the entrance is
guarded by boulders, but not blocked. She grabs a handful
of ivy and pulls it down as hard as she can, clearing not only

the doorway but the window that sits on a stone ledge above it.

The sun is edging up, approaching the horizon. She runs down the dark passageway – about sixty feet long and so tight that at one point she has to turn sideways to pass. She comes to a small chamber shaped like a cross. There are large basins, too. For what purpose? She can't imagine. She thinks of the Saint Wi statue in the crypt where Bradwell first started to pray. She thinks of the boy in the morgue and her grandfather, who performed so many funerals but never had one of his own, and of her mother and Sedge, whose bodies joined the soil of the forest floor.

'The ceiling,' she whispers to Fignan. He shines the light overhead, and there is a corbelled arch, the stones neatly fitted in place to keep the whole structure tight and sound. She wishes she weren't alone. She wants Bradwell, El Capitan, and Helmud to see this. She imagines the ghostly girls, their faces staring out from the walls of the stone cottage. They would be proud of her.

I'm here, she wants to tell them.

She tells Fignan to power off. 'There can't be any light.'

And seconds later, it's dark.

She sits down, her back to one of the walls. She hears Bradwell's voice in her head: *The box we stored God in kept getting smaller . . . until only a speck of God still exists, maybe only an atom.*

Right now she's sure that at least one atom of God survived, because how else can she explain that – as the sun climbs the sky and then pours light into the small window above the door and shines down the passageway, illuminating a bright, glowing strip on the floor – she's sure that this is a holy place?

Fignan sits beside her. 'You're not a box,' she says, repeating Walrond's message. 'You're a key.' But the truth is she has no idea how he's going to become a key. She feels a rise of panic.

She's put her faith in a box. A box filled with information, but a box nonetheless.

Fignan seems to know his role. He buzzes to the middle of the chamber. A thin glass lens rises up from his center on a long, thin arm. The lens is almost as wide as Pressia's doll-head fist. Fignan holds the lens steady. The light thrown from the sun pours through the lens.

Pressia holds her breath. She feels the cold stone through her coat. She keeps her eyes on Fignan as the sunlight fills the lens and illuminates the floor.

At first, she sees nothing – only the floor made of pulverized stones or maybe hard-packed clay.

But then, there's something iridescent. Some pattern on the ground shines.

She hears a voice. Footsteps at the entrance. The light flickers as someone's body casts a shadow for a second or two. Pressia holds her breath. *Go away*, she urges. *Leave!*

The floor illuminates again, and there are three interlocked spirals – altogether they're about a foot wide. Pressia crawls to the spot on the ground and touches the spirals. She pushes on the hard dirt, hears the voice again down the long, tunneled entrance, but she can't make out any words. She wants to dip back out of sight into the alcove of the cross, but she can't afford to hide.

'You're a key!' she says to Fignan, and with a buzz, small tools emerge from the box. He starts to dig into the ground where the iridescent spirals are lit up. He strikes metal, revealing three concentric circles, like the stone carvings. 'What is this, Fignan? What are these shapes?'

Fignan doesn't respond. It's as if he's concentrating on absorbing the light.

She hears footsteps pounding toward her. She tells Fignan to turn off his power again. The chamber is lit by the rising sun. Pressia picks up Fignan, slips around the corner of one of the alcoves, and holds him high over her head, pressing as hard as she can with her doll-head fist.

'Who's there?' It's a man's voice. 'Who is it?'

The figure, short and stocky, is standing just a foot away, breathing hard, his white shirt lit up by the morning sun – a shirt so bright white that she's not sure she's ever seen something that brilliant. For the briefest flash of a moment, she hopes that this is her father – Hideki Imanaka – and she freezes. But she knows the chances of this are impossibly small.

She draws in a breath, arches her back, raises Fignan as high as she can, and brings the box down – heavy and sharp – on the back of the man's head. He pitches forward and catches himself with one hand on the stone wall. He reaches up and touches the blood that's already seeping from the gash, wetting his thick gray hair, and stares at his hand. He isn't fused to anything, but he isn't a Pure either. The pitted scars of burns ride up one side of his face, but his skin holds a strange golden hue. He manages to say, 'Who?' but then he slides down the wall, his loose white shirt billowing, then he lands hard on his back, on top of the three grooved spirals.

Pressia listens for more voices and footfalls. She hears nothing. She sets Fignan back on the ground. Her hand is shaking. Even her heart feels like it's trembling.

She reaches down and tries to push the man off the three grooved spirals. He's heavier than she thought he'd be. She sits and shoves him with her boots, using all the strength left in her legs. He budges a little. She shoves again, and he budges a little more. The sleeve of his shirt is now mud-stained. She keeps pushing and finally the three spirals are exposed.

'Fignan,' she says, breathlessly. 'Don't stop now.'

Fignan beeps. He buzzes to the triple spiral. A thin chest plate retracts. A grooved metal spiral – just one – appears on a long robotic arm. Pressia bends down and brushes the pebbles away. Fignan fits his spiral into the center spiral and it locks in place with a series of clicks. With a quick jolt, Fignan pushes on the spiral, which makes the three spirals turn a few inches, interlocking. Pressia reaches down and pulls on the edge of one of the spirals. It opens while still attached on one side by hinges that connect to a box buried underground. The three spirals are decorating the lid of the box.

Fignan shines a light inside the box, which is made of metal – cold and damp. Within it, Pressia sees a pale square. She reaches in and pulls out an envelope. It has one word scribbled on the front of it: *Cygnus*.

Pressia grips the letter, holds it for a second to her chest, then rips it open. Inside, there's one sheet of blue-lined paper ripped from a notebook. Written on it, in a messy scrawl, are numbers and letters separated by parentheses, pluses, and minuses. A formula.

The formula.

The man on the ground lets out a moan. She quickly folds the sheet, slips it back into the envelope, and shoves the envelope into her pocket.

Fignan buzzes to the man.

'No!' Pressia whispers harshly.

But Fignan doesn't listen. He reaches out and pulls a few strands of bloody hair from the man's head, testing DNA, as he did to Bradwell, Pressia, and Partridge.

Pressia stands up and walks to the man's limp body. His cheeks are ruddy, his lashes dark. His white shirt is handmade. It laces up the front instead of using buttons and is loose at the collar, the result of Pressia's shoving him with her boots. The collar is so loose that she sees the rise and fall of the man's bare chest.

And as Fignan lets out a sharp beep, she kneels next to the man and sees a row of six small squares embedded in his chest – two of them pulsing.

'One of the Seven,' she whispers.

And Fignan says, 'Bartrand Kelly.'

She reaches out and touches his shirt. Bartrand Kelly – a man who knew her mother and her father. One of the Seven.

One of the pulses belongs to Ghosh. Who knows where she is?

The other belongs to Hideki Imanaka, Pressia's father.

She stares at the two pulses. Her father is still alive. This pulse is her only tie to him.

Bartrand Kelly moans. There are more voices down the passageway and what sounds like the braying of an animal.

Pressia grabs Fignan and gets on her feet. She doesn't know whose side Kelly's on, after all. His eyes flit open. He stares up into the corbelled ceiling and then he sees Pressia. She raises Fignan again over her head, but half heartedly.

'Wait a minute. Steady now,' he says. He lifts himself to one elbow and holds out his hand.

'Are you Bartrand Kelly?' she says.

'Who's asking?' He blinks and rubs his eyes.

'Where is Hideki Imanaka?'

'Imanaka?' he says, as if he hasn't heard the name in years. 'How do you know Imanaka?'

She hears the voices coming closer now. She hears footsteps moving down the corridor. 'Where is he?' she shouts.

'Why do you want to know?' he says.

'He's my father,' she says. My father. *My father.* The words feel foreign in her mouth. 'He's my father,' she says again and her chest seizes, but she refuses to cry.

Bartrand Kelly stares at her face. He whispers, 'Emi Brigid Imanaka,' the name Pressia was given at birth, the name that was obliterated by the Detonations, the girl she never got to be. 'Is it really you?'

He reaches for her and she steps backward. The fact that he's alive means that he might have made a special deal with Willux. She has the formula in her pocket. She has the vials strapped to her ribs. If Kelly has ties to Willux and if Kelly captures her, Willux would have everything she's risked her life for.

She grips Fignan and takes off down the corridor but is blocked by a man and a woman – both young and strong. The man grabs her by the wrist of her doll-head fist. His grip is leathery and callused. He pulls the doll head up and gasps when he sees it.

The woman stares at the doll head too. 'Who are you?' she says but in a tone that almost sounds like she's asking, What are you? Neither of them has fusings either, as far as Pressia can tell, yet in the light of dawn she sees that these two also have some scars and burns – but that same golden tint to their skins.

'Let go of me!' Pressia shouts.

'Kelly?' the woman yells. 'Are you okay?'

Pressia tries to wrench her arm loose. She's cold and tired. Her muscles burn. The welts on her body ache.

'Leave her alone!' Bartrand Kelly calls out. 'Let her go!'

The man stares at Pressia's face for a moment and then loosens his grip. Pressia shoves her way past the two of them, runs down the passageway jaggedly, bumping against the stone walls pressing in on either side, toward the light.

She hears thudding, the strange braying again. She puts one hand on the stone and steps out into the fresh air, the sun, the new day.

And there, standing in front of her, is a horse.

This horse seems like a miracle – its existence alone, its wide barrel of ribs, its dark mane, its long, elegant legs that taper to delicately thin ankles. A wide, dark scar runs the length of its body, which is otherwise covered in velvety fur. Its ears twitch and rotate. Its breath fogs the air.

The horse is fitted with a saddle but isn't tied to anything. Pressia walks to it quickly, spreads one hand to its ribs, which are warm. They rise and fall. She can hear the voices inside the tomb. Coming closer?

She's never ridden a horse before. Her grandfather told her the story of pony rides at one of her birthday parties, but that was a lie from the life she never had. She thinks of the twisted bodies of the horses on the tilted merry-go-round.

This horse is a miracle meant for her.

She grabs a knob at the front of the saddle with her good hand, holds Fignan in the other arm, and hoists herself up. She's surprised by how tall the horse is, how regal. She picks up the reins and nudges the horse with her boots. 'Go,' she says.

The horse takes a few steps.

She nudges the horse again more urgently. She leans forward and whispers, 'Go! Please go!'

She hears the voices clearly now.

She gives the horse a little kick and cries out, 'Go!'

And as the man and the woman, who are propping Bartrand Kelly up between them, emerge from the passageway, the horse starts to gallop. Pressia grips the horse's ribs between her legs, tries to keep her balance while holding Fignan tightly to her chest. She leans down close to the horse's mane. The wind in her hair, her eyes streaming tears, she says, 'Go, go! Keep going!'

PARTRIDGE

LYDA MERTZ

By THE TIME THE CAMERAS click on, Partridge and Iralene
are sitting on the edge of his bed. Ever since he saw the eye of the
doll in his mind – its glassy bead, the fringe of plastic eyelashes,
the mechanism of the eyelid caked with ash – he's seen other
things, in sharp, vivid detail.

A sheep with gnarled and twisted horns.

Splintered glass covering some kind of map.

A man carrying another spindly man on his back.

And Lyda Mertz. He's sure it was her face, but her head was
shaved, her face streaked with dirt, and she was holding a long
spear in a bleak, windswept dust bowl, as if he'd really been with
her to Nebraska, a version of it blasted to charred prairies. Is this
what she looks like now that she's outside the Dome?

Each image begins with a flare, like a trick of light – a brilliant
glow that funnels down to one small detail. It's like being in a
dark room in a thunderstorm, and there's that first bolt that
illuminates what your eyes are focused on before the light is gone.

'Take it,' Iralene says, and she shoves the handheld at him, its motor humming. One red light flashes on it like a beacon. Before the cameras clicked on, he told her that he was seeing things now, without context – just jarring images with no sense of correlation, one and then the next. She told him not to let on, not in front of the cameras.

But now this. He knows what the red light means: a message from his father. His father told him he'd be brought back in soon, in the hope of salvaging his brain's synaptic firings. But that's not what he's going in for. His father wants to kill him.

'Press play,' Iralene says, trying to sound chipper. 'Let's hear it.'

He looks up at the cameras and wonders if whoever's watching thinks that Iralene turned the cameras off so they could be alone. Iralene's hair even looks authentically messy.

A bird with a metal beak and hinged jaw.

A black car in a cloud of dust.

His father's face, looking raw and shiny as if covered in a thin membrane of fake skin.

The memories come in clusters, unpredictably, in flashes, and then stop as abruptly as they started. He remembers the coding sessions – how they threw strange memories at you – but these are more like attacks. They don't feel familiar at all – except Lyda Mertz. Yes, he remembers her from the girls' academy, but not like this – not dirty and armed. Yet that's the image he wants to return. Lyda with a shaved head and a spear. He wants to linger there. Does he love her? Is that the source of his lovesickness? Lyda Mertz? He's supposed to go back and save her. But this image isn't of someone who needs saving.

'Play it,' Iralene says, guiding him along with simple instructions.

He hits the red button. His father's voice fills the room. 'We'll need you at the medical center bright and early at seven a.m. It's good news all around, Partridge. They're sure that they can do a lot of quick repairs. It's a tune-up. You'll have to be put under, but it will be fast and painless. I'll be there when you wake up. I look forward to being reunited with you, son.'

'Well,' Iralene says, 'there you have it! Isn't this great news?'

Partridge nods. He tries to muster some kind of enthusiasm. Even a smile would help. But he can't. 'I'm tired,' he says. He wishes he didn't have the pill, didn't know it existed.

'It's late. I'll let you rest,' Iralene says.

'I don't want to go to sleep.' He's afraid of the memories that might bubble up, mixed with dreams. If he could order dreams, he'd ask for Lyda Mertz – her and her alone. But he knows that's not how the subconscious likes to play things.

'You should try to sleep. Tomorrow's a big day. You'll want to be ready for it.' Iralene stands up. She reaches into a pretend pocket and lifts her hand. 'I offer you a pocketful of sweet dreams!'

He lifts his hand and she pretends to tuck the sweet dreams into it, but what she means is, *The pill is in your pocket, the one that can kill your father and end all of this.* She means, *Use it.*

EL CAPITAN

VINES

EL CAPITAN HAS BEEN staggering, falling, calling Bradwell's name in the darkness surrounding the airship for what seems like hours. No response. Bradwell is out there, somewhere, but all El Capitan has heard is the occasional rustle of leaves and, now that it's dawn, the chatter of birds.

His head throbs. Twice, he's thrown up. With the dim glow of sunrise, he can finally search the ground for tracks. He's on his hands and knees, looking at the dirt, hoping to find an imprint of a boot sole. Helmud feels heavier on El Capitan's back than ever before – even when El Capitan was just a boy still covered in burns from the Detonations, when he was barely able to hold Helmud up for much longer than a few minutes at a time. His vision blurs then doubles.

He blinks hard and squints. He knows why he's out here searching for Bradwell and why he hasn't given up. He doesn't want to tell Pressia that Bradwell's dead. He doesn't want to break her heart like that. He saw them in the underpass. He knows the way she looks at Bradwell. She might love him and she'll never love El Capitan, but El Capitan loves her and couldn't stand to see her suffer another loss. He imagines the look on her face upon telling her the news. It breaks him. He has to keep searching.

'Helmud,' he says. 'Tell me what you see.'

'You see,' Helmud says.

'There's no time for that shit now, Helmud!' El Capitan says. 'I need you.'

'I need you,' Helmud says.

They need each other. They always have and always will. Maybe he should just be happy with that fact. Not everyone gets to need someone and to be needed permanently, forever. He should let Pressia go. He shouldn't have ever hoped for her to begin with.

He crawls toward trees. The spastic shadows of flying birds skitter across the ground. There's cawing overhead. He thinks, *If Bradwell's dead, I'll have to tell Pressia and then I'll have to comfort her*. It's a cruel thing to imagine, but there it is – her head on his shoulder. He strokes her hair.

'No,' he mutters aloud. 'Don't.'

'Don't,' Helmud says, as if he can read his mind.

'You're right, Helmud,' El Capitan says, but some adrenaline has already kicked in. It's like his body has already started to wish Bradwell dead and gone, and there's nothing his conscience can do about it. He keeps on crawling. His elbow buckles and he falls but then slowly straightens up. 'Keep your eyes peeled,' he says. 'Don't stop looking.'

And then Helmud tightens his arms around El Capitan and says, 'Stop looking.'

El Capitan freezes. He stares down at the muddy, ivy-covered dirt and sees a waxy leaf smeared with blood. He pinches the stem of the ivy leaf and holds it up. The thin coating of blood is almost dried. 'Where the hell is he?'

'Where the hell is he.' Helmud points across the rest of the field into the stand of trees.

And now El Capitan can see the boot tracks, skidding through the dirt, trampling the ivy. He sees the outline of Bradwell's body, the shape of it, wound in vines. His face is expressionless – asleep? Dead?

El Capitan struggles to his feet and tries to run, but the forest tilts. He looks up at the sky to get his bearings. The birds, flushed from the trees, scatter across the sky. One spreads its wings and pinwheels, downward, or is that his vision? El Capitan falls hard on his shoulder. 'Bradwell!' he shouts. 'Bradwell!'

He breathes hard and gets up on his knees. One foot on the ground, he stands and walks – a zigzag path. He sees Bradwell's body. His vision jumps and stutters.

As he makes his way to him, he sees that the ivy is wrapped tightly around his arms and legs, strapped around his chest and throat. And barbed. My God, who did this to him? And how? The thorns have cut into his skin. There's been a slow and steady loss of blood. Bradwell is pale. His eyes are closed. His rifle is a few feet away, covered in vines too. Maybe he had no knife.

El Capitan falls to his knees. He puts his hand on Bradwell's face. It's cold. The thought appears in his mind: He killed Bradwell. He imagined him dead and now he's dead. It's his fault. 'I didn't mean it,' he says to Helmud.

'Mean it!' Helmud says.

And Helmud's voice is so angry and strong that it makes El Capitan's head jerk up. 'Okay,' he says. 'Okay.' And he regains his composure. He reaches under the ivy circling Bradwell's throat and tries to find a pulse.

At first, nothing. But then he pushes harder and he feels it – slow and weak. He's alive! 'Come on, Bradwell!' He lifts Bradwell's heavy head. Bradwell coughs and then his eyes open.

'Cap, Helmud,' he whispers. 'My brothers.'

'That's right,' El Capitan says. 'Your brothers are here.' He reaches for the knife in his belt loop, but it's gone. Where is it? Back in the airship? Did it come loose when he fell? Did Helmud disarm him when he was out cold? 'Helmud,' he says, 'I need a knife. I need a goddamn knife?'

'My knife,' Helmud says, 'my goddamn knife.' He pulls out his whittling knife and hands it to El Capitan.

'Yes,' El Capitan says. He's glad he gave Helmud a knife, that he trusted him with it. He wants to look his brother in the eyes. It's not easy to do. He says, 'Thank you, Helmud,' and he means, *Thank you for everything* – not just for giving him this knife, but also for cutting the spider from his leg, for tending to him in the airship, for being his brother – always there.

'Thank you,' Helmud says, and El Capitan is sure that Helmud's thank-you means as much as El Capitan's does.

El Capitan starts to cut the vines – first the ones around Bradwell's neck. But as soon as they snap loose, they seem to grow again, quickly. They dig their thorns into Bradwell's skin, fresh punctures, and claw their way back into place. Bradwell is so dazed that he barely winces. His eyes are now distant, his breath coming in short pants.

Dizzy and exhausted, El Capitan keeps cutting, but it seems to do more harm than good – each new thorn creates a new perforation, a new trickle of blood. Feeling helpless, he lets the knife fall to the ground. He props Bradwell up, shoulder-to-shoulder, wraps his arm around his ribs, which are encased in vines. He can see Bradwell's birds wrestling the confining weave across his back. 'We won't leave you,' he says to Bradwell. 'We're here together.'

And that's when he notices the first tickle of a vine slip over his wrist; then it cinches like a tight cuff, the thorns pricking his skin. El Capitan doesn't jerk away, doesn't have much fight left in him. 'We're staying with you,' he says again.

'Staying with you,' Helmud says.

Bradwell blinks twice. His eyes close and his chin dips to his chest.

And as the vines wind up El Capitan's arm and start to encircle his legs, he knows this is how he and Bradwell will be tied together, forever, with thorns and vines and blood. This is a kind of brotherhood that El Capitan understands. To be bound. He looks through the trees, across the field back at the airship – lolled heavily on its side. His head is impossibly heavy. He rests it on Bradwell's shoulder, and Helmud rests his head on El Capitan's shoulder as the vines keep curling around them, faster and faster, like being woven into a barbed web. He imagines Pressia seeing them, at first, from a distance – upright and together. She'll assume that they're alive, sitting at the edge of the field, like three brothers, talking – maybe talking about her. She's the one who binds them.

The thorns begin to feel like teeth, offering a sharp, gnawing pain. The vines are alive, carnivorous. They're being eaten.

If they're dead when Pressia reaches them, at least she'll know they died together.

Helmud bucks and jerks on his back as if he's just now understanding that this is the end. 'Stay here?' he says. 'Stay?'

'We can't leave,' El Capitan says.

'Leave!' Helmud shouts.

'No, Helmud.' El Capitan is sure that they aren't going to make it. He says, 'We'll die here.'

'No,' Helmud says.

'This is it for us,' El Capitan says.

'No!' Helmud says breathlessly.

And then El Capitan sees a speck on the horizon. Some creature charging toward them. He thinks for a moment that it's Death. Didn't it gallop toward the dead and steal their souls? His grandmother told him stories about Death. His grandmother, who pressed flowers in books.

'Death is coming,' El Capitan says, 'to steal our souls.'

'Steal our souls?' Helmud is shaking.

El Capitan closes his eyes. 'Steal our souls,' he whispers, as if it's his final order. 'Steal our souls!'

And then as everything goes dark, he hears a voice – clear and sweet as an angel's voice. It is his brother, singing the way he used to sing for their mother, the beautiful voice that made her cry. Maybe Helmud is an angel after all. Maybe that's who he's been all along.

LYDA

JUMPSUIT

LYDA COMES TO when the water hits her. It's cold at first, maybe meant to wake her up. She's in a white stall as small as a closet, with nozzles pointed at her – dozens of them. There's a silver door handle in front of her. She reaches for it, but slips. She's naked. She sees the bloat of her tender stomach. It isn't obvious, but maybe they've done tests on her while she was knocked out. Her inner arm feels bruised. Do they know she's pregnant?

The nozzles spray foam that smells strongly of the academy swimming pool, rubbing alcohol, and other acrid chemicals. She coughs and gags. Her eyes burn.

And then the water turns hot. The small room fills quickly with steam.

When the nozzles finally shut off, she reaches for the door handle again. As she suspects, it's locked. A drawer opens from the wall. There's a white jumpsuit from the rehabilitation center and a head scarf. She's back where she started.

She picks up the clothes, starts to put them on. As she zips the jumpsuit, she imagines her stomach growing round and taut, filling it up. What will a child conceived out there amid the wretches look like? Maybe she's a wretch now too. Dome officials wouldn't let a child of hers be born in the Dome, would they?

The handle turns. The door opens. A voice says, 'Step outside.'

But there is no outside. She steps out of one small enclosed space into another enclosed space. The air has no motion at all. It's sterile and static. The Dome is the real wasteland. She remembers telling Partridge about the snow globe – she's trapped again, except there isn't even the watery swirl of fake, wet snow.

PRESSIA

PROMISE ME

PRESSIA'S GOTTEN USED TO the horse's stride, its pounding hooves, its snorting breaths. As Fignan gives directions, she tugs the reins and the horse responds immediately. It feels like she was meant to ride this horse. The formula in her pocket, the two remaining vials pressed close to her skin, she feels strong and powerful.

She sees the airship first. In broad daylight, it looks worse for wear. Toppled and rocked to one side, the ship's tanks look fragile and exposed. It hits her with full force that it might not matter if she has the formula and the vials – not if they can't get the airship back into the air. They'll be stuck here forever.

Shaken, she scans the field that rises to a hill and then the distant perimeter of trees.

That's when she sees what seems like a three-headed Groupie, furred in greenery. She pulls back on the reins, and the horse slows. It isn't a Groupie. She sees the pale faces – Bradwell, El Capitan, Helmud. She gives the horse a kick and gallops toward them.

This close, she can see that only Bradwell's face is blanched and slack. El Capitan and Helmud are looking at her, but with a distant look in their eyes as if they aren't really seeing her at all. The blood on the gauze wrapped around El Capitan's head has hardened and blackened. She pulls back on the reins. The horse stops; she swings her leg off and slides to the ground. She sets Fignan down and runs to them. 'What happened? What is this?'

'Souls,' El Capitan whispers.

'Souls,' Helmud says.

She sees the knife on the ground, picks it up, and almost starts to saw at the vines, but El Capitan shouts, 'No. It only gets worse. They grow back.'

'What do you mean?'

He just shakes his head. 'Don't.'

She kneels, reaches up, and holds Bradwell's face in her hands. 'Bradwell!' she shouts. She cups her hand to his parted lips and feels the faintest hint of warm breath. 'He's alive.'

'We're bound,' El Capitan says. 'We'll die together.'

'No,' she says, and she stares at the vines, looping endlessly around their bodies. 'There has to be a root. If I can get to that . . .'

'Steal our souls,' El Capitan says.

'Souls,' Helmud says.

She runs her eyes over the vines frantically, searching for a common source. She puts her fingertips on a thin vine, hoping for some sense of a pulse, some energy she can follow. Finally, she feels more tension in one of the vines. She follows the tension as the vine winds down Bradwell's body, across his chest, over one hip, around his leg. She keeps with this one vine, feeling a vibration as if the cord is really alive, as if somewhere – maybe deep in the earth itself – it has a beating heart.

As the vine cuffs Bradwell's ankle and then passes down below the heel of his boot, she grabs the knife again. She pins the vine to the ground with her doll-head fist and cuts it as fast as she can. The vine snaps and recoils into the ground with the hiss of a snake.

The thorns break, suddenly brittle and dry. She rips a fistful of vines from Bradwell's chest and then another from El Capitan's shoulder all the way down his arm.

Once his arm is loose, he starts clawing at the vines on his and Helmud's bodies but Bradwell slumps to the ground. Pressia now sees all the blood. Thousands of tiny cuts all over him. She rolls him to his side. The birds are limp on his back. If they die, does that mean he will too?

She cups his face. 'Bradwell!' she says. 'Bradwell!'

He doesn't wake up, doesn't move.

'Cap,' she says.

El Capitan shakes his head. 'Don't make me say those words.'

'Those words,' Helmud says.

'He's not going to die!' Pressia says. 'I won't let him.' She grips his shirt, pierced with holes and wet with blood. 'Bradwell! I'm here! It's Pressia!' Her voice cracks. 'Itchy knee!' She shouts the words from her dream of telephone poles, the words they said together when they thought they would freeze to death in each other's arms. 'Sun, she go!'

His eyes flutter open and squint. He purses his lips and whispers, 'Did you get it?'

'I did. Yes.' Her hands are shaking. There's too much blood. The center of his shirt is soaked. She finds a small hole, rips his shirt wide open. Along the center of his chest, the thorns have chewed an incision as if he were cut by a knife, as if the thorns were serrated like teeth.

She starts crying. 'It's okay,' she says, 'it's okay. It's okay.'

'Pressia,' Bradwell says. 'I'm not going to make it. But you will. You'll save them.'

'No!' she says. 'El Capitan, tell him that it's going to be okay!'

El Capitan shakes his head. He stands up heavily, steadying himself by holding on to the trunk of a lean tree. 'I can't.' He reaches out to another tree. He staggers toward the horse, standing elegantly in the field. She knows that he's giving her privacy. He's telling her that now is the time to say what she needs to say – including goodbye.

This makes her angry. She isn't saying goodbye, because this isn't the end. She puts her hands on Bradwell's face. She's crying – hot, angry tears. She's crying so hard that she can barely speak. 'You're going to be okay. You can't die.'

'It's not up to you,' he says.

She curls forward, feeling her mother's vials dig sharply into her ribs, and she remembers the Dust near the amusement park, how its hand healed and swelled, strong and muscled. She has two of her mother's syringes. They push the body to self-generate cells. Why not Bradwell's wounds? 'I can fix this!' She lifts her sweater and unwinds the cloth that holds the vials in place. She holds them up. 'Look.'

He shakes his head. 'I want to die Pure, Pressia.'

She shakes her head. 'The drugs can be dangerous, but this is the time to take that risk.'

'I'm Pure already. You are too. Let me die that way.' He reaches up and touches her face. 'Promise me.'

She nods. She'll agree with anything he says. She wants him to stay with her. 'Okay,' she says, as if she's negotiating with him. 'Just promise me you'll stay awake. Don't leave me.'

He shakes his head. 'You'll miss me,' he says.

'Listen to me, Bradwell! You can't go.'

But he closes his eyes. His face looks calm, peaceful. She whispers, 'No, no, no.' She couldn't save her mother or Sedge. There was nothing she could do. But this time there is. She looks at Bradwell's face, the two beautiful scars running down his cheek. She promised she'd let him die Pure. She promised.

But she's desperate. She'll never have this moment back – the moment when he can still be saved. She sets down the syringes, pulls off his coat, and rips a tear in the back of his shirt, exposing his bloody back and the three birds, their bodies entwined forever with his. Two look dead already. Their claws stiff, their eyes glassy. But the third ruffles its wings and blinks at her.

She picks up one of the syringes. Her hands are shaking so badly that she can barely uncap the needle. Quickly, she fills it with the contents of the vial. She pushes the thumb rest just enough so that the plunger releases a small bead of thick, golden liquid.

She promised to let him die Pure, but she didn't promise to let the birds die too. They're connected – Bradwell and the birds – forever. She'll inject the birds. It's a loophole, a crazy loophole.

She wedges the needle under the feathers on the back of one of the birds and slowly injects it with about a third of the serum. The bird opens its wings and jerks and bucks for a moment or two and then settles down. She injects the second bird and then the third until the syringe is empty.

She crawls over Bradwell's legs to face him again, and she runs her hand through his hair. 'Bradwell,' she whispers.

He doesn't move. He doesn't blink. His lips are parted but he's not going to speak.

She sobs, her ribs convulsing. Her heart throbs in her chest. She covers her mouth with her hand and then tells herself that he's going to come back. She can't lose him, not now. They've come so far.

He's coming back.

He's coming back.

She lies down on the bloody ground, the curve of her body against the curve of his.

He's coming back.

She pulls his arm, heavy with muscle, around her waist. She stares out into the field. El Capitan and Helmud are standing by the horse, whose muzzle is bent to the grass.

And then she hears a breath. Bradwell's arm tightens around her. His hand curls into a fist.

She turns her head.

His eyes are wide.

He moans and then cries out in pain. Even under the dried blood, she can see the wound on his bare chest – the skin and exposed muscle – stitching itself back together. Each small nick tightens to a hardened knot of skin.

Bradwell says her name, just once. 'Pressia.'

She hears her name in the distance too. It's El Capitan. She hears a pretty voice ringing through the trees, singing her name. Could it be Helmud's?

She stands up and sees El Capitan loping toward her. 'He's back!' she shouts. 'I brought him back!'

El Capitan's face is ghostly white, frozen in a grim mask. Terrified. 'What did you do?' he says as he reaches her.

And then she hears a feathery shudder – like the thrum of a massive handheld fan. She touches the tree beside her, afraid to turn around. She feels the rough bark under her hand. She looks at El Capitan. His mouth is opened as if he's about to speak, but he can't.

She has to turn and see what he sees. She feels sick, but she twists her head, looks back over her shoulder.

There is Bradwell – alive but in anguish. He writhes on the ground, flexes, and throws his head back in pain. He staggers to his feet, his bare chest ripped open and now sealing itself, blood-caked, knitting into a long, dark scar. His arms look stronger and, for a second, it seems like he's wearing a thick, dark cape – a feathered cape.

But Pressia knows that it's not a cape. She knows that the birds have taken hold. What else did she think would happen? She isn't sure, but not this . . .

Arching from his back in either direction are wings, large and sleek – and not just one set. No. Six wings start to riot on his back. His whole body shaking violently, he looks at Pressia. 'What did you do to me?'

For a few moments, her voice is lost in her throat, and then finally she's able to tell him, 'I brought you back.'

PARTRIDGE

KISS

BECKLEY IS THERE IN THE MORNING, knocking on the door with what sounds like the butt of his gun. Partridge is dressed. The pill sits in the envelope in one pocket of his pants, and the list is in the other. He should destroy the list, but he can't. He needs to have some kind of truth he can hold on to.

When Partridge opens the door, he's not surprised to find Iralene standing in the hall, her arms folded on her chest, her eyes darting around nervously.

'You ready?' Beckley says.

Partridge nods, but he's not ready. He spent the night trying to apply logic to the situation, and he decided that his father isn't going to kill him. His pinky – nearly grown back now, its nail bud forming above the final knuckle – and his memory swiped clean are proof. His father wouldn't do these things if he was going to kill him. Why bother? He's decided that Iralene must have gotten it all wrong somehow. Still, he doesn't leave the pill behind. Is there some nagging doubt in his mind? Maybe.

They use the private routes to the medical center and arrive a little early. A tech ushers the three of them to a private room. 'You can wait out here,' she says to Beckley. 'Guard the door.'

The room is small and beige. There's a bed covered in a sheet of white, crinkly paper, a few chairs, a computer fitted into the wall. 'I'd like to see my father before this starts,' Partridge says.

'That's not part of the plan.'

'We're here early, and he's here, isn't he?'

The tech nods but looks flustered. 'I can't okay that kind of thing.'

'I'd like to see Dr Weed, then,' Partridge says.

'I don't think Dr Weed was planning a consult before the procedure. You'll talk to him after.'

Iralene links her arm around Partridge's and gives him a small pinch just above his elbow. She says to the tech, 'You know who this is, right? Or, should I say, who he's going to be one day? One day soon, you realize. Very soon.'

The tech gives a smile that's more of a twitch in one rouged cheek. 'Partridge Willux,' she says. 'Of course I know.'

'And you know that his father's will and testament is in order. It's been signed. The transfer of power to his son will be immediate. Do you understand what I'm getting at? So Partridge would like to see his father, okay' – she leans forward, reading the tech's name tag – 'Rosalinda Crandle?'

'I'll contact Dr Weed. I'll ask for his permission,' she says. 'Excuse me.' She hurries out of the room, which is outfitted with a camera mounted in one corner.

Partridge pulls Iralene in close. He touches her cheek lightly and hides his face by nuzzling her neck. He whispers in her ear, 'I'm not going to do it. He's not going to kill me. It doesn't add up.'

She smiles – for the sake of the camera. She kisses him on the cheek and whispers, 'You haven't figured it out yet?'

He shakes his head.

She hugs him tightly. She cups her hand to his ear and says, 'He wants to live forever. He wants his brain to continue on. His body won't let this happen. But yours . . .'

Partridge's chest courses with burning heat. *My body*, he thinks. *My father needs my body.* And suddenly everything clicks into place. This is why he's transferring power to Partridge. He will *be* Partridge. He's going to attempt a transplant. Jesus, is that what Arvin Weed's team of researchers figured out? Is that why he was being congratulated at the engagement party? When his father's brain is transplanted into Partridge's body, he wants a pinky that's fully intact? Partridge leans into Iralene. He feels dizzy and sick. 'Why didn't you tell me earlier?'

'I told you he was going to kill you. I don't like to give any more information than I need to at any given moment. Sometimes your secrets are your only value.'

He looks at Iralene. 'But that means . . . you'd be . . .'

'This was always part of his plan,' she says, her breath warm on his neck. 'I was meant for you, but if he could get the transplant perfected, then . . .'

'For him?'

'It's my role.'

'And your mother?'

'Her duty will have been served. She will no longer require resources.'

Partridge feels sick. He wants to bash the camera, punch the computer, shove over the examination table.

'You were right,' she whispers to Partridge, playing with his hair. 'Willux framed my father. He put him in jail so he could have my mother. It started long ago and far away. Kill him.' Her voice is low. 'Do it.'

He recognizes the pit of fury in her. He has it himself, and it burns now. For himself, for Iralene, for all the survivors and all those in the Dome who've lost the ones they've loved. For his mother and brother. Loss. So much loss.

But there are things that still don't sit right. 'His brain,' Partridge says. 'It has to be deteriorating alongside all his organs, if not even faster. He had *brain* enhancements, after all. Why would he think that moving his RCD-ravaged brain into my body would work?'

Iralene pulls away and grasps his pinky. 'As long as some healthy part of his brain is still intact, as long as it has conditions where it can thrive . . .'

Weed can regrow his brain from the healthy part remaining? If he can manage this kind of re-creation with a pinky, maybe he can do it with brain tissue too. 'Okay,' Partridge concedes, but there's one fact that still doesn't make sense. 'I know why my father might want to have a scarless body to move into, but why swipe my memory? It doesn't make sense.'

'Do you really expect to understand your father?' Iralene stares at him, steely-eyed. She places her hand on his chest. She whispers, 'All I know is that you'll have forty seconds before the capsule dissolves and releases the poison. If you don't want the cameras to see, you should . . .' But she doesn't finish the sentence. Instead she rises on her tiptoes and gives him a light kiss on the lips.

There's a knock at the door.

The tech pokes her head in. 'Dr Weed wanted you to know that your father is also having a light procedure done today.

Something cosmetic. He will be under. But since you haven't seen him in a long time, Dr Weed has indicated his approval of a short visit.'

'Good,' Partridge says. Weed. Is this some small concession? Is this, in the end, his role – to provide this small window, an opportunity for Partridge to kill his father?

'Beckley will lead you there. But first, you need to be in scrubs.'

'Is my father contagious?' This could be the worst thing you can accuse someone of in the Dome.

'No, but we don't want you to get him sick.'

'Tell him I want to see him without all that stuff on unless he's too weak.'

This flusters the tech even more. She looks at Iralene, who simply smiles at her. She scurries off and disappears. Finally, she returns and only nods.

'Good,' Partridge says. He feels like he's won a small battle of wills. It's good to keep his father a little off balance.

When they walk down the hall, Partridge notices people crowding together, whispering.

'What's going on?' Partridge asks.

'Nothing,' Beckley whispers.

'I want to know.'

'A prisoner brought in from the outside. A wretch.' Docs are running in and out. There are technicians on hand, a few of them wearing full contamination suits.

'A wretch?' Iralene says.

'What are you talking about?' Partridge says. 'How could a wretch get into the Dome?'

Beckley shakes his head and smirks. 'I've got orders not to talk. This is high-level-clearance information.'

'But Beckley, I'm scared,' Iralene says. She stops walking and grabs hold of Beckley's biceps. Her eyes are suddenly filled with tears. Partridge isn't sure how she does it.

'Don't be, Iralene,' Beckley says. 'Supposedly there was an attack on the Dome, but it didn't accomplish much. They hauled in one wretch for questioning and probably to make an example out of her.'

'Her?' Partridge says.

'Well, yeah,' Beckley says, 'but you wouldn't know it was a girl, what with her hair buzzed like it is.'

'I want to see her,' Partridge says.

'I thought you wanted to see your father,' Beckley says.

'Partridge,' Iralene says, 'we should stick to the plan.'

Partridge can't help it. He's compelled. A girl from the outside, a girl with a buzzed head. He has to see her. He starts walking fast toward the clutch of doctors and technicians standing in front of an open door. Beckley catches up with him and jerks him backward, hard.

Partridge spins with great speed and grabs Beckley by the throat. He applies steady pressure. Partridge says in a low gruff voice, 'You're here to protect me, remember that?'

Beckley jerks his head – a slight nod.

Partridge lets go and calls out down the hall, 'What's going on here?'

The doctors and technicians glance at one another. 'A medical case,' one of them says.

'I want to see the patient!' Partridge says, striding up to them.

'You can't. There's the possibility of contagion,' one of the doctors says.

'Contagion?' Partridge asks.

'She's been on the outside, sir. She needs . . .' The technician stalls mid-sentence and looks around, unsure of how much he's supposed to divulge.

'What?'

A doctor steps forward, blocking Partridge from the door. 'Medical intervention.'

Mummy molds. Beautiful barbarism. A knife.

Partridge shoves the doctor in the chest. He slams into a wall and falls to the floor. Other techs grab hold of Partridge from behind, but he shakes one loose and grabs the other's coat until Partridge has flipped him over his back and he's sprawled on the ground.

Partridge rushes into the room. There's a glass window separating him from Lyda. She's sitting on the edge of a metal examination table. She's wearing a white suit and paper slippers.

The doctor shouts at everyone to disperse. 'Go on! Go about your business!' He steps into the room. Iralene follows him with quick, mincing steps. Beckley guards the door, making sure everyone does, in fact, disperse.

The doctor lowers his voice, trying not to shout. 'You can't be in here! Do you understand me?'

Partridge ignores him.

'It's a one-way observation mirror. She can't see you,' the doctor says.

He knocks on the glass, and Lyda looks up.

Her dress, the feel of it in his hands as they dance under a ceiling of fake stars.

'We have to go, Partridge,' Iralene says.

Partridge ignores Iralene. He's staring at Lyda. Her sharp cheekbones, her blue eyes. *A child's body fused to a mother's body. Lyda stooping to talk to the child, cupping its chin in her hands. Lyda walking across an ashen desert, running back to him, kissing him in a gust of wind.* She's looking in Partridge's direction – but her eyes scan past him, almost through him. He feels that sharp pang, that vague feeling of loss and lovesickness, but now it has a name – Lyda. And that sense of grief that made his body feel waterlogged, heavy and deadened – he knows what's caused it: that face. Her face. 'Why is she here? What's wrong with her?'

The doctor sighs. 'It seems she's been impregnated while on the outside. We don't know what kind of creature might be taking root. Most likely the child is the result of a rape, as we all well know what the wretches are capable of.'

Partridge feels like the wind has been pounded from his lungs. 'What did you say?'

'Pregnant, sir. The wretch who was once Pure is pregnant.'

Partridge tries to swallow, but his throat is dry. His lungs are still, airless. Everything feels like it's come to a stop: Lyda is pregnant. His eyes fill with light. *A windswept sky, a loud battle, an old weary house, a room with no roof, a rusty brass frame with no bed. Lyda and him, under his coat. Skin on skin.* 'I have to talk to her.'

'Partridge, no,' Iralene says softly. Beckley walks into the room. 'Tell him, Beckley. He can't talk to the wretch! Not now!'

'Not before you see your father,' Beckley says. 'There's no way. He's going to undergo surgery and so are you. You can't risk contagion.'

'Get out!' Partridge says. He looks at Iralene and says, 'Iralene! Get out! You know what this means to me! Get out!'

Iralene cries out. She turns, dizzily, and reaches for Beckley's shoulder. She misses but he catches her as she stumbles out of the room, onto her hands and knees on the tile floor. The doctor rushes to her side. She looks at Partridge for a moment and then rolls her eyes back in her head and goes limp.

She's faked it. He's sure. Iralene might be brilliant.

This gives Partridge time to slam the door and lock it. He tries to take a deep breath but his lungs feel shallow. Lyda's pregnant. It's not some creature. It's their child, together.

They're in the wrecked subway car again. 'Paper snowflakes,' he hears himself saying. 'Is that all it would take to make you happy?' And Lyda whispers, 'Yes. And you.' She kisses him. 'This.'

He pulls the square-shaped list from his pocket. It's the only paper he has. He folds it into triangular sections. He tears off the tip, chews small holes from the sides quickly with his teeth, then rips the other end jaggedly.

He takes the envelope out of his other pocket and slides the list into it. He extracts the small capsule and puts it back in his pocket. He seals the envelope.

He opens the door. There's Iralene in the hall, having survived her fit quite well. She's been given a folding chair. Beckley stands by her side. The doctor is holding her wrist, taking her pulse. When Partridge walks out of the room, she stands up, jerking her arm from the doctor, and walks up close to Partridge.

He hands her the envelope. She holds it to her heart with one hand and wraps her other arm around him. 'Don't ever get mad with me again,' she says.

He whispers in her ear, 'Iralene, I want the girl to have this. Got it?' Iralene nods.

'I trust you,' he says. 'Do you trust me?'

She nods again. Sometimes he forgets how pretty she is, perfect really, and it catches him off guard even under all that meticulous makeup – her petite features, her pert chin, her white, shiny teeth. She's smiling at him, but the sadness in her eyes is plain. Whatever happens next will change them. Partridge kisses her cheek. It surprises her. She touches the spot.

He turns and walks down the hall. People scatter as he

approaches. Soon, Beckley's at his side. They walk in silence. The power dynamic has shifted. Beckley's a little afraid of him now.

He guides Partridge through the halls, then stops in front of a door.

'This is it?'

Beckley nods. Partridge can't tell if Beckley hates him or grudgingly respects him.

Partridge opens the door and Beckley follows him into his father's room. There's another guard beside his father's bed. 'I need a moment alone with him,' he says to Beckley. 'Take this guard with you.'

Beckley meets Partridge's eye, and for a second Partridge wonders if Beckley is going to challenge him. Partridge holds his gaze. 'I want both of you guarding the door,' he says. 'I want this private time with my father protected.'

'Of course,' Beckley finally says, and he nods to the other guard. They both walk out.

Partridge walks up to the rectangular plastic tent surrounding his father's bed. The tent itself seems to breathe. It's alive with beeping, humming machinery, and the huff and hiss of a small iron box around his father's ribs. This all feels familiar. Partridge has been here before.

He has to confront his father. But he can't commit murder. He doesn't have it in him. And he can't believe Iralene's story – not completely – because it still doesn't make sense; why would his father go to the trouble of having his memory swiped if he was only going to cast his brain off?

He pulls back one side of the plastic tent. His father's eyes are closed. His own skin is rejecting him – it's all either raw or blackened. Both hands have curled inward and are tucked under his chin. Even in sleep, he shakes and trembles – a palsy that won't quit.

But the sight of his father's body, so twisted, so ruptured and wasted, shocks tears to his eyes. This is his father. This is his body. This is death. His father's skin, festering as if scalded from within, some of it covered in a plasticine gauze. It shines.

Blood – a fine mist of it exploding, filling the air. His mother's blood. His brother's blood. He remembers cameras – not the kind in this room but the tiny lenses in his sister's eyes. He's shouting. He's crazed. He finally stops and there's his sister's face, her eyes, the doll – he sees that too. Lyda is there, calling his name, except this memory is silent.

Partridge reaches into his pocket. He feels the capsule with the tip of his index and middle fingers. There are cameras in every corner of the room, as well as within the tent itself – even without them, he wouldn't do it. He's no murderer. This is the difference between his father and himself. He can't allow that difference to erode. He shakes his head and pulls his hand out of his pocket. He won't do it.

His father's eyes open then. 'Partridge?' His voice is a raw chirp.

'Dad.'

His father twitches the fingers on one of his blackened, curled hands, coaxing Partridge closer. 'I have something I need before . . .'

'Before what?'

'Before the end.' Whose end? His father's? Partridge's? The difference between a murderer and the murdered, the difference between evil and good – it feels as see-through and flimsy as a damp veil.

'What is it?' Partridge asks.

His father looks stricken. His face clouds over with physical pain, or is it an emotion? His father clenches his eyes, juts out his jaw, and then finally says, 'I want your forgiveness.'

This is what his father wants? Forgiveness for all his horrific acts, for millions of deaths, for what?

'Tell me,' his father says, 'tell me you love me.'

Partridge tears away from his father's bedside rail. He wheels around the room, the shiny white tile seeming to spin around him. This was why his father wanted Partridge's memory swiped clean. He wants Partridge to know only what he knew before he left. His father wants forgiveness for some petty crimes, the normal ones sons harbor against their fathers. He wants false absolution, the words of forgiveness to pass over his son's lips – forgiveness that would ride out and cover his infinite sins.

And after he gets forgiveness, his father can take over his body. Partridge braces himself with his shoulder against the wall. His father is choosing to make his own truth – a truth where his son loves him and forgives him. He feels a trickle of sweat run down his back. His pulse is loud and quick. He reaches into his pocket. There is the pill, just at the tips of his fingers.

'Partridge,' his father calls to him. 'Come here.'

Partridge wipes sweat from his face. His fingers nudge the pill. And then he pinches it between his index and middle fingers and folds it into the center of his palm, holding it in his fist. He walks back to the bedside but can't look at his father's ravaged skin and curled hands.

'That's all you want?' he says to his father, breathless. 'Just forgiveness? Just for me to tell you that I love you?'

His father nods, his eyes wet with tears.

Partridge raises his fist to his mouth, pretends to cough, and pops the capsule under his tongue. The cameras bear down. He tucks the slick pill into his cheek.

Forty seconds will pass before the pill dissolves. Partridge won't need forty seconds.

He grabs the bed rails. He imagines for a moment his father taking over his body, his life. He imagines his father living out a future with Iralene. His father touching her with Partridge's hands. And Partridge's own brain . . . gone? Suspended? He imagines Lyda – never seeing her again.

His mother dead.

His brother dead.

The entire world dead, dead, dying, and dead.

He leans over the rails. The blood pounds in his face, his neck. He whispers to his father, 'You'll never understand love. But I'll forgive you – with a kiss.'

His father never kissed him and Sedge as kids; he never hugged them. He taught them to shake hands, like men. But this is on Partridge's terms, this absolution, and as he leans down and gives his father a kiss, he blows the capsule from his mouth past his father's lips to the back of his father's throat. 'Forgive you?' Partridge says. 'Forgive me? What's it matter now?'

His father's throat hitches. He swallows. His raw, red-rimmed eyes go wide. He recognizes this moment. He knows what Partridge has done. He lifts his claw of a hand and grasps his son's shirt.

'You *are* my son,' he says. 'You are mine.'

LYDA

TREMBLE

AND AN ENVELOPE SHOOTS into the room from under the door. It glides for a moment, catching air, and then slides to a stop. Lyda stares at it – plain and white, an ordinary envelope with a slight bulkiness in its middle.

She picks it up. She imagines it's some kind of invitation, but she knows she's never going to be invited anywhere here.

She slides one finger under the back flap, peeling it up.

A torn piece of folded paper, words written in pencil. It looks worn out, pocked with holes.

She picks it up and unfolds it.

A small paper snowflake. Her heart starts thrumming.

She sees the ghostly imprint of words in reverse. She flips it over and sees those words floating on the page.

Lyda. She sees her own name. A few numbers, as if this is a list. The words *capsules* and *memory*.

There's only one explanation for this snowflake.

She looks up at the one-way mirror. Is he there? Has he seen her?

It's his gift to her, the one he promised to give her back when they were in the subway car. He kissed her on the lips so softly. She lifts her fingers to her mouth, remembering the kiss. He's with her. He knows she's here. They're still bound.

The paper snowflake trembles in her hand. She loses her grip on it and it sways on the air, back and forth, falling to the floor.

PRESSIA

WINGS

It's QUIET. BRADWELL LIES on the ground bare-chested. His ribs – larger now, heavier – rise and fall quickly. But he's otherwise still. Pressia has been keeping watch and finally she crawls to him. The wind ruffles his hair, his wings, one of which is curled around his shoulder – a feathered vault protecting his body. The scar rides up the center of his chest. She touches it, and without opening his eyes, he winces.

El Capitan sits with his brother's back resting against a tree, his fists clenching dirt. Maybe El Capitan does love her. She thinks of Bradwell, El Capitan, and Helmud bound in vines, dying. She has to believe that it's better this way. Better. It has to be.

Fignan churns his wheels. There's nowhere to go. The horse whinnies. It wags its mane, which falls along its thick neck. A giant animal with a giant heart. She hasn't told them where the horse came from or about the people she saw in the sacred mound. Kelly is here and alive. They aren't alone. And yet it feels like they are completely alone on this earth, cut off.

She hears the sound of her own heart in her ears – her ragged, wild, beating heart. It's the same sound she heard underwater when she was drowning – the deep bass thrum, the rest of the world gone nearly silent. She broke her word to someone she loves.

She *loves* Bradwell.

There it is. The truth of it. It isn't a weakness and it doesn't take courage. Her love for him simply is. They didn't die together on the forest floor, their bodies covered in ice. She couldn't let him die here, without her. Is that a selfish love? If it is, she's guilty of it. She can't apologize for saving him, for turning him into this creature with three giant winged birds in his back.

She leans down over Bradwell, holding tight to the last remaining vial, the formula still deep in her pocket, and she whispers, 'You're still Pure. It's only the inside that counts. You taught me that.'

She saved him – whether he wanted to be saved or not. There's been too much loss.

He's alive. Sedge isn't. Her grandfather isn't. Her mother isn't. What would her mother tell her? Her mother is unknowable. What would her grandfather say? Nothing. He would hold her tight, the way he did from the beginning when she was just a stranger to him, a lost little girl who didn't even speak English. Itchy knee sun she go.

She thinks of Partridge. Where is he now? Did he ever really think she could get this far? Will she ever be able to get back?

For some reason she can't explain, she knows that they will return. There's something calling her home.

Maybe it's Wilda and all the others like her. Pressia might be able to save them still.

Pressia no longer believes solely in this world. It's a myth. It's a dream. And Newgrange is a place touched by a world beyond. Maybe, here, fireflies still exist; maybe somewhere there are blue butterflies – real ones. Maybe one day she will see her father and he will hug her and she will hear the beating of his actual heart. She isn't alone. She is part of a constellation. Scattered stars – lit souls, brightly burning.

'Itchy knee,' she says to Bradwell.

And his lips tremble. He whispers, 'Sun, she go.'

The End of Book Two

ACKNOWLEDGMENTS

So many people go into the brute work of this creation. I want to thank my steadfast agents Nat Sobel, Judith Weber – their entire team – and Justin Manask. I'm deeply thankful to Hachette – Jaime Levine, Jaime Raab, Beth deGuzman, Selina McLemore, and the brilliant art department – as well as Hachette UK, in particular Hannah Sheppard and Ben Willis and all of my dedicated foreign editors. Thank you Karen Rosenfelt, Rodney Ferrell, and Emmy Castlen for believing in the cinematic possibilities. I'm incredibly thankful for Heather Whitaker, who might just one day let me read her work.

I'm thankful for the work of Andrew Collins, in particular his book *The Cygnus Mystery: Unlocking the Ancient Secret of Life's Origins in the Cosmos*. Again, I'd like to thank Charles Pellegrino for his book *Last Train from Hiroshima*, which is still not currently available, but I hope for a revised edition to hit the shelves once more. Thank you Cheryl Fitch for inviting me into the Florida State University Molecular Cloning Facility for a tour. To the tour guide at Newgrange who took us in and to the kid who jumped up and down in the dark chamber, setting off his light-up sneakers. (Ireland, my soul sways.) Special thanks to Rick Wilber. I'm thankful for the vast collection of colleagues at Florida State University – the breadth and depth of their work inspires. And, oddly, I want to thank St. Andrew's School. It's been a long time, but it's all still there.

My family. You, kids. Dave. I love you tenderly. When I'm weary, I remember that I'm building this for you.

And again, the Pure Trilogy is something that wouldn't exist without my father, Bill Baggott – too gentle for wolves, you are the wisest man I know. You taught me to be curious and critical and brave. You remain my favorite interpretive dancer and the best model I know for living heart-first. I am so deeply indebted, for everything.

Peace.